The Doctor
A Tale Of The Rockies

by

Ralph Connor

The Doctor
A Tale Of The Rockies
by Ralph Connor

Copyright © 2024

All Rights reserved.

ISBN: 978-93-65783-08-7

Published by

DOUBLE 9 BOOKS

2/13-B, Ansari Road
Daryaganj, New Delhi – 110002
info@double9books.com
www.double9books.com
Tel. 011-40042856

This book is under public domain

ABOUT THE AUTHOR

Charles William Gordon, CMG, commonly known as Ralph Connor, was a Canadian novelist who used the Connor pen name while simultaneously serving as a church leader, first in the Presbyterian and later in the United Church of Canada. Gordon was born in Glengarry County, Canada West. He was the son of Rev. Daniel and Mary Robertson Gordon. His father was a Free Church of Scotland missionary in Upper Canada. While at Knox College, Gordon was impressed by Superintendent Robertson's presentation on the issues in the West, which led him to pursue his summer mission work there and, eventually, to dedicate his life working for reform and mission in Western Canada. Gordon felt called to become one of these missionaries, establishing not only churches, but also Christian social and moral change in Western Canada. To that purpose, Gordon completed his theological schooling in Edinburgh, Scotland, where he was strengthened in his resolve to introduce the church to Western Canada. During the 1870s and 1880s, theological attitudes in Scotland shifted toward liberalism. Gordon was very interested in the endeavor to harmonize ancient Christian doctrine with modern achievements such as science and evolution. He became a powerful advocate for Western social change and church unity.

CONTENTS

I
THE OLD STONE MILL

There were two ways by which one could get to the Old Stone Mill. One, from the sideroad by a lane which, edged with grassy, flower-decked banks, wound between snake fences, along which straggled irregular clumps of hazel and blue beech, dogwood and thorn bushes, and beyond which stretched on one side fields of grain just heading out this bright June morning, and on the other side a long strip of hay fields of mixed timothy and red clover, generous of colour and perfume, which ran along the snake fence till it came to a potato patch which, in turn, led to an orchard where the lane began to drop down to the Mill valley.

At the crest of the hill travellers with even the merest embryonic aesthetic taste were forced to pause. For there the valley with its sweet loveliness lay in full view before them. Far away to the right, out of an angle in the woods, ran the Mill Creek to fill the pond which brimmed gleaming to the green bank of the dam. Beyond the pond a sloping grassy sward showed green under an open beech and maple woods. On the hither side of the pond an orchard ran down hill to the water's edge, and at the nearer corner of the dam, among a clump of ancient willows, stood the Old Stone Mill, with house attached, and across the mill yard the shed and barn, all neat as a tidy housewife's kitchen. To the left of the mill, with its green turf-clad dam and placid gleaming pond, wandered off green fields of many shading colours, through which ran the Mill Creek, foaming as if enraged that it should have been even for a brief space paused in its flow to serve another's will. Then, beyond the many-shaded fields, woods again, spruce and tamarack, where the stream entered, and maple and beech on the higher levels. That was one way to the mill, the way the farmers took with their grist or their oats for old Charley Boyle to grind.

The other way came in by the McKenzies' lane from the Concession Line, which ran at right angles to the sideroad. This was a mere foot path, sometimes used by riders who came for a bag of flour or meal when the barrel or bin had unawares run low. This path led through the beech and maple woods to the farther end of the dam, where it divided, to the right if one wished to go to the mill yard, and across the dam if one wished to reach the house. From any point of view the Old Stone Mill, with its dam and pond, its surrounding woods and fields and orchard, made a picture of rare loveliness, and suggestive of deep fulness of peace. At least, the woman standing at the dam, where the shade of the willows fell, found it so. The beauty, the quiet of the scene, rested her; the full sweet harmony of those many voices in which Nature pours forth herself on a summer day, stole in upon her heart and comforted her. She was a woman of striking appearance. Tall and straight she stood, a figure full of strength; her dark face stamped with features that bespoke her Highland ancestry, her black hair shot with silver threads, parting in waves over her forehead; her eyes deep set, black and sombre, glowing with that mystic light that shines only in eyes that have for generations peered into the gloom of Highland glens.

"Ay, it's a bonny spot," she sighed, her rugged face softening as she gazed. "It's a bonny spot, and it would be a sore thing to part it."

As she stood looking and listening her face changed. Through the hum of the mill there pierced now and then the notes of a violin.

"Oh, that weary fiddle!" she said with an impatient shake of her head. But in a few moments the impatience in her face passed into tender pity. "Ah, well, well," she sighed, "poor man, it is the kind heart he has, whateffer."

She passed down the bank into the house, then through the large living-room, speckless in its thrifty order, into a longer room that joined house to mill. She glanced at the tall clock that stood beside the door. "Mercy me!" she cried, "it's time my own work was done. But I'll just step in and see—" She opened the door leading to the mill and stood silent. A neat little man with cheery, rosy face, clean-shaven, and with a mass of curly hair tinged with grey hanging about his forehead, was seated upon a chair tipped back against the wall, playing a violin with great vigour and unmistakable delight.

"The mill's a-workin', mother," he cried without stopping his flying fingers, "and I'm keepin' my eye upon her."

She shook her head reproachfully at her husband. "Ay, the mill is workin' indeed, but it's not of the mill you're thinking."

"Of what then?" he cried cheerily, still playing.

"It is of that raising and of the dancing, I'll be bound you."

"Wrong, mother," replied the little man exultant. "Sure you're wrong. Listen to this. What is it now?"

"Nonsense," cried the woman, "how do I know?"

"But listen, Elsie, darlin'," he cried, dropping into his Irish brogue. "Don't you mind—" and on he played for a few minutes. "Now you mind, don't you?"

"Of course, I mind, 'The Lass o' Gowrie.' But what of it?" she cried, heroically struggling to maintain her stern appearance.

But even as she spoke her face, so amazing in its power of swiftly changing expression, took on a softer look.

"Ah, there you are," cried the little man in triumph, "now I know you remember. And it's twenty-four years to-morrow, Elsie, darlin', since—" He suddenly dropped his violin on some meal bags at his side and sprang toward her.

"Go away with you." She closed the door quickly behind her. "Whisht now! Be quate now, I'm sayin'. You're just as foolish as ever you were."

"Foolish? No mother, not foolish, but wise yon time, although it's foolish enough I've been often since. And," he added with a sigh, "it's not much luck I've brought you, except for the boys. They'll do, perhaps, what I've not done."

"Whisht now, lad," said his wife, patting his shoulder gently, for a great tenderness flowed over her eloquent face. "What has come to you to-day? Go away now to your work," she added in her former tone, "there's the hay waiting, you know well. Go now and I'll watch the grist."

"And why would you watch the grist, mother?" said a voice from the mill door, as a young man of eighteen years stepped inside. He was his mother's son. The same swarthy, rugged face, the same deep-set, sombre eyes, the same suggestion of strength in every line of his body, of power in every move he made and of passion in every glance. "Indeed, you will do no such thing. Dad'll watch the grist and I'll slash down the hay in no time. And do you know, mother," he continued in a tone of suppressed excitement, "have you heard the big news?" His mother waited. "He's coming home to-day. He's coming with the Murrays, and Alec will bring him to the raising."

A throb of light swept across the mother's face, but she only said in a voice calm and steady, "Well, you'd better get that hay down. It'll be late enough before it is in."

"Listen to her, Barney," cried her husband scornfully. "And she'll not be going to the raising today, either. The boy'll be home by one in the morning, and sure that's time enough."

Barney stood looking at his mother with a quiet smile on his face. "We will have dinner early," he said, "and I'll just take a turn at the hay."

She turned and entered the house without a word, while he took down the scythe from its peg, removed the blade from the snath and handed it to his father.

"Give it a turn or two," he said; "you're better than me at this."

"Here then," replied his father, handing him the violin, "and you're better at this."

"They would not say so to-night, Dad," replied the lad as he took the violin from his father's hands, looking it over reverently. In a very few minutes his father came back with the scythe ready for work; and Barney, fastening it to the snath, again set off up the lane.

II
THE DAUGHTER OF THE MANSE

Two hours later, down from the dusty sideroad, a girl swinging a milk pail in her hand turned into the mill lane. As she stepped from the glare and dust of the highroad into the lane, it seemed as if Nature had been waiting to find in her the touch that makes perfect; so truly, in all her fresh daintiness, did she seem a bit of that green shady lane with its sweet fragrance and its fresh beauty.

It had taken sixteen years of wholesome country life to round that supple form into its firm lines of grace, and to tint those moulded cheeks with the dainty bloom that seemed a reflection from the thistle heads that nodded at her through the snake fence. It had taken sixteen years of pure-hearted, joyous living to lend those eyes, azure as the sky above, their brave, clear glance; sixteen years of unsullied maidenhood to endow her with that divine something of mystery which, with its shy reserve and fearless trust, awakens reverence and rebukes impurity as with the vision of God.

Her sunbonnet, fallen back from her yellow hair, shining golden in the sun, revealed a face strong, brave and kind, with just a touch of pride. The pride showed most, however, in the poise of her head and the carriage of her shoulders. But when the mobile lips parted in a smile over the straight rows of white teeth one forgot the pride and thought only of the soft persuasive lips.

As she sprang up the green turf, she drew in deep breaths of clover-scented air, and exclaimed aloud, "Oh, this is good!" She peeped through the snake fence at the luscious rich masses of red clover. "What a bed!" she cried; "I believe I'll try it." Over the fence she sprang, and in a thorn tree's shade, deep in the fragrant blossoms, she stretched herself at full length upon her back. For some minutes she lay in the luxury of that fragrant bed looking up through the spreading thorn tree branches to the blue sky with its floating, fleecy clouds far overhead. The lazy drone of the bees in the clover beside her, the languorous summer airs swaying into gentle nodding the timothy stalks just above her head, and all the soothing sounds of a summer morning, that many-voiced choir that sings to the great God Nature's glad content that all is so very good, rested and comforted the girl's heart and body, making her know as she had not known before how very weary she had been and how deep an ache her heart had held.

"Oh, it's good!" she cried again, stretching her hands at full length above her head. "I wish I could stay for one whole day, just here in the clover with the bees and the birds and the trees and the clouds and the blue sky, no children, no dinner, no tidying up."

As she lay there it seemed to her as if she had thrown off for the moment the load she had been carrying for many months. For a year she had tried to fill in the minister's household her mother's place. Without a day's warning the burden had been laid upon her shoulders, but with the fine courage that youth and love combine to give, denying herself even the poor luxury of indulgence of the grief that had fallen upon her young heart, she had given herself, without thought of anything heroic in her giving, to the caring for the house and the household, and the comforting as best she could of her father, suddenly bereft of her who had been to him not wife alone, but comrade and counsellor as well. Without a thought, she had at once surrendered all the bright plans that she, with her mother, had cherished for the cultivation of her varied talents, and had turned to the dull, monotonous routine of household duties with never a thought but that she must do it. There was no one else.

"I believe I am tired," she said again aloud; then letting her heart follow her eyes into and beyond the blue above her, she cried softly, "O mother, how tired you must have been with it all, and how much you did for me! For me, great, big lump that I am! Dear little mother. Oh, if I had only known! Oh, we were all so thoughtless!" She stretched up her hands again to the blue sky with its fleecy clouds. "For your sake, mother dear," she whispered. Not often had any seen those brave eyes dim with tears. Not often since that day when they had carried her mother out from the Manse and left her behind with the weeping, clinging children, and even now she hastily wiped the tears away, chiding herself the while. "I never saw HER cry," she said to herself, "not once, except for some of us. And I will try. I MUST try. It is hard to give up," and again the tears welled up in the brave blue eyes. "Nonsense," she cried impatiently, sitting up straight, "don't be a big, selfish baby. They're just the dearest little darlings in the world, and I'll do my best for them."

Her moment of self-pity was gone in a flood of shamed indignation. She locked her hands round her knees and looked about her. "It is a beautiful world after all. And how near the beauty is to us; just over the fence and you are in the thick of it. Oh, but this is great!" Once more she rolled in an ecstasy of luxurious delight in the clover and lay again supine, revelling in that riot of caressing sounds and scents.

"Kir-r-r-ink-a-chink, kir-r-r-ink-a-chink—"

She sprang up alert and listening. "That is old Charley, I suppose, or Barney, perhaps, sharpening his scythe." She climbed up the conveniently jutting ends of the fence rails and looked over the field.

"It's Barney," she said, shading her eyes with her hand; "I wonder he does not cut his fingers." She sat herself down upon the top rail and leaned against the stake.

"My! what a sweep," she said in admiring tones as the young man swayed to and fro in all the rhythmic grace of the mower's stride, swinging easily now backward the curving blade and then forward in a cutting sweep, clean and swift, laying the even swath. Alas! the clattering machine-knives have driven off from our hay-fields the mower's art with all its rhythmic grace.

Those were days when men were famous according as they could "cut off the heels of a rival mower." There are that grieve that, one by one, from field and from forest, are banished those ancient arts of daily toil by which men were wont to prove their might, their skill of hand and eye, their invincible endurance. But there still offer in life's stern daily fight full opportunity to prove manhood in ways less picturesque perhaps, but no less truly testing.

Down the swath came Barney, his sinewy body swinging in very poetry of motion.

"Doesn't he do it well!" said the girl, following with admiring eyes every movement of his well-poised frame. "How big he is! Why—" and her blue eyes widened with startled surprise, "he's almost a man!" The tint of the thistle bloom deepened in her cheek. She glanced down and made as if to spring to the ground; then settling herself resolutely back against her fence stake, she exclaimed, "Pshaw! I don't care. He is just a boy. Anyway, I'm not going to mind Barney Boyle."

On came the mower in mighty sweeps, cutting the swath clean out to the end.

"Well done!" cried the girl. "You'll be cutting off Long John's heels in a year or so."

"A year or so! If I can't do it to-day I never can. But I don't want to blow."

"You needn't. They're all talking about you, with your binding and pitching and cradling, and what not."

"They are, are they? Who is good enough to waste breath on me?"

"Oh, everybody. The McKenzie girls were just telling me the other day."

"Oh, pshaw! I ran away from their crowd, but that's nothing."

"And I suppose you have not an idea how nice you look as you go swinging along?"

"Do I? That's the only time then."

"Oh, now you're fishing, and I'm not going to bite. Where did you learn the scythe?"

"Where? Right here where we had to, Dick and I. By the way, he's coming home to-day." He glanced at her face quickly as he said this, but her face showed only a frank pleasure.

"To-day? Good. Won't your mother be glad?"

"Yes. And some other people, too," said Barney.

"And who, particularly?"

A sudden shyness seemed to seize the young man, but recovering himself, "Well, I guess I will, myself, a little. This is the first time he has ever been away. We never slept a night apart from each other as long as I can mind till he went to college last year. He used to put his arm just round me here," touching his breast. "I'll tell you the first nights after he went I used to feel for him in the dark and be sick to find the place empty."

"Well," said the girl doubtfully, "I hope he won't be different. College does make a difference, you know."

"Different! Dick! He'd better not. I'll thrash the daylights out of him. But he won't be different. Not to us, nor," he added shyly, "to you."

"Oh, to me?" She laughed lightly. "He had better not try any airs with me."

"What would you do?" inquired Barney. "You couldn't take it out of his hide."

"Oh, I'd fix him. I'd take him down," she replied with a knowing shake of her head.

"Poor Dick! He's in for a hard time," replied Barney. "But nothing can change Dick. And I am awful glad he's coming to-day, in time for the raising, too."

"The raising? Oh, yes. The McLeods'. Yes, I remember. And," regretfully, "a big supper and a big spree afterwards in the new barn."

"Are not you going?" inquired Barney.

"I don't know. They want me to go to help, but I don't think I'll go. I don't think father would like me to go, and," —a pause— "anyway, I don't think I can get away."

"Oh, pshaw! Get Old Nancy in. She can take care of the children for once. You would like the raising. It's great fun."

"Oh! wouldn't I, though? It's fine to see them racing. They get so wild and yell so."

"Well, come on then. You must come. They'll all be disappointed, if you don't. And Dick is coming that way, too. Alec Murray is to bring him on his way home from town." Again Barney glanced keenly at her face, but he saw only puzzled uncertainty there.

"Well, I don't know. We'll see. At any rate, I must go now."

"Wait," cried Barney, "I'll go with you. We're having dinner early to-day." He hung up the scythe in the thorn tree and threw the stone at the foot.

"I wish you would promise to come," he said earnestly.

"Do you, really?" The blue eyes turned full upon him.

"Of course I do. It will be lots better fun if you are there." The frank, boyish honesty of his tone seemed to disappoint the blue eyes. Together in silence they set off down the lane.

"Well," she said, resuming their conversation, "I don't think I can go, but I'll see. You'll be playing for the dancing, I suppose?"

"No. I won't play if Dan is around, and I guess he'll be there. I may spell him a little perhaps."

"Then you'll be dancing yourself. You're great at that, I know."

"Me? Not much. It's Dick. Oh, he's a dandy! He's a bird! You ought to see him! I'll make him do the Highland Fling."

"Oh, Dick, Dick!" she cried impatiently, "everything is Dick with you."

Barney glanced at her, and after a moment's pause said, "Yes. I guess you're right. Everything is pretty much Dick with me. Next to my mother, Dick is the finest in all the world."

At the crest of the hill they stood looking silently upon the scene spread out before them.

"There," said Barney, "if I live to be a hundred years, I can't forget that," and he waved his hand over the valley. Then he continued, "I tell you what, with the moon just over the pond there making a track of light across the pond—" She glanced shyly at him. The sombre eyes were looking far away.

"I know," she said softly; "it must be lovely."

Through the silence that followed there rose and fell with musical cadence a call long and clear, "Who-o-o-hoo."

"That's mother," said Barney, answering the call with a quick shout. "You'll be in time for dinner."

"Dinner!" she cried with a gasp. "I'll have to get my buttermilk and other things and hurry home." And she ran at full speed down the hill and into the mill yard, followed by Barney protesting that it was too hot to run.

"How are you, Mrs. Boyle?" she panted. "I'm in an awful hurry. I'm after father's buttermilk and that recipe, you know."

Mrs. Boyle's eyes rested lovingly upon her flushed face.

"Indeed, there's no hurry, Margaret. Barney should not be letting you run."

"Letting me!" she laughed defiantly. "Indeed, he had all he could do to keep up."

"And that I had," said Barney, "and, mother, tell her she must come to the raising."

"And are you not going?" said the older woman.

"I don't think so. You know father—well, he wouldn't care for me to be at the dance."

"Yes, yes, I know," quickly replied Mrs. Boyle, "but you might just come with me and look quietly on. And, indeed, the change will be doing you good. I will just call for you, and speak to your father this afternoon."

"Oh, I don't know, Mrs. Boyle. I hardly think I ought."

"Hoots, lassie! Come away, then, into the milk-house."

Back among the overhanging willows stood the little whitewashed log milkhouse, built over a little brook that gurgled clear and cool over the gravelly floor.

"What a lovely place," said Margaret, stepping along the foot stones.

"Ay, it's clean and sweet," said Mrs. Boyle. "And that is what you most need with the milk and butter."

She took up an earthen jar from the gravelly bed and filled the girl's pail with buttermilk.

"Thank you, Mrs. Boyle. And now for that recipe for the scones."

"Och, yes!" said Mrs. Boyle. "There's no recipe at all. It is just this way—" And she elucidated the mysteries of sconemaking.

"But they will not taste a bit like yours, I'm sure," cried Margaret, in despair.

"Never you fear, lassie. You hurry away home now and get your dinner past, and we will call for you on our way."

"Here, lassie," she cried, "your father will like this. It is only churned th' day." She rolled a pat of butter in a clean linen cloth, laid it between two rhubarb leaves and set it in a small basket.

"Good-bye," said the girl as she kissed the dark cheek. "You're far too kind to me."

"Poor lassie, poor lassie, I would I could be kinder. It's a good girl you are, and a brave one."

"Not very brave, I fear," replied the girl, as she quickly turned away and ran up the hill and out of sight.

"Poor motherless lassie," said Mrs. Boyle, looking after her with loving eyes; "it's a heavy care she has, and the minister, poor man, he can't see it. Well, well, she has the promise."

III
THE RAISING

The building of a bank-barn was a watershed in farm chronology. Toward that event or from it the years took their flight. For many summers the big boulders were gathered from the fields and piled in a long heap at the bottom of the lane on their way to their ultimate destination, the foundation of the bank-barn. During the winter, previous the "timber was got out." From the forest trees, maple, beech or elm—for the pine was long since gone—the main sills, the plates, the posts and cross-beams were squared and hauled to the site of the new barn. Hither also the sand from the pit at the big hill, and the stone from the heap at the bottom of the lane, were drawn. And before the snow had quite gone the lighter lumber—flooring, scantling, sheeting and shingles—were marshalled to the scene of action. Then with the spring the masons and framers appeared and began their work of organising from this mass of material the structure that was to be at once the pride of the farm and the symbol of its prosperity.

From the very first the enterprise was carried on under the acknowledged, but none the less critical, observation of the immediate neighbourhood. For instance, it had been a matter of free discussion whether "them timbers of McLeod's new barn wasn't too blamed heavy," and it was Jack McKenzie's openly expressed opinion that "one of them 'purline plates' was so all-fired crooked that it would do for both sides at onct." But the confidence of the community in Jack Murray, framer, was sufficiently strong to allay serious forebodings. And by the time the masons had set firm and solid the many-coloured boulders in the foundation, the community at large had begun to take interest in the undertaking.

The McLeod raising was to be an event of no ordinary importance. It had the distinction of being, in the words of Jack Murray, framer, "the biggest thing in buildin's ever seen in them parts." Indeed, so magnificent were its dimensions that Ben Fallows, who stood just five feet in his stocking soles, and was, therefore, a man of considerable importance in his estimation, was overheard to exclaim with an air of finality, "What! two twenty-foot floors and two thirty-foot mows! It cawn't be did." Such was, therefore, the magnitude of the undertaking, and such the far-famed hospitality of the McLeods, that no man within the range of the family acquaintance who was not sick, or away from home, or prevented by some special act of Providence, failed to appear at the raising that day.

It was still the early afternoon, but most of the men invited were already there when the mill people drove up in the family democrat. The varied shouts of welcome that greeted them proclaimed their popularity.

"Hello, Barney! Good-day, Mrs. Boyle," said Mr. McLeod, who stood at the gate receiving his guests.

"Ye've brought the baby, I see, Charley, me boy," shouted Tom Magee, a big, good-natured son of Erin, the richness of whose brogue twenty years of life in Canada had failed to impoverish.

"We could hardly leave the baby at home to-day," replied the miller, as with tender care he handed the green bag containing his precious violin to his wife.

"No, indeed, Mr. Boyle," replied Mr. McLeod. "The girls yonder would hardly forgive us if Charley Boyle's fiddle were not to the fore. You'll find some oats in the granary, Barney. Come along, Mrs. Boyle. The wife will be glad of your help to keep those wild colts in order yonder, eh, Margaret, lassie?"

"Indeed, it is not Margaret Robertson that will be needing to be kept in order," replied Mrs. Boyle.

"Don't you be too sure of that, Mrs. Boyle," replied Mr. McLeod. "A girl with an eye and a chin like that may break through any time, and then woe betide you."

"Then I warn you, don't try the curb on me," said Margaret, springing lightly over the wheel and turning away with Mrs. Boyle toward the house, which was humming with that indescribable but altogether bewitching medley of sounds that only a score or two of girls overflowing with life can produce.

"Come along, Charley," roared Magee. "We're waitin' to make ye the boss."

"All right, Tom," replied the little man, with a quiet chuckle. "If you make me the boss, here's my orders, Up you get yourself and take hold of the gang. What do you say, men?"

"Ay, that's it." "Tom it is." "Jump in, Tom," were the answering shouts.

"Aw now," said Tom, "there's better than me here. Take Big Angus there. He's the man fer ye! Or what's the matter wid me frind, Rory Ross? It's the foine boss he'd make fer yez! Sure, he'll put the fire intil ye!"

There was a general laugh at this reference to the brilliant colour of Rory's hair and face.

"Never you mind Rory Ross, Tom Magee," said the fiery-headed, fiery-hearted little Highlander. "When he's wanted, ye'll not find him far away, I'se warrant ye."

There was no love lost between the two men. Both were framers, both famous captains, and more than once had they led the opposing forces at raisings. The awkward silence following Rory's hot speech was relieved by Charley Boyle's ready wit.

"We'll divide the work, boys," he said. "Some men do the liftin' and others the yellin'. Tom and me'll do the yellin'."

A roar of laughter rose at Tom's expense, whose reputation as a worker was none too brilliant.

"All right then, boys," roared Tom. "Ye'll have to take it. Git togither an' quit yer blowin'." He cast an experienced eye over the ground where the huge timbers were strewn about in what to the uninitiated would seem wild confusion.

"Them's the sills," he cried. "Where's the skids?"

"Right under yer nose, Tom," said the framer quietly.

"Here they are, lads. Git up thim skids! Now thin, fer the sills. Grab aholt, min, they're not hot! All togither-r-r—heave! Togither-r-r—heave! Once more, heave! Walk her up, boys! Walk her up! Come on, Angus! Where's yer porridge gone to? Move over, two av ye! Don't take advantage av a little man loike that!" Angus was just six feet four. "Now thin, yer pikes! Shove her along! Up she is! Steady! Cant her over! How's that, framer? More to the east, is it? Climb up on her, ye cats, an' dig in yer claws! Now thin, east wid her! Togither-r-r—heave! Aw now, where are ye goin'? Don't be too rambunctious! Ye'll be afther knockin' a hole in to-morrow mornin'. Back a little now! Whoa! How's that, framer? Will that suit yer riverence? All right. Now thin, the nixt! Look lively there! The gurls are comin' down to pick the winners, an a small chance there'll be fer some of yez."

And so with this running fire of exhortation, more or less pungent, the sills were got in place upon the walls, pinned and spliced.

"Now thin, min fer the bints!"

The "bents" were the cross sections of heavy square timbers which, fastened together with cross ties, formed the framework of the barn. Dividing his men into groups, the bents were put together on the barn floor, and, one by one, raised into their places, each one being firmly joined to the one previously erected.

"Mind yer braces, now, an' yer pins!" admonished Tom. "We don't want no slitherin' timbers round here when we get into the ruction a little later on!"

In spite of all Tom's tumultuous vocal energy, it was nearly five before the last bent was reached. One by one they had fitted into their places, but not without some few hitches, each of which was the occasion for an outburst of exhortations on the part of the boss, more or less sulphurous, although the presence of the ladies interfered very considerably with Tom's fluency in this regard. He worked his men like galley slaves, and rowed them unmercifully. But for the most part they took it all with good humour, though some few who had the misfortune to fall specially under his tongue began to show signs that the lash had bitten into the raw. The timbers of the last bent were specially heavy, and the men, more or less fagged with their hard driving, didn't spring to their work with the alacrity that Tom deemed suitable.

"At it, min!" he roared. "Snatch it alive! Begob, ye'd think it was plate glass ye're liftin', ye're so tinder about it! Now thin! Togither-r-r—heave! Once again, heave! Ye didn't git it an inch that time! Stidy there a minute! Here you min on that pike, what in the blank, blank are ye bunchin' in one ind loike a swarm av bees on a cowld day! Shift over there, will ye!"

In obedience to the word two pike-poles were withdrawn at the same moment, leaving only a single pike with Big Angus and two others to sustain the full weight of the heavy timbers. Immediately the bent swayed backward as if to fall upon the throng below. Some of the men sprang back from under the huge bent. It was a moment of supreme peril.

"Howld there, fer yer lives, ye divils!" howled Tom, "or the hull of ye'll be in hell in two howly minutes."

At the cry Barney and Rory sprang to Angus's side and threw themselves upon the pike. Immediately they were followed by others, and the calamity was averted.

"Up wid her now thin, me lads, God bliss ye!" cried Tom. But there was a new note in Tom's voice, the note that is heard when men stand in the presence of serious danger. There was no more pause. The bent was walked up to its place, pinned and made secure. Tom sprang down from the building, his face white, his voice shaking. "Give me yer hand, Barney Boyle, an' yours, Rory Ross, for be all the saints an' the Blessid Virgin, ye saved min's lives this day!"

Around the two crowded the men, shaking their hands and clapping them on the back with varied exclamations. "You're the lads!" "Good boys!" "You're the stuff!" "Put it there!"

"What are ye doin' to us?" cried Rory at last; "I didn't see anything happen. Did you, Barney?"

"We did, though," answered the crowd.

For once Tom Magee was silent. He walked about among the crowd chewing hard upon his quid of tobacco, fighting to recover his nerve. He had seen as no other of the men the terrible catastrophe from which the men had been saved. It was Charley Boyle that again relieved the strain.

"Did any of you hear the cowbell?" he said. "It strikes me it's not quitting time yet. Better get your captains, hadn't you?"

"Rory and Tom for captains!" cried a voice.

"Not me, by the powers!" said Tom.

"Oh, come on, Tom. You'll be all right. Get your men."

"All right, am I? Be jabbers, I couldn't hit a pin onct in the same place, let alone twice. By me sowl, min, it's a splash of blood an' brains I've jist been lookin' at, an' that's true fer ye. Take Barney there. He's the man, I kin tell ye."

This suggestion caught the crowd's fancy.

"Barney it is!" "Rory and Barney!" they yelled.

"Me!" cried Barney, seeking to escape through the crowd. "I have never done anything but carry pins and braces at a raising all my life."

There was a loud laugh of scorn, for no man in all the crowd had Barney's reputation for agility, nerve and quickness.

"Carry pins, is it?" said Tom. "Ye can carry yer head level, me boy. So at it ye go, an' ye'll bate Rory fer me, so ye will."

"Well then," cried Barney, "I will, if you give me first choice, and I'll take Tom here."

"Hooray!" yelled Tom, "I'm wid ye." So it was agreed, and in a few minutes the sides were chosen, little Ben Fallows falling to Rory as last choice.

"We'll give ye Ben," said Tom, whose nerve was coming back to him. "We don't want to hog on ye too much."

"Never you mind, Ben," said Rory, as the little Englishman strutted to his place among Rory's men. "You'll earn your supper to-day with the best of them."

"If I cawn't hearn it I can heat it, by Jove!" cried Ben, to the huge delight of the crowd.

And now the thrilling moment had arrived, for from this point out there was to be a life-and-death contest as to which side should complete each its part of the structure first. The main plates, the "purline" plates, posts and braces, the rafters and collar beams, must all be set securely in position. The side whose last man was first down from the building after its work was done claimed the victory. In two opposing lines a hundred men stood, hats, coats, vests and, in case of those told off to "ride" the plates, boots discarded. A brawny, sinewy lot they were, quick of eye and steady of nerve, strong of hand and sure of foot, men to be depended upon whether to raise a barn or to build an empire. The choice of sides fell to Rory, who took the north, or bank, side.

"Niver fret, Barney," cried Tom Magee, who in the near approach of battle was his own man again. "Niver ye fret. It's birrds we are, an' the more air for us the better."

Between the sides stood the framer ready to give the word.

"Aren't they splendid!" said Margaret in a low tone to Mrs. Boyle, her cheek pale and her blue eyes blazing with excitement. "Oh, if I were only a boy!"

"Ay," said Mrs. Boyle, "ye'd be riding the plate, I doubt."

"Wouldn't I, though! My! they're fine!" answered the girl, with her eyes upon Barney. And more eyes than hers were upon the young captain, whose rugged face showed pale even at that distance.

"Now then, men," cried the framer. "Mind your pins. Are you ready?" holding his hat high in the air.

"Ready," answered Rory.

Barney nodded.

"Git then!" he cried, flinging his hat hard on the ground. Like hounds after a hare in full sight, like racers springing from the tape, they leaped at the timbers, every man to his place, yelling like men possessed. At once the admiring female friends broke into rival camps, wildly enthusiastic, fiercely partisan.

"Well done, Rory! He's up first!" cried a girl whose brilliant complexion and still more brilliant locks proclaimed her relationship to the captain of the north side.

"Huh! Barney'll soon catch him, you'll see," cried Margaret. "Oh, Barney, hurry! hurry!"

"Indeed, he will need to hurry," cried Rory's sister, mercilessly exultant. "He's up! He's up!"

Sure enough, Rory, riding the first half of his plate over the bent, had just "broken it down," and in half a minute, seized by the men detailed for this duty, it was in its place upon the posts. Like cats, three men with mauls were upon it driving the pins home just as the second half was making its appearance over the bent, to be seized and placed and pinned as its mate had been.

"He's won! He's won!" shrieked Rory's admiring faction.

"Barney! Barney!" screamed his contingent reproachfully.

"Well done, Rory! Keep at it! You've got them beaten!"

"Beaten, indeed!" was the scornful reply. "Just wait a minute."

"They're at the 'purlines'!" shrieked Rory's sister, and her friends, proceeding to scream wildly after the female method of expressing emotion under such circumstances.

"My!" sniffed a contemptuous member of Barney's faction, suffering unutterable pangs of humiliation. "Some people don't mind making a show of themselves."

"Oh, Barney! why don't you hurry?" cried Margaret, to whose eager spirit Barney's movements seemed painfully and almost wilfully slow.

But Barney had laid his plans. Dividing his men into squads, he had been carrying out the policy of simultaneous preparation, and while part of his men had been getting the plates to their places, others had been making ready the "purlines" and laying the rafters in order so that, although beaten by Rory in the initial stages of the struggle, when once his plates were in position, while Rory's men were rushing about in more or less confusion after their rafters, Barney's purlins and rafters moved to their positions as if by magic. Consequently, though when they arrived at the rafters Barney was half a dozen behind, the rest of his rafters were lifted almost as one into their places.

At once the ranks of Barney's faction, which up to this point had been enduring the poignant pangs of what looked like humiliating defeat, rose in a tumult of triumph to heights of bliss inexpressible, save by a series of ear-piercing but altogether rapturous shrieks.

"They're down! They're down!" screamed Margaret, dancing in an ecstasy of joy, while hand over hand down posts, catching at braces, slipping, sliding, springing, the men of both sides kept dropping from incredible distances to the ground. Suddenly through all the tumultuous shouts of victory a heart-rending scream rang out, followed by a shuddering groan and dead silence. One-half of Rory's purlin plate slipped from its splicing, the pin having been neglected in the furious haste, and swinging free, fell crashing through the timbers upon the scurrying, scrambling men below. On its way it swept off the middle bent Rory, who was madly entreating a laggard to drop to the earth, but who, flung by good fortune against a brace, clung there. On the plate went in its path of destruction, missing several men by hairs' breadths, but striking at last with smashing cruel force across the ankle of poor little Ben Fallows, in the act of sliding down a post to the ground. In a moment two or three men were beside him. He was lifted up groaning and screaming and carried to an open grassy spot. After some moments of confusion Barney was seen to emerge from the crowd and hurry after his horse. A stretcher was hastily knocked together, a mattress and pillow placed thereon, to which Ben, still groaning piteously, was tenderly lifted.

"I'll go wid ye," said Tom Magee, throwing on his coat and hat.

Before they drove out of the yard the little Englishman pulled himself together. "Stop a bit, Barney," he said. He beckoned Rory to his side. "Tell them," he said between his gasps, "not to spoil their supper for me. I cawn't heat my share, but I guess perhaps I hearned it."

"And that you did, lad," cried Rory. "No man better, and I'll tell them."

The men who were standing near and who had heard Ben's words broke out into admiring expletives, "Good boy, Benny!" "Benny's the stuff!" till finally someone swinging his hat in the air cried, "Three cheers for Benny!" and the feelings of the crowd, held in check for so many minutes, at length found expression in three times three, and with the cheers ringing in his ears and with a smile upon his drawn face, poor Ben, forgetting his agony for the time, was borne away on his three-mile drive to the doctor.

The raising was over, but no man asked which side had won.

IV
THE DANCE

The dance was well on when Barney and Tom drove up to the McLeods' gate. They were met by Margaret and Barney's mother, who, with a group of girls and Mr. McLeod, had been waiting for them. As they drove into the yard they were met at once with eager questions as to the condition and fate of the unhappy Ben.

"Ben, is it?" said Tom. "Indeed, it's a hero we've discovered. He stud it like a brick. An' I'm not sure but there are two av thim," he said, jerking his thumb toward Barney. "Ye ought to have seen him stand there houldin' the light an' passin' the doctor sthrings, an' the blood spoutin' like a stuck pig. What happened afther, it's mesilf can't tell ye at all, for I was restin' quietly by mesilf on the floor on the broad av me back, an' naither av thim takin' annythin' to do wid me except to drown me wid watther betune times. Indeed, it's himsilf is the born doctor, an' so he is," continued Tom, warming to his theme, "for wid his hands red wid blood an' his face as white as yer apron, ma'am, niver a shiver did he give until the last knot was tied an' the last stitch was sewed. Bedad! there's not a man in the county could do the same."

There was no stopping Tom in his recital, and after many attempts Barney finally gave it up, and began unhitching his horse. Meantime the sound of the dancing had ceased, and suddenly up through the silence there rose a voice in song to the accompaniment of some stringed instrument. It was an arresting voice. The group about the horse stood perfectly still as the voice rose and soared and sank and rose again in an old familiar plantation air.

"Who in thunder is that?" cried Barney, turning to his mother.

But his mother shook her head. "Indeed, I know not, but it's likely yon strange girl that came out from town with the Murrays."

"I know," cried Teenie Ross, Rory's sister, with a little toss of her head, "Alec told me. She is the girl who has come to take the teacher's place for a month. She is the niece of Sheriff Hossie. Her father was a colonel in the Southern army, California or Virginia or some place, I don't just remember.

Oh! I know all about her, Alec told me," continued Teenie with a knowing shake of her ruddy curls. "And she'll have a string of hearts dangling to her apron, if she wears one, before the month is out, so you'd better mind out, Barney."

But Barney was not heeding her. "Hush!" he said, holding up his hand, for again the voice was rising up clear and full into the night silence. Even Teenie's chatter was subdued and no one moved till the verse was finished.

"She'll be needing a boarding house, Barney," continued Teenie wickedly. "You'll just need to take her with you to the Mill."

"Indeed, and there will be no such lassie as yon in my house," said the mother, speaking sharply.

"She has no mother," said Margaret softly, "and she will need a place."

"Yes, that she will," replied Mrs. Boyle, "and I know very well where she will be going, too, and you with four little ones to do for, not to speak of the minister, the hardest of the lot." Mrs. Boyle was evidently seriously angered.

"Man! What a voice!" breathed Barney, and, making fast the horse to the waggon, he set off for the barn apparently oblivious of all about him.

"Begorra, ma'am, an' savin' yer prisince, there's nobody knows what's in that lad. But he'll stir the world yit, an' so he will. An' that's what the ould Doctor said, so it was."

When Barney reached the barn floor the Southern girl had just finished her song, and with her guitar still in her hands was idly strumming its strings. The moonlight fell about her in a flood so bright as to reveal the ivory pallor of her face and the lustrous depths of her dark eyes. It was a face of rare and romantic beauty framed in soft, fluffy, dark hair, brushed high off the forehead and gathered in a Greek knot at the back of her head. But besides the beauty of face and eyes, there was an air of gentle, appealing innocence that awakened the chivalrous instincts latent in every masculine heart, and a lazy, languorous grace that set her in striking contrast to the alert, vigorous country maids so perfectly able to care for themselves, asking odds of no man. When the singing ceased Barney came out of the shadow at his father's side, and, reaching for the violin, said, "Let me spell you a bit, Dad."

At his voice Dick, who was across the floor beside the singer, turned quickly and, seeing Barney, sprang for him, shouting, "Hello! you old whale, you!" The father hastily pulled his precious violin out of danger.

"Let go, Dick! Let go, I tell you!" said Barney, struggling in his brother's embrace; "stop it, now!"

With a mighty effort he threw Dick off from him and stood on guard with an embarrassed, half-shamed, half-indignant laugh. The crowd gathered near in delighted expectation. There was always something sure to happen when Dick "got after" his older brother.

"He won't let me kiss him," cried Dick pitifully, to the huge enjoyment of the crowd.

"It's too bad, Dick," they cried.

"So it is. But I'm not going to be put off. It's a shame!" replied Dick, in a hurt tone. "And me just home, too."

"It's a mean shame, Dick. Wouldn't stand it a minute," cried his sympathisers.

"I won't either," cried Dick, preparing to make an attack.

"Look here, Dick," cried Barney impatiently, "just quit your nonsense or I'll throw you on the floor there and sit on you. Besides, you're spoiling the music."

"Well, well, that's so," said Dick. "So on Miss Lane's account I'll forbear, provided, that is, she sings again, as, of course, she will."

It was Dick's custom to assume command in every company where he found himself.

"What is it to be? 'Dixie'?"

"Yes! Yes!" cried the crowd. "'Dixie.' We'll give you the chorus."

After a little protest the girl struck a few chords and dashed off into that old plantation song full of mingling pathos and humour. Barney picked up his father's violin, touched the strings softly till he found her key and then followed in a subdued accompaniment of weird chords. The girl turned herself toward him, her beautiful face lighting up as if she had caught a glimpse of a kindred spirit, and with a new richness and tenderness she poured forth the full flood of her song. The crowd were entranced with delight. Even those who had been somewhat impatient for the renewal of the dance joined in calls for another song. She turned to Dick, who had resumed his place beside her. "Who is the man you wanted so badly to kiss?" she asked quietly.

"Who?" he cried, so that everyone heard. "What! don't you know? That's Barney, the one and only Barney, my brother. Here, Barney, drop your fiddle and be introduced to Miss Iola Lane, late from Virginia, or is it Maryland? Some of those heathen places beyond the Dixie line."

Barney dropped the violin from his chin, came over the floor, and awkwardly offered his hand. With easy, lazy grace she rose from the block where she had been sitting.

"You accompany beautifully," she said in her soft Southern drawl; "it's in you, I can see. No one can ever be taught to accompany like that."

"Oh, pshaw! That's nothing," said Barney, eager to get back again to his shadow, "but if you don't mind I'll try to follow you if you sing again."

"Certainly," cried Dick, "she'll sing again. What will you give us now, white or black?"

"Plantation, of course," said Barney brusquely.

"All right. 'Kentucky home,' eh?" cried Dick.

The girl looked up at him with a saucy, defiant look. "Do they all obey you here?"

"Ask them."

"That's what," cried Alec Murray, "especially the girls."

She hesitated a few moments, evidently meditating rebellion, then turning to Barney, who was playing softly the air that had been asked for, "You, too, obey, I see," she said.

"Generally—, always when I like," he replied, continuing to play.

"Oh, well," shrugging her shoulders, "I suppose I must then." And she began:

"The sun shines bright on de old Kentucky home."

Again that hush fell upon the crowd. The face of the singer, with its dark, romantic beauty touched with the magic of the moonlight, the voice soft, mellow, vibrant with passion, like the deeper notes of a 'cello, supported by the weird chords of Barney's violin, held them breathless. No voice joined in the chorus. As she sang, the subtle telepathic waves came back from her audience to the girl, and with ever-deepening passion and abandon she poured forth into the moonlit silence the full throbbing tide of song. The old air, simple and time-worn, took on a new richness of tone colour and a fulness of volume suggestive of springs of unutterable depths. Even Dick's gay air of command surrendered to the spell. As before, silence followed the song.

"But you did not do your part," she said, smiling up at him with a very pretty air of embarrassment.

"No," said Dick solemnly, "we didn't dare."

"Sing again," said Barney abruptly. His voice sounded deep and hoarse, and Dick, looking curiously at him, said apologetically, "Music, when it's good, makes him quite batty."

But Iola ignored him. "Did you ever hear this?" she said to Barney. She strummed a few chords on her guitar. "It's only a little baby song, one my old mammy used to sing."

"Sleep, ma baby, close youah lil winkahs fas',

Loo-la, Loo-la, don' you gib me any sass.

Youah mammy's ol', an' want you to de berry las',

So, baby, honey, let dose mean ol' angels pass.

CHORUS:

"Sleep, ma baby, mammy can't let you go.

Sleep, ma baby, de angels want you sho!

De angels want you, guess I know,

But mammy hol' you, hol' you tight jes' so.

"Sleep, ma baby, close youah lil fingahs, Meah,

Loo-la, Loo-la, tight about ma fingahs heah,

De dawk come close, but baby don' you nebbeh feah,

Youah mammy'll hol' you, hol' you till de mawn appeah.

"Sleep, ma baby, why you lie so col', so col'?

Loo-la, Loo-la, do Massa want you for His fol'?

But, baby, honey, don' you know youah mammy's ol'

An' want you, want you, oh, she want you jes' to hol'."

A long silence followed the song. The girl laid her guitar down and sat quietly looking straight before her, while Barney played the refrain over and over. The simple pathos of the little song, its tender appeal to the mother-chords that somehow vibrate in all human hearts, reached the deep places in the honest hearts of her listeners and for some moments they stood silent about her. It was with an obvious effort that Dick released the tension by crying out, "Partners for four-hand reel." Instantly the company resolved itself into groups of four and stood waiting for the music.

"Strike up, Barney," cried Dick impatiently, shuffling before Iola, whom he had chosen for his partner. But Barney, handing the violin to his father, slipped back into the shadow where his mother and Margaret were standing. The boy's face was pale through its swarthy tan.

"Come away," he said to his mother in a strained, unnatural voice.

"Isn't she beautiful?" cried Margaret impulsively.

"Is she? I didn't notice. But great goodness! What a voice!"

"Um, some will be thinking so, I doubt," said Mrs. Boyle grimly, with a sharp glance at her son.

But Barney had become oblivious to her words and glances. He moved away as in a dream to make ready for the home going of his party, for soon the dancers would be at Sir Roger's. Nor did he waken from his dream mood during the drive home. He could hear Dick chattering gaily to Margaret and his mother of his College experiences, but except for an occasional word with his father he sat in silence, gazing not upon the fields and woods that lay in all their moonlit glory about them, but upon that new world, vast, unreal, yet vividly present, whose horizon lay beyond the line of vision, the world of his imagination, where he must henceforth live and where his work must lie. For the events of the afternoon had summoned a new self into being, a self unfamiliar, but real and terribly insistent, demanding recognition. He could not analyse the change that had come to him, nor could he account for it. He did not try to. He lived again those great moments when, having been thrust by chance into the command of these fifty mighty men, he had swung them to victory. He remembered the ease, the perfect harmony with which his faculties had wrought through those few minutes of fierce struggle. Again he passed through the awful ordeal of the operation, now holding the light, now assisting with forceps or cord or needle, now sponging away that ghastly red flow that could not be stemmed. He wondered now at his self-mastery. He could see again his fingers, bloody, but unshaking, handing the old doctor a needle and silk cord. He remembered his surprise and pity, almost contempt, for big Tom Magee lying on the floor unable to lift his head; remembered, too, the strange absence of anything like elation at the doctor's words, "My boy, you have the nerve and the fingers of a surgeon, and that's what your Maker intended you to be."

But he let his mind linger long and with thrilling joy through the interlude in the dance. Every detail of that scene stood clearly limned before his mind. The bare skeleton of the new harp, the crowding, eager, tense faces of the listeners, his mother's and Margaret's in the hindmost row, his brother standing in the centre foreground, the upturned face of the singer with its pale romantic loveliness, all in the mystery of the moonlight, and, soaring over all, that clear, vibrant, yet softly passionate, glorious voice. That was the final magic touch that rolled back the screen and set before him the new world which must henceforth be his. He could not explain that touch. The songs were the old simple airs worn threadbare by long use in the countryside. It was certainly not the songs. Nor was it the singer. Curiously enough, the girl, her personality, her character, worthy or unworthy, had only a subordinate place in his thought. He was conscious of her presence there as a subtle yet powerful influence, but as something detached from the upturned face illumined in the soft moonlight and the stream of heart-shaking song. She was to him thus far simply a vision and a voice, to which all the psychic element in him made eager response. As he drove into the quiet Mill yard it came upon him with a shock of pain that with the old life he had done forever. He felt himself already detached from it. The new self looking out upon its new world had shaken off his boyhood as the bursting leaf shakes off the husks of spring.

As Dick's gay exclamation of delight at sight of the old home fell upon his ear a deeper pain struck him, for he vaguely felt that while his brother still held his place in the centre of the stage, that stage had immeasurably extended and was now peopled with other figures, shadowy, it is true, but there, and influential. His brother, who with his mother, or, indeed, perhaps more than his mother, had absorbed his boyish devotion, must henceforth share that devotion with others. Upon this thought his brother's voice broke in.

"What's the matter, old chap? Is there anything wrong?"

The kindly tone stabbed like a knife.

"No, no. Nothing, Dick."

"Yes, but there is. You're not the same." At the anxious appeal in the voice Barney stood for a moment steadily regarding his brother, for whom he could easily give his life, with a troubled sense of change that he could not analyse to himself, much less explain to his brother.

"I don't know, Dick—I can't tell you—I don't think I am the same." A look of startled dismay fell swiftly down upon the frank, handsome face turned toward him.

"Have I done anything, Barney?" said the younger boy, his dismay showing in his tone.

"No, no, Dick, boy, it has nothing to do with you." He put his hands on his brother's shoulders, the nearest thing to an embrace he ever allowed himself. "It is in myself; but to you, my boy, I am the same." His speech came now hurriedly and with difficulty: "And whatever comes to me or to you, Dick, remember I shall never change to you—remember that, Dick, to you I shall never change." His breath was coming in quick gasps. The younger boy gazed at his usually so undemonstrative brother. Suddenly he threw his arms about his neck, crying in a broken voice, "You won't, Barney, I know you won't. If you ever do I don't want to live."

For a single moment Barney held the boy in his arms, patting his shoulder gently, then, pushing him back, said impatiently, "Well, I am a blamed old fool, anyway. What in the diggins is the matter with me, I don't know. I guess I want supper, nothing to eat since noon. But all the same, Dick," he added in a steady, matter-of-fact tone, "we must expect many changes from this out, but we'll stand by each other till the world cracks."

After Dick had gone upstairs with his father, Barney and his mother sat together talking over the doings of the day after their invariable custom.

"He is looking thin, I am thinking," said the mother.

"Oh, he's right enough. A few days after the reaper and a few meals out of your kitchen, mother, and he will be as fit as ever."

"That was a fine work of yours with the doctor." The indifferent tone did not deceive her son for a moment.

"Oh, pshaw, that was nothing. At least it seemed nothing then. There were things to be done, blood to be stopped, skin to be sewed up, and I just did what I could." The mother nodded slightly.

"You did no more than you ought, and that great Tom Magee might be doing something better than lying on his back on the floor like a baby."

"He couldn't help himself, mother. That's the way it struck him. But, man, it was fine to see the doctor, so quick and so clever, and never a slip or a stop." He paused abruptly and stood upright looking far away for some moments. "Yes, fine! Splendid!" he continued as in a dream. "And he said I had the fingers and the nerve for a surgeon. That's it. I see now—mother, I'm going to be a doctor."

His mother stood and faced him. "A doctor? You?"

The sharp tone recalled her son.

"Yes, me. Why not?"

"And Richard?"

Her son understood her perfectly. His mind went back to a morning long ago when his mother, putting his younger brother's hand in his as they set forth to school for the first time, said, "Take care of your brother, Bernard. I give him into your charge." That very day and many a day after he had stood by his brother, had fought for him, had pulled him out of scraps into which the younger lad's fiery temper and reckless spirit were frequently plunging him, but never once had he consciously failed in the trust imposed on him. And as Dick developed exceptional brilliance in his school work, together they planned for him, the mother and the older brother, the mother painfully making and saving, the brother accepting as his part the life of plodding obscurity in order that the younger boy might have his full chance of what school and college could do for him. True to the best traditions of her race, the mother had fondly dreamed of a day when she should hear from her son's lips the word of life. With never a thought of the sacrifice she was demanding, she had drawn into this partnership her elder son. And thus to the mother it seemed nothing less than an act of treachery, amounting to sacrilege, that Barney for a single moment should cherish for himself an ambition whose realisation might imperil his brother's future. Barney needed, therefore, no explanation of his mother's cry of dismay, almost of horror. He was quick with his answer.

"Dick? Oh, mother, do you think I was forgetting Dick? Of course nothing must stop Dick. I can wait—but I am going to be a doctor."

The mother looked into her son's rugged face, so like her own in its firm lines, and replied almost grudgingly, "Ay, I doubt you will." Then she added hastily, as if conscious of her ungracious tone, "And what for should you not?"

"Thank you, mother," said her son humbly, "and never fear we'll stand by Dick."

Her eyes followed him out of the room and for some moments she stood watching the door through which he had passed. Then, with a great sigh, she said aloud: "Ay, it is the grand doctor he will make. He has the nerve and the fingers whatever." Then after a pause she added: "And he will not fail the laddie, I warrant."

V
THE NEW TEACHER

The new teacher was distinctly phenomenal from every point of view. Her beauty was a type quite unusual where rosy-cheeked, deep-chested, sturdy womanhood was the rule. Even the smallest child was sensible of the fascination of her smile, which seemed to emanate from every feature of her face, so much so that little Ruby Ross was heard to say: "And do you know, mother, she smiles with her nose!" The almost timid appeal in her gentle manner stirred the chivalry latent in every boy's heart. Back of her appealing gentleness, however, there was a reserve of proud command due to the strain in her blood of a regnant, haughty, slave-ruling race. But in her discipline of the school she had rarely to fall back upon sheer authority. She had a method unique, but undoubtedly effective, based upon two fundamental principles: regard for public opinion, and hope of reward. The daily tasks were prepared and rendered as if in the presence of the great if somewhat vague public which at times she individualized, as she became familiar with her pupils, in the person of father or mother or trustee, as the case might be. And with marvellous skill she played this string, albeit occasionally she struck a false note.

"What would your father think, Lincoln?" she inquired reproachfully of little Link Young. Link's father was a typical Down Easterner, by name Jabez Young or, as he was more commonly known, "Maine Jabe," for his fondness of his reminiscence of his native State. "What would your father think if he saw you act so rudely?"

"Dad wouldn't care a dang."

Instantly conscious of her mistake, she hastened to recover.

"Well, Lincoln, what do you think I think?"

Link's Yankee assurance sank abashed before this direct personal appeal. He hung his head in blushing silence.

"Do you know, Lincoln, you might come to be a right clever gentleman if you tried hard." A new idea lodged itself under Link's red thatch of hair and a new motive stirred in his shrewd little soul. Here was one visibly present whose good opinion he valued. At all costs that good opinion he must win.

The whole school was being consciously trained for exhibition purposes. The day would surely come when before the eyes of the public they would parade for inspection. Therefore, it behooved them to be ready.

But more important in enforcing discipline was the hope of reward. This principle was robbed of its more sordid elements by the nature of the reward held forth. A day of good conduct and of faithful work invariably closed with an hour devoted to histrionic and musical exercise. To recite before the teacher and to hear the teacher recite was worth considerable effort. To sing with the teacher was a joy, but to hear the teacher sing to the accompaniment of her guitar was the supreme of bliss. It was not only an hour of pleasure to the pupils, but an hour of training as well. She initiated them into the mysteries of deep breathing, chest tones, phrasing, and expression, and such was their absorbing interest in and devotion to this study, that in a few weeks truly remarkable results were obtained. The singing lesson invariably concluded with a plantation song from the teacher; and with her memory-gates wide open to the sunny South of her childhood, and with all her soul in her voice, she gave them her best, holding them breathless, laughterful, or tear-choked, according to her mood and song.

It was by such a song that Mr. Jabez Young, driving along the road on his way to the store, was suddenly arrested and rendered incapable of movement till the song was done. In amazed excitement he burst forth to old Hector Ross, the Chairman of the Trustee Board, who happened to be in the store:

"Gol dang my cats! What hev yeh got in the school up yonder? Say! I couldn't git my team to move past that there door!"

"What's matter, Mr. Young?"

"Why, dang it all! I'll report to the Reeve. Fust thing yeh know there'll be a string-a-teams from here to the next concession blockin' that there road in front of the school!"

"Why, what's the matter with the school, Mr. Young?" inquired old Hector, in anxious surprise.

"Why, ain't ye heard her? Say! down in Maine I paid a dollar one 'time to hear a big singer, forgit her name, but she was 'lowed to be the dangdest singer in all them parts. But, Gol dang my cats to cinders! she ain't any more like that there teacher of yours than my old Tom cat's like the angel that leads the choir in Abram's bosom!"

"That is very interesting, Mr. Young. And I suppose you won't mind paying a little extra school rate now," said Hector, with a shrewd twinkle in his eye.

"Extra school rate! I tell yeh what, I'll charge up my lost time to the trustees! But danged if I wouldn't give a day's pay to hear that song again!"

In application of this principle of reward for merit, the teacher introduced a subordinate principle which proved effective when all else failed. The school was made corporately and jointly responsible for the individual. The offence of one was the offence of all, the merit of one the merit of all. Thus every pupil was associated with her in the business of securing good lessons and exemplary conduct. As the day went on each misdemeanour was gravely, and in full view of the school, marked down upon the blackboard. The merits obtained by any pupil were in like manner recorded. The day closing with an adverse balance knew no hour of song. Woe to the boy who, dead to all other motives of good conduct, persisted in robbing the school of its hour of delight. In the case of Ab Maddock, big, impudent, and pachydermous, it took Dugald Robertson, the minister's son, just half an hour's hard fighting to extract a promise of good behaviour. Dugald was in the main a thoughtful, peaceable boy, the most advanced pupil in the entrance class, and a great mathematician. At first he was inclined to despise the teacher, setting little store by her beautiful face and fascinating smile, for on the very first day he discovered her woful mathematical inadequacy. Arithmetic was her despair. With algebraic formulae and Euclid's propositions her fine memory saved her. But with quick intuition she threw herself frankly upon the boy's generosity, and in the evenings together they, with Margaret's assistance, wrestled with the bewildering intricacies of arithmetical problems. Her open confession of helplessness, and her heroic attempts to overcome her defects, made irresistible appeal to the chivalrous heart of the little Highland gentleman. Thenceforth he was her champion for all that was in him.

But the teacher's weakness in mathematics was atoned for, if atonement there be for such a weakness, by the ample strength of her endowments in those branches of learning in which imagination and artistic sensibility play any large part. And a far larger part, and far more important, do these Divine gifts play than many wise educationists conceive. The lessons in history, in geography, and in reading ceased to be mere memory tasks and became instinct with life. The whole school would stay its ordinary work to listen while the teacher told tales of the brave days of old to the history class, or transformed the geography lessons into excursions among people of strange tongues dwelling in far lands. But it was in the reading lessons that her artistic talents had full play. The mere pronouncing and spelling of words were but incidents in the way of expression of thought and emotion. After a whole week of drilling which she would give to a single lesson, she would arrest the class with the question, "What is the author seeing?" and with the further question, "How does he try to show it to us?" Reading, to her, consisted in the ability to see what the author saw and the art of telling it, and to set forth with grace that thing in the author's words.

In the writing class her chief anxiety was to avoid blots. Every blot might become an occasion of humiliation to teacher and pupils alike. "Oh, this will never do! They must not see this!" she would cry, rubbing out with infinite care and pains the blot, and rubbing in the horror of such a defilement being paraded before the eyes of the vague but terrible "they."

Thus the pathway trodden in the school routine was, perchance, neither wide nor far extended, but it was thoroughly well trodden. As a consequence, when the day for the closing exercises came around both teacher and pupils had become so thoroughly familiar with the path and so accustomed to the vision of the onlooking public that they faced the ordeal without dread, prepared to give forth whatever of knowledge or accomplishment they might possess.

A fortunate rainy day, making the hauling of hay or the cutting of fall wheat equally impossible, filled the school with the parents and friends of the children. The minister and the trustees were dutifully present. Of the mill people Dick and his mother appeared, Dick because his mother insisted that a student should show interest in the school, his mother because Dick refused to go a step without her. Barney came later, not because of his interest in the school, but chiefly, he declared to himself, conscious of the need of a reason, because there was nothing much else to do. The presence of "Maine" Jabe might be taken as the high water mark of the interest aroused throughout the section in the new teacher and her methods.

The closing exercises were, with a single exception, a brilliantly flawless exhibition. That exception appeared in the Euclid of the entrance class. The mathematics were introduced early in the day. The arithmetic, which dealt chiefly with problems of barter and sale of the various products of the farm, was lightly and deftly passed over. The algebra class was equally successful. In the Euclid class it seemed as if the hitherto unbroken success would come to an unhappy end in the bewilderment and confusion of Phoebe Ross, from whom the minister had asked a demonstration of the pons asinorum. But the blame for poor Phoebe's bewilderment clearly lay with the minister himself, for in placing the figure upon the board with the letters designating the isosceles triangle he made the fatal blunder of setting the letter B at the right hand side of the base instead of at its proper place at the left, as in the book. The result was that the unhappy Phoebe, ignoring the figure upon the board and depending entirely upon her memory, soon plunged both the minister and herself into confusion hopeless and complete. But the quick eye of the teacher had detected the difficulty, and, going to the board, she erased the unfamiliar figure, saying, as she did so, in her gentle appealing voice, "Wait, Phoebe. You are quite confused, I know. We shall wipe the board clean and begin all over." She placed the figure upon the board with the designating letters arranged as in the book. "Now, take your time," she said with deliberate emphasis. "Let A, B, C be an isosceles triangle." And thus, with her feet set firmly upon the familiar path, little Phoebe slipped through that desperate maze of angles and triangles with an ease, speed, and dexterity that elicited the wonder and admiration of all present, the minister, good man, included. Upon Barney, however, who understood perfectly what had happened, the incident left a decidedly unpleasant impression. Indeed, the superficiality of the mathematical exercises as a whole awakened within him a feeling of pain which he could not explain.

When the reading classes were under review the school passed from the atmosphere of the superficial to that of the real. Never had such reading been heard in that or in any other common school. The familiar sing-song monotony of the reading lesson was gone and in its place a real and vivid picturing of the scenes described or enacted. It was all simple, natural, and effective.

The exercises attained an easy climax with the recitations and singing which closed the day. Here the artistic gifts of the teacher had full scope. There was an absence of all nervous dread in the performers. By some marvellous power she caught hold and absorbed their attention so that for her chiefly, if not entirely, they recited or sang. In the singing, which terminated the proceedings, the triumph of the day was complete. A single hymn, two or three kindergarten action songs, hitherto unheard in that community, a rollicking negro chorus; and, at the last, "for the children and the mothers," the teacher said, one soft lullaby in which for the first time the teacher's voice was heard, the low, vibrant tones filling the room with music such as in all their lives they had never listened to. It was a fine sense of artistic values that cut out the speeches and dismissed the school in the ordinary way. The full tide of their enthusiasm broke upon her as minister, trustees, parents, and all crowded about her, offering congratulations. Her air of shy grace with just a touch of nonchalant reserve served in no small degree to heighten the whole effect of the day.

The mill people walked home with the minister and Margaret.

"Isn't she a wonder?" cried Dick. "What has she done to those little blocks? Why, they don't seem the same children!"

"Yes, yes," replied the minister, "it is quite surprising, indeed."

"In their mathematics, though, there was some thin skating there for a while," continued Dick.

"Yes, yes, the little lassie became confused. But she recovered herself cleverly."

"Yes, indeed," said Dick, with a slight laugh. "That was a clever bit of work on the part of the teacher."

"Oh, shut up, Dick!" said Barney sharply.

"Oh, well," replied Dick, "no one expects mathematics from a girl, anyway."

"Do you hear the conceit of him?" said his mother indignantly, "and Margaret there can show all of you the way."

"Yes, that's true, mother, but Margaret is a wonder, too. But whatever you say, the reciting and singing were good. Even little Link Young was quite dramatic. They say that 'Maine' Jabe for the first time in his life is quite reckless in regard to the school rates."

"We will just wait a year," said his mother. "It is a new broom that sweeps clean."

"Now, mother, you are too hard to please."

"Perhaps," she replied, grimly closing her lips.

As they reached the manse gate the minister, who had evidently been pondering Dick's words, said, "Well, Mrs. Boyle, we have had a delightful afternoon, whatever, a remarkable exhibition. Yes, yes. And after all it is a great matter that the children should be taught to read and recite well. And it was no wonder that the poor thing would seek to make it easy for the little girl. And Margaret will need to take Dugald over his mathematics, I fear, before he goes up to the entrance." At which remark the painful feeling which the reciting and singing had caused Barney to forget for the time, returned with even greater poignancy.

But in all the section there was only one opinion, and that was that, at all costs, the teacher's services must be retained. For once, the trustees realised that no longer would they depend for popularity upon the sole qualification of their ability to keep down the school rate. It was, perhaps, not the most diplomatic moment they chose for the securing of the teacher's services for another year. It might be that they were moved to immediate action by the apparent willingness on her part to leave the matter of re-engagement an open question. On all hands, however, they were applauded as having done a good stroke of business when, there and then, they closed their bargain with the teacher, although at a higher salary, as it turned out, than had ever been paid in the section before.

VI
THE YOUNG DOCTOR

Barney's jaw ran along the side of his face, ending abruptly in a square-cut chin, the jaw and chin doing for his face what a ridge and bluff of rock do for a landscape. They suggested the bed rock of character, abiding, firm, indomitable. Having seen the goal at which he would arrive, there remained only to find the path and press it. He would be a doctor. The question was, how? His first step was to consult the only authority available, old Doctor Ferguson. It was a stormy interview, for the doctor was of a craggy sort like Barney himself, with a jaw and a chin and all they suggested. The boy told his purpose briefly, almost defiantly, as if expecting scornful opposition, and asked guidance. The doctor flung difficulties at his head for half an hour and ended by offering him money, cursing his Highland pride when the boy refused it.

"What do I want with money?" cried the doctor. He had lost his only son three years before. "There's only my wife. And she'll have plenty. Money! Dirt, fit to walk on, to make a path with, that's all! Had my boy lived, God knows I'd have made him a surgeon. But—" Here the doctor snorted violently and coughed, trumpeting hard with his nose. "Confound these foggy nights! I'll put you through."

"I'll pay my way," said Barney almost sullenly, "or I'll stay at home."

"What are you doing here, then?" he roared at the boy.

"I came to find out how to start. Must a man go to college?"

"No," shouted the doctor again; "he can be a confounded fool and work up by himself, a terrible handicap, going up for the examinations till the last year, when he must attend college."

"I could do that," said Barney, closing his jaws.

The doctor looked at his face. The shut jaws looked more than ever like a ledge of granite and the chin like a cliff. "You can, eh? Hanged if I don't believe you! And I'll help you. I'd like to, if you would let me." The voice ended in a wistful tone. The boy was touched.

"Oh, you can!" he cried impulsively, "and I'll be awfully thankful. You can tell me what books to get and sometimes explain, perhaps, if you have time." His face went suddenly crimson. He was conscious of asking a favour.

The old doctor sat down, rejoicing greatly in him, and for the first time treated him as an equal. He explained in detail the course of study, making much of the difficulties in the way. When he had done he waved his hand toward his library.

"Now, there are my books," he cried; "use them and ask me what you will. It will brush me up. And I'll take you to see my cases and, by God's help, we'll make you a surgeon! A surgeon, sir! You've got the fingers and the nerves. A surgeon! That's the only thing worth while. The physician can't see further below the skin than anyone else. He guesses and experiments, treats symptoms, trys one drug then another, guessing and experimenting all along the line. But the knife, boy!" Here the doctor rose and began to pace the floor. "There's no guess in the knife point! The knife lays bare the evil, fights, eradicates it! Look at that boy Kane, died three weeks ago. 'Inflammation,' said the physician. Treated his symptoms properly enough. The boy died. At the postmortem"—here the doctor paused in his walk, lowering his voice almost to a whisper while he bent over the boy—"at the post-mortem the knife discovered an abscess on the vermiform appendix. The discovery was made too late." These were the days before appendicitis became fashionable. "Now, listen to me," continued the doctor, even more impressively, "I believe in my soul that the knife at the proper moment might have saved that boy's life! A slight incision an inch or two long, the removal of the diseased part, a few stitches, and in a couple of weeks the boy is well! Ah, boy! God knows I'd give my life to be a great surgeon! But He didn't give me the fingers. Look at these," and he held up a coarse, heavy hand; "I haven't the touch. And besides, He brought me my wife, the best thing I've got in the world, and my baby, which settled the surgeon business forever. Now listen, boy! You've got the nerve—plenty of men have that—but you've also got the fingers, which few men have. With your touch and your steady nerve and your mechanical ingenuity—I've seen your machines, boy—you can be a great surgeon! But you must know your subject. You must think, dream, sleep, eat, drink bones and muscles and sinews and nerves. Push everything else aside!" he cried, waving his great hands. "And remember!"—here his voice took a solemn tone—"let nothing share your heart with your knife! Leave the women alone. A woman has no business in science. She distracts the mind, disturbs the liver, absorbs the vital powers, besides paralysing the finances. For you, let there be one woman, your mother, at least till you are a surgeon. Now, then, there are my books and all my spare time at your command." At these words the boy's face, which had caught the light and glow of the old man's enthusiasm, fell.

"Well, what now?" cried the doctor, reading his face like a book.

"I have no right to take your books or your time."

The doctor sprang to his feet with an oath. The boy also rose and faced him, almost as if expecting a blow. For a moment they stood steadfastly regarding each other, then the doctor's old face relaxed, his eyes softened. He put his big hand on the boy's shoulder.

"Now, by the Lord that made you and me!" he said, "we were meant for a team, and a team we'll make. I'll help you and I'll make you pay." The boy's face brightened.

"How?" he cried eagerly.

"We'll change work." The doctor's old eyes began to twinkle. "I want fall ploughing done and my cordwood hauled."

"I'll do it!" cried Barney. A light broke in his eyes and flooded his face. At last he saw his path.

"Here," said the doctor, taking down a book, "here's your Gray." And turning the leaves, "Here's what happened to Ben Fallows. Read this. And here's the treatment," pulling down another book and turning to a page, "Read that. I'll make Ben your first patient. There's no money in it, anyway, and you can't kill him. He only needs three things, cleanliness, good cheer, and good food. By and by we'll get him a leg. Here's that Buffalo doctor's catalogue. Take it along. Now, boy, I'll work you, grind you, and you'll go for your first examination next spring."

"Next spring!" cried Barney, aghast, "not for three years."

"Three years!" snorted the doctor, "three fiddlesticks! You can do this first examination by next spring."

"Yes. I could do it," said Barney slowly.

The doctor cast an admiring glance at the line of jaw on the boy's face.

"But there's the mortgage and there's Dick's college."

"Dick's college? Why Dick's and not yours?"

The boy's rugged face changed. A tender light fell over it, filling in its cracks and canyons.

"Because—well, because Dick must go through. Dick's clever. He's awful clever." Pride mingled with the tenderness in look and tone. "Mother wants him to be a minister, and," he added after a pause, "I do, too."

The old doctor turned from him, stood looking out of the window a few minutes, and then came back. He put his hands on the boy's shoulders. "I understand, boy," he said, his great voice vibrating in deep and tender tones, "I, too, had a brother once. Make Dick a minister if you want, but meantime we'll grind the surgeon's knife."

The boy went home to his mother in high exultation.

"The doctor wants me to look after Ben for him," he announced. "He is going to show me the dressings, and he says all he wants is cleanliness, good cheer, and good food. I can keep him clean. But how he is to get good cheer in that house, and how he is to get good food, are more than I can tell."

"Good cheer!" cried Dick. "He'll not lack for company. How many has she now, mother? A couple of dozen, more or less?"

"There are thirteen of them already, poor thing."

"Thirteen! That's an unlucky stopping place. Let us hope she won't allow the figure to remain at that."

"Indeed, I am thinking it will not," said his mother, speaking with the confidence of intimate knowledge.

"Well," replied Dick, with a judicial air, "it's a question whether it's worse to defy the fate that lurks in that unlucky number, or to accept the doubtful blessing of another twig to the already overburdened olive tree."

"Ay, it is a hard time she is having with the four babies and all."

"Four, mother! Surely that's an unusual number even for the prolific Mrs. Fallows!"

"Whisht, laddie!" said his mother, in a shocked tone, "don't talk foolishly."

"But you said four, mother."

"Twins the last twice," interjected Barney.

"Great snakes!" cried Dick, "let us hope she won't get the habit."

"But, mother," inquired Barney seriously, "what's to be done?"

"Indeed, I can't tell," said his mother.

"Listen to me," cried Dick, "I've got an inspiration. I'll undertake the 'good cheer.' I'll impress the young ladies into this worthy service. Light conversation and song. And you can put up the food, mother, can't you?"

"We will see," said the mother quietly; "we will do our best."

"In that case the 'food department' is secure," said Dick; "already I see Ben Fallows making rapid strides toward convalescence."

It was characteristic of Barney that within a few days he had all three departments in full operation. With great tact he succeeded in making Mrs. Fallows thoroughly scour the woodwork and whitewash the walls in Ben's little room, urging the doctor's orders and emphasizing the danger of microbes, the dread of which was just beginning to obtain in popular imagination.

"Microbes? What's them?" inquired Mrs. Fallows, suspiciously.

"Very small insects."

"Insects? Is it bugs you mean?" Mrs. Fallows at once became fiercely hostile. "I want to tell yeh, young sir, ther' hain't no bugs in this 'ouse. If ther's one thing I'm pertickler 'bout, it's bugs. John sez to me, sez 'e, 'What's the hodds of a bug or two, Hianthy?' But I sez to 'im, sez I, 'No bugs fer me, John. I hain't been brought up with bugs, an' bugs I cawn't an' won't 'ave.'"

It was only Barney's earnest assurance that the presence of microbes was no impeachment of the most scrupulous housekeeping and, indeed, that these mysterious creatures were to be found in the very highest circles, that Mrs. Fallows was finally appeased. With equal skill he inaugurated his "good food" department, soothing Mrs. Fallows' susceptibilities with the diplomatic information that in surgical cases such as Ben's certain articles of diet specially prepared were necessary to the best results.

Not the least successful part of the treatment prescribed was that furnished by the "good cheer" department. This was left entirely in Dick's charge, and he threw himself into its direction with the enthusiasm of a devotee. Iola with her guitar was undoubtedly his mainstay. But Dick was never quite satisfied unless he could persuade Margaret, too, to assist in his department. But Margaret had other duties, and, besides, she had associated herself more particularly with Mrs. Boyle in the work of supplementing Mrs. Fallows' somewhat unappetising though entirely substantial meals with delicacies more suited to the sickroom. Dick, however, insisted that with all that Iola and himself in the "good cheer" department and Barney in what he called the "scavenging" department could achieve, there was still need of Margaret's presence and Margaret's touch. Hence, before the busy harvest time came upon them, he made a practice of calling at the manse, and, relieving her of the duty of getting to sleep little five-year-old Tom, with whom he was first favourite, he would carry her off to the Fallows household, whither Barney and Iola had preceded them.

Altogether the "young doctor," as Ben called him, had reason to be proud of the success he was achieving with his first patient. The amputation healed over and the bone knit at the first intention, and in a few weeks Ben was far on the way to convalescence. He was never weary in his praises of the "young doctor." It was the "young doctor" who, by changing the bandages, had eased him of the intolerable pain which followed the first dressing. It was the "young doctor" who had changed the splints, shaping them cunningly to fit the limb, bringing ease where there had been chafing pain.

"Let 'em 'ave the old doctor if they want," was Ben's final conclusion, "but fer me, the young doctor, sez I."

VII
THE GOOD CHEER DEPARTMENT

The "good cheer" department, while ostensibly for Ben's benefit, wrought profit and cheer for others besides. What Dick got of it no one but himself knew, for that young man, with all his apparent frankness, kept the veil over his heart drawn close. To Barney, absorbed in his new work, with its wealth of new ideas and his new ambitions, the "good cheer" department was chiefly valued as an important factor in Ben's progress. To Iola it brought what to her was the breath of life, admiration, gratitude, affection. But Margaret perhaps more than any, not even excepting Ben himself, gathered from this department what might be called its by-products. The daily monotony of her household duties bore hard upon her young heart. Ambitions long cherished, though cheerfully laid aside at the sudden call of duty, could not be quite abandoned without a sense of pain and loss. The break offered by the work of the department in the monotony of her life, the companionship of its members, and, as much as anything, the irresistible appeal to her keen sense of humour by the genial, loquacious, dirty but irresistibly cheery Mrs. Fallows, far more than compensated for the extra effort which her membership in the department rendered necessary.

It was the evening following that of the school closing that Dick with Margaret and Iola were making one of their customary calls at the Fallows cottage. It would be for Iola the last visit for some weeks, as she was about to depart to town for her holidays.

"I have come to say good-bye," she announced as she shook hands with Mrs. Fallows.

"Good-bye, dear 'eart," said that lady, throwing up her hands aghast; "art goin' to leave us fer good?"

"No, nothing so bad," said Dick; "only for a few weeks, Mrs. Fallows. The section couldn't do without her, and the trustees have decided that they wouldn't let her out of sight till they had put a string on her."

"Goin' to come back again, be yeh? I did 'ear as 'ow yeh was goin' to leave. My little Joe was that broken-'earted, an' 'e declared to me as 'ow 'e wouldn't go to school no more."

"I don't wonder," said Dick. "Why, if the trustees hadn't engaged her, as 'Maine Jabe' said, 'there'd be the dangdest kind of riot in the section.'"

"Don't listen to him, Mrs. Fallows. I'm going in to sing to Ben, if I may."

"An' that yeh may, bless yer 'eart!" said Mrs. Fallows, picking up a twin from the doorway to allow Iola and Dick to pass into the inner room. "Ther' now," she continued to Margaret, who was moving about putting things to rights, "don't yeh go tirin' of yerself. I know things is in a muss. Some'ow by Saturday night things piles up terr'ble, an' I'm that tired I don't seem to 'ave no 'eart to straighten 'em up. Jest look at that 'ouse! I sez to John, sez I, 'I cawn't do no 'ousekeepin' with all 'em children 'bout my feet. An', bless their 'earts! it's all I kin do to put the bread in their mouths an keep the rags on their backs.' But John sez to me, sez 'e, 'Don't yeh worry, lass, 'bout the rags. Keep 'em full,' sez 'e, 'a full belly never 'eeds a bare back,' sez 'e. That's 'is way. 'E's halways a-comin' over somethin' cleverlike, is John. Lard save us! will yeh listen to that, now!" she continued in an awestruck undertone, as Iola's voice came in full rich melody from the next room. "An' Ben is fair raptured with 'er. Poor Benny! it's a sore calamity 'as overtaken 'im, a-breakin' of 'is leg an' a-mutilatin' of 'isself. It does seem as if the Lard 'ad give me som'at more'n my share. Listen to that ther'. Bless 'er dear 'eart; Benny fergits 'is hamputation an' 'is splits."

"His splints," cried Margaret; "are they all right now?"

"Yes. Since the young doctor—that's w'at Benny calls 'im—change 'em. Oh, that's a clever young man! Benney, 'e sez, 'Give me the young doctor,' sez 'e. Yeh see," continued Mrs. Fallows confidentially, and again lowering her voice impressively, "yeh see, 'is leg 'urt most orful at first, an' Benny cried to me, 'It's in me toes, mother, it's in me toes.' 'Why, Benny,' sez I to 'im, 'yeh hain't got no toes, Benny.' 'That's w'ere it 'urts,' sez 'e, 'toes or no toes.' An' father 'e wakes right up an' 'erd w'at Benny was cryin', an' sez 'e, 'Benny's right enough. 'Is toes'll 'urt till they're rotted away in the ground.' An' 'e tells as 'ow 'is sister's holdest boy got 'is leg hamputated, poor soul! an' 'ow 'is toes 'urted till they was took an' buried an' rotted away. Some doctors don't bury 'em, an' they do say," and here Mrs. Fallows' voice dropped quite to a whisper, "as 'ow that keeps 'em sore all the longer. Well, jest as father was speakin' in comes the doctor 'isself, an' father 'e told 'im as 'ow Benny was feelin' the pain in 'is toes. 'In yer toes, Benny?' sez the doctor surprised-like. 'Tain't yer toes, Ben.' 'Well, I guess it's me as is doin' the feelin',' sez Ben quite sharp, 'an' it's in me toes the feelin' is.' Then father 'e spoke up. 'E's a terr'ble man fer hargument, is father. 'Doctor,' sez 'e, 'is them toes buried, if I might be so bold?' 'Cawn't say,' sez the doctor quite hindifferent, though 'e must 'a' knowed. 'Well, my opinion is,' sez father, ''e'll feel them toes till they're took an' buried an' rotted away in the ground.' An' then 'e tells 'bout 'is sister's boy. 'Nonsense,' sez the doctor, 'tain't 'is toes at all. 'Is toes 'as nothin' to do with it.' 'W'at then?' asks father quite polite. 'It's the feelin' of 'is toes 'e's feelin'.' ''Ow can 'e 'ave any feelin' of 'is toes if 'e hain't got no toes?' 'Well,' sez the doctor, ''is feelin's hain't in 'is toes at all.' 'Well, that's w'ere mine is,' sez father. 'W'en I 'urts my toes it's in my toes I feel 'em. W'en I 'urts my 'and, it's my 'and.' 'My dear sir,' sez the doctor calm-like, 'it hain't in yer 'and, nor yet in yer toes, but in yer brain, in yer mind, yeh feel the pain.' 'P'raps,' sez Ben quite short again. My! 'e WAS short! 'But the feelin' in my mind is that my toes is 'urtin' most orful, an' I'd like to 'ave 'em buried if it's goin' to 'elp any.' 'Oh, come, Benny, that's all nonsense, yeh know,' sez the doctor, puttin' 'im off. But father is terr'ble persistent, an' 'e keeps on an' sez, 'Don't 'is mind know 'e hain't got no toes, doctor? 'Ow can 'is mind feel 'is toes 'urt w'en 'is mind knows 'e hain't got no toes to 'urt?' 'It hain't 'is toes, I tell yeh,' sez the doctor quite short, 'jest the feelin' of 'is toes in 'is mind.' 'The feelin' of 'is toes in 'is mind?' sez father. 'But 'e hain't got no toes to give 'im the feelin' of 'is toes in 'is mind or henywheres else.' 'Dummed old fool!' sez the doctor, quite losin' 'is temper, fer father is terr'ble provokin'. 'It's the feelin' 'is toes used to give 'im, an' that same feelin' of toes keeps up after 'is toes is gone.' 'Well,' sez father, an' me tryin' to ketch 'is eye to make 'im stop, 'I don't git no feelin' of toes till me toes is 'urt. If I don't 'urt 'em, I don't git no feelin' of toes. 'Ow are yeh goin' to start that ther' toe feelin' 'thout no toes to start it?' 'Yeh don't need no toes to start it,' sez the doctor, 'it's the old feelin' of toes a-keepin' up.' 'Ther' hain't no—' 'Look 'ere,' sez 'e, 'I tell yeh it hain't toes, it's the nerves of the toes reachin' up to the brain. Don't yeh see? W'en the toes are 'urt the nerves sends word up to the brain jest like the telegraph.' Then father 'e ponders aw'ile. 'W'ere's them nerves, doctor?' sez 'e. 'In the toes.' 'In the toes? Then w'en them toes is gone them nerves is gone, hain't they?' 'Yes.' 'But the nerve feelin' is ther' still.' This puzzles father some. 'Then,' sez 'e, 'the feelin's in the nerves, an' if ther's no nerves, no feelin's.' 'That's so,' sez the doctor. 'W'en them toes is gone, doctor, the nerves is gone. 'Ow could ther' be any feelin's?' 'Look 'ere,' sez the doctor, an' I was feared 'e was gettin' real mad, 'jest quit it right now.' 'Well, well. All right, doctor,' sez father quite polite, 'I've got a terr'ble inquirin' mind, an' I jest wanted to know.' Then the doctor 'e did seem a little ashamed of 'isself, an' 'e set right down an' sez 'e, 'Look a-'ere, Mr. Fallows, I'll hexplain it to yeh. It's like the telegraph wire. 'Ere's a station we'll call Bradford, an' 'ere's a station we'll call London. Hevery station 'as 'is own call. Bradford station, we'll say, 'as a call X Y Z, an' w'enever X Y Z sounds yeh know that's Bradford a-speakin'. So if yeh 'eerd X Y Z in London yeh'd know somethin' was wrong with Bradford.' 'But if ther' hain't any,' breaks in father, who was gettin' impatient. 'Shut up! will yeh?' sez the doctor, 'till I git through. Well; all 'long that Bradford line yeh can give that Bradford call. D'yeh see?' 'Can yeh make that Bradford call houtside of Bradford?' sez father. 'Well,' sez the doctor, an' 'e seemed quite puzzled, 'e did, 'I suppose yeh can. Any kind of a bang'll do along the line. Now ther's Benny's toes, w'en they git 'urt they sounds up to the brain, "Toes! Toes! Toes!" an' all 'long that toe line yeh can git the same call to the brain.' This keeps father quiet a long time, then sez 'e, 'I say, doctor, is ther' many of them nerves?' ''Undreds of 'em.' 'Hevery part of the body got nerves?' 'Yes.' 'Hankles? calves? shins?' 'Yes, all got nerves.' 'Well, doctor,' sez father, quite triumphant, 'w'en yeh cut through hankles, shins, an' heverythin', all them nerves begin to shout, don't they?' 'Yes,' sez the doctor, not seein' w'ere father was at. 'Then,' sez 'e quick-like, 'w'at makes 'em all shout "Toes?" W'y don't the brain 'ear "Hankle" or "'Eel"?' Then the old doctor 'e did git mad an' 'e did swear at father most orful. But father, 'e knows 'ow to conduct 'isself, an' sez 'e quite dignified, 'I 'ope as 'ow I know 'ow to treat a gentleman.' This pulls the old doctor up an' 'e sez, 'I beg yer pardon, Mr. Fallows,' sez 'e. 'Don't mention it,' sez father. Then the doctor went on quite nice, 'Yeh see, Mr. Fallows, the truth is, we don't hunderstand these things very well,' sez 'e. 'Well, doctor,' sez father, 'it would 'a' saved a lot of trouble if yeh'd said so at the first.' An' 'e said no more, but I seed 'im thinkin' 'ard, an' w'en the doctor was goin' 'e speaks up sez, sez 'e, 'I think I know w'y it's the shoutin' of toes keeps up an' not 'eels or hankles,' sez 'e. 'W'en my thirteen gits a-shoutin' in this little 'ouse, yeh cawn't 'ear the old woman or me. Ther's thirteen of 'em. An' I suppose w'en them toes gits a-shoutin' yeh cawn't 'ear nothin' of hankle, or 'eel, but it's all toes. Ther's five to one. But, doctor,' 'e sez, as 'e druv' away, 'if it's not too bold, would yeh mind buryin' them toes?'"

"But," said Mrs. Fallows, pulling herself up, "I do talk. But poor Benny, 'e kep' a-cryin' with 'is toes till that ther' blessed young lady come, the young doctor fetched 'er, an' the minit she begin to sing, poor Benny 'e fergits 'is toes an' 'e soon falls off to sleep, the first 'e 'ad fer two days an' two nights. Poor dear! An' 'e hain't ever done talkin' 'bout that very young lady an' the young doctor. An' a lovely pair they'd make, poor souls."

Margaret was conscious of a sudden pang at this grouping of names by Mrs. Fallows, but before she had time to analyse her feelings Iola reappeared.

"Well, good-bye," said Mrs. Fallows. "Yeh'll come agin w'en yeh git back. Good-bye, Miss," she said to Margaret. "It does seem to give me a fresh start w'en yeh put things to rights."

It was not till that night when she was in her own room preparing for bed that Margaret had time to analyse that sudden pang.

"It can't be that I am jealous," she said. "Of course, she is far more attractive than I am and why shouldn't everyone like her better?" She shook her fist at her reflection in the glass. "Do you know, you are as mean as you can be," she said viciously.

At that moment there came from Iola's room the sound of soft singing.

"It's no wonder," said Margaret as she listened to the exquisite sound, "it's no wonder that she could catch poor Ben and his mother with a voice like that. Yes, and—and the rest of them, too."

In a few minutes there was a tap at her door and Iola came in, her hair hanging like a dusky curtain about her face. Margaret uttered an involuntary exclamation of admiration.

"My! you are lovely!" she cried. "No wonder everyone loves you." With a sudden rush of penitent feeling for her "mean thoughts" she put her arms about Iola and kissed her warmly.

"Lovely! Nonsense!" she exclaimed, surprised at this display of affection so unusual for Margaret, "I am not half so lovely as you. When I see you at home here with all the things to worry you and the children to care for, I think you are just splendid and I feel myself cheap and worthless."

Margaret was conscious of a grateful glow in her heart.

"Indeed, my work doesn't amount to much, washing and dusting and mending. Anybody could do it. No one would ever notice me. Wherever you go the people just fall down and worship you." As she spoke she let down her hair preparatory to brushing it. It fell like a cloud, a golden-yellow cloud, about her face and shoulders. Iola looked critically at her.

"You are beautiful," she said slowly. "Your hair is lovely, and your big blue eyes, and your face has something, what is it? I can't tell you. But I believe people would come to you in difficulty. Yes. That's it," she continued, with her eyes on Margaret's face, "I can please them in a way. I can sing. Yes, I can sing. Some day I shall make people listen. But suppose I couldn't sing, suppose I lost my voice, people would forget me. They wouldn't forget you."

"What nonsense!" said Margaret brusquely. "It is not your voice alone; it is your beauty and something I cannot describe, something in your manner that is so fetching. At any rate, all the young fellows are daft about you."

"But the women don't care for me," said Iola, with the same slow, thoughtful voice. "If I wanted very much I believe I could make them. But they don't. There's Mrs. Boyle, she doesn't like me."

"Now you're talking nonsense," said Margaret impatiently. "You ought to have heard old Mrs. Fallows this evening."

"Now," continued Iola, ignoring her remark, "the women all like you, and the men, too, in a way."

"Don't talk nonsense," said Margaret impatiently. "When you're around the boys don't look at me."

"Yes, they do," said Iola, as if pondering the question. "Ben does."

Margaret laughed scornfully. "Ben likes my jelly."

"And Dick does," continued Iola, "and Barney." Here she shot a keen glance at Margaret's face. Margaret caught the glance, and, though enraged at herself, she could not prevent a warm flush spreading over her fair cheek and down her bare neck.

"Pshaw!" she cried angrily, "those boys! Of course, they like me. I've known them ever since I was a baby. Why, I used to go swimming with them in the pond. They think of me just like—well—just like a boy, you know."

"Do you think so? They are nice boys, I think, that is, if they had a chance to be anything."

"Be anything!" cried Margaret hotly. "Why, Dick's going to be a minister and—"

"Yes. Dick will do something, though he'll make a funny clergyman. But Barney, what will he be? Just a miller?"

"Miller or whatever he is, he'll be a man, and that's good enough," replied Margaret indignantly.

"Oh, yes, I suppose so. But it's a pity. You know in this pokey little place no one will ever hear of him. I mean he'll never make any stir." To Iola there was no crime so deadly as the "unheard of." "And yet," she went on, "if he had a chance—"

But Margaret could bear this no longer. "What are you talking about? There are plenty of good men who are never heard of."

"Oh," cried Iola quickly, "I didn't mean—of course your father. Well, your father is a gentle man. But Barney—"

"Oh, go to bed! Come, get out of my room. Go to bed! I must get to sleep. Seven o'clock comes mighty quick. Good-night."

"Don't be cross, Margaret. I didn't mean to say anything offensive. And I want you to love me. I think I want everyone to love me. I can't bear to have people not love me. But more than anyone else I want you." As she spoke she turned impulsively toward Margaret and put her arms around her neck. Margaret relented.

"Of course I love you," she said. "There," kissing her, "good-night. Go to sleep or you'll lose your beauty."

But Iola clung to her. "Good-night, dear Margaret," she said, her lips trembling pathetically. "You are the only girl friend I ever had. I couldn't bear you to forget me or to give up loving me."

"I never forget my friends," cried Margaret gravely. "And I never cease to love them."

"Oh, Margaret!" said Iola, trembling and clinging fast to her, "don't turn from me. No matter what comes, don't stop loving me."

"You little goose," cried Margaret, caressing her as if she were a child, "of course I will always love you. Good-night now." She kissed Iola tenderly.

"Good-night," said Iola. "You know this is my last night with you for a long time."

"Not the very last," said Margaret. "We go to the Mill to-morrow night, you remember, and you come back here with me. Barney is going to have Ben there for nursing and feeding."

Next day Barney had Ben down to the Mill, and that was the beginning of a new life to Ben in more ways than one. The old mill became a place of interest and delight to him. Perhaps his happiest hours were spent in what was known as Barney's workroom, where were various labour-saving machines for churning, washing, and apple-paring, which, by Barney's invention, were run by the mill power. He offered to connect the sewing machine with the same power, but his mother would have none of it.

Before many more weeks had gone Ben was hopping about by the aid of a crutch, eager to make himself useful, and soon he was not only "paying his board," as Barney declared, but "earning good wages as well."

The early afternoon found Margaret and Iola on their way to the Mill. It was with great difficulty that Margaret had been persuaded to leave her home for so long a time. The stern conscience law under which she regulated her life made her suspect those things which gave her peculiar pleasure, and among these was a visit to the Mill and the Mill people. It was in vain that

Dick set before her, with the completeness amounting to demonstration, the reasons why she should make that visit. "Ben needs you," he argued. "And Iola will not come unless with you. Barney and I, weary with our day's work, absolutely require the cheer and refreshment of your presence. Mother wants you. I want you. We all want you. You must come." It was Mrs. Boyle's quiet invitation and her anxious entreaty and command that she should throw off the burden at times, that finally weighed with her.

The hours of that afternoon, spent partly in rowing about in the old flat-bottomed boat seeking water lilies in the pond, and partly in the shade of the big willows overlooking the dam, were full of restful delight to Margaret. It was one of those rare summer evenings that fall in harvest weather when, after the burning heat of the day, the cool air is beginning to blow across the fields with long shadows. When their work was done the boys hurried to join the little group under the big willows. They were all there. Ben was set there in the big armchair, Mrs. Boyle with her knitting, for there were no idle hours for her, Margaret with a book which she pretended to read, old Charley smoking in silent content, Iola lazily strumming her guitar and occasionally singing in her low, rich voice some of her old Mammy's songs or plantation hymns. Of these latter, however, Mrs. Boyle was none too sure. To her they bordered dangerously on sacrilege; nor did she ever quite fully abandon herself to delight in the guitar. It continued to be a "foreign" and "feckless" sort of instrument. But in spite of her there were times when the old lady paused in her knitting and sat with sombre eyes looking far across the pond and into the shady isles of the woods on the other side while Iola sang some of her quaint Southern "baby songs."

Under Dick's tuition the girl learned some of the Highland laments and love songs of the North, to which his mother had hushed him to sleep through his baby years. To Barney these songs took place with the Psalms of David, if, indeed, they were not more sacred, and it was with a shock at first that he heard the Southern girl with her "foreign instrument" try over these songs that none but his mother had ever sung to him. Listening to Iola's soft, thrilling voice carrying these old Highland airs, he was conscious of a strange incongruity. They undoubtedly took on a new beauty, but they lost something as well.

"No one sings them like your mother, Barney," said Margaret after Dick had been drilling Iola on some of their finer shadings and cadences, "and they are quite different with the guitar, too. They are not the same a bit. They make me see different things and feel different things when your mother sings."

"Different how?" said Dick.

"I can't tell, but somehow they give me a different taste in my mouth, just the difference between eating your mother's scones with rich creamy milk and eating fruit cake and honey with tea to drink."

"I know," said Barney gravely. "They lose the Scotch with the guitar. They are sweet and beautiful, wonderful, but they are a different kind altogether. To me it's the difference between a wood violet and a garden rose."

"Listen to the poetry of him. Come, mother," cried Dick, "sing us one now."

"Me sing!" cried the mother aghast. "After yon!" nodding toward Iola. "You would not be shaming your mother, Richard."

"Shaming you, indeed!" cried Margaret, indignantly.

"Do, Mrs. Boyle," entreated Iola. "I have never heard you sing. Indeed, I did not know you could sing."

Something in her voice grated upon Barney's ear, but he spoke no word.

"Sing!" cried Dick. "You ought to hear her. Now, mother, for the honor of the heather! Give us 'Can Ye Sew Cushions?' That's a 'baby song,' too."

"No," said Barney quietly, "Sing 'The Mac'Intosh,' mother." And he began to play that exquisite Highland lament.

It was not her son's entreaty so much as something in the soft drawl of the Southern girl that made Mrs. Boyle yield. Something in that tone touched the pride in the old lady's Highland blood. When Barney reached the end of the refrain his mother took up the verse with the violin accompanying.

Her voice lacked fulness and power. It was worn and thin, but she had the exquisite lilting note of the Highland maids at their milking or of the fisher folk at the mending of their nets. Clear and sweet and with a penetrating pathos indescribable, the voice rose and fell in all the quaint turns and quavers and cadences that a tune takes on with age. As she sang her song in the soft Gaelic tongue, with hands lying idly in her lap, with eyes glowing in their gloomy depths, the spell of mountain and glen and loch fell upon her sons and upon the girl seated at her feet, while Iola's great lustrous eyes, fastened upon the stranger's face, softened to tears.

"Oh, that is too lovely!" cried Iola, when the song was done, clapping her hands. "No, not lovely. That is not the word. Sad, sad." She hid her face in her hands one impulsive moment, then said softly, "I could never do that. Never! Never! What is it you put into the song? What is it?" she cried, turning to Barney.

"It's the moan of the sea," said Barney gravely.

"It gives a feller a kind of holler pain inside," said Ben Fallows. "There hain't no words fer it."

"Sing again," entreated Iola, all the lazy indifference gone from her voice. "Sing just one more."

"This one, mother," said Barney, playing the tune, "your mother used to sing, you know, 'Fhir a Bhata'."

> *"How often haunting the highest hilltop,*
>
> *I scan the ocean thy sail to see;*
>
> *Wilt come to-night, Love? wilt come to-morrow?*
>
> *Wilt ever come, love, to comfort me?*
>
> *Fhir a bhata, na horo eile,*
>
> *Fhir a bhata, na horo eile,*
>
> *Fhir a bhata, na horo eile,*
>
> *O fare ye well, love, where'er ye be."*

For some moments they sat quiet with the spell of the dreamy, sad music upon them.

"One more, mother," entreated Dick.

"No, laddie. The night is falling. There's work to-morrow for you. Aye, and for Margaret here."

Iola rose and came timidly to Mrs. Boyle. "Thank you," she said, lifting up her great, dark eyes to the old woman's face, "you have given me great pleasure to-night."

"Indeed, and you're welcome, lassie," said Mrs. Boyle, smitten with a sudden pity for the motherless girl. "And we will be glad to see ye when ye come back again."

For this, too, it was that Iola as well as Margaret could never forget that afternoon.

"And now, ladies and gentlemen," cried Dick, striking an attitude, "though the 'good cheer' department may seem to have accomplished the purpose for which it was organised, it cannot be said to have outlived its usefulness, in that it appears to have created for itself a sphere of operations from which it cannot be withdrawn without injury to all its members. I, therefore, respectfully suggest that the department be organised upon a permanent basis with headquarters at the Mill and my humble self at its head. All who agree will say 'Aye'."

"Aye," said Barney with prompt heartiness.

"Me, too," cried Iola, holding up both hands.

"Mother, what do you say?"

"Aye, laddie. There's much need for good cheer in the world."

"And you?" turning to Margaret, who stood with Mrs. Boyle's arm thrown about her, "how do you vote?"

"This member needs it too much" — with a somewhat uncertain smile — "to say anything but 'Aye'."

"Then," said Dick solemnly, "the 'good cheer' department is hereby and henceforth organised as a permanent institution in the community here represented, and we earnestly hope that its members will continue in their faithful adherence thereto, believing, as we do, that loyalty to this institution will be its highest reward."

But none of them knew what potencies of joy and of pain lay wrapped up for them all in that same department of "good cheer."

VIII
BEN'S GANG

The harvest time in Ontario is ever a season of delightful rush and bustle. The fall wheat follows hard upon the haying, and close upon the fall wheat comes the barley, then the oats and the rest of the spring grain.

It was this year to be a more than usually busy time for the Boyle boys. They had a common purse, and out of that purse the payments on the mortgage must be met, as well as Dick's college expenses. For the little farm, with the profits from the mill, could do little more than provide a living for the family. Ordinarily the lads worked for day's wages, the farmers gladly paying the highest going, for the boys were famous binders and good workers generally. This year, however, they had in mind something more ambitious.

"Mother," said Dick, "did you hear of the new harvesting gang?"

"And who might they be?" asked his mother, always on the lookout for some nonsense from her younger son.

"Boyle and Fallows—or Fallows and Boyle, I guess it will be. Ben's starting with us Monday morning."

"Nonsense, laddie. There will be no reaping for Ben this year, I doubt, poor fellow; and, besides, I will be needing him for myself."

"Yes. But I am in earnest, mother. Ben is to drive the reaper for us. He can sit on the reaper half a day, you know. At least, his doctor here says so. And he will keep us busy."

"If I cawn't keep the two of you a-humpin', though you are some pumpkins at bindin', I hain't worth my feed."

"But, Barney," remonstrated his mother, "is he fit to go about that machine? Something might happen the lad."

"I don't think there is any danger, mother. And, besides, we will be at hand all the time."

"And what will two lads like you do following the machine all day? You will only be hurting yourselves."

"You watch us, mother," cried Dick. "We'll be after Ben like a dog after a coon."

"Indeed," said his mother. "I have heard that it takes four good men to keep up to a machine. It was no later than yesterday that Mr. Morrison's Sam was telling me that they had all they could do to follow up, the whole four of them."

"Huh!" grunted Dick scornfully, "I suppose so. Four like Fatty Morrison and that gang of his!"

"Hush, laddie. It is not good to be speaking ill of your neighbours," said his mother.

"It's not speaking ill to say that a man is fat. It's a very fine compliment, mother. Only wish someone could say the same of me."

"Indeed, and you would be the better of it," replied his mother compassionately, "with your bones sticking through your skin!"

It was with the spring crop that Ben Fallows began his labours; and much elevated, indeed, was he at the prospect of entering into partnership with the Boyle boys, who were renowned for the very virtues which poor Ben consciously lacked and to which, in the new spirit that was waking in him, he was beginning to aspire. For the weeks spent under Barney's care and especially in the atmosphere of the Mill household had quickened in Ben new motives and new ambitions. This Barney had noticed, and it was for Ben's sake more than for their own that the boys had associated him with them in their venture of taking harvesting contracts. And as the summer went on they found no reason to regret the new arrangement. But it was at the expense of long days and hard days for the two boys following the reaper, and often when the day's work was done they could with difficulty draw their legs home and to bed. Indeed, there were nights when Dick, hardly the equal of his brother in weight and strength, lay sleepless from sheer exhaustion, while Barney from sympathy kept anxious vigil with him. Morning, however, found them stiff and sore, it is true, but full of courage and ready for the renewal of the long-drawn struggle which was winning for them not only very substantial financial profits, but also high fame as workers. The end of the harvest found them hard, tough, full of nerve and fit for any call within the limit of their powers. It was Ben who furnished the occasion of such a call being made upon them. A rainy day found him at the blacksmith shop with the Mill team waiting to be shod. The shop was full of horses and men. A rainy day was a harvest day for the blacksmith. All odd jobs allowed to accumulate during the fine weather were on that day brought to the shop.

Ben, with his crutch and his wooden leg, found himself the centre of a new interest and sympathy. In spite of the sympathy, however, there was a disposition to chaff poor Ben, whose temper was brittle, and whose tongue took on a keener edge as his temper became more uncertain. Withal, he had a little man's tendency to brag. To-day, however, though conscious of the new interest centring in him, and though visibly swollen with the importance of his new partnership with the Boyle boys, he was exhibiting a dignity and self-control quite unusual, and was, for that very reason, provocative of chaff more pungent than ordinary.

Chief among his tormenters was Sam Morrison, or "Fatty" Morrison, as he was colloquially designated. Sam was one of four sons of "Old King" Morrison, the richest and altogether most important farmer in the district. On this account Samuel was inclined to assume the blustering manners of his portly, pompous, but altogether good-natured father, the "Old King." But while bluster in the old man, who had gained the respect and esteem that success generally brings, was tolerated, in Sammy it became ridiculous and at times offensive. The young man had been entertaining the assembled group of farmers and farm lads with vivid descriptions of various achievements in the harvest field on the part of himself or some of the members of his distinguished family, the latest and most notable achievement being the "slashing down and tying up" of a ten-acre field of oats by the four of them, the "Old King" himself driving the reaper.

"Yes, sir!" shouted Sammy. "And Joe, he took the last sheaf right off that table! You bet!"

"How many of you?" asked Ben sharply.

"Just four," replied Sammy, turning quickly at Ben's unexpected question.

"How many shocking?" continued Ben, with a judicial air.

"Why, none, you blamed gander! An' kep' us humpin', too, you bet!"

"I guess so," grunted Ben, "from what I've seed."

Sam regarded him steadfastly. "And what have you 'seed,' Mr. Fallows, may I ask?" he inquired with fine scorn.

"Seed? Seed you bindin', of course."

"Well, what are ye hootin' about?" Sam was exceedingly wroth.

"I hain't been talking much for the last hour." In moments of excitement Ben became uncertain of his h's. "I used to talk more when I wasn't so busy, but I hain't been talkin' so much this 'ere 'arvest. We hain't had time. When we're on a job," continued Ben, as the crowd drew near to listen, "we hain't got time fer talkin', and when we're through we don't feel like it. We don't need, to."

A general laugh of approval followed Ben's words.

"You're right, Ben. You're a gang of hustlers," said Alec Murray. "There ain't much talkin' when you git a-goin'. But that's a pretty good day's work, Ben, ten acres."

Ben gave a snort. "Yes. Not a bad day's work fer two men." He had no love for any of the Morrisons, whose near neighbours he was and at whose hands he had suffered many things.

"Two men!" shouted Sammy. "Your gang, I suppose you mean."

Suddenly Ben's self-control vanished. "Yes, by the jumpin' Jemima!" he cried, facing suddenly upon Sam. "Them's the two, if yeh want to know. Them's binders! They don't stop, at hevery corner to swap lies an' to see if it's goin' to ran. They keep a-workin', they do. They don't wait to cool hoff before they drink fer fear they git foundered, as if they was 'osses, like you fellers up on the west side line there." Ben threw his h's recklessly about. "You hain't no binders, you hain't. Yeh never seed any."

At this moment "King" Morrison himself entered the blacksmith shop.

"Hello, Ben! What's eatin' you?" he exclaimed.

Ben grew suddenly quiet. "Makin' a bloomin' hass of myself, I guess," he growled.

"What's up with Benny? He seems a little raised," said the "Old King," addressing the crowd generally.

"Oh, blowin' 'bout his harvestin' gang," said his son Sam.

"Well, you can do a little blowin' yourself, Sammy."

"Guess I came by it natcherly n'ough," said Sam. He stood in no awe of his father.

"Blowin's all right if you can back it up, Sammy. But what's the matter, Benny, my boy? We're all glad to see you about, an' more'n that, we're glad to hear of your good work this summer. But what are they doin' to you?"

"Doin' nothin'," broke in Sam, a little nettled at the "Old King's" kindly tone toward Ben. "He's blowin' round here to beat the band 'bout his gang."

"Well, Sam, he's got a right to blow, for they're two good workers."

"But they can't bind ten acres a day, as Ben blows about."

"Well, that would be a little strong," said the "Old King." "Why, it took my four boys a good day to tie up ten acres, Ben."

"I'm talkin' 'bout binders," said Ben, in what could hardly be called a respectful tone.

"Look here, Ben, no two men can bind ten acres in a day, so just quit yer blowin' an' talk sense."

"I'm talkin' 'bout binders," repeated Ben stubbornly.

"And I tell you, Ben," replied the "Old King," with emphasis, "your boys—and they're good boys, too—can't tie no ten acres in a day. They've got the chance of tryin' on that ten acres of wheat on my west fifty. If they can do it in a day they can have it."

"They wouldn't take it," answered Ben regretfully. "They can do it, fast enough."

Then the "Old King" quite lost patience. "Now, Ben, shut up! You're a blowhard! Why, I'd bet any man the whole field against $50 that it can't be done."

"I'll take you on that," said Alec Murray.

"What?" The "Old King" was nonplussed for a moment.

"I'll take that. But I guess you don't mean it."

But the "Old King" was too much of a sport to go back upon his offer. "It's big odds," he said. "But I'll stick to it. Though I want to tell you, there's nearer twelve acres than ten."

"I know the field," said Alec. "But I'm willing to risk it. The winner pays the wages. How long a day?" continued Alec.

"Quit at six."

"The best part of the day is after that."

"Make it eight, then," said the "Old King." "And we'll bring it off on Monday. We're thrashing that day, but the more the merrier."

"There's jest one thing," interposed Ben, "an' that is, the boys mustn't know about this."

"Why not?" said Alec. "They're dead game."

"Oh, Dick'd jump at it quick enough, but Barney wouldn't let 'im risk it. He's right careful of that boy."

After full discussion next Sabbath morning by those who were loitering, after their custom, in the churchyard waiting for the service to begin, it was generally agreed that the "Old King" with his usual shrewdness had "put his money on the winning horse." Even Alec Murray, though he kept a bold face, confided to his bosom friend, Rory Ross, that he "guessed his cake was dough, though they would make a pretty big stagger at it."

"If Dick only had Barney's weight," said Rory, "they would stand a better chance."

"Yes. But Dick tires quicker. An' he'll die before he drops."

"But ten acres, Alec! And there's more than ten acres in that field."

"I know. But it's standing nice, an' it's lighter on the knoll in the centre. If I can only get them goin' their best clip—I'll have to work it some way. I'll have to get Barney moving. Dick's such an ambitious little beggar he'd follow till he bust. The first thing," continued Alec, "is to get them a good early start. I'll have a talk with Ben."

As a result of his conversation with Ben it was hardly daylight on Monday morning when Mrs. Boyle, glancing at her clock, sprang at once from her bed and called her sons.

"You're late, Barney. It's nearly six, and you have to go to Morrison's to-day. Here's Ben with the horses fed."

"Why, mother, it's only five o'clock by my watch."

"No, it's six."

Upon comparison Ben's watch corresponded with the clock. Barney concluded something must be wrong and routed Dick up, and with such good purpose did they hasten through breakfast that in an hour from the time the boys were called they were standing in the field waiting for Ben to begin the day's work.

After they had been binding an hour Alec Murray appeared on the field. "I'm going to shock," he announced. "They've got men enough up at the thrashing, an' the 'Old King' wants to get this field in shock by to-morrow afternoon so he can get it thrashed, if you hustlers can get it down by then." Alec was apparently in great spirits. He brought with him into the field a breezy air of excitement.

"Here, Ben, don't take all day oiling up there. I guess I'm after you to-day, remember."

"Guess yeh'll wait till it's tied, won't yeh?" said Ben, who thoroughly understood Alec's game.

"Don't know 'bout that. I may have to jump in an' tie a few myself."

"Don't you fret yourself," replied Dick. "If you shock all that's tied to-day you'll need to hang your shirt on the fence at night."

"Keep cool, Dick, or you'll be leavin' Barney too far behind. You tie quicker than him, I hear."

"Oh, I don't know," said Dick modestly, though quite convinced in his own mind that he could.

"Dick's a little quicker, ain't he?" said Alec, turning to Barney.

"Oh, he's quick enough."

"Did you never have a tussle?" inquired Alec, snatching up a couple of sheaves in each arm and setting them in their places in the shock with a quick swing, then stepping off briskly for others.

"No," said Barney shortly.

"I guess he didn't want you to hurt yourself," he suggested cunningly to Dick. "When a fellow isn't very strong he's got to be careful." This was Dick's sensitive point. He was not content to do a man's work in the field, but he was miserable unless he took first place.

"Oh, he needn't be afraid of hurting me," he said, taking Alec's bait. "I've worked with him all harvest and I'm alive yet." Unconsciously Dick's pace quickened, and for the next few minutes Barney was left several sheaves behind.

"He's just foolin' with you, Dick," jeered Alec. "He wouldn't hurt you for the world."

Unconsciously by his hustling manner and by his sly suggestion of superiority now to one and again to the other, he put both boys upon their mettle, and before they were aware they were going at a racing pace, though neither would acknowledge that to the other. Alec kept following them close, almost running for his sheaves, flinging a word of encouragement now to one, now to the other, shouting at Ben as he turned the corners, and by every means possible keeping the excitement at the highest point. But he was careful not to overdrive his men. By a previous arrangement and without serious difficulty he had persuaded Teenie Ross, who had come to assist the Morrison girls at the threshing, to bring out a lunch to the field at ten o'clock. For half an hour they sat in the long grass in the shade of a maple tree eating the lunch which Dick at least was beginning to feel in need of. But not a minute more did Alec allow.

"I'm going to catch you fellows," he said, "if I've to take off my shirt to do it."

Dick was quick to respond and again set off at full speed. But the grain was heavier than Alec had counted upon, and when the noon hour had arrived he estimated that the grain was not more than one-third down. A full hour and a half he allowed his men for rest, cunningly drawing them off from the crowd of threshers to a quiet place in the orchard where they could lie down and sleep, waking them when time was up that there should be no loss of a single precious moment. As they were going out to the field Alec suggested that instead of coming back for supper at five, according to the usual custom, they should have it brought to them in the field.

"It's a long way up to the house," he explained, "and the days are getting short." And though the boys didn't take very kindly to the suggestion, neither would think of opposing it.

But in spite of all that Alec and Ben could do, when the threshers knocked off work for the day and sauntered down to the field where the reaping was going on, it looked as if the "Old King" were to win his bet.

"Keep out of this field!" yelled Alec, as the men drew near; "you're interferin' with our work. Come, get out!" For the boys had begun to take it easy and chatting with some of them.

"Get away from here, I tell you!" cried Alec. "You line up along the fence and we'll show you how this thing should be done!"

Realizing the fairness of his demand, the men retired from the field. The long shadows of the evening were falling across the field. The boys were both showing weariness at every step they took. Alec was at his wit's end. The grain was all cut, but there was still a large part of it to bind. He determined to take the boys into his confidence. He knew all the risk there was in this step. Barney might refuse to risk an injury to his brother. It was Alec's only chance, however, and walking over to the boys, he told them the issue at stake.

"Boys," he said, "I don't want you to hurt yourselves. I don't care a dern about the money. I'd like to beat 'Old King' Morrison and I'd like to see you make a record. You've done a big day's work already, and if you want to quit I won't say a word."

"Quit!" cried Dick in scorn, kindling at Alec's story. "What time have we left?"

"We have till eight o'clock. It's now just seven."

"Come on then, Barney!" cried Dick. "We're good for an hour, anyway."

"I don't know, Dick," said Barney, hesitating.

"Come along! I can stand it and I know you can." And off he set again at racing pace and making no attempt to hide it.

In half an hour there were still left them, taking two swaths apiece, the two long sides and the two short ends.

"You can't do it, boys," said Alec regretfully. "Let 'er go."

"Yes, boys," cried the "Old King," who, with the crowd, had drawn near, "you've done a big day's work. You'll hurt yourselves. You've earned double pay and you'll get it."

"Not yet," cried Dick. "We'll put in the half hour at any rate. Come on, Barney! Never mind your rake!"

His face looked pale and worn, but his eyes were ablaze with light, and but for his pale face there was no sign of weariness about him. He flung away his rake and, snatching up a band, kicked the sheaf together, caught it up, drew, tied, and fastened it as with one single act.

"We'll show them waltz time, Barney," he called, springing toward the next sheaf. "One"—at the word he snatched up and made the band, "two"—he passed the band around the sheaf, kicking it at the same time into shape, "three"—he drew and knotted the band, shoving the end in with his thumb. After him went Barney. One—two—three! and a sheaf was done. One—two—three! and so from sheaf to sheaf. It took them fifteen minutes to go down the long side. Dick, who had the inside, finished and sprang to his place at the outer side.

"Get inside!" shouted Barney, "let me take that swath!"

"Come along!" replied Dick, tying his sheaf.

"Fifteen minutes left, boys! I believe you're going to do it!" At this Ben gave a yell.

"They're goin' to do it!" he shouted, stumping around in great excitement.

"Double up, Dick!" cried Barney, carrying one sheaf to the next and tying them both together. Dick followed Barney's example, but here his brother's extra strength told in the race. Close after them came the crowd, Alec leading them, watch in hand, all yelling.

"Two minutes for that end, boys!" cried Alec, as they reached the corner. "You're goin' to do it, my hearties! You're goin' to do it!" They had thirteen minutes in which to bind a side and an end.

"They can't do it, Alec," said the "Old King." "They'll hurt themselves. Call them off!"

"Are you all right, Dick?" cried Barney, swinging on to the outer swath.

"All right," panted his brother, striding in at his side.

"Come on! We'll do it, then!" replied Barney.

Side by side they rushed. Sheaf by sheaf they tied together, Barney gradually gaining by the doubling process.

"Don't wait for me," gasped Dick, "if you can go faster!"

"One minute and a half, boys, if you can stand it!" cried Alec, as they reached the last corner. "One minute and a half, and we win!"

There remained five sheaves on the outer of Barney's two swaths, two on the inner of Dick's. In all, nine for Barney, six for Dick. The sheaves were comparatively small. Springing at this swath, Barney doubled the first two, the second two, the third two, and putting the last three together swung in upon Dick's swath where there were two sheaves left.

"Don't you touch it!" gasped Dick angrily.

"How's the time, Alec?" panted Barney.

"Half a minute."

Before he spoke, Dick flung himself on his last two sheaves, crying, "Out of the way there!" snatched his band, passing it around the sheaf, tied it, flung it over his shoulder, and stood with his hands on his knees, his breath coming in sobbing gasps.

For a few minutes the men went wild. Barney stepped to Dick's side, and patting him on the shoulder, said, "Great man, Dick! But I was a fool to let you!"

"That's what you were!" cried the "Old King," slapping Dick on the back, "but there's the greatest day's work ever done in these parts. The wheat's yours," he said, turning to Alec, "but begad! I wish it was goin' to them that won it!"

"An' that's where it is going," said Alec, "every blamed sheaf of it, to Ben's gang."

"We'll take what's coming to us," said Barney shortly.

"I told yeh so," said Ben regretfully.

"Why, don't you know it was for you I took the bet?" said Alec, angry that he should be balked in his good intention to help the boys.

"We'll take our wages," repeated Barney in a tone that settled the controversy. "The wheat is not ours."

"Then it ain't mine," said Alec, disgusted, remembering in how great peril his $50 had been.

"Well, boys," said the "Old King," "it ain't mine. We'll divide it in three."

"We'll take our wages," said Barney again, in sullen determination.

"Confound the boy!" cried the "Old King." "What'll we do with the wheat? I say, we'll give it to Ben; he's had hard luck this year."

"No, by the jumpin' Jemima Jebbs!" said Ben, stumping over to Barney's side. "I stand with the boss. I take my wages."

"Well, dog-gone you all! Will you take double pay, then? There's two days' good work there. And the rest we'll give to the church. Good thing the minister ain't here or he'd kick, too!"

"But," added the "Old King," turning to his son Sam, "after this you crawl into your shell when there's any blowin' bein' done about Ben's gang."

IX
LOVE'S TANGLED WAYS

The mill lane was prinked with all the June flowers. Over the snake fence massed the clover, red and white. Through the rails peeped the thistle bloom, pink and purple, and higher up above the top rail the white crest of the dogwood slowly nodded in the breeze this sweet summer day. In the clover the bumblebees, the crickets, and the grasshoppers boomed, chirped, crackled, shouting their joy to be alive in so good a place and on so good a day. Above, the sky was blue, pure blue, and all the bluer for the specks of cloud that hung, still-poised like white-winged birds, white against the blue. Last evening's rain had washed the world clean. The sky, the air, the flowers, the clover, red and white, the kindly grass that ran green everywhere under foot, the dusty road, all were washed clean. In the elm bunches by the fence, in the maples and thorns, the birds, their summer preoccupations forgotten at the bidding of this new washed day, recalled their spring songs and poured them forth with fine careless courage.

In tune to this brave symphony of colour and song, and down this flower-prinked, song-filled, clean washed, grassy lane stepped Dick this summer morning, stepped with the spring and balance of the well-trained athlete, stepped with the step of a man whose heart makes him merry music. A clean-looking man was Dick, harmonious with the day and with the lane down which he stepped. Against the grey of his suit his hands, his face, and his neck, where the negligee shirt fell away wide, revealing his strong, full curves spreading to the shoulders, all showed ruddy brown. He was a man good to look upon, with his springy step, his tan skin, his clear eye, but chiefly because out of his clear eye a soul looked forth clean and unafraid upon God's good world of wholesome growing things.

From his three years of 'varsity life he came back unspoiled to his boyhood's love of the open sky and of all things under it. He had just come through a great year in college, his third, the greatest in many ways of the college course. His class had thrust him into a man's place of leadership in that world where only manhood counts, and he had "made good." In the literary, in the gym, on the campus he had made and held high place, and on the class lists, in spite of his many distractions, he had ranked a double first. Best of all, it filled him with warm gratitude to remember that none of his fellows had grudged him any of his good things. What a decent lot they were! It humbled him to think of their pride in him. He would not disappoint them. Noblesse oblige.

At the crest of the hill he paused to look back, and here the pain that had been running below his consciousness, like the minor strain in rich music, came to the top. This was Barney's spot. At this spot Barney always made him pause to look back upon the old mill in its frame of beauty. Poor Barney! Twice he had gone down to the exams, and twice he had failed. Of all in the home circle only Dick could understand the full bitterness of the cup of humiliation that his brother had put silently to his lips and drained. To his mother, the failure brought no surprise, and she would have been glad enough to have him give up "his notion of being a doctor and be content with the mill." She had no ambitions for poor Barney, who was "a quiet lad and well-doing enough," an encomium which stood for all the virtues removed from any touch of genius. She was not hurt by his failure. Indeed, she could hardly understand how deep the shame had gone into his proud, reserved heart. His father did not talk about it, but carried him off to look at some of the mill machinery which had gone wrong, and it was only by a gentler tone in his voice that Barney knew that his father understood. But Dick, with his fuller knowledge of college life, realized as none other of them did the extent of Barney's miserable sense of defeat.

And now, as he looked back upon the mill, Barney's pain became his anew. The causes of his failure were not far to seek. "He had no chance!" said Dick aloud, leaning upon the top rail and looking with gloomy eyes upon the scene of beauty before him. Things had changed since old Doctor Ferguson's time. The scientific basis of medicine was coming to its place in medical study, and the old doctor's contempt for these new-fangled notions had wrought ill for Barney. Dick remembered how he had gone, hot with indignation for his brother, to the new English professor in chemistry, whose papers were the terror of all pass men and, indeed, all honour men who stuck too closely to the text-book. He remembered the Englishman's drawling contempt as, after looking up Barney's name and papers, he dismissed the matter with the words, "He knows nothing whatever about the subject, couldn't conduct the simplest experiment, don't you know." Poor Barney! the ancient and elementary chemistry of Dr. Ferguson seemed to hold not even the remotest affinity to that which Professor Fish expected. Dick was glad this morning that he had had sense enough to hold his tongue in the professor's presence. It comforted him to recall the generous enthusiasm with which Dr. Trent, the most brilliant surgeon on the staff, had recalled Barney's name.

"Your brother, is he? Well, sir, he's a wonder!"

"Fish doesn't think so," Dick had replied.

"Oh! Fish be hanged!" the doctor had answered, with the fine contempt of a specialist in practical work for the theorist in medicine. "He has some idiotic notions in his head that he plucks men for not knowing. I don't say they are not necessary, but useful chiefly for examination purposes. Send your brother down. Send him down. For if ever I saw an embryonic surgeon, he's one! When he comes, bring him to me."

"He'll come," Dick had answered, his face hot to think that it was for his sake Barney had remained grinding at home.

"And he's going this fall," said Dick aloud, "or no 'varsity for me." He pulled a letter out of his pocket. It was from his football comrade, young Macdonald, offering, in his father's name, to Barney and himself positions in one of the lumber mills far up the Ottawa, where, by working overtime, there was a chance of making $100 a month and all found. "And we'll make it go," said Dick. "There's $300 apiece for us, and that's more than we want. Poor old chap!" he continued, musing aloud, "he'll get his chance at last. Besides, we'll get him away from that girl, confound her! though I'm afraid it's no use now."

A deeper pain surged up from the bottom of Dick's heart. "That girl" was Iola. The night before, as they were driving home in the growing dark, with halting words and with shamed face, as if he were doing his brother a wrong, Barney had confided to him that Iola and he had come to an understanding of their mutual love. Dick remembered this morning, and he would remember to his dying day, the sense of loss, of being forsaken, that had smitten him as he cried, "Oh, Barney! is it possible?" Then, as Barney had gone on to explain how it had come about, almost apologizing, as it seemed to Dick, for his weakness, Dick, seeing in the gloom a gleam of hope, had cried, "We'll get you out of it, Barney. I'll help you this summer." And then again the inevitableness of what had taken place had come over him at Barney's reply: "But, Dick, I don't want to get out of it." At that moment Dick's world changed. No longer was he first with his brother. Iola had taken his place. In vain Barney, guessing the thought in his heart, had protested with eager, almost piteous, appeal that Dick would be the same to him as ever. In the first acute moment of his pain he had cried out some quick word of bitter reproach, but the look on Barney's face had checked him. He was glad now that he had said nothing against the girl. And as he thought of her in the saner light of the morning, he felt that he could not be quite fair to her, and yet he wished it had been some other than Iola. "It's that confounded voice of hers, and her eyes, and her whole get-up. She's got something diabolically fetching about her." Then, as if he had gone too far, he continued, still musing aloud, "She's good enough, I guess, but not for Barney." That was one of the bitter things that had survived the night. She was not good enough for his brother, his hero, his beau ideal of high manhood ever since he could think. "But there is no one good enough for Barney," he continued, "except—yes—there is one—Margaret—she is good enough—even for Barney." As Barney among men, so Margaret among women had stood with Dick, peerless. And all his life he had put these two together. Even as a little fellow, when saying his prayers to his mother, next in the list to Barney's name had always come Margaret's. She was like Barney in so many ways; strong like Barney in her relentless devotion to duty; she had Barney's fine sense of honour, of righteousness, and Barney's superb courage, and, more than anything else, the same unfathomable heart of love. One could never get to the bottom of it. No matter what the drain, there would still be love there.

It was the thought of Margaret that had set his heart singing within him this morning. Even last night, after the first few moments of pain, the thought of Margaret had come to him, bringing an odd sense of happiness, and early this morning the first consciousness of loss, that had made him tighten his arm hard about his brother, had been followed by that feeling of happiness, indefinable at first, but soon traced to the thought of Margaret. For the first time in his life he thought of her unrelated to Barney. He had always loved Margaret, rejoiced in her high spirit, her courage, her downright sincerity, her deep heart, but never for himself, always for Barney. The first resentment that Barney should have passed her by for one like Iola had given way to a timid fluttering of heart that strengthened and deepened to a great joy that the way to Margaret for him stood open. For himself, now, he might love her. With such marvellous swiftness does love work that, when his mother bade him go "pay his duty to the minister," his heart responded with so great a leap of joy that he found himself glancing quickly at the faces of those about him, sure that they must have noticed.

And now he was on his way to Margaret. It was as if he had to make acquaintance of her. He wondered how she would greet him and he wondered what he should say to her. What would she be doing now? He glanced at his watch. It was just ten o'clock. The morning work would be done. She might come for a little stroll in the woods at the back of the manse, but he would say nothing to her to-day. He would wait and watch to read her heart. He sprang up the bank, that ran along beside the fence, to go on his way. A gleam of white through the snake fence against the pink of the clover caught his eye. Under the thorn tree—he knew the spot well—and upon the grass, lay a girl. "By Jove!" he whispered, his heart stopping, thumping, then rushing, "it is Margaret." He would creep up and surprise her. The deep grass deadened his footfalls. He was close to her. He held his breath. She lay asleep, one arm under her head, the other flung wide in an abandonment of weariness. He stood gazing down upon her. Pale she looked to him, and thin and weary. The lines about her mouth and eyes spoke of cares and of griefs, too. How much older she was than he had thought! "Poor girl! she has been having a hard time! It's a shame, a downright shame! And she's only a child yet!" At the thought of her long sacrifice for those three past years a great pity stole into his heart. At that touch of pity the love that had ever filled his heart, dammed back for so long by his regard for his brother's rights, suddenly finding its new channel, burst forth and swept like a torrent through his being. He lost grip of himself and, before he knew, he had bent over the sleeping girl and kissed her lips. A long shivering sigh shook her. "Barney," she murmured, a slight smile playing about her lips. She opened her eyes. A moment she lay looking up into Dick's face, then, suddenly wide awake, she sat upright.

"You! Dick!" she cried, surprise, indignation, shame, mingling in her voice. "You—you dare to—"

"Yes, Margaret," said Dick, aghast at what he had done, "I couldn't help it. You looked so sweet and so sad, and—and I love you so much."

"You," cried the girl again, as if she could find no other word. "What did you say?"

"I said, Margaret," he replied, gathering his courage together, "that I love you so much."

"You love me?" she gasped.

"Yes, I love you. I never knew till last night."

"Last night?" she echoed, with her eyes upon his face, now grown pale, but illuminated with a light she had never seen there before.

"Yes, last night. It was always there, Margaret," he hurried to say, "but only last night I found out I might love you. I never let myself go. I thought I had no right. I mean I thought Barney—" At the mention of his brother's name, the face that had been white with a look almost of horror flamed quickly with red. "Last night," continued Dick, wondering at the change in her, "I found out, and this morning, Margaret, the whole world is just humming with joy because I know I may love you all I want to. Oh, it's great! I never imagined a fellow could hold so much love or so much joy.

Do you understand me, Margaret? Do you knew what I am talking about?" Margaret's face had grown pale and haggard, as with pain, and her eyes were wide open with pity.

"Yes, Dick," she said slowly, "I know. I have just been learning." The brave lips quivered, but she kept firm hold of herself. "I know all the joy and—all the pain." She stopped short at the look in Dick's face. The buoyant, glad light flickered and went out. A look of perplexity, of great fear, and then of desolation, like that on her own face, spread over his. He knew her too well to misunderstand her meaning. She leaned over to him, still kneeling in the grass. "Oh, Dick, dear!" she cried, taking his hand in hers with a mother-touch and tone, "must you suffer, too? Oh, don't say you must! Not with my pain, Dick! Not with my pain!" Her voice rose in a cry, broke into a sob, but still she held him with her eyes.

"Do you say I must?" he answered in a hoarse tone. "I love you with all my heart."

"Oh, don't Dick, dear," she pleaded, "don't say it!"

"Yes, I will," he said, recovering his voice, "because it's true. And I'm glad it's true. I'm glad that I can at last let myself love you. It was only last night when Barney told me about Iola, you know."

"Yes, yes," she said hurriedly.

"I had always thought that it was you, and I was glad to think so for Barney. But last night"—here a quick flash of joy came into his face at the memory—"I found out, and this morning I could hardly help shouting it as I came along to you." He paused, and, leaning toward her, he took her hand. "Don't you think, Margaret, you might perhaps some time." The piteous entreaty in his voice broke down the girl's proud courage.

"Oh, Dick! Oh, Dick!" she sobbed, "don't! Don't ask me!" Her sobs came tempestuously.

He put his arms about her and, stroking her yellow hair, gently said, "Never mind, little girl. Don't do that! I can't stand that, and—well, I won't bother you a bit with my affair. Don't think about me. I'll get hold of myself. There now—hush, hush, girlie. Don't cry like that!" He held her close to him, caressing her till she grew quiet.

At length she drew away, saying, "I don't know why I should act like this. I haven't cried for a year. I think I am tired. It has been a hard winter, Dick. They used to play and sing together for hours. Oh, it was wonderful music, but I could have shrieked aloud. Don't think me horrid," she went on hurriedly. "I wonder I am not ashamed to tell you. But I never let anyone know, neither of them nor anyone else. Mind you that, Dick, no one knows." She sat up straight, her courage coming back. "I never meant to tell you, Dick, but you know you took me unaware." A little smile was struggling to the corners of her mouth and a faint flush touched her pale cheek. "But I am glad you know. And, Dick, can't we go back? Won't you forget what you have said?" Dick had been looking at her, wondering at her courage and self-command, but in his eyes a look of misery that went to the girl's heart.

"Forget!" he cried. "Tell me how."

She shook her head, and then, reading his eyes, she cried aloud, "Oh, Dick! must we go on and on like this?" She pressed her hands hard upon her heart. "There's a sore, sore pain right here," she said. "Is there to be no rest, no relief from it? It's been there for two years." She was fast losing her grip of herself again. Once more he caught her in his strong brown hands.

"Now, Margaret dear, don't do that! We'll help each other somehow. God—yes, God will help us if He takes any interest in us at all. He can't let us go on like this!"

The words steadied her.

"I know, Dick," she said, a sudden quiet falling upon her, "there has been no one else for all these months, and He has helped me. He will help you, too. Come," she continued, "let us go."

"No, sit down and talk," replied Dick. He looked at his watch. "A quarter after ten," he said, in surprise. "Can the whole world change in one little quarter of an hour?" he asked, looking up at her, "it was ten when I stopped at the hill."

"Come, Dick," she said again, "we'll talk another time, I can't trust myself just now. I was going to your mother's."

But Dick remained kneeling in the grass where he was. It seemed to him as if he had been in some strange land remote from this common life, and he shrank from contact with the ordinary day and its ordinary doings.

"I can't, Margaret," he said. "You go. Let me fight it out."

She knew too well where he was. "No, Dick, I will not leave you here. Come, do." She went quickly to him, kneeled down, put her arms about his neck and kissed him. "Help me, Dick," she whispered.

It was the word he needed. He threw his arms about her, kissed her once, and then, as if seized with a frenzy of passion, he kissed, again and again, her hair, her face, her hands, her lips, murmuring in hoarse, passionate tones, "I love you! I love you!" For a few moments she suffered him, and then gently pushed him back and drew apart from him. Her action recalled him to himself.

"Forgive me, Margaret," he cried brokenly, "I'm a great, selfish brute. I think only of myself. Now I'm ready to go. And when I weaken again, don't think me quite a cad."

He sprang up, threw back his shoulders as if adjusting them to a load, gave her his hand, and lifted her up, and together they set off down the lane, the shadow a little lighter as each felt the other near.

X
FOR A LADY'S HONOUR

"Are you going to Trinity convocation tomorrow?" asked Dr. Bulling of Iola.

They were sitting in what Iola called her studio. A poor little room it was, but suggesting in every detail the artistic taste of its occupant. Its adornments, the luxurious arrangement of cushions in the cosey corner, the prints upon the walls, and the books on the little table, spoke of a pathetic attempt to reproduce the surroundings of luxurious art without the large outlay that art demands. At one side of the room stood a piano with music lying carelessly about. In another corner was Iola's guitar, which she seldom used now except when intimate friends gathered for one of the little suppers she loved to give. Then she took it up to sing the mammy songs of her childhood. On the side opposite to that on which the piano stood was a little fireplace. It was the fireplace that had determined the choice of the room.

As Dr. Bulling asked his question Iola's lace lit up with a sudden splendour.

"Yes, of course," she cried.

"And why 'of course'?" inquired the doctor.

"Why? Because a great friend of mine is to receive his degree and his gold medal."

"And who is that, pray?"

"Mr. Boyle."

"Oh, you know him? Clever chap, they say. Can't say I know him. Have seen him a few times in the hospital with Trent. Struck me as rather crude. From the country, some place, isn't he?"

"Yes," replied Iola, with ever so slight a hesitation, "he is from the country, where I met him five—yes, it is actually five—years ago. So you see he is quite an old friend. And as for being crude, I think you can hardly call him that. Of course, he is not one of society's darlings, a patron of art, and a rising member of his profession as yet"—this with a little bow to her visitor—"but some day he will be great. And, besides, he is very nice."

"Of that I have no doubt," said the doctor, "seeing he is a friend of yours. But how are you going? Some friends of mine are to be there and will be glad to call for you." The doctor could hardly prevent a tone of condescension, almost of patronage, in his voice.

"You are very kind," said Iola, with just enough reserve in her manner to make the doctor conscious of his tone, "but I am going with friends."

"Friends?" inquired the doctor. "And who, may I ask?" There was an almost rude familiarity in his tone, but Iola only smiled at him the more sweetly.

"Oh, very dear friends, and very old friends, and friends of Mr. Boyle. In fact, his brother, a theological student, and a Miss Robertson. I think you have met her. She is a nurse in the General Hospital."

"Nurse Robertson?" said Bulling. "Oh, yes, I know her. Pretty much of a saint, isn't she?"

"A saint?" cried Iola, for the first time throwing energy into her voice. "Yes, a saint. But the best and sweetest and kindest and jolliest girl I know."

"I should hardly have called her jolly," said the doctor, with an air of dismissing her.

"Oh, she is!" cried Iola, enthusiastically, her large eyes glowing eager enthusiasm. "You ought to have seen her at home. Why, at sixteen years she took charge of her father's manse and the children in the most wonderful way. Looked after me, too."

"Poor girl!" murmured the doctor. "She had a handful, sure enough."

"Yes, you may say so. Then her father went on a trip to the old country, and, to the surprise of everybody, brought back a new wife."

"And put the girl's nose out of joint," said the doctor.

"Well, hardly that. But there was no longer need for her at home, and, on the whole, she felt better to be independent, and so here she has been for the last two years. She shares my room when she is at home, which is not often, and still takes care of me."

"Most fortunate young lady she is," murmured the doctor.

"So I am going with them," continued Iola.

"Then I suppose nobody will see you." The doctor's tone was quite gloomy.

"Why, I love to see all my friends."

"It will be the usual thing," said the doctor, "the same circle crowding you, the same impossibility of getting a word with you."

"That depends on how much you—" cried Iola, throwing a swift smile at him.

"How much I want to?" interrupted the doctor eagerly. "You know quite well I—"

"How much time there is. You see, one can't be rude. One must speak to all one's friends. But, of course, one can always plan one's time. How ever," she continued, "one can hardly expect to see much of the very popular Dr. Bulling, whose attention is always so fully taken up."

"Oh, rot!" said the doctor. "I say, can't we get off a little together? There are nice quiet nooks about the old building."

"Oh, doctor, how shocking!" But her eyes belied her voice, and the doctor departed with the lively expectation of a very pleasant convocation day at Trinity.

The convocation passed off with the usual uproar on the part of the students and the usual long-suffering endurance on the part of the dean and faculty and those who were fortunate, or unfortunate, enough to be the orators of the day, the fervent enthusiasm of the undergraduate body finding expression, now in college songs, whose chief characteristic was the vigour with which they were rendered, personal remarks in the way of encouragement, deprecation, pity, or gentle reproof to all who had to take part in the public proceedings, and at intervals in wildly uproarious applause and cheers at the mention of the name of some favourite. At no point was the fervour greater than when Barney was called to receive his medal. To the little group of friends at the left of the desk, consisting of his brother, Margaret, and Iola, it seemed as if the cheering that greeted Barney's name was almost worthy of the occasion. Dr. Trent presented him, and as he spoke of the difficulties he had to contend with in the early part of his course, of the perseverance and indomitable courage the young man had shown, and the singular, indeed the very remarkable, ability he had manifested in the special line of study for which this medal was granted, the dead silence that pervaded the room was even more eloquent than the tumult of cheers that followed Dr. Trent's remarks and that continued until Barney had taken his place again among the graduating class.

Then someone called out, "What's the matter with old Carbuncle?" eliciting the usual vociferous reply, "He's all right!"

"By Jove," said Dick to Margaret, who sat next him, "isn't that great? And the old boy deserves it every bit!" But Margaret made no reply. She was sitting with her eyes cast down, pale except for a spot of red in each cheek. At Dick's words she glanced at him for a moment, and he noticed that the large blue eyes were full of tears.

"It's all right, little girl," he whispered, giving her hand a little pat. He dared say no more, for the sight of her face and the look in her eyes set his own heart beating and gave him a choke in his throat.

On the other side of Margaret sat Iola, her face radiant with pride and joy, and as Barney reached his seat, turning half around and in the face of the whole company, she flashed him a look and a smile so full of pride and love that it seemed to him at that moment as if all he had endured for the last three years were quite worth while.

After the formal proceedings were over, Dr. Bulling made his way to the little group about Barney.

"Congratulations, Boyle," he said, in the somewhat patronizing manner of a graduate of some years' standing to one who holds his parchment in his hand and wears his still blushing honours as men wear new clothes, "that was a remarkable fine reception you had to-day."

Barney's brief word of acknowledgment showed his resentment of Bulling's tone and his dislike of the man. It angered Barney to observe the familiar, almost confidential, manner of Dr. Bulling with Iola, but it made him more furious to notice that, instead of resenting, Iola seemed to be pleased with his manner. Just now, however, she was giving herself to Barney. Her pride in him, her joy in him, and her quiet appreciation of him, were evident to all, so evident, indeed, that after a few words Dr. Bulling took himself off.

"Brute!" said Barney as the doctor retired.

"Why, I am sure he seems very nice," said Iola, raising her eyebrows in surprise.

"Nice!" said Barney contemptuously. "If you knew how the men speak of him about town you wouldn't call him nice. He has money, and he's in the swim, but he's a beast, all the same."

"Oh, Barney, you mustn't say so!" cried Iola, "for you know he's been a great friend to me. He has been very kind. I am quite devoted to him." Something in the tone of her voice, and more in the smile which she gave Barney, took the sting out of her words.

Before many minutes had passed the little group was broken up, chiefly because of the fact that Iola was soon surrounded by a circle of her own admiring friends, and among them the most insistent was Dr. Bulling, who finally, with bluff, good-natured but almost rude aggressiveness, carried her off to the tearoom. It took all the joy out of the day for Barney, and on his behalf, for Margaret and Dick, that for the rest of the afternoon Iola's attention was entirely absorbed by Dr. Bulling and his little coterie of friends.

And this feeling of disappointment in Iola and of resentment against Dr. Bulling he carried with him to a little stag dinner by the hospital staff at the Olympic that evening. The dinner was due chiefly to the exertions of Dr. Trent, and was intended by him not only to bring into closer touch with each other the members of the hospital staff, but also to be a kind of introduction of Barney to the inner circle of medical men in the city. For the past year Barney had acted as his clerk, almost as his assistant, and, indeed, Dr. Trent had made the formal proposition of an assistantship to him. Out of compliment to Barney, Dick had been invited, and young Drake also, who owed his parchment that day to Barney's merciless grinding in surgery, and perhaps more to his steadying friendship. Dr. Bulling, who, more for his great wealth and his large social connection than for his professional standing, had been invited, was present with Foxmore, Smead, and others who followed him about applauding his coarse jokes and accepting his favours. The dinner was purely informal in character, the menu well chosen, the wines abundant, and the drinking hard enough with some, with the result that as the dinner neared its end the men, and especially the group about Bulling, became more and more hilarious. Barney, who was drinking water and keeping his hand upon Drake's wineglass, found his attention divided between his conversation with Trent and the talk of Bulling, who, with his friends, sat across the table. As this group became more boisterous, they absorbed to themselves the attention of the whole company. Conscious of the prestige his wealth and social position accorded him, and inflamed by the wine he was drinking, Bulling became increasingly offensive. The talk degenerated. The stories and songs became more and more coarse in tone. It was Barney's first experience of a dinner of this kind, and it filled him with disgust and horror. Even Trent, by no means inexperienced in these matters, was disgusted with Bulling's tone. Following Barney's glances and aware of his wandering attention, he was about to propose a breakup of the party when he was arrested by a look of rigid and eager attention upon the face of his friend.

"Disgusting brute!" said Trent, in a low voice.

But Barney heeded him not. His attention was concentrated upon Bulling. He had his glass in his hand.

"Here's to the Lane!" he was saying, "the sweetest little Lane in all the world!"

"She's divine!" replied Foxmore. "And what a voice! She'll make Canada famous some day. Where did you discover her, Bulling?"

"In church," replied Bulling solemnly, to the uproarious delight of his followers. "That's right," he continued, "heard her sing, set things in motion, and now she's the leading voice in the cathedral. Introduced her to a few people, and there she is, the finest thing in her line in the city! Yes, and some day on the continent! A dear, sweet little lane it is," he continued in a tone of affectionate proprietorship that made Barney grind his teeth in furious rage.

"That she is," said Smead enthusiastically, "and thoroughly straight, too!"

"Oh," said Foxmore, "there's no lane but has a turning. And trust Bulling," he added coarsely, "for finding it out."

"Well," said Bulling, with a knowing smile, "this little Lane is straight. Of course there may be a slight deflection. Nature's lines run in curves, you know." And again his wit provoked applauding laughter. But before the laughter had quite faded out a voice was heard, clear and cutting.

"Dr. Bulling, you are a base liar!" The words were plainly audible to every man in the room. A dead silence fell upon the company.

"What?" said the doctor, sitting up straight, as if he had not heard aright.

"I say you are a cowardly liar!"

"What the deuce do you mean?"

"You have just made an insinuation against the honour of a young lady. I say again you are a mean and cowardly liar. I want you to say so."

For a moment or two Bulling's surprise kept him silent.

"Quite right," said Trent. "Beastly cad!"

Then Dr. Bulling broke forth. "You impertinent young cub! What do you mean?"

For answer, Barney seized Drake's wineglass, half full of wine, and flung glass and contents full in Bulling's face. In an instant every man was on his feet. Above the din rose Foxmore's voice.

"Give it to him Bulling! Give it to the young prig!"

The Doctor: A Tale Of The Rockies | 83

"No hurry about this, boys," said Bulling quietly; "I'll make him eat his words before he's half an hour older."

Meantime Dick was entreating his brother. "Let me at him. He's a great knocker. Held the 'varsity championship. You don't know anything about it. Let me at him, Barney. I can do him up." Dick had been 'varsity champion in his own time. But Barney put Dick aside with quiet, stern words.

"Don't interfere, Dick. No matter what happens, don't interfere to-night. I won't have it, Dick, remember. It may take us an hour or it may take all night, but he'll say he lied before I'm through with him."

Meantime the men, and chief among them Trent, were seeking to appease the doctor and to patch up the peace.

"If he apologizes I shall let the young cub off," were the doctor's terms.

"If he says he lied," was Barney's condition.

"Don't disturb yourselves, gentlemen," said Bulling; "it will not take more than two minutes, and then we can finish our smoke."

The moment they stood facing each other Barney rushed, only to receive a heavy blow which hurled him backward. It was plain he knew nothing of the game. It was equally plain that the doctor was entirely master of it. Again and again Barney rushed in wildly, the doctor easily blocking, avoiding and sending in killing blows, till at length bloody, dazed, panting, Barney had to lean against his friends to recover his wind and strength. Opposite him, cool, smiling, and untouched, stood his adversary.

"This is easy, boys," he smiled. "Now, you young whipper-snapper," he continued, addressing Barney, "perhaps you've had enough. Let me tell you, it's time for you to quit fooling, or, by the Eternal, I'll send you to sleep!" As he spoke he closed his teeth with a savage snap.

"Will you say you're a liar?" said Barney, facing his opponent again, and disregarding Dick's entreaties and warnings.

"Ah, quit it!" said the doctor contemptuously, "Come along, you fool, if you must have it!"

Once more Barney rushed. As he did so Bulling stopped him with a heavy left-hander on the face which sent him reeling backward, quickly following with his right and again with a last terrific blow upon the jaw of his dazed and reeling victim. Barney fell with a crash upon the floor, and lay quiet. With a cry Dick sprang at Bulling, but half a dozen men pulled him off.

"Let him come," said Bulling, with a laugh, "I've a very fine assortment of the same kind. Families supplied on reasonable terms."

Meantime, while the men were struggling with Dick, Dr. Trent and Drake were trying to revive poor Barney, bathing his face and hands.

"Stand back! Don't crowd about, men! Bring me a little brandy, someone," said Dr. Trent. "A more cowardly brute I've never seen. You're a disgrace to the profession, Bulling."

"Oh, thanks. I don't need your credentials, Trent," said Bulling cynically.

But Trent, ignoring him, devoted himself to Barney, who showed signs of reviving. It was some minutes, however, before he could sit up. Meanwhile Bulling with his friends retired to the lavatory.

"Here, Boyle," said Treat, holding a glass to his lips as Barney sat up, "a little more brandy and water."

For a few moments after he drank the liquor Barney sat gazing stupidly about. Then, as full consciousness returned, cried out, "Where is he? He's not gone?" He seized the glass of brandy and water from Dr. Treat's hands and drank it off. "Get me another," he said. "Is he gone?" he repeated, making an effort to rise.

"Never mind, Boyle, he's gone."

"Wait till another day, Barney," entreated Dick. "Never mind to-night."

At this moment the sound of Dr. Bulling's voice, followed by loud laughter, came from the lavatory. At once Barney stood up, walked to the table, poured out a glass of brandy and drank it raw. For a minute he stood stretching his arms.

"Ah, that's better," he said, and started toward the lavatory, but Dick clung to him.

"Barney, listen to me," he entreated, his voice coming in broken sobs. "He'll kill you. Let me take your place."

"Dick, keep out of it," said Barney. "Don't worry. He'll hurt me no more, but he'll say it before I'm done." And, throwing off the restraining hands, he made his way into the lavatory. Dr. Bulling was arranging his collar before a glass. As Barney entered he turned around.

"I'm sorry, Boyle," he began, "but you brought it on yourself, you know."

Barney walked straight up to him.

"I didn't hear you say you are a liar."

"Look here," cried Bulling, "haven't you got enough. Be thankful you're not killed. Go on! Get home! I don't run a butcher shop!"

"Will you say you're a liar and a cowardly liar?"

Barney's voice had in it the ring of cold steel.

"I say, boys," said Bulling, appealing to the crowd, "keep this fool off. I don't want to kill him."

Foxmore, with some of the others, approached Barney.

"Now, Boyle, quit it," said Foxmore. "There's no use, you see." He laid his hand on Barney's arm.

Barney put his hand against his breast, appearing to brush him aside, but Foxmore touched nothing till he struck the wall ten feet away.

"Get back!" cried Barney, springing away from the men approaching him. As he spoke, he seized a small oak dressing table by one of its legs, swung it round his head, dashed it to pieces on the marble floor, and, putting his foot upon the wreckage, with one mighty wrench had the leg free in his hand.

"You men stand back," he said in a low voice, "and don't any of you interfere."

Amazed at this exhibition of furious strength, the men started back to their places, leaving a wide space about him.

"Good heavens!" said Bulling, his face turning a shade pale, "the man is mad! Call a policeman, some of you."

"Drake, lock that door and bring me the key," said Barney.

As Barney put the key in his pocket and turned again toward Bulling, the latter's pallor increased. "I take you men to witness," he said, appealing to the company, "if murder is done I'm not responsible. I'm defending my life. Remember, I'll strike to kill."

"No, Dr. Bulling," said Barney, handing his club to Drake, "you won't strike at all. I've had my lesson. You'll strike me no more. The boxing exhibition is over. This is a fight till you can fight no more."

The doctor's nerve was fast going. Barney stood cool, quiet, and terrible.

"I'll give you your chance once again," he said. "Will you say you are a cowardly liar?"

Dr. Bulling glanced at the group back of him, read pain in their faces, hesitated a moment, then, pulling himself together, said, with an evident effort at bluster, "Not by a — — sight! Come on! Take your medicine!" But the lesson of the last half hour had not been lost on Barney. Up and down the long room, circling about his man, feinting to draw his attack, eluding, and again feinting, Barney kept his antagonist in such rapid motion and so intensely on the alert that his wind began to fail him, and it soon became evident that he could not stand the pace for very long.

"You've got him!" cried Dick, in an ecstasy of expectation. "Keep it up, Barney! That's the game! You'll have him in five minutes more!"

"Quite evident," echoed Dr. Trent quietly, hugely enjoying the change in the situation.

Dr. Bulling heard the words. His pallor deepened. Red blotches began to appear on his cheek. The sweat stood out upon his forehead. His breath came in short gasps. He knew he could not last much longer. His only hope lay in immediate attack. He must finish off his man within the next minute or accept defeat. Nature was now taking revenge upon him for his long outraging of her laws. Barney, on the other hand, though bruised and battered about the face, was stepping about easily and lightly, without any sign of the terrible punishment he had suffered. Reading his opponent's face he knew that the moment for a supreme effort had arrived, and waited for his plan to develop. There was only one thing for Bulling to do. Edging his opponent toward the corner and summoning his fast failing strength for a final attack, he forced him hard back into the angle of the wall. He had him now. One clean blow and all would be over.

"Look out, Barney!" yelled Dick.

Suddenly, as if shot from a steel spring, Barney crouched low and leaped at his man, and disregarding two heavy blows, thrust one long arm forward and with his sinewy fingers gripped his enemy's throat. "Ha!" he cried with savage exultation, holding off his foe at arm's length. "Now! Now! Now!" As he uttered each word between his clenched teeth he shook the gasping, choking wretch as a dog shakes a rat. In vain his victim struggled to get free, now striking wild and futile blows, now clutching and clawing at those terrible gripping fingers. His face grew purple; his tongue protruded; his breath came in rasping gasps; his hands fell to his side. "Keep your hands so," hissed Barney, loosening his grip to give him air. "Ha! would you? Don't you move!" gripping him hard again. "There!" loosening once more, "now, are you a liar? Speak quick!" The blue lips made an attempt at the affirmation of which the head made the sign. "Say it again. Are you a liar?" Once more the head nodded and the lips attempted to speak. "Yes," said Barney, still through his clenched teeth, "you are a cowardly liar!" The words came forth with terrible deliberation. "I could kill you with my hands as you stand. But I won't, you cur! I'll just do this." As he spoke he once more tightened his grip upon the throat and swung his open hand on the livid cheek.

"For God's sake, Boyle," cried Foxmore, "let up! That's enough!"

"Yes, it's enough," said Barney, flinging the semi-conscious man on the floor, "it's enough for him. Foxmore, you laughed, I think, when he uttered that lie," he said in a voice smooth, almost sweet, but that chilled the hearts of the hearers, "you laughed. You were a beastly cad, weren't you? Speak!"

"What? I—I—" gasped Foxmore, backing into the corner.

"Quick, quick!" cried Barney, stepping lightly toward him on his toes, "say it quick!" His fingers were working convulsively.

"Yes, yes, I was!" cried Foxmore, backing further away behind the others.

"Yes," cried Barney, his voice rising hoarse, "you would all of you laugh at that brute ruin the name and honour of a lonely girl!" He walked up and down before the group which stood huddled in the corner in abject terror, more like a wild beast than a man. "You're not fit to live! You're beasts of prey! No decent girl is safe from you!" His voice rose loud and thin and harsh. He was fast losing hold of himself. His ghastly face, bloody and horribly disfigured, made an appalling setting for his blazing eyes. Nearer and nearer the crowd he walked, gnashing and grinding his teeth till the foam fell from his lips. The wild fury of his Highland ancestors was turning him into a wild beast with a wild beast's lust of blood. Further and further back cowered the group without a word, so utterly panic-stricken were they.

"Barney," said Dick quietly, "come home." He stopped short, with a mighty effort recalling his reason. For a few moments he stood silent looking at the floor, then, raising his eyes, he let them rest upon the doctor, who was leaning against the wall, and, without a word, turned and slowly passed out of the room.

"Gad!" said Foxmore, with a horrible gasp of relief, "if the devil looks like that I never want to see him."

XI
IOLA'S CHOICE

Iola was undoubtedly pleased; her lips parting in a half smile, her eyes shining through half-closed lids, her whole face glowing with a warm light proclaimed the joy in her heart. The morning letters lay on her table. She sat some moments holding one which she had opened, while she gazed dreamily out through the branches of the big elms that overshadowed her window. She would not move lest the dream should break and vanish. As she lay back in her chair looking out upon the moving leaves and waving boughs, she allowed the past to come back to her. How far away seemed the golden days of her Southern childhood. Almost her first recollection of sorrow, certainly the first that made any deep impression upon her heart, was when the men carried out her father in a black box and when, leaving the big house with the wide pillared veranda, she was taken to the chilly North. How terribly vivid was the memory of her miserable girlhood, poverty pressed and loveless, her soul beating like a caged bird against the bars of the cold and rigid discipline of her aunt's well-ordered home. Then came the first glad freedom from dependence when first she undertook to earn her own bread as a teacher. Freedom and love came to her together, freedom and love and friendship in the Manse and the Old Stone Mill. With the memory of the Mill, there rose before her, clear-limned and vividly real, one face, rugged, strong, and passionate, and the thought of him brought a warmer light to her eyes and a stronger beat to her heart. Every feature of the moonlight scene on the night of the barn-raising when first she saw him stood out with startling distinctness, the new skeleton of the barn gleaming bony and bare against the sky, the dusky forms crowding about, and, sitting upon a barrel across the open moonlit space of the barn floor, the dark-faced lad playing his violin and listening while she sang. At that point it was that life for her began.

A new scene passed before her eyes. It was the Manse parlour, the music professor with dirty, claw-like fingers but face alight with rapturous delight playing for her while she sang her first great oratorio aria. She could feel to-day that mysterious thrill in the dawning sense of new powers as the old man, with his hands upon her shoulders, cried in his trembling, broken voice, "My dear young lady, the world will listen to you some day!" That was the beginning of her great ambition. That day she began to look for the time when the world would come to listen. Then followed weary days and weeks and months and years, weary with self-denials new to her and with painful struggling with unmusical pupils, for she needed bread; weary with heart-breaking strivings and failings in the practice of her art, but, worst of all, weary to heart-break with the patronage of the rich and flattering friends—how she loathed it—of whom Dr. Bulling was the most insistent and the most objectionable. And then this last campaign, with its plans and schemes for a place in the great Philharmonic which would at once insure not only her standing in the city, but a New York engagement as well. And now the moment of triumph had arrived. The letter she held in her hand was proof of it. She glanced once more at the written page, her eye falling upon a phrase here and there, "We have succeeded at last—the Duff Charringtons have surrendered—you only want a chance—here it is— you can do the part well." She smiled a little. Yes, she knew she could do the part. "And now let nothing or nobody prevent you from accepting Mrs. Duff Charrington's invitation for next Saturday. It is a beautiful yacht and well found, and I am confident the great lady will be gracious—bring your guitar with you, and if you will only be kind, I foresee two golden days in store for me." She allowed a smile slightly sarcastic to curl her lips.

"The doctor is inclined to be poetical. Well, we shall see. Saturday? That means Sunday spent on board the yacht. I wish they had it made another day. Margaret won't like it, and Barney won't either."

For a moment or two she allowed her mind to go back to the Sundays spent in the Manse. She had never known the meaning of the day before. The utter difference in feeling, in atmosphere, between that day and the other days of the week, the subduing quiet, the soothing peace, and the sense of sacredness that pervaded life on that day, made the Sabbaths in the Manse like blessed isles of rest in the sea of time. Never, since her two years spent there, had she been able to get quite away from the sense of obligation to make the day differ from the ordinary days of the week. No, she was sure Barney would not like it. Still, she could spend its hours quietly enough upon the yacht.

She picked up another letter in a large square envelope, the address written in bold characters. "This is the Duff Charrington invitation, I suppose," she said, opening the letter. "Well, she does it nicely, at any rate, even if, as Dr. Bulling suggests, somewhat against her inclination."

Again she sat back in silent dreaming, her eyes looking far away down the coming years of triumph. Surely enough, the big world was drawing near to listen. All she had read of the great queens of song, Patti, Nilsson, Rosa, Trebelli, Sterling, crowded in upon her mind, their regal courts thronged by the great and rich of every land, their country seats, their luxurious lives. At last her foot was in the path. It only remained for her to press forward. Work? She well knew how hard must be her daily lot. Yes, but that lesson she had learned, and thoroughly well, during these past years, how to work long hours, to deny herself the things her luxurious soul longed for, and, hardest of all, to bear with and smile at those she detested. All these she would endure a little longer. The days were coming when she would have her desire and do her will.

She glanced at the other letters upon the table. "Barney," she cried, seizing one. An odd compunction struck into her heart. "Barney, poor old boy!" A sudden thought stayed her hand from opening the letter. Where had Barney been in this picture of the future years upon which she had been feasting her soul? Aghast, she realized that, amid its splendid triumphs, Barney had not appeared. "Of course, he'll be there," she murmured somewhat impatiently. But how and in what capacity she could not quite see. Some prima donnas had husbands, mere shadowy appendages to their courts. Others there were who found their husbands most useful as financial agents, business managers, or upper servants. Iola smiled a proud little smile. Barney would not do for any of these discreetly shadowy, conveniently colourless or more useful husbands. Would he be her husband? A warm glow came into her eyes and a flush upon her cheek. Her husband? Yes, surely, but not for a time. For some years she must be free to study, and—well, it was better to be free till she had made her name and her place in the world. Then when she had settled down Barney would come to her.

But how would Barney accept her programme? Sure as she was of his great love, and with all her love for him, she was a little afraid of him. He was so strong, so silently immovable. Often in the past three years she had made trial of that immovable strength, seeking to draw him away from his work to some social engagement, to her so important, to him so incidental. She had always failed. His work absorbed him as her art had her, but with a difference. With Barney, work was his reward; with her, a means to it. To gain some further knowledge, to teach his fingers some finer skill, that was enough for Barney. Iola wrought at her long tasks and practised her unusual self-denials with her eye upon the public. Her reward would come when she had brought the world, listening, to her feet. Seized in the thrall of his work, Barney grimly held to it, come what might. No such absorbing passion possessed Iola. And Iola, while she was provoked by what she called his stubbornness, was yet secretly proud of that silently resisting strength she could neither shake nor break. No, Barney was not fitted for the role of the shadowy, pliant, convenient husband.

What, then, in her plan of life would be his place? It startled her to discover that her plan had been complete without him. Complete? Ah, no. Her life without Barney would be like a house without its back wall. During these years of study and toil, while Barney could only give her snatches of his time, she had come to feel with increasing strength that her life was built round about him. When others had been applauding her successes, she waited for Barney's word; and though beside the clever, brilliant men that moved in the circle into which her art had brought her he might appear awkward and dull, yet it was Barney who continued to be the standard by which she judged men. With all his need of polish, his poverty of small talk, his hopeless ignorance of the conventions, and his obvious disregard of them, the massive strength of him, his fine sense of honour, his chivalrous bearing toward women, added a touch of reverence to the love she bore him. But more than all, it was to Barney her heart turned for its rest. She knew well that she held in all its depth and strength his heart's love. He would never fail her. She could not exhaust that deep well. But the question returned, where would Barney be while she was being conducted by acclaiming multitudes along her triumphal way? "Oh, he will wait—we will wait," she corrected, shrinking from the heartlessness of the former phrasing. How many years she could not say. But deep in her heart was the determination that nothing should stand in the way of the ambition she had so long cherished and for which she had so greatly endured.

She opened the note with lingering deliberation as one dallies with an approaching delight.

"MY DEAR IOLA: I have always told you the truth. I could not see you last evening, nor can I to-day, and perhaps not for a day or two, because my face is disfigured. These are the facts: At the dinner, night before last, Dr. Bulling lied about you. I made him swallow his lie and in the process got rather badly marked, though not at all hurt. The doctor and his friends will, I think, guard their tongues in future, at least in my hearing. Dr. Bulling is a man of vile mind and of unclean life. He should not be allowed to appear with decent people. I have written to forbid him ever approaching you in public. You will know how to treat him if he attempts it. This will be a most disgusting business to you. I hate to make you suffer, but it had to be done, and by no one but me. Would I could bear it all for you, my darling. The patronage of these people, I mean Dr. Bulling's set, cannot, surely, be necessary to your success. Your great voice needs not their patronage; if so, failure would be better. When I am fit for your presence I shall come to you. Good-bye. It is hard not to see you. Ever yours,

"Barney."

Alas! for her dreams. How rudely they were dispelled! Alas! for her castle in Spain. Already it was tottering to ruin, and by Barney's hand. She read the note hurriedly again.

"He wants me to break with Dr. Bulling." She recalled a sentence in the doctor's letter. "Let no one or nothing keep you from accepting this invitation." "He's afraid Barney will keep me back. Nonsense! How stupid of Barney! He is so terribly particular! He doesn't understand these things. There has been a horrid row of some kind and now he asks me to cut Dr. Bulling!" She glanced at Barney's letter. "Well, he doesn't ask me, but it's all the same—'you will know how to treat him.' He's too proud to ask me, but he expects me to. It would be sheer madness! Wouldn't the Duff Charrington's and Evelyn Redd be delighted! It is preposterous! I must go! I shall go!"

Rarely did Iola allow herself the luxury of a downright burst of passion. With her, it was hardly ever worth while to be seriously angry. It was so much easier to avoid straight issues. But to-day there was no avoiding. She surprised herself with a storm of indignant rage so heart-shaking that after it had passed she was thankful she had been alone.

"What's the matter with me?" she asked herself. She did not know that the whole volume of her ambition, which had absorbed so great a part of her life, had come, in all its might, against the massive rock of Barney's will. He would never yield, she knew well. "What shall I do?" she cried aloud, beginning to pace the room. "Margaret will tell me. No, she would be sure to side with Barney. She would think it was wicked to go on Sunday, anyway, and, besides, she has Barney's rigid notions about things. I wish I could see Dick. Dick will understand. He has seen more of this life and—oh, he's not so terribly hidebound. And I'll get Dick to see Barney." She would not acknowledge that she was grateful that Barney could not come to see her, but she could write him a note and she could send Dick to him, and in the meantime she would accept the invitation. "I will accept at once. I wish I had before I read Barney's note. I really had accepted in my mind, and, besides, the arrangements were all made. I'll write the letters now." She hastened to burn her bridges behind her so that retreat might be impossible. "There," she cried, as she sealed, addressed, and stamped the letters, "I wish they were in the box. I'm awfully afraid I'll change. But I can't change! I cannot let this chance go! I have worked too long and too hard! Barney should not ask it!" A wave of self-pity swept over her, bringing her temporary comfort. Surely Barney would not cause her pain, would not force her to give up her great opportunity. She sought to prolong this mood. She pictured herself a forlorn maiden in distress whom it was Barney's duty and privilege to rescue. "I'll just go and post these now," she said. Hastily she put on her hat and ran down with the letters, fearing lest the passing of her self-pity might leave her to face again the thought of Barney's inevitable and immovable opposition.

"There, that's done," she said to herself, as the lid of the post box clicked upon her letters. "Oh, I wonder—I wish I hadn't!" What she had feared had come to pass. She had committed herself, and now her self-pity had evaporated and left her face to face with the inevitable results. With terrible clearness she saw Barney's dark, rugged face with the deep-seeing eyes. "He always makes you feel in the wrong," she said impatiently. "You can never think what to say. He always seems right, and," she added honestly, "he is right generally. Never mind, Dick will help me." She shook off her load and ran on. At her door she met Dr. Foxmore.

"Ah, good-morning," smiled the doctor, showing a double row of white teeth under his waxed mustache. "And how does the fair Miss Lane find herself this fine morning?"

It took the whole force of Iola's self-mastery to keep the disgust which was swelling her heart from showing in her face. Here was one of Dr. Bulling's friends, one of his toadies—and he had a number of them—who represented to her all that was most loathsome in her life. The effort to repress her disgust, however, only made her smile the sweeter. Foxmore was greatly encouraged. It was one of his fixed ideas that his manner was irresistible with "the sex." Bulling might hold over him, by reason of his wealth and social position, but give him a fair field without handicap and see who would win out!

"I was about to do myself the honour and the pleasure of calling upon you this morning."

"Oh, indeed. Well—ah—come in." Iola was fighting fiercely her loathing of him. It was against this man and his friends that Barney had defended her name. She led the way to her studio, ignoring the silly chatter of the man following her upstairs, and by the time he had fairly got himself seated she was coolly master of herself.

"Just ran in to give you the great news."

"To wit?"

"Why, don't you know? The Philharmonic thing is settled. You've got it."

Iola looked blank.

"Why, haven't you heard that the Duff Charringtons have surrendered?" Iola recognized Dr. Bulling's words.

"Surrendered? Just what, exactly?"

"Oh, d-dash it all! You know the big fight that has been going on, the Duff Charringtons backing that little Redd girl."

"Oh! So the Duff Charringtons have been backing the little Redd girl? Miss Evelyn Redd, I suppose? It sounds a little like a horse race or a pugilistic encounter."

"A horse race!" he exclaimed. "Ha, ha, ha! A horse race isn't in it with this! But Bulling pulled the wires and you've got it."

"But this is extremely interesting. I was not aware that the soloists were chosen for any other reason than that of merit."

In spite of herself Iola had adopted a cool and somewhat lofty manner.

"Oh, well, certainly on merit, of course. But you know how these things go." Dr. Foxmore was beginning to feel uncomfortable. The lofty air of this struggling, as yet unrecognized, country girl was both baffling and exasperating. "Oh, come, Miss Lane," he continued, making a desperate effort to recover his patronizing tone, "you know just what we all think of your ability."

"What do you think of it?" Iola's tone was calmly curious.

"Why, I think—well—I know you can do the work infinitely better than Evelyn Redd."

"Have you heard Miss Redd in oratorio? I know you have never heard me."

"No, can't say I have; but I know your voice and your style and I'm confident it will suit the part."

"Thank you so much," said Iola sweetly; "I am so sorry that Dr. Bulling should have given so much time, and he is such a busy man."

"Oh, that's nothing," waved Dr. Foxmore, recovering his self-esteem, "we enjoyed it."

"How nice of you! And you were pulling wires, too, Dr. Foxmore?"

"Ah, well, we did a little work in a quiet way," replied the doctor, falling into his best professional tone.

"And this yachting party, I suppose Dr. Bulling and you worked that, too? Really, Dr. Foxmore, you have no idea what a relief it is to have one's affairs taken charge of in this way. It quite saves one the trouble of making up one's mind. Indeed, one hardly needs a mind at all." Iola's face and smile were those of innocent childhood. Dr. Foxmore shot a suspicious glance at her and hastened to change the subject.

"Well, you will go next Saturday, will you not?"

"I am really a little uncertain at present," replied Iola.

"Oh, you must, you know! Mrs. Duff Charrington will be awfully cut up, not to speak of Bulling. He had no end of trouble to bring it off."

"You mean, to persuade Mrs. Duff Charrington to invite me?"

"Oh, well," said the doctor, plunging wildly, "I wouldn't put it that way. But the whole question of the Philharmonic was involved, and this invitation was a flag of truce, as it were."

"Your metaphors certainly have a warlike flavour, Dr. Foxmore; I cannot pretend to follow the workings of your mind. But seeing that this invitation has been secured at the expense of such effort on the part of Dr. Bulling and yourself, I rather think I shall decline it." In spite of all she could do, Iola could not keep out of her voice a slightly haughty tone. Dr. Foxmore's sense of superiority was fast deserting him. "And as to the Philharmonic solos," continued Iola, "if the directors see fit to make me an offer of the part I shall consider it."

"Consider it!" gasped Dr. Foxmore. It was time this young girl with her absurd pretensions were given to understand the magnitude of the favour that Dr. Bulling and himself were seeking to confer upon her. He became brutal. "Well, all I say is that if you know when you are well off, you'll take this chance."

Iola rose with easy grace and stood erect her full height. Dr. Foxmore had not thought her so tall. Her face was a shade paler than usual, her eyes a little wider open, but her voice was as smooth as ever, and with just a little ring as of steel in it she inquired, "Did you come here this morning to make this threat, Dr. Foxmore?"

"I came," he said bluntly, "to let you know your good fortune and to warn you not to allow any of your friends to persuade you against your own best interests."

"My friends?" Iola threw her head slightly backward and her tone became frankly haughty.

"Oh, I know your friends, and especially—I may as well be plain—that young medical student, Boyle, don't like Dr. Bulling, and might persuade you against this yacht trip."

Iola was furiously aware that her face was aflame, but she stood without speaking for a few moments till she was sure her voice was steady.

"My FRIENDS would never presume to interfere with my choosing."

"Well, they presume, or at least that young Boyle presumed, to interfere once too often for his own good. But he'll probably be more careful in future."

"Mr. Boyle is a gentleman in whom I have the fullest confidence. He would do what he thought right."

"He will probably correct his judgments before he interferes with Dr. Bulling again." The doctor's tone was insolently sarcastic.

"Dr. Bulling?"

"Yes. He was grossly insulting and Dr. Bulling was forced to chastise him."

"Chastise! Mr. Boyle!" cried Iola, her anger throwing her off her guard. "That is quite impossible, Dr. Foxmore! That could not happen!"

"But I am telling you it did! I was present and saw it. It was this way—"

Iola put up her hand imperiously. "Dr. Foxmore," she said, recovering her self-command, "there is no need of words. I tell you it is quite impossible! It is quite impossible!"

Dr. Foxmore's face flushed a deep red. He flung aside the remaining shreds of decency in speech.

"Do you mean to call me a liar?" he shouted.

"Ah, Dr. Foxmore, would you also chastise me as well?"

The doctor stood in helpless rage looking at the calm, smiling face.

"I was a fool to come!" he blurted.

"I would not presume to contradict you, nor to stand in the way of returning wisdom."

The doctor swore a great oath under his breath and without further words strode from the room.

Iola stood erect and silent till he had disappeared through the open door. "Oh!" she breathed, her hands fiercely clenched, "if I were a man what a joy it would be just now!" She shut the door and sat down to think. "I wonder what did happen? I must see Dick at once. He'll tell me. Oh, it is all horribly loathsome!" For the first time she saw herself from Dr. Bulling's point of view. If she sang in the Philharmonic it would be by virtue of his good offices and by the gracious permission of the Duff Charringtons. That she had the voice for the part and that it was immeasurably better than Evelyn Redd's counted not at all. How mean she felt! And yet she must go on with it. She would not allow anything to stand in the way of her success. This was the first firm stepping-stone in her climb to fame. Once this was taken, she would be independent of Bulling and his hateful associates. She would go on this yacht trip. She need not have anything to do with Dr. Bulling, nor would she, for Barney would undoubtedly be hurt and angry. It looked terribly like disloyalty to him to associate herself on terms of friendship with the man who had beaten him so cruelly. Oh, how she hated herself! But she could not give up her chance. She would explain to Barney how helpless she was and she would send Dick to him. He would listen to Dick.

Poor Iola! Without knowing it, she was standing at the cross roads making choice of a path that was to lead her far from the faith, the ideals, the friends she now held most dear. Through all her years she had been preparing herself for this hour of choice. With her, to desire greatly was to bend her energies to attain. She would deeply wound the man who loved her better than his own life; but the moment of choice found her helpless in the grip of her ambition. And so her choice was made.

XII
HE THAT LOVETH HIS LIFE

Mrs. Duff Charrington at close range was not nearly so formidable as when seen at a distance. The huge bulk of her, the pronouncedly masculine dress and manner, the loud voice, the red face with its dark mustache line on the upper lip, all of which at a distance were calculated to overawe if not to strike terror to the heart of the beholder, were very considerably softened by the shrewd, kindly twinkle of the keen grey eyes which a nearer view revealed. Her welcome of Iola was bluff and hearty, but she was much too busy ordering her forces and disposing of her impedimenta, for she was her own commodore, to pay particular attention in the meantime to her guests. The wharf at which the Petrel was tied was crowded this Saturday afternoon with various parties of excursionists making for the steamers, ferries, yachts, and other craft that lay along the water front. Already the Petrel had hoisted her mainsail and, under the gentle breeze, was straining upon her shore lines awaiting the word to cast off. As Iola stood idly gazing at the shifting scene, wondering how Dick had succeeded on his mission to his brother, she observed Dr. Bulling approaching with his usual smiling assurance. Just as he was about to speak, however, she noticed him start and gaze fixedly toward the farther side of the wharf. Iola's eye, following his gaze, fell upon the figure of a man pushing his way through the crowd. It was Barney. She saw him pause, evidently to make inquiry of a dockhand. With a muttered oath, Bulling sprang to the aft line.

"Let go that line, Murdoff!" he shouted to the man at the bow. "Look lively, there!"

As he spoke he cast off the stern line and seized the wheel, making it imperative that Murdoff should execute his command in the liveliest manner. At once the yacht swung out and began to put a space of blue water between herself and the dock. She was not a moment too soon, for Barney, having received his direction, was coming at a run, scattering the crowd to right and left. As he arrived at the dock edge he caught sight of Iola and Dr. Bulling. He took a step backwards and made as if to attempt the spring. Iola's cry, "Don't, Barney!" arrested Mrs. Duff Charrington's attention.

"What's up?" she shouted. "How's this? We're off! Bulling, what the deuce—who gave orders?"

Mrs. Duff Charrington for once in her life was, as she would have said herself, completely flabbergasted. At a single glance she took in the white face of Iola, and that of Dr. Bulling, no less white.

"What's up?" she cried again. "Have you seen a ghost, Miss Lane? You, too, Bulling?" She glanced back at the clock. "There's someone left behind! Who is that young man, Daisy? Why, it's our medallist, isn't it? Do you know him, Bulling? Shall we go back for him?"

"No, no! For Heaven's sake, no! He's a madman, quite!"

"Pardon me, Dr. Bulling," said Iola, her voice ringing clear and firm in contrast with Bulling's agitated tone, "he is a friend of mine, a very dear friend, and, I assure you, very sane." As she spoke she waved her hand to Barney, but there was no answering sign.

"Your friend, is he?" said Mrs. Duff Charrington. "Then doubtless very sane. Does he want you, Miss Lane? Shall we go back for him?"

"No, he doesn't want me," said Iola.

"Mrs. Charrington," said Dr. Bulling, "he has a grudge against me because of a fancied insult."

"Ah," said Mrs. Duff Charrington, "I understand. What do you say, Miss Lane? We can easily go back."

"Oh, let us not talk about it, Mrs. Charrington," said Iola hurriedly; "he is gone."

"As you wish, my dear. Daisy, take Dr. Bulling down to the cabin. I declare he looks as if he needed bracing up. I shall take the wheel."

"Mrs. Charrington," said Iola in a low voice, as Bulling disappeared down the companionway, "that was Mr. Boyle, my friend, and I want you to think him a man of the highest honour. But he doesn't like Dr. Bulling. He doesn't trust him."

"My dear, my dear," said Mrs. Charrington brusquely, "don't trouble yourself about him. I haven't lived fifty years for nothing. Oh! these men, these men! They take themselves too seriously, the dear creatures. But they are just like ourselves, with a little more conceit and considerably less wit. And they are not really worth all the trouble we take for them. I must get to know your medallist, my dear. That was a strong face and an honest face. I have heard John rave about him. John is my young son, first year in medicine. His judgment, I confess, is not altogether reliable—worships brawn, and there are traditions afloat as to that young man's doings when they were initiating him. But I have no doubt that, however sane on other subjects, he is quite mad about you, and, hang me! if I can wonder. If I were a young man I'd get my arms round you as soon as possible."

As she chattered along, Iola found her heart warm to Mrs. Duff Charrington, who, with all her sporty manners and masculine ways, was an honest soul, with a shrewd wit and a kindly heart.

"I'm glad now I came," said Iola gratefully; "I was afraid you weren't—" She paused abruptly in confusion.

"Oh, I'm not so bad as I'm painted, I assure you."

"Oh, dear Mrs. Charrington, it was not you I was afraid of, it was what Dr. Bulling—" Again Iola hesitated.

"Don't bother telling me," said Mrs. Duff Charrington, observing her confusion. "No doubt Bulling gave you to understand that he worked me to invite you. Confess now." There was a shrewd twinkle in her keen grey eye. "Bulling is a liar, a terrible liar, with large possibilities of self-appreciation. But he had nothing to do with this invitation, though he flatters himself he had. He's not without ability, but he can't teach his grandmother to suck eggs. I'll tell you why you are here. I pride myself upon having an eye for a winner, and I pick you as one, and that's why you are to sing in the Philharmonic. Evelyn Redd has a pretty voice. She is a niece of a very dear friend, and for a time I thought she might do. But she has no soul, no passion, and music, like a man, must have passion. Music without passion is a crime against art. So I just told Duff, he's chairman, you know, of the Board of Directors, that she was impossible and that we must have you. I have heard you sing, my dear, and I know the singer's face and the singer's throat and eye. You have them all. You have the voice and the temperament and the passion. You'll be great some day, much greater than I, and, with the hope of sharing your glory, I have decided to put my money on you."

Iola murmured some words of thanks, not knowing just what to say, but Mrs. Duff Charrington waved them aside.

"Purely selfish," she said, "purely selfish, my dear. Now don't let Bulling worry you. I pick him for a winner, too. He has force. He'll be a power in the country. Inclines to politics. He's a kind of brute, of course, but he'll succeed, for he has wealth and social prestige, neither to be sniffed at, my child. But, especially, he has driving power. But I'll have my eye on him this trip, so enjoy your outing."

Mrs. Duff Charrington was as good as her word. She knew nothing of the finesse of diplomacy in the manipulation of her company. Her method was straightforward dragooning. Observing the persistent attempts of Dr. Bulling during the early part of the trip to secure Iola for a tete-a-tete, she called out across the deck in the ears of the whole company, "See here, Bulling, I won't have you trying to monopolise our star. We're out for a good time and we're going to have it. Miss Lane is not your property. She belongs to us all." Thenceforth Dr. Bulling, with what grace he could summon, had to content himself with just so much of Iola's company as his hostess decided he should have.

It was Iola's first experience of yachting, and it brought her a series of sensations altogether new and delightful. As the yacht skimmed, like a great white-winged bird, over the blue waters of Ontario, the humming breeze, the swift rush through the parting waves, the sense of buoyant life with which the yacht seemed to be endowed made her blood jump. She abandoned herself to the joys of the hour and became the life and soul of the whole party. And were it not for Barney's haunting face, the two days' outing would have been for Iola among the happiest experiences of her life. But Barney's last look across the widening strip of water pursued her and filled her with foreboding. It was not rage; it was more terrible than rage. Iola shuddered as she recalled it. She read in it the despair of renunciation. She dreaded meeting him again, and as the end of her trip drew near her dread increased.

Nor did Mrs. Duff Charrington, who had become warmly interested in the girl during the short voyage, fail to observe her uneasiness and to guess the cause. Foremost among the crowd awaiting them at the dock, Iola detected Barney.

"There he is," she cried under her breath.

"My dear," said Mrs. Duff Charrington, who was at her side, "it is not possible that you are afraid, and of a man! I would give something to have that feeling. It is many years since a man could inspire me with any feeling but that of contempt or of kind pity. They are really silly creatures and most helpless. Let me manage him. Introduce him to me and leave him alone."

Mrs. Duff Charrington's confidence in her superior powers was more than justified. Through the crowd and straight for Iola came Barney, his face haggard with two sleepless nights. By a clever manoeuvre Mrs. Duff Charrington swung her massive form fair in his path and, turning suddenly, faced him squarely. Iola seized the moment to present him. Barney made as if to brush her aside, but Mrs. Duff Charrington was not of the kind to be lightly brushed aside by anyone, much less by a young man of Barney's inexperience.

"Ah, young man," she exclaimed, "I think I have seen you before." The strong grip of her hand and the loud tone of her voice at once arrested his progress and commanded his attention. "I saw you get your medal the other day, and I have heard my young hopeful rave about you—John Charrington, you know, medical student, first year. He is something of a fool and a hero-worshipper. You, of course, won't have noticed him."

Barney halted, gazed abstractedly at the strong face with the keen grey eyes compelling his attention, then, with an effort, he collected his wits.

"Charrington? Yes, of course, I know him. Very decent chap, too. Don't see much of him."

"No, rather not. He doesn't haunt the same spots. The dissecting-room wouldn't recognize him, I fancy. He's straight-going, however, but he can't pass exams. Good thing, too, for unless he changes considerably, the Lord pity his patients." She became aware of a sudden hardening in Barney's face and a quick flash in his eye. Without turning her head she knew that Dr. Bulling was approaching Iola from the other side. She put her hand on Barney's arm. "Mr. Boyle, please take Miss Lane to my carriage there? Bulling," she said, turning sharply upon the doctor, "will you help Daisy to collect my stuff? I am sure things will be left on the yacht. There are always some things left. Servants are so stupid." There was that in her voice that made Bulling stand sharply at attention and promptly obey. And ere Barney knew, he was leading Iola and Mrs. Duff Charrington to the waiting carriage.

"So sorry I didn't know you were a friend of Miss Lane's, or we would have had you on our trip, Mr. Boyle," said Mrs. Duff Charrington as he closed the carriage door.

"I thank you. But I am very busy, and, besides, I would not fit in with some of your party." There was war in Barney's tone.

"Good Heavens, young man!" cried Mrs. Duff Charrington, in no way disturbed, "you don't expect to make the world fit in with you or you with the world, do you? Life consists in adjusting one's self. But you will be glad to know that Miss Lane has made us all have a very happy little holiday."

"Of that I am sure," cried Barney gravely.

"And we gave her, or we tried to give her, a good time."

"It is for that some of us have lived." Barney's deep voice, thrilling with sad and tender feeling, brought the quick tears to Iola's eyes. To her, the words had in them the sound of farewell. Even Mrs. Duff Charrington was touched. She leaned over the carriage door toward him.

"Mr. Boyle, I am taking Miss Lane home to dinner. Come with us."

Barney felt the kindly tone. "Thank you, Mrs. Charrington, it would give none of us pleasure, and I have much to do. I am leaving to-morrow for Baltimore."

Iola could not check a quick gasp. Mrs. Duff Charrington glanced at her white face.

"Young man," she said sternly, leaning out toward him and looking Barney in the eyes, "don't be a fool. The man that would, from pique, willingly hurt a friend is a mean and cruel coward."

"Mrs. Charrington," replied Barney in a steady voice, "I have just come from an operation by which a little girl, an only child, has lost her arm. It was the mother that desired it, not from cruelty, but from love. It is because it is best, that I go to-morrow. Good-bye." Then turning to Iola he said, "I shall see you to-night." He lifted his hat and turned away.

"Drive home, Smith," said Mrs. Charrington sharply; "the others will find their way."

"Take me home," whispered Iola, with dry lips.

"Do you love him?" said Mrs. Duff Charrington, taking the girl's hand in hers.

"Ah, yes. I never knew how much."

"Tut! tut! child, the world still moves. Baltimore is not so far and he is only a man." Mrs. Duff Charrington's tone did not indicate a high opinion of the masculine section of humanity. "You'll just come with me for dinner and then I shall send you home. Thank God, we can still eat."

For some minutes they drove along in silence.

"Yes," said Mrs. Charrington, following up the line of her thought, "that's a man for you—thinks the whole world moves round the axis of his own life. But I like him. He has a good face. Still," she mused, "a man isn't everything, although once I—but never mind, there is always a way of bringing them to time."

"You don't know Barney, Mrs. Charrington," said Iola; "nothing can ever change him."

"Pish! You think so, and so, doubtless, does he. But none the less it is sheer nonsense. Can you tell me the trouble?"

"No, I think not," said Iola softly.

"Very well. As you like, my dear. Few things are the better for words. If ever you wish to come to me I shall be ready. Now let us dismiss the thing till after dinner. Disagreeable thoughts hinder digestion, I have found, and nothing is quite worth that."

With such resolution did she follow her own suggestion that, during the drive and throughout the dinner hour and, indeed, until the moment of her departure, Iola was not permitted to indulge her anxious thoughts, but with Mrs. Duff Charrington's assistance she succeeded in keeping them deep in her heart under guard.

As Mrs. Duff Charrington kissed her good-night she whispered:

"Don't face any issue to-night. Don't settle anything. Give time a chance. Time is a wonderfully wise old party."

And Iola, sitting back in the carriage, decided she would act upon the advice which suited so thoroughly her own habit of mind. That Barney had made up his mind to a line of action she knew. She would set herself to gain time, and yet she was fearful of the issue of the interview before her. The fear and anxiety which she had been holding down for the last two hours came over her in floods. As she thought of Barney's last words she found herself searching wildly, but in vain, for motives with which to brace her strength. If he had only been angry! But that sad, tender solicitude in his voice unnerved her. He was not thinking of himself, she knew. He was, as ever, thinking of and for her.

A storm of wind and rain was rapidly drawing on, but she heeded not the big drops driving into her face, nor did she notice that before she reached her door she was quite wet. She found Barney waiting for her. As she entered he arose and stood silent.

"Barney!" she exclaimed, and paused, waiting. But there was no reply.

"Oh, Barney!" she cried again, her voice quivering, "won't you tell me to come?"

"Come," he said, holding out his arms.

With a little cry of timid joy she ran to him, wreathed her arms about his neck, and clung sobbing. For some moments he held her fast, gently caressing with his hand her face and her beautiful hair till she grew quiet. Then disengaging her arms, he kissed her with grave tenderness and put her away from him.

"Go and take off your wet things first," he said.

"Say you forgive me, Barney," she whispered, putting her arms again about his neck.

"That's not the word," he replied sadly; "there's nothing to forgive. Go, now!"

She hurried away, praying that Barney's mood might not change. If she could only get her arms about his neck she could win and hold him, and, what was far more important, she could conquer herself, for great as she knew her love to be, she was fully aware of the hold her ambition had upon her and she dreaded lest that influence should become dominant in this hour. She knew well their souls would reach each other's secrets, and according to that reading the issue would be.

"I will keep him! I will keep him!" she whispered to herself as she tore off her wet clothing. "What shall I put on?" She could afford to lose no point of vantage and she must hasten. She chose her simplest gown, a soft creamy crepe de chene trimmed with lace, and made so as to show the superb modelling of her perfect body, leaving her arms bare to the elbow and falling away at the neck to reveal the soft, full curves where they flowed down to the swell of her bosom. She shook down her hair and gathered it loosely in a knot, leaving it as the wind and rain had tossed it into a bewildering tangle of ringlets about her face. One glance she threw at her mirror. Never had she appeared more lovely. The dead ivory of her skin, relieved by a faint flush in her cheeks, the lustrous eyes, now aglow with passion, all set in the frame of the night-black masses of her hair—this, and that indescribable but all-potent charm that love lends to the face, she saw in her glass.

"Ah, God help me!" she cried, clasping her hands high above her head, and went forth.

These few moments Barney had spent in a fierce struggle to regain the mastery over the surging passion that was sweeping like a tempest through his soul. As her door opened he rose to meet her; but as his eyes fell upon her standing in the soft rose-shaded light of the room, her attitude of mute appeal, the rare, rich loveliness of her face and form again swept away all the barriers of his control. She took one step toward him. With a swift movement he covered his face with his hands and sank to his chair.

"O God! O God! O God!" he groaned. "And must I lose her!"

"Why lose me, Barney?" she said, gliding swiftly to him and dropping to her knees beside him. "Why lose me?" she repeated, taking his head to her heaving bosom.

The touch of pity aroused his scorn of himself and braced his manhood. Not for himself must he think now, but for her. The touch of self makes weak, the cross makes strong. What matter that he was giving up his life in that hour if only she were helped? He rose, lifted her from her knees, set her in a chair, and went back to his place.

"Barney, let me come to you," she pleaded. "I'm sorry I went—"

"No," he said, his voice quiet and steady, "you must stay there. You must not touch me, else I cannot say what I must."

"Barney," she cried again, "let me explain."

"Explain? There is no need. I know all you would say. These people are nothing to you or to me. Let us forget them. It matters not at all that you went with them. I am not angry. I was at first insane, I think. But that is all past now."

"What is it, Barney?" she asked in a voice awed by the sadness and despair in the even, quiet tone.

"It is this," he replied; "we have come to the end. I must not hold you any more. For two years I have known. I had not the courage to face it. But, thank God, the courage has come to me these last two days."

"Courage, Barney?"

"Yes. Courage to do right. That's it, to do right. That is what a man must do. And I must think for you. Our lives are already far apart and I must not keep you longer."

"Oh, Barney!" cried Iola, her voice breaking, "let me come to you! How can I listen to you saying such terrible things without your arms about me? Can't you see I want you? You are hurting me!"

The pain, the terror in her voice and in her eyes, made him wince as from a stab. He seemed to hesitate as if estimating his strength. Dare he trust himself? It would make the task infinitely harder to have her near him, to feel the touch of her hands, the pressure of her body. But he would save her pain. He would help her through this hour of agony. How great it was he could guess by his own. He led her to a sofa, sat down beside her, and took her in his arms. With a long, shuddering sigh, she let herself sink down, with muscles relaxed and eyes closed.

"Now go on, dear," she whispered.

"Poor girl! Poor girl!" said Barney, "we have made a great mistake, you and I. I was not made for you nor you for me."

"Why not?" she whispered.

"Listen to me, darling. Do I love you?"

"Yes," she answered softly.

"With all my heart and soul?"

"Yes, dear," she answered again.

"Better than my own life?"

"Yes, Barney. Oh, yes," she replied with a little sob in her voice.

"Now we will speak simple truth to each other," said Barney in a tone solemn as if in prayer, "the truth as in God's sight."

She hesitated. "Oh, Barney!" she cried piteously, "must I say all the truth?"

"We must, darling. You promise?"

"Oh-h-h! Yes, I promise." She flung her arms upward about his neck. "I know what you will ask."

"Listen to me, darling," he said again, taking down her arms, "this is what I would say. You have marked out your life. You will follow your great ambition. Your glorious voice calls you and you feel you must go. You love me and you would be my wife, make my home, mother my children if God should send them to us; but both these things you cannot do, and meantime you have chosen your great career. Is not this true?"

"I can't give you up, Barney!" she moaned.

To neither of them did it occur as an alternative that Barney should give up his life's work to accompany her in the path she had marked. Equally to both this would have seemed unworthy of him.

"Is not this true, Iola?" Barney's voice, in spite of him, grew a little stern. And though she knew it was at the cost of life she could not deny it.

"God gave me the voice, Barney," she whispered.

"Yes, darling. And I would not hinder you nor turn you from your great art. So it is better that there should be no bond between us." He paused a moment as if to gather his strength together for a supreme effort. "Iola, when you were a girl I bound you to me. Now you are a woman, I set you free. I love you, but you are not mine. You are your own."

Convulsively she clung to him moaning, "No, no, Barney!"

"It is the only way."

"No, not to-night, Barney!"

"Yes, to-night. To-morrow I go to Baltimore. Trent has got me an appointment in Johns Hopkins. You will never forget me, but your life will be full again of other people and other things." He hurried his words, seeking to strike the note of her ambition and so turn her mind from her present pain. "Your Philharmonic will bring you fame. That means engagements, great masters, and then you will belong to the great world." How clearly he had read her mind and how closely he had followed the path she herself had outlined for her feet! He paused, as if to take breath, then hurried on again as through a task. "And we will all be proud of you and rejoice in your success and in your—your—your—happiness." The voice that had gone so bravely and so relentlessly through the terrible lesson faltered at the word and broke, but only for an instant. He must think of her. "Dick will be here," he went on, "and Margaret, and soon you will have many friends. Believe me, it is the best, Iola, and you will say it some day."

Like a flash of inspiration it came to her to say, "No, Barney, you are not helping me to my best."

In his soul he felt that it was a true word. For a moment he had no answer. Eagerly she followed up her advantage.

"And who," she cried, "will help me up and take care of me?"

Ah, she struck deep there. Who, indeed, would care for her, guard her against the world with its beasts of prey that batten their lusts upon beauty and innocence? And who would help her against herself? The desire to hold her for himself and for her sprang up fierce within him. Could he desert her, leave her to fight her fights, to find her way through the world's treacherous paths alone? That was the part of his renunciation that had been the heart of his pain. Not his loss, but her danger. Not his loneliness, but hers. For a moment he forgot everything. All the great love in him gathered itself together and massed its weight behind this desire to protect her and to hold her safe.

"Could you, Iola," he cried hoarsely, "don't you think you could let me care for you? Couldn't you come to me, give me the right to guard you? I can make wealth, great wealth, for you. Can't you come?"

Wildly, with the incoherent logic and eloquence of great passion, he poured forth his soul's desire for her. To work for her, to suffer for her, to live for her, yes, and to give himself to her and to keep her only for himself! Helpless in the sweeping tide of his mighty passion, he poured forth his words, pleading as for his life. By an inexplicable psychic law the exhibition of his passion calmed hers. The sight of his weakness brought her strength. For one fleeting moment she allowed her mind to rest upon the picture his words made of a home, made rich with the love of a strong man, and sweet with the music of children's voices, where she would be safe and sheltered in infinite peace and content. But only for a moment. Swifter than the play of light there flashed before her another scene, a crowded amphitheatre of faces, tier upon tier, eager, rapt, listening, and upon the stage the singer holding, swaying, compelling them to her will. Barney felt her relaxed muscles tone up into firmness. The force of her ambition was being transmitted along those subtle spiritual nerves that knit soul and mind and body into one complex whole, into the very sinews and muscles of her frame. She had hold of herself again. She would set herself to gain time.

"Let us wait, Barney," she said, "let us take time."

An intangible something in her tone pulled him to a sharp stop. What a weak fool he had been and how he had been thinking of himself! He sat up, straight and strong, his own man again.

"Forgive me, darling," he said, a faint, wan smile flitting across his face. "I was weak and selfish. I allowed myself to think for a moment that it might be, but now I know we must say good-bye to-night."

"Good-bye?" The sting of her pain made her irritable. He was so stubborn. "Surely, Barney, it is unreasonable to ask me to decide at once to-night."

He rose to his feet and lifted her gently.

"You have decided. You have already chosen your life's path, and it lies apart from mine. Let me go quietly away." His voice was toneless, passionless. His fight of two days and two nights had left him exhausted. His apparent apathy chilled her to the heart. It was a supreme moment in their lives, and yet she could not fan her soul's fires into flame. He was tearing up the roots of his love out of her life, but there was no acute sense of laceration. The inevitable had come to pass. A silence, dense and throbbing, fell upon them. Outside the storm was lashing the wet leaves against the window.

"If ever you should want me to come to you, Iola, one word will bring me. I shall be waiting, waiting. Remember that, always waiting." He tightened his arms about her and without passion, but gravely, tenderly he lifted her face. "Good-bye, my love," he said, and kissed her lips. "My heart's love!" Once more he kissed her. "My life! My love!"

She let the full weight of her body lie in his arms, lifeless but for the eyes that held his fast and for the lips that gave him back his kisses. Gently he placed her on the couch.

"God keep you, darling," he whispered, bending over her and touching her dusky hair with his lips.

He found his hat, walked with unsteady feet as a man walks under a heavy load, her eyes following his every step, and reached the door. There he paused, his hand fumbling at the knob, opened the door, halted yet an instant, but without turning he passed out of her sight.

An hour later Margaret came in and found her sitting where Barney had left her, dazed and tearless.

"He is gone," she said dully.

Margaret turned upon her. "Gone? Yes. I have just seen him."

"And I love him," continued Iola, looking up at her with heavy eyes.

"Love him! You don't know what love means! Love him! And for your paltry, selfish ambition you send from you a man whose shoes you are not worthy to tie!"

"Oh, Margaret!" cried Iola piteously.

"Don't talk to me!" she replied, her lip quivering. "I can't bear to look at you!" and she passed into her room.

It was intolerable to her that this girl should have regarded lightly the love she herself would have died to gain. But long after Iola had sobbed herself to sleep in her arms Margaret lay wakeful for her own pain and for that of the man she loved better than her life.

But next day, as Iola was planning to go to the station, Margaret would not have it.

"Why should you go? You have nothing to say but what would give him pain. Do you want him to despise you and me to hate you?"

But Iola was resolved to have her way. It was Mrs. Duff Charrington who fortunately intervened and carried Iola off with her to spend the afternoon and evening.

"Just a few musical friends, my dear. So brush up and come away. Bring your guitar with you."

Iola demurred.

"I don't feel like it."

"Tut! Nonsense! The lovelorn damsel reads well in erotic novels, but remember this, the men don't like stale beer."

This bit of worldly wisdom made Iola put on her smartest gown and lay aside the role she had unconsciously planned to adopt, so that even Mrs. Duff Charrington had no fault to find with the sparkling animation of her protegee.

But to the three who stood together waiting for the train to pull out that night there was only dreary, voiceless misery. There was no pretence at anything but misery. To the brothers the moment of parting would be the end of all that had been so delightful in their old life. The days of their long companionship were over, and to both the thought brought grief that made words impossible. Only Margaret's presence forced them to self-control. As to Margaret, Dick alone knew the full measure of her grief, and her quiet, serene courage filled him with amazed admiration. At length came the call of the bustling, businesslike conductor, "All aboard!"

"Good-bye, Margaret," said Barney simply, holding out his hand. But the girl quietly put back her veil and lifted up her face to him, her brave blue eyes looking all their love into his, but her lips only said, "Good-bye, Barney."

"Good-bye, dear Margaret," he said again, bending over her and kissing her.

"Me, too, Barney," said Dick, his tears openly streaming down his face. "I'm a confounded baby! But hanged if I care!"

At Dick's words all Barney's splendid self-mastery vanished. He threw his arms about his brother's neck, crying "Good-bye, Dick, old man. We've had a great time together; but oh, my boy, my boy, it's all come to an end!"

Already the train was moving.

"Go, old chap," cried Dick, pushing him away but still clinging to him. And then, as Barney swung on to the step he called back to them what had long been in his heart to say.

"Look after her, will you?"

"Yes, Barney, we will," they both cried together. And as they stood gazing through dimming tears after the train as it sped out through the network of tracks and the maze of green and red lights, they felt that a new bond drew them closer than before. And it was the tightening of that bond that brought them all the comfort that there was in that hour of misery unspeakable.

XIII
A MAN THAT IS AN HERETIC REJECT

The college year had come to an end. The results of the examinations had been published. The Juniors were preparing to depart for their summer work in the mission field. Of the graduating class, some were waiting with calm confidence the indications of the will of Providence as to their spheres of labour, a confidence undoubtedly strengthened by certain letters in their possession from leading members of influential congregations. Others were preparing with painful shrinking of heart to tread the weary and humiliating "trail of the black bag," while others again, to whom had come visions of high deeds and sounds of distant battle, were making ready outfits supposed to be suitable for life and work in the great West, or in the far lands across the sea.

Two high functions of college life yet remained, one, the Presbytery examination, the other, Professor Macdougall's student party. The annual examination before Presbytery was ever an event of nerve-racking uncertainty. It might prove to be an entirely perfunctory performance of the most innocuous kind. On the other hand, it might develop features of a most sensational and perilous nature. The college barometer this year was unusually depressed, for rumour had gone abroad that the Presbytery examination was to be of the more serious type. It was a time of searchings of heart for those who had been giving, throughout the session, undue attention to the social opportunities afforded by college life, and more especially if they had allowed their contempt for the archaic and oriental to become unnecessarily pronounced. To these latter gentlemen the day brought gloomy forebodings. Even their morning devotions, which were marked by unusual sincerity and earnestness, failed to bring them that calmness of mind which these exercises are supposed to afford. For their slender ray of hope that their memory of the English text might not fail them in the hour of trial was very materially clouded by the dread that in their embarrassment they might assign a perfectly correct English version to the wrong Hebrew text. The result of such mischance they would not allow themselves to contemplate. On the other hand, however, there was the welcome possibility that they might be so able to dispose themselves among the orientalists in their class that a word dropped at a critical moment might save them from this mischance. And there was the further, and not altogether unreal, ground of confidence, that the examiner himself might be uneasily conscious of the ever-present possibility that some hidden Hebrew snag might rudely jag a hole in his own vessel while sailing the mare ignotum of oriental literature. Of course, the examination would also include other departments of sacred learning, for it was the province and duty of Presbytery to satisfy itself as to the soundness in the faith of the candidates before them. On this score, however, few indulged serious anxiety. Once the Hebraic shoals and snags were safely passed, both examiner and examined could disport themselves with a jaunty self-confidence born of a thorough acquaintance with the Shorter Catechism received during the plastic years of childhood.

It was, however, just in these calm waters that danger lurked for Boyle. On the side of scholarship he was known to be invulnerable. Boyle was the hero and darling of the college men, more especially of the "sinners" among them, not simply by reason of his prowess between the goal posts where, times without number, he had rescued the college from the contempt of its foes; but quite as much for the modesty with which he carried off his brilliant attainments in the class lists. Throughout the term, in the college halls after tea, there had been carried on a series of discussions extending over the whole range of the "fundamentals," and Boyle had the misfortune to rouse the wrath and awaken the concern of Finlay Finlayson, the champion of orthodoxy. Finlay was a huge, gaunt, broad-shouldered son of Uist, a theologian by birth, a dialectician by training, and a man of war by the gift of Heaven. Cheerfully would Finlay, for conscience' sake, have given his body to the flames, as, for conscience' sake, he had shaken off the heretical dust of New College, Edinburgh, from his shoes, unhesitatingly surrendering at the same time, Scot though he was, a scholarship of fifty pounds. The hope that he had cherished of being able to find, in a colonial institution of sacred learning, a safe haven where he might devote himself to the perfecting of the defences of his faith within the citadel of orthodoxy was rudely shattered by the discovery that the same heresies which had driven him from New College had found their way across the sea and were being championed by a man of such winning personality and undoubted scholarship as Richard Boyle. The effect upon Finlayson's mind of these discussions carried on throughout the term was such that, after much and prayerful deliberation, and after due notice to the person immediately affected, he discovered it to be his duty to inform the professor in whose department these subjects lay of the heresies that were threatening the very life of the college, and, indeed, of the Canadian Church.

The report of his interview with the professor came back to college through the realistic if somewhat irreverent medium of the professor's son, Tom, presently pursuing a somewhat leisurely course toward a medical degree. As Tom appeared in the college hall he was immediately surrounded by an eager crowd, the most eager of whom was Robert Duff, the sworn ally of Mr. Finlayson.

"Did Finlayson see your father?" inquired Mr. Duff anxiously.

"Sure thing," answered Tom.

"And did he inform him of what has been going on in this college?"

"You bet your life! Give him the whole tip!"

"And what did the professor say?" inquired Mr. Duff, with bated breath.

"Told him to go to the devil."

"To what?" gasped Mr. Duff, to whom it appeared for the moment that the foundations of things in heaven and on earth had indeed been removed. It was only after the shout of laughter on the part of the "sinners" had subsided that Mr. Duff realised that it was the spirit only, and not the ipsissima verba, of the devout and reverent professor, that had been translated in the vigorous vernacular of his son.

Unhappily, however, for Boyle, the report of his heretical tendencies had reached other ears than those of the sane and liberal-minded professor, those, namely, of that stern and rigid churchman, the Rev. Alexander Naismith, some time minister of St. Columba's. Not through Finlayson, however, be it understood, did this report reach him. That staunch defender of orthodoxy might, under stress of conscience, find it his duty to inform the proper authority of the matter, but sooner than retail gossip to the hurt of his fellow-student he would have cut off his big, bony right hand.

The Rev. Alexander Naismith was a little man with a shrill voice, which gained for him the cognomen of "Squeaky Sandy," and a most irritatingly persistent temper. Into his hands, while candidates and examiners were disporting themselves in the calm waters of Systematic Theology, fell poor Dick, to his confusion and the temporary withholding of his license. It was impossible but that in the college itself, and in the college circles of society, this event should become a subject of much heated discussion.

Professor Macdougall's student parties were not as other student parties. They were never attended from a sense of duty. This was undoubtedly due, not so much to the popularity of the professor with his students, as to the shrewd wisdom and profound knowledge of human nature generally and of student nature particularly, on the part of that gentle lady, the professor's wife. Mrs. Macdougall was of the old school, with very beautiful if very old-fashioned notions of propriety. Her whole life was one poetic setting forth of the manners and deportment proper to ladies, both young and old. But none the less her shrewd mother wit and kindly heart instructed her in things not taught in the schools. The consequence was that, while she herself sat erect in fine scorn of the backs of her straight-backed Sheratons, her drawing-room was furnished with an abundance of easy chairs and lounges, and arranged with cosey nooks and corners calculated to gratify the luxurious tastes and lazy manners of a decadent generation. Her shrewd wit was further discovered in the care she took to assemble to her evening parties the prettiest, brightest, wickedest of the young girls in the wide circle of her friends. As young Robert Kidd put it with more vigour than grace, "There were no last roses in her bunch." Moreover, the wise little lady took pains to instruct her young ladies as to their duties toward the young men of the college.

"You must exert yourselves, my dears," she would explain, "to make the evening pleasant for the young men. And they require something to distract their attention from the too earnest pursuit of their studies."

And it is a tradition that so heartily did the young ladies throw themselves into this particular duty that there were, even of the saintliest of the saints, who found it necessary to take their lectures in absentia for at least two days in order that they might recover from the all too successful distractions of the Macdougall party.

Among the guests invited was Margaret, beloved for her own sake, but even more for the sake of her mother, who had been Mrs. Macdougall's college companion and lifelong cherished friend. The absorbing theme of conversation, carried on in a strictly confidential manner, was the sensational feature of the Presbytery examination. The professor himself was deeply grieved, and no less so his stately little lady, for to both of them Dick was as a son. But from neither of them could Margaret extract anything but the most meagre outline of what had happened. For full details of the whole dramatic scene she was indebted to Robert Kidd, second year theologue, whose brown curly locks and cherubic face and fresh innocence of manner won for him the sobriquet of "Baby Kidd," or more shortly, "Kiddie."

"Tell us just what happened," entreated Miss Belle Macdougall, with a glance of such heart-penetrating quality that Kiddie promptly acquiesced.

"Well, I'll tell you," he said, adopting a low confidential tone. "I could see from the very start that old Squeaky Sandy was out after Dick. He couldn't get him on his Hebrew, so the old chap lay low till everything was lovely and they were falling on each others' necks over the Shorter

Catechism, and things every fellow is supposed to be quite safe on. All at once Sandy squeaked in, 'Mr. Boyle, will you kindly state what you consider the correct theory of the Atonement?' 'I don't know,' said Boyle; 'I haven't got any.' By Jove! everyone sat up. 'You believe in the doctrine, I suppose?' Boyle waited a while and my heart stopped till he went on again. 'Yes, sir, I believe in it.' 'How is that, sir? If you believe in it you must have a theory. What do you believe about it?' 'I believe in the fact. I don't understand it, and I have no theory of it as yet.' And Boyle was as gentle as a sucking dove. Then the Moderator, decent old chap, chipped it."

"Who was it?" inquired Miss Belle.

"Dr. Mitchell. Fine old boy. None too sound himself, I guess. Pre-mill, too, you know. Well, he chipped in and got him past that snag. But old Sandy was not done yet by a long shot. He went after Boyle on every doctrine in the catalogue where it was possible for a man to get off the track, Inspiration, Inerrancy, the Mosaic Authorship, and the whole Robertson Smith business. You know that last big heresy hunt in Scotland."

"No," said Miss Belle, "I don't know. And you don't, either, so you needn't stop and try to tell us."

"I don't, eh?" said Bob, who was finding it difficult to keep himself in a perfectly sane condition under the bewildering glances of Miss Belle's black eyes. "Well, perhaps I don't. At any rate, I couldn't make you understand."

"Hear him!" said Miss Belle, with supreme scorn. "Go on. We are interested in Boyle, aren't we, Margaret?"

"Well, where was I? Oh, yes. Well, sir, in about five minutes it seemed to me that Boyle's theology was a tattered remnant. Some of the brethren interfered, explaining and apologizing for the young man after their kindly custom, but Squeaky wouldn't have it. 'This is most serious, Mr. Moderator!' he sung out. 'This demands the most searching investigation! We all know what is going on in the Old Land, how the great doctrines of our faith are being undermined by so-called scholarship, which is nothing less than blasphemy and impudent scepticism.' And so he went on shrieking more and more wildly a lot of tommy-rot. But the worst was yet to come. All at once Sandy changed his line of attack and proceeded to take Boyle on the flank. 'Mr. Boyle, are you a smoker?' he asked. 'Yes,' stammered poor Boyle, getting red in the face, 'I smoke some.' 'Are you a total abstainer?' And then Boyle got on to him, and I saw his head go back for the first time. Before this he had been sitting like a convicted criminal. 'No, sir,' he answered, turning square around and facing old Squeaky, 'I am not pledged to total abstinence.' Don't suppose he ever took a drink in his life. 'Did you ever attend the theatre?' This was the limit. It seemed to strike the brethren all at once what the old inquisitor was driving at. The words were hardly out of his mouth when there was a weird sound, a cross between a howl and a roar, and Grant was at the Moderator's desk. It will always be a mystery to me how he got there. There were three pews between him and the desk, and I swear he never came out into the aisle. 'Mr. Moderator, I protest', he shouted. And then the dust began to fly. Say! it was a regular sand storm! About the only thing visible was the lightning from Grant's eyes. By Jingo! 'Mr. Moderator, I protest,' he cried, when he could get a hearing, 'against these insinuations. We all know what Mr. Naismith means by this method of inquisition. But let me tell Mr. Naismith—' Don't know what in thunder he was going to tell him, for the next few moments they mixed it up good and hot. Say! it was a circus with all the monkeys loose and the band playing seventeen tunes all at once! But finally Grant had his say and treated the Presbytery to a pretty full disquisition of his own theology, and when he was done my pity was transferred from Boyle to him, for it seemed that on every doctrine where Boyle was a heretic Grant had gone him one better. And I believe the whole Presbytery were vastly relieved to discover how slight, by contrast, were the errors to which Boyle had fallen. Then Henderson, good old soul, took his innings and poured on oil, with the result that Boyle was turned over to a committee—and that's where he is now. But he'll never appear. He's going in for journalism. The Telegraph wants him."

"Journalism?" cried Margaret faintly. She was thinking of the dark-faced old lady up in the country who was counting the days till her son should be sent forth a minister of the Gospel.

"Yes," said Kiddie. "And there's where he'll shine. See what he's done with the Monthly. He's got great style. But wasn't there a row at the college!" continued Kiddie. "Old Father Finlayson there," nodding across the room at the Highlander, who was engaged in what appeared to be an extremely interesting conversation with his hostess, "orthodox old beggar as he is, was ready to lead a raid on Squeaky Sandy's house. You know he has been at war with Boyle all winter on every and all possible themes. But he fights fair, and this hitting below the belt was too much for him. He was raging up and down the hall like a wild man when Boyle came in. 'Mr. Boyle,' he roared, rushing up to him and seizing him by the hand and working it like a pump-handle in a fire, 'it was a most iniquitous proceeding! I wish to assure you I have no sympathy whatever with that sort of thing!' And so he went on till he had Boyle almost in tears. By Jove! he's a rum old party! Look at his socks, will you!"

The young ladies glanced across and beheld in amused but amazed horror the Highlander's great feet encased in a new pair of carpet slippers adorned with pink roses and green ground, which made a startling contrast with his three-ply worsted stockings, magenta in colour, which his fond aunt had knit as part of his outfit for the Arctic regions of Canada.

"You may laugh," continued Bob. "So would I yesterday. But, by Jingo! he can wear magenta socks on his head if he likes for me! He's all white, and he has the heart of a gentleman!" Little Kidd's voice went shaky and his eyes had the curious shine that appeared in them only in moments of deepest excitement, but if he had only known it, he had never been so near storming the gate of Miss Belle's heart as at that moment. She showed her sympathy with Kiddie's attitude by giving Mr. Finlayson "the time of his life," as Kiddie himself remarked. So assiduously, indeed, did she devote herself to the promotion of Mr. Finlayson's comfort and good cheer that that gentleman's fine sense of honour prompted him to inform her incidentally of the existence of Miss Jennie McLean, who was to "come out to him as soon as he was placed." He was surprised, but entirely delighted, to discover that this announcement made no difference whatever in Miss Belle's attentions. At the supper hour, however, Miss Belle, moved by Kiddie's lugubrious countenance, yielded her place to Margaret, who continued the operation of giving Mr. Finlayson "the time of his life." But not a word could she extract from him regarding the heresy case, for, with a skill that might have made a Queen's Counsel green with envy, he baffled her leading questions with a density of ignorance unparalleled in her experience, until she let it be known that Dick was an old schoolmate and dear friend. Then Mr. Finlayson poured forth the grief and rage swelling in his big heart at the treatment his enemy had received and his anxious concern for his future both here and hereafter. In a portion of this concern, at least, Margaret shared. And as Mr. Finlayson continued to unburden himself, during the walk home, regarding the heresies in Edinburgh from which he had fled and the heresies that had apparently taken possession of Dick's mind, her heart continued to sink within her, for it seemed that the opinions attributed to Dick were subversive of all she had held true from her childhood. With such intelligence and sympathy, however, did she listen to Mr. Finlayson discoursing, that that gentleman carried back with him to college a heart somewhat lightened of its burden, but withal seriously impressed with the charm and the mental grasp of the young ladies of Canada. And so enthusiastically did he dwell upon this theme in his next letter, that Miss Jessie McLean set herself devoutly to pray, either that Finlayson might soon be placed, or that the professors might cease giving parties.

The brand of heresy almost invariably works ill to him who bears it. For if he be young and shallow enough to enjoy the distinction, it will only increase his vanity and render his return to sure and safe paths more difficult. But if his doubts are to him a grief and a horror of darkness, the brand will burn in and drive him far from his fellows, and change the kindly spirit in him to bitterness unless, perchance, he light upon a friend who gives him love and trust unstinted and links him to wholesome living. After all, in matters of faith every man must blaze his own path through the woods and make his own clearing in which to dwell. And he may well thank God if his path lead him some whither where there is space enough to work his day's work and light enough to live by.

With Dick it was mostly dark, for it was not given him to have a friend who could understand. But he was not allowed to feel himself to be quite abandoned, for in the darkest of his hours there stood at his side Margaret Robertson, whose strong, cheery good sense and whose loyalty to right-doing helped him and strengthened him and so made it possible to wait till the better day dawned.

XIV
WHOSOEVER LOOKETH UPON A WOMAN

The Journalistic World has its own diversity of mountain and plain, and its own variety of inhabitants. There are its mountain ranges and upland regions of clear skies and pure airs, where are wide outlooks and horizons whose dim lines fade beyond the reach of clear vision. Amid these mountain ranges and upon these uplands dwell men among the immortals to whom has come the "vision splendid" and whose are the voices that in the crisis of a man or of a nation give forth the call that turns the face upward to life eternal and divine. To these men such words as Duty, Honour, Patriotism, Purity, stand for things of intrinsic value worth a man's while to seek and, having found, to die for.

Level plains there are, too, where harvests are sown and reaped. But there these same words often become mere implements of cultivation, tools for mechanical industries or currency for the conduct of business. Here dwell the practical men of affairs, as they love to call themselves, for whom has faded the vision in the glare of opportunism.

And far down by the water-fronts are the slum wastes where the sewers of politics and business and social life pour forth their fetid filth. Here the journals of yellow shade grub and fatten. In this ooze and slime puddle the hordes of sewer rats, scavengers of the world's garbage, from whose collected stores the editor selects his daily mess for the delectation of the great unwashed, whether of the classes or of the masses, and from which he grabs in large handfuls that viscous mud that sticks and stings where it sticks.

The Daily Telegraph was born yellow, a frank yellow of the barbaric type that despises neutral tints. By the Daily Telegraph things were called by their uneuphemistic names. A spade was a spade, and mud was mud, and nothing was sacred from its sewer rats. The highest paid official on its staff was a criminal lawyer celebrated in the libel courts. Everybody cursed it and everybody read it. After a season, having thus firmly established itself in the enmities of the community, and having become, in consequence, financially secure, it began to aspire toward the uplands, where the harvests were as rich and at the same time less perilous as well as less offensive in the reaping. It began to study euphemism. A spade became an agricultural implement and mud alluvial deposit. Having become by long experience a specialist in the business of moral scavenging, it proceeded to devote itself with most vehement energy to the business of moral reform. All indecencies that could not successfully cover themselves with such gilding as good hard gold can give were ruthlessly held up to public contempt. It continued to be cursed, but gradually came to be respected and feared.

It was to aid in this upward climb that the editor of the Daily Telegraph seized upon Dick. That young man was peculiarly fitted for the part which was to be assigned to him. He was a theological student and, therefore, his ethical standards were unimpeachable. His university training guaranteed his literary sense, and his connection with the University and College papers had revealed him a master of terse English. He was the very man, indeed, but he must serve his apprenticeship with the sewer rats. For months he toiled amid much slime and filth, breathing in its stinking odours, gaining knowledge, it is true, but paying dear for it in the golden coin of that finer sensibility and that vigorous moral health which had formerly made his life, to himself and to others, a joy and beauty. For the slime would stick, do what he could, and with the smells he must become so familiar that they no longer offended. That delicate discrimination that immediately detects the presence of decay departed from him, and in its place there developed a coarser sense whose characteristic was its power to distinguish between sewage and sewage. Hence, morality, with him, came to consist in the choosing of sewage of the less offensive forms. On the other hand, consciousness of the brand of heresy drove him from those scenes where the air is pure and from association with those high souls who by mere living exhale spiritual health and fragrance.

"We do not see much of Mr. Boyle these days, Margaret," Mrs. Macdougall would say to her friend, carefully modulating her tone lest she should betray the anxiety of her gentle, loyal heart. "But I doubt not he is very busy with his new duties."

"Yes, he is very busy," Margaret would reply, striving to guard her voice with equal care, but with less success. For Margaret was cursed, nay blessed, with that heart of infinite motherhood that yearns over the broken or the weak or the straying of humankind, and makes their pain its own.

"Bring him with you to tea next Sabbath evening, my dear," the little lady would say, with never a quiver or inflection of voice betraying that she had detected the girl's anxiety for her friend.

But more infrequently, as the days went on, could she secure Dick for an hour on Sabbath evening in the quiet, sweet little nook of the professor's dining-room. He was so often held by his work, but more often by his attendance upon Iola, for between Iola and him there had grown up and ripened rapidly an intimacy that Margaret regarded with distrust and fear. How she hated herself for her suspicions! How she fought to forbid them harbour in her heart! But how persistently they made entrance and to abide.

The World of Fashion is, for the most part, a desert island of gleaming sands, at times fanned by perfume-laden zephyrs and lapped by shining waters. Then those who dwell there disport themselves, careless of all save the lapping, shining waters and the gleaming sands out of which they build their sand castles with such concentrated eagerness and such painful industry. At other times there come tempests, sudden and out of clear skies, which sweep, with ruthless besom, castles and castle-builders alike, and leave desolation and empty spaces for a time.

A silly world it is, and hard of heart, and like to die of ennui at times. And hence it welcomes with pathetic joy all who can bring some new fancy or trick to their castle-building, rejecting all other without remorse. To this World of Fashion Iola had offered herself, giving freely her great voice and her superb body, now developed into the full splendour of its rich and sensuous beauty. And how they gathered about her and gave her unstinted their flatteries and homage, taking toll the while of the very soul-stuff in her. Devoutly they worshipped at the shrine of that heavenlike and heaven-given instrument wherewith she could tickle their senses, rejoicing, during the pauses of their envies and hatreds, such among them as were female, and of their lusts and despairs such as were male, in her warm flesh tints and full flesh curves and the draperies withal wherewith, with consummate art, she revealed or enhanced the same. For Iola was possessed of a fatal, maddening beauty, and an alluring fascination of manner that wrought destruction among men and fury among women.

To Dick, who, with his brilliant talents, shed lustre upon her courts, Iola gave chief place in her train, yet in such manner as that her preference for him neither lessened the number nor checked the ardour of her devotees. He was her friend of childhood days, her good friend, but nothing more. Upon this basis of a boy and girl friendship was established an intimacy which seemed to render unnecessary those conventions, unreal and vexing in appearance, but which, as the wise old world has proved, man and woman with the dread potencies of passion slumbering within them cannot afford to despise. By their mutual tastes, as by their habits of life, Iola and Dick were brought into daily association. Under Dick's guidance she read and studied the masters of the English drama. For she had her eye now upon the operatic stage and was at present devoting herself to the great musical dramas of Wagner. Together they took full advantage of the theatre privileges which Dick's connection with the press gave him. And at those festive routs by which society amuses and vexes itself they were constantly thrown together. Dick was acutely and growingly sensitive to the influence Iola had upon him. Her beauty disturbed him. The subtle potency that exhaled from her physical charms affected him like draughts of wine. Away from her presence he marvelled at himself and scorned his weakness; but once within sound of her voice, within touch of her hand, her power reasserted itself. The mystery of the body, its subtle appeal, its terrible potency, allured and enslaved him. Against this infatuation of Dick's, Margaret felt herself helpless. She well knew that Dick's love for her had not changed, except to grow into a bitter, despairing intensity that made his presence painful to her at times. This very love of his closed her lips. She could only wait her time, meanwhile keeping such touch with him as she could, bringing to him the wholesome fragrance of a pure heart and the strength and serenity of a life devoted to well doing.

Something would occur to recall him to his better self. And something did occur. Almost a year had elapsed since Barney had gone out of Iola's life in so tragic a way. Through all the months of the year he had waited, longing and hoping for the word that might recall him to her, until suspense became unbearable even for his strong soul. Hence it was that Iola received from him a letter breathing of love so deep, so tender, and withal so humble, that even across the space that these months had put between Barney and herself, Iola was profoundly stirred and sorely put to it to decide upon her answer. She took the letter to Margaret and read her such parts as she thought necessary. "A year has gone. It seems like ten. I have waited for your word, but none has come. Looking back upon that dreadful night I sometimes think I may have been severe. If so, my punishment has been heavy enough to atone. Tell me, shall I come to you? I can offer you a home even better than I had hoped a year ago. I am offered a lectureship here with an ample salary, or an assistantship on equal terms, by Trent. I have discovered that I am in the grip of a love beyond my power to control. In spite of all that my work is to me, I find myself looking, not into the book before me, but into your eyes—I may be able to live without you, but I cannot live my best. I don't see how I can live at all. It seems as if I could not wait even a few days for your word to come. Darling, my heart's love, tell me to come."

"How can I answer a letter like that?" said Iola to Margaret.

"How?" exclaimed Margaret. "Tell him to come. Wire him. Go to him. Anything to get him to you."

Iola mused a while. "He wants me to marry him and to keep his house."

"Yes," said Margaret, "he does."

"Housekeeping and babies, ugh!" shuddered Iola.

"Yes," cried Margaret, "ah, God, yes! Housekeeping and babies and Barney! God pity your poor soul!"

Iola shrank from the fierce intensity of Margaret's sudden passion.

"What do you mean?" she cried. "Why do you speak so?"

"Why? Can't you read God's meaning in your woman's body and in your woman's heart?"

From Margaret Iola got little help. Indeed, the gulf between the two was growing wider every day. She resolved to show her letter to Dick. They were to go that evening to the play and after the play there would be supper. And when he had taken her home she would show him the letter.

On their way home that evening as they were passing Dick's rooms, he suddenly remembered that a message was to be sent him from the office.

"Let us run in for a moment," he said.

"I think I had better wait you here," replied Iola.

"Nonsense!" cried Dick. "Don't be a baby. Come in."

Together they entered and, laying aside her wrap, Iola sat down and drew forth Barney's letter.

"Listen, Dick. I want your advice." And she read over such portions of Barney's letter as she thought necessary.

"Well?" she said, as Dick remained silent.

"Well," replied Dick, "what's your answer to be?"

"You know what he means," said Iola a little impatiently. "He wants me to marry him at once and to settle down."

"Well," said Dick, "why not?"

"Now, Dick," cried Iola, "do you think I am suited for that kind of life? Can you picture me devoting myself to the keeping of a house tidy, the overseeing of meals? I fancy I see myself spending the long, quiet evenings, my husband busy in his office or out among his patients while I dose and yawn and grow fat and old and ugly, and the great world forgetting. Dick, I should die! Of course, I love Barney. But I must have life, movement. I can't be forgotten!"

"Forgotten?" cried Dick. "Why should you be forgotten? Barney's wife could not be ignored and the world could not forget you. And, after all," added Dick, in a musing tone, "to live with Barney ought to be good enough for any woman."

"Why, how eloquent you are, Dick!" she cried, making a little moue. "You are quite irresistible!" she added, leaning toward him with a mocking laugh.

"Come, let us go," said Dick painfully, conscious of her physical charm. "We must get away."

"But you haven't helped me, Dick," she cried, drawing nearer to him and laying her hand upon his arm.

The perfume of her hair smote upon his senses. The beauty of her face and form intoxicated him.

He knew he was losing control of himself.

"Come, Iola," he said, "let us go."

"Tell me what to say, Dick," she replied, smiling into his face and leaning toward him.

"How can I tell you?" cried Dick desperately, springing up. "I only know you are beautiful, Iola, beautiful as an angel, as a devil! What has come over you, or is it me, that you should affect me so? Do you know," he added roughly, lifting her to her feet, his breath coming hard and fast, "I can hardly keep my hands off you. We must go. I must go. Come!"

"Poor child," mocked Iola, still smiling into his eyes, "is it afraid it will get hurt?"

"Stop it, Iola!" cried Dick. "Come on!"

"Come," she mocked, still leaning toward him.

Swiftly Dick turned, seized her in his arms, his eyes burning down upon her mocking face. "Kiss me!" he commanded.

Gradually she allowed the weight of her body to lean upon him, drawing him steadily down toward her the while, with the deep, passionate lure of her lustrous eyes.

"Kiss me!" he commanded again. But she shook her head, holding him still with her gaze.

"God in heaven!" cried Dick. "Go away!" He made to push her from him. She clasped him about the neck, allowing herself to sink in his arms with her face turned upward to his. Fiercely he crushed her to him, and again and again his hot, passionate kisses fell upon her face.

Conscious only of the passion throbbing in their hearts and pulsing through their bodies, oblivious to all about them, they heard not the opening of the door and knew not that a man had entered the room. For a single moment he stood stricken with horror as if gazing upon death itself. Turning to depart, his foot caught a chair. Terror-smitten, the two sprang apart and stood with guilt and shame stamped upon their ghastly faces.

"Barney!" they cried together.

Slowly he came back to them. "Yes, it is I." The words seemed to come from some far distance. "I couldn't wait. I came for my answer, Iola. I thought I could persuade you better. I have it now. I have lost you! And" — here he turned to Dick — "oh, my God! My God! I have lost my brother, too!" he turned to depart from him.

"Barney," cried Dick passionately, "there was no wrong! There was nothing beyond what you saw!"

"Was that all?" inquired his brother quietly.

"As God is in heaven, Barney, that was all!"

Barney threw a swift glance round the room, crossed to a side table, and picked up a Bible lying there. He turned the leaves rapidly and handed it to his brother with his finger upon a verse.

"Read!" he said. "You know your Bible. Read!" His voice was terrible and compelling in its calmness.

Following the pointing finger, Dick's eyes fell upon words that seemed to sear his eyeballs as he read, "Whosoever looketh on a woman to lust after her, hath committed adultery with her already in his heart." Heart-smitten, Dick stood without a word.

"I could kill you now," said the quiet, terrible voice. "But what need? To me you are already dead."

When Dick looked up his brother had gone. Nerveless, broken, he sank into a chair and sat with his face in his hands. Beside him stood Iola, pale, rigid, her eyes distended as if she had seen a horrid vision. She was the first to recover.

"Dick," she said softly, laying her hand upon his head.

He sprang up as if her fingers had been red-hot iron and had burned to the bone.

"Don't touch me!" he cried in vehement frenzy. "You are a devil! And I am in hell! In hell! do you hear?" He caught her by the arm and shook her. "And I deserve hell! Hell! Hell! Fools! no hell?" He turned again to her. "And for you, for this, and this, and this," touching her hair, her cheek, and her heaving bosom with his finger, "I have lost my brother—my brother—my own brother—Barney. Oh, fool that I am! Damned! Damned! Damned!"

She shrank back from him, then whispered with pale lips, "Oh, Dick, spare me! Take me home!"

"Yes, yes," he cried in mad haste, "anywhere, in the devil's name! Come! Come!" He seized her wrap, threw it upon her shoulders, caught up his hat, tore open the door for her, and followed her out.

"Can a man take fire into his bosom and not be burned?" And out of the embers of his passion there kindled a fire that night that burned with unquenchable fury for many a day.

XV
THE SUPERINTENDENT'S METHODS

The Superintendent was spending the precious hours of one of his rare visits at home in painful plodding through his correspondence. For it was part of the sacrifice his work demanded, and which he cheerfully made, that he should forsake home and wife and children for his work's sake. The Assembly's Convener found him in the midst of an orderly confusion of papers of different sorts.

"How do you do, sir?" The Superintendent's voice had a fine burr about it that gripped the ear, and his hand a vigour and tenacity of hold that gripped the outstretched hand of the Assembly's Convener and nearly brought the little man to the floor. "Sit down, sir, and listen to this. Here are some of the compensations that go with the Superintendent's office. This is rich. It comes from my friend, Henry Fink, of the Columbia Forks in the Windermere Valley. British Columbia, you understand," noticing the Convener's puzzled expression. "I visited the valley a year ago and found a truly deplorable condition of things. Men had gone up there many years ago and settled down remote from civilization. Some of them married Indian wives and others of them ought to have married them, and they have brought up families in the atmosphere and beliefs of the pagans. Would you believe it, I fell in with a young man on the trail, twenty years of age, who had never heard the name of our Saviour except in oaths? He had never heard the story of the Cross. And there are many others like him. At the Columbia Forks the only institution that stands for things intellectual is a Freethinkers' Club, the president of which is a retired colonel of the British Army, a man of fine manners, of some degree of intelligence and reading, but, I have reason to believe, of bad life. His is the dominant influence in the community if we except my friend, Mr. Henry Fink, or, as he is known locally, 'Hank Fink.' Hank is a character, I assure you. A Yankee from the Eastern States, the son of a Scotch mother. Has a cattle ranch, runs a store which supplies the scattered ranchers, prospectors, and miners with the necessaries of life, and keeps a stopping place. Is postmaster, too. In fact, Hank is pretty much the whole village. He has lived in that country some fifteen years. Has a good Canadian wife, and a flock of small children. He is a rara avis in that country from the fact that he hates whiskey. He hates it almost as much as he does Colonel Hicks and his Freethinking Club. When I visited the village, for some reason or other Hank took me up, the Scotch blood in him possibly recognising kinship. He gave me his store to preach in, took me all about the country, and in a week had a mission organized on a sound financial basis. His methods were very simple, very direct, and very effective. He estimated the amount each man should pay and announced this fact to the man, who generally acquiesced. I didn't probe too deeply into Hank's motives, but it seemed to give him considerable satisfaction to learn that Colonel Hicks was filled with indignant and scornful rage at the proposal to establish a Christian mission in that remote valley. It grieved the Colonel to think that after so many years of immunity they should at last be called upon to tolerate this particularly offensive appendage to an effete civilization. I noticed that Hank's English always broke down in referring to the Colonel. Well, we sent in Finlayson a year ago this spring, you remember. Strong man, good preacher, conscientious fellow. Thought he would do great work. You know Finlayson? Well, this is the result." Here he picked up Hank's letter. "This would hardly do for the Home Mission report," continued the Superintendent, with a twinkle in his keen grey eyes:

"COLUMBIA FORKS, WINDERMERE, B. C.

"DEAR SIR:—I take my pen to write you a few lines to let you know how things is goin'. Well, sir, I want to tell you this station is goin' to the devil. [Judging from what I saw of the place, it hadn't far to go.] Your preacher ain't worth a cuss. I don't say he ain't good fer some people, but he ain't our style. [Mr. Finlayson would doubtless agree with that.] He means well, but he ain't eddicated up to the West. You remember how we got the boys all corralled up nice an' tame when you was here. Well, he's got 'em wild. Couldn't reach 'em with a shotgun. He throwed hell fire at 'em till they got scart an' took to the hills till you can't get near 'em no more'n mountain goats. So they have all quit comin'—I don't count Scotty Fraser, for he would come, anyway—except me an' Monkey Fiddler an' his yeller dog. You can always count on the dog. Now, sir, this is your show, not mine. But I was born an' raised a Presbyteryn down East, an' though I haven't worked hard at the business for some years, it riles me some to hear Col. Hicks an' a lot of durned fools that has got smarter than God Almighty Himself shootin' off against the Bible an' religion an' all that. [We needn't read too closely between the lines at this point.] Send a man that don't smell so strong of sulphur an' brimstone, who has got some savey, an' who will know how to handle the boys gentle. They ain't to say bad, but just a leetle wild. Send him along, an' we will stay with him an' knock the tar out of that bunch of fools.

"Yours most respeckfully,

"HENRY FINK.

"P. S. When are you comin' into the valley again? If you could arrange to spend a month or two I'll guarantee we will have 'em all in nice shape.

"Yours respeckfully,

"HENRY FINK."

"I don't think you can count much from the support of a man like that," said the assembly's Convener; "I don't think he shows any real interest in the work."

"My dear sir," said the Superintendent, "don't you know he is the Chairman of our Board of Management, a most regular attendant upon ordinances and contributes most liberally to our support? And while these things in the East wouldn't necessarily indicate a change of heart, they stand for a good deal west of the Great Divide. And, at any rate, in these matters we remember gratefully the word that is written, 'He that is not against us is on our part.'"

"Well, well," said the Assembly's Convener, "it may be so. It may be so. But what's to be done with Finlayson? And where will you get a successor for him?"

"We can easily place Finlayson. He is a good man and will do excellent work in other fields. But where to get a man for Windermere is the question. Do you know anyone?"

The Assembly's Convener shook his head sadly.

"There appears to be no one in sight," said the Superintendent. "I have a number of applications here," picking up a good-sized bundle of neatly folded papers, "but they are hardly the kind to suit conditions at Windermere. Numbers of them feel themselves specially called of God to do mission work in large centres of population. Others are chiefly anxious about the question of support. One man would like to be in touch with a daily train service, as he feels it necessary to keep in touch with the world by means of the daily newspaper. A number are engaged who want to be married. Here's Mr. Brown, too fat. No move in him. Here's McKay—good man, earnest, but not adaptable, like Finlayson; won't do. Here's Garton— fine fellow, would do well, but hardly strong enough. So what are you to do? I have gone over the whole list of available men and I cannot find one suitable for Windermere."

In this the Assembly's Convener could give him no help. Indeed, from few did the Superintendent receive assistance in the securing of men for his far outposts.

Assistance came to him from an unexpected quarter. He was to meet the Assembly's Convener and some members of the Committee that evening at Professor Macdougall's for tea. The Superintendent's mind could not be kept long away from the work that was his very life, and at the table the conversation turned to the question of the chronic difficulty of securing men for frontier work, which had become acute in the case of Windermere. Margaret, who had been invited to assist Mrs. Macdougall in the dispensing of her hospitality, was at once on the alert. Why could not Dick be sent? If only that Presbytery difficulty could be got over he might go. That he would be suited for the work she was well assured, and equally certain was she that it would be good for him.

"It would save him," Margaret said to herself with a sharp sting at her heart, for she had to confess sadly that Dick had come to the point where he needed saving. She had learned from Iola the whole miserable story of Barney's visit, of his terrible indictment of his brother and the final break between them, but she had seen little of him during the past six months. From that terrible night Dick had gone down in physical and in moral health. Again and again he had written Barney, but there had been no reply. Hungrily he had come to Margaret for word of his brother, hopeful of reconciliation. But of late he had given up hope and had ceased to make inquiry, settling down into a state of gloomy, remorseful grief into which Margaret felt she dare not intrude. He occasionally met Iola at society functions, but there was an end of all intimacy between them. His only relief seemed to be in his work, and he gave himself to that with such feverish energy that his health broke down, and under Margaret's persuasion he was now at home with his mother. Thence he had written once to say that his days were one long agony. She remembered one terrible sentence. "Everything here, the house, the mill, my father's fiddle, my mother's churn, the woods, the fields, everything, everything shrieks 'Barney' at me till I am like to go mad. I must get away from here to some place where he has never been with me."

It required some considerable skill to secure the Superintendent that evening for a few minutes alone. In whatever company he was, he was easily the centre of interest. But Margaret, even in the early days of the Manse, had been a favourite with him, and he was not a man to forget his friends. He had the rare gift of gripping them to him with "hooks of steel." Hence, he had kept in touch with her during the latter years, pitying the girl's loneliness as much as his admiration for her cheery courage and her determined independence would allow him. When Margaret found her opportunity she wasted no time.

"I have a man for you for Windermere," were her opening words.

"You have? Where have you got him? Who is he? And are you willing to spare him? Few young ladies are. But you are different from most." The Superintendent was ever a gallant.

"You remember Mr. Boyle who graduated a year ago?" Her words came hurriedly and there was a slight flush on her cheek. "There was some trouble about his license at Presbytery. That horrid old Mr. Naismith was very nasty, and Dick, Mr. Boyle, I mean—we have always been friends," she hastened to add, explaining her deepening blush, "you know his mother lived at the Mill near us. Well, since that day in Presbytery he has never been the same. His work—he is on the Daily Telegraph, you know—takes him away from—from—well, from Church and that kind of thing, and from all his friends."

"I understand," said the Superintendent, with grave sympathy.

"And he's got to be very different. He had some trouble, great trouble, the greatest possible to him. Oh, I may as well tell you. The brothers—you remember the doctor, Barney?"

"Very well," replied the Superintendent. "Strong man. Where is he now?"

"He went to Europe. Well, the brothers were everything to each other since little fellows together. Oh, it was beautiful! I never saw anything like it anywhere. They had a misunderstanding, a terrible misunderstanding. Dick was in the wrong." The Superintendent shot a keen glance at her. "No," she said, answering his glance, the colour in her face deepening into a vivid scarlet, "it was not about me, not at all. I can't tell you about it, but that, and his trouble with the Presbytery, and all the rest of it are just killing him. And I know if he got back to his own work again and away from home it would save him, and his mother, too, for she is breaking her heart. Couldn't you get him out there?"

The Superintendent saw how hard a task it had been for her to tell the story, and the sight of her eager face, the big blue eyes bright, and the lips quivering with the intensity of her feeling, deeply touched him.

"It might be possible," he said.

"Oh, I know the Presbytery difficulty," cried Margaret, with a desperate note in her voice.

"That could be arranged, I have no doubt," said the Superintendent, brushing aside that difficulty with a wave of the hand. "The question is, would he be willing to go?"

"Oh, he would go, I am sure. If you saw him and if you told him those stories about the need there is, I am sure he would go. Could you see him? There is no use to write. I do wish you could. He is such a fine boy and his mother is so set upon his being a minister." The blue eyes were bright with tears she was too brave to let fall.

"My dear young lady," said the Superintendent, his deep voice growing deeper under the intensity of his feelings, "I would do much for your sake and for your mother's. I am to visit your home early next month. I shall make it a point to see Mr. Boyle, and I promise you I shall get him if it is possible."

The sudden lifting of the burden from her heart deprived the girl of speech, but she shyly put out her hand and touched the long, sinewy fingers that lay within reach of hers in a timid caress. Instantly the fingers closed upon her hand in a grasp so strong that it seemed to drive the conviction into her heart that somehow this strong man would find a way by which Dick could be saved.

How, or by what arguments, the Superintendent overcame Dick's objections, Margaret never learned. But the full bitter tale of reasons against his ever taking up his work again, with which Dick had made himself so familiar during the past dark, dreary months, were one by one removed, and when the Superintendent left the Old Stone Mill he had secured his missionary for Windermere. It gave the Superintendent acute satisfaction to remember the flash of his missionary's blue eyes as, in answer to the warning, "You will have a hard fight of it, remember," the reply came, "A hard fight? Thank God!"

Before the year was over it fell that the Windermere valley came to be one of the mission fields that gladdened the hearts of the Home Mission Committee of the Calgary Presbytery, and especially of its doughty Convener. In the Convener's study, eight by ten, the report from the Windermere field was discussed with the ubiquitous and indefatigable Superintendent.

"An extremely gratifying record," said the Superintendent, "especially when one considers its disorganized condition a year ago."

"Yes, it's a good report," assented the Convener. "We had practically no support a year ago. Our strongest man—"

"Fink?"

"Yes. You know Hank, I see. Well, Hank's enthusiasm and devotion were hardly of what you would call the purest type. But whatever his motive, he stood by the missionary, and, do you know, it is a splendid testimony of the power of the Gospel to see the change in that same shrewd old sinner. Yes, sir, give the Gospel a chance and it will do its work." The Convener, who hated all cant and canting phrases with a perfect hatred, rarely allowed himself the luxury of an emotional outbreak. But the case of Hank Fink seemed to reach the springs of feeling that he kept hidden in the deep heart of him.

"So Boyle has done well?" said the Superintendent. "I am very glad of it. Very glad of it, for his own sake, for his mother's, and for the sake of another."

"Yes," replied the Convener, "Boyle has done a fine bit of work. He lived all summer on his horse's back and in his canoe, followed the prospectors up into the gulches and the miners to their mines, if you can call them mines, left a magazine here, a book there, a New Testament next place. And once he got his grip on a man, he never let him go. Hank told me how he found a man sick in a camp away up in a gulch and how he stayed with him for more than a week, then brought him down on his horse's back to the Forks. Yes, it's a good record. A church built at the north end of the field, another almost completed at the Forks. Really, it was very fine," continued the Convener, allowing his enthusiasm to rise. "It renews one's faith in the reality of religion to see a man jump into his work like that. They didn't pay him his salary the first half year, but he omitted to mention that in his report."

The Superintendent sat up straight. "Is he behind yet?"

"No. I mentioned the matter to Fink and explained that if the field failed it was Boyle that would suffer. His language—well," the Convener laughed reminiscently, "you have seen Hank?"

"Yes. I've seen him, I've heard him, and I've read him. But let us hope that his deeds will atone in a measure for his broken English. But," continued the Superintendent, "you have had Boyle ordained, have you not?"

"Yes. We got him ordained," replied the Convener, beginning to chuckle. A delighted, choking chuckle it was. Any missionary who had worked in his Presbytery would recognize the Convener in the dark by that chuckle. It began, if one were quick to observe, with a wrinkling about the corners of the sharp blue eyes, then became audible in a succession of small explosions that seemed to have their origin in the region of the esophagus and to threaten the larynx with disruption, until relief was found in a wide-throated peal that subsided in a second series of small explosions and gradually rumbled off into silence somewhere in the region of the diaphragm, leaving only the wrinkles about the corners of the blue eyes as a kind of warning that the whole process might be repeated upon sufficient provocation. "Yes, we got him ordained," he repeated when the chuckle had passed. "I was glad of your explanatory note about him. It guided us in our arrangements for examination."

"What happened?" inquired the Superintendent, leaning forward. He dearly loved a yarn, and he sorely hated to lose any of the more humorous incidents of missionary life, not only for the joy they brought him, but also because they furnished him with ammunition for his Eastern campaigns.

"Well, it was funny," said the Convener, his lips twitching and his eyes wrinkling, "though at one time it looked like an Assembly case with all seven of us up before the bar. You know McPherson, our latest importation in the way of ordained men? Somehow he had got wind of Boyle's trouble with the Presbytery in the East. McPherson is a fine fellow and doing good work."

"Yes," assented the Superintendent, "he's a fine fellow, but his conscience gives him a hard time now and then and works over time for other People."

"Well," continued the Convener, "McPherson came to me about the matter in very considerable anxiety. I put him off, consulted with McTavish and Murray, and we decided that Boyle was too good a man to lose, and as to his heresy, it was not hurting Windermere as far as we could learn. So it happened"—here the Convener pulled himself up short to suppress the chuckle that threatened—"it happened that just as the examination was beginning McPherson was called out, and before he had returned the trials for license and ordination had been sustained. I think on the whole McPherson was relieved, but there were some funny moments after he came back into court."

"Heresy-hunting doesn't flourish in the West," said the Superintendent. "There's no time for it. Some of the Eastern Presbyteries have too many men with more time on their hands than sense in their heads."

"Certainly there was no time lost in this case," replied the Convener. "We knew Boyle's scholarship was right. We knew his heart was sound. We knew he was doing good work for us and we knew we wanted him. We were not anxious to know anything else."

"What we want for the West," said the Superintendent, his voice vibrating in a deeper tone, "is men who have the spirit of the Gospel with the power to preach it and the love of their fellowmen, with tact to bring it to bear upon them. A little heresy, more or less, won't hurt them. Orthodoxy is my doxy, heterodoxy the other fellow's."

"In Boyle's case, I believe he was helped by his touch of heresy. It gave him a kind of brotherly feeling with all heretics. It was that more than anything else that broke up the Freethinkers' Club."

"Ah," said the Superintendent, bending eagerly forward, again on the scent, "I didn't hear that."

"Yes," said the Convener, "Fink told me about it. Boyle went to their meetings. He found them revelling in cheap scepticism of the Ingersollian type. He took the attitude of a man seeking after a working theory of life, and that attitude he stuck to—his real attitude, mind you. He encouraged them to talk, combated none of their positions and, as Hank said, 'coaxed them out into deep water and had them froggin' for their lives. He was the biggest Freethinker in the bunch.' They invited him to give a series of lectures. He did so, and that settled the Freethinkers' Club. He never blamed them for doubting anything, and I believe that's right." The Convener was a bit of a heretic himself and, consequently, carried a tender heart toward them. "Let a man doubt till he finds his faith. And that was Boyle's line. He let them doubt, but he insisted that they should have something positive to live by."

"Our friend Hank," said the Superintendent, "would be delighted."

"Delighted? I should say so. But Hank 'joins trembling with his mirth,' for Boyle got after him with the same demands."

The Superintendent was filled with delighted pride in his missionary. "That's the kind of man we want. He ought to do well in your railroad field."

"Yes," replied the Convener hesitatingly. "You think he ought to go? Windermere will be furious. I wouldn't care to go in there after Boyle is removed."

"It is hard on Windermere, but Windermere mustn't be selfish. That railroad work is most pressing, and only a man like Boyle will do. There will be from three to five thousand men in there this winter between Macleod and Kuskinook. We dare not neglect them. I have had correspondence with Fahey, the General Manager for the Crow's Nest line, and he is not unfriendly, though he would prefer us to send in medical missionaries. But that work he and his contractors ought to look after."

"There is a terrible state of things in the eastern division, I fear, from all reports," replied the Convener. "By the way, there is a young English doctor working on that eastern division from the MaCleod end who is making a great stir. Bailey is his name, I believe. He began as a navvy, but finding a lot of fellows sick, and the doctor a poor drunken fellow, Bailey, it appears, stood it as long as he could, then finally threw him out of the camp and installed himself in his place. The contractor backed him up and he has revolutionized the medical work in that direction. Murray told me the most wonderful tales about him. He must be a remarkable man. Gambles heavily, but hates whiskey and won't have it near the camp. You ought to look him up when you go in."

"I will. These camp doctors are a poor lot and the railroad people ought to feel disgraced in employing them. They draw their fifty cents per man a month, but their practice is shameful. It is a delicate matter, but I shall take this up with Fahey when I see him. He is a rough diamond, but he is fair and he won't stand any nonsense."

"And you think Boyle ought to go in?"

"Yes. On the whole, I think Boyle must go. These are a fine body of men and must be looked after. A weaker man would make a mess of things. Boyle is the man for the work. How did he seem? Cheerful?"

"No, I shouldn't call him so. But he is vastly better than when he came to us. He was low in health, I think, and his face haunted me for weeks. He strikes me as a man with a tragedy in his life."

The Superintendent said nothing. He had, in large degree, the rare gift of silence. Even with his trusted lieutenants he would break no confidence. But before he slept that night he wrote two letters, and after he had sealed and stamped them he placed them, with a pile already written, on the table and sat back in his chair indulging himself in a few moments of reverie. He saw the orderly, well-kept kitchen in the Old Stone Mill and, bending over his letter a woman, dark-faced and stern, her wavy, black hair heavily streaked with white, for during the past years the sword had pierced her heart. He saw the light break upon her tragic Highland face as she read of her boy and his well doing. With glad heart she had given him up, and now, with humble joy, she would read that her offering had been accepted.

The other letter brought to him the Macdougalls' drawing-room with all its beautiful appointments and the face of a young girl pleading for her friend. He still could see the quivering lips and hear the words of her invincible faith, "I know that if he got at his own work again it would save him." He could still feel the grateful, timid pressure of her fingers as he had pledged her his word that her desire should be fulfilled. He had kept his word and her faith had not been put to shame.

XVI
THE CHALLENGE OF DEATH

"Be aisy now, ye little divils. Sure ye'd think it wuz the ould Nick himself ye're dodgin'."

Thus Tommy Tate, teamster along the Tote road between the Maclennan camps, admonished his half-broken bronchos.

"Stiddy now. The saints be good t'us! Will we iver git down this hill alive? Hould back, will yez? There, now. The saints be praised! that's over. How are ye now, Scotty? If ye're alive, kick me fut. Hivin be praised! He's there yit," said Tommy to himself. "We're on the dump now, Scotty, an' we won't be long, me bhoy, till we see the lights av Swipey's saloon. Git along there, will ye!"

The bronchos after their fifteen-mile drive along the unspeakable bush roads, finding the smooth surface of the railway grade beneath their feet, set off at a good lope. It was now quite dark. The snow was driving bitterly in Tommy's face, but that stout little Irishman cared nothing for himself. His concern was for the man lying under the buffalo robes in the sleigh. Mile after mile the bronchos kept up their tireless lope, encouraged by the cheery admonitions and the cracking whip of their driver.

"Begob, but it's cowld enough to freeze the tail aff a brass monkey. I'll jist be afther givin' the lad a taste."

He tied the reins to the seat, gave his bronchos a parting lash, took a flask from his pocket, and got down on his knees beside the sick man.

"Here, Scotty," he said coaxingly, "take another taste. It'll put life into ye." The sick man tried to swallow once, twice, choked hard, then shook his head. "Now, God be merciful! an' can't ye swally at all? An' the good stuff it is, too! Thry once more, Scotty darlin'. Ye'll need it an' we're not far aff now." Once more the sick man made a desperate effort. He got a little of the whiskey down, then turned away his head. The tender-hearted little Irishman covered him over carefully and climbed into his seat. "He couldn't swally it," he said to himself in an awed voice, putting the flask to his own lips, "Begorra, an' it's near the Kingdom he must be!" To Tommy it appeared an infallible sign of approaching dissolution that a man should reject the contents of his flask. He gave himself to the business of getting out of the bronchos all the speed they had. "Come on, now, me bhoys!" he shouted through the gale, "what are ye lookin' at? Sure, there's nothin' purtier than yerselves can be seen in the dark. Hut, there! Kick, wud ye? Take that, thin, an' larn manners! Now ye're beginin' to move! Hooray!"

So with voice and lash Tommy continued to urge his team till they came out into a clearing at the far end of which twinkled the lights of the new railroad town being built about Maclennan's camp No. 1.

"Hivin be praised! we're there at last. Begob, it's mesilf that thought ye'd moved to the ind of nowhere. We're here, Scotty, me man. In ten howly minutes we'll have ye by the fire an' the docthor puttin' life into ye wid a spoon. Are ye there, Scotty?" But there was no movement in response. "Howly Mary! Give us a little more speed!" He stood up over his team, lashing and yelling till the tired beasts were going at full gallop. As he drew near the camp the sound of singing came on the driving wind. "Now the divil fly away wid the whiskey! It's pay day an' the camp's loose. God send, there's a quiet spot to be found near at hand!"

Through the driving snow could be seen the dim, black outlines of the various structures of the pioneer town. First came the camp building, the bunkhouse, grub-house, office, blacksmith shop, and beyond these the glaring lights of a couple of saloons, while back nearer timber the "red lights," the curse and shame of railroad, lumber, and mining camps in British Columbia then and unto this day, cast their baleful lure through the snowy night.

At full gallop Tommy drove his bronchos up to the door of the first saloon and before they were well stopped burst open the door, crying out, "Give us a hand here, min, for the love o' God!" Swipey, the saloon-keeper, came himself to the door.

"What have you there, Tommy?" he asked.

"It's mesilf don't know. It wuz alive when we started out. Are ye there, Scotty?" There was no answer. "The saints be good to us! Are ye alive at all?" He lifted back the buffalo robe from the sick man's face and he found him breathing heavily, but unable to speak. "Where's yer doctor?"

"Haven't seen him raound," said Swipey. "Have you, Shorty?"

"Yes," replied the man called Shorty. "He's in there with the boys."

Tommy swore a great oath. "Like our own docthor, he is, the blank, dirty suckers they are! Sure, they'd pull a bung hole out be the roots!"

"He's not that way," replied Swipey, "our doctor."

"Not much he ain't!" cried Shorty. "But he's into the biggest game with 'Mexico' an' the boys ye ever seen in this camp."

"Fer the love av Hivin git him!" cried Tommy. "The man is dyin'. Here, min, let's git him in."

"There's no place here for a sick man," said the saloon-keeper.

"What? He's dyin', I'm tellin' ye!"

"Well, this ain't no place to die in. We ain't got time." An angry murmur ran through the men about the door. "Take him up to the bunk-house," said the saloon-keeper to Tommy with a stream of oaths. "What d'ye want to come monkeyin' raound my house for with a sick man? How do you know what he's got?"

"What differ does it make what he's got?" retorted Tommy. "Blank yer dirty face fer a bloody son of a sheep thief! It's plinty of me money ye've had, but it's no more ye'll git! Where'll I take the man to?" he cried, appealing to the crowd. "Ye can't let him die on the street!"

Meantime Shorty had found the doctor in a small room back of the bar of the "Frank" saloon, seated at a table surrounded by six or eight men with a deck of cards in his hand, deep in a game of "Black Jack" for which he held the pot. Opposite him sat "Mexico," the type of a Western professional gambler and desperado, his swarthy face adorned with a pair of sweeping mustaches, its expressionless appearance relieved by a pair of glittering black eyes. For nine hours the doctor had not moved from his chair, playing any who might care to chip in to the game. For the last hour he had been winning heavily, till, at his right hand, he had a heap of new crisp bills lately from the Bank of Montreal, having made but a slight pause in the grimy hands of the railroad men on their way to his. At his left hand stood a glass of water with which, from time to time, he moistened his lips. His face was like a mask of death, colourless and empty of feeling, except that in the black eyes, deep-set and blood-shot, there gleamed a light as of madness. The room was full of men watching the game and waiting an opportunity to get into it.

"The doctor's wanted!" shouted Shorty, bursting into the room. Not a head turned, and but for a slight flicker of impatience the doctor remained unmoved.

"There's a man dyin' out here from No. 2," continued Shorty.

"Let him go to hell, then, an' you go, too!" growled out "Mexico," who had for the greater part of the evening been playing in bad luck, but who had refused to quit, waiting for the turn.

"He's out here in the snow," continued Shorty, "an' he's chokin' to death, an' we don't know what to do with him."

The doctor looked up from his hand. "Put him in somewhere. I'll be along soon."

"They won't let him in anywhere. They're all afraid, an' he's chokin' to death."

The doctor turned down his cards. "What do you say? Choking to death?" He passed his hand over his eyes. His professional instinct began to assert itself.

"Yes," continued Shorty. "There's somethin' wrong with him; he can't swallow. An' we can't git him in."

The doctor pushed back his chair. "Here, men," he said, "I'm going to quit."

A chorus of oaths and imprecations greeted his proposal.

"You can't quit now!" growled "Mexico" fiercely, like a dog that is about to lose a bone. "You've got to give us a chance."

"Well, here's your chance then," cried the doctor. "Let's stop this tiddle-de-winks game. You can't have up more than a hundred apiece. I'll put my pile against your bets, there's three thousand if there's a dollar, and quit. Come on."

The greatness of the opportunity staggered them.

Then they flung themselves upon it. "It's a go!" "Come on!" "Give us your cards!" Quickly the cards were dealt. One by one the men made up their hands. The crowd about crushed in upon them in breathless excitement. Never had there been seen in that camp so reckless a stake.

"Now, then, show down," growled "Mexico."

The doctor laid down his cards face up. One by one they compared their hands. He had won. With an oath "Mexico" made a grab for the pile, reaching for his hip at the same time with the other hand, but the doctor was first, and before anyone could move or speak "Mexico" was lying in the corner, his toes quivering above his upturned chair.

"Look after the brute, someone. He doesn't understand the game," said the doctor with cool contempt, crumpling up the bills and pushing them down into his pocket. "Where's your sick man?"

"This way, doctor," said Shorty, hurrying out toward the sleigh. The doctor passed him on a run.

"What does this mean?" he cried. "Why haven't you got him inside somewhere?"

"That's what I say, docthor," answered Tommy, "but the bloody haythen wudn't let him in."

"How's this, Swipey?" said the doctor sternly, turning to the saloon-keeper, who still stood in the door.

"He's not comin' in here. How do I know what he's got?"

"I'll take that responsibility," replied the doctor. "In he goes. Here, take him up on the robe, men. Steady, now."

Swipey hesitated a moment, but before he could make up his mind what to do, the doctor was leading his men with their burden past the bar door.

"Show us a room at the back, Swipey, upstairs. It must be warm. Be quick about it."

Swearing deep oaths, Swipey led the way. "It must be warm, eh? Want a bath in it next, I suppose."

"This will do," said the doctor when they reached the room. "Now, clear out, men. I want one of you. You'll do, Shorty." Without hurry, but with incredible speed and dexterity, he had the man undressed and in bed between heated blankets. "Now, hold the light. We'll take a look at his throat. Heavens above! Stay here, Shorty, till I come back."

He ran downstairs, and, bareheaded as he was, plunged through the storm to his office, returning in a few minutes with his medical bag and two hot-water bottles.

"We're too late, Shorty, I fear, but we'll do our best. Get these full of hot water for me."

"What is it, Doctor?" cried Shorty anxiously.

"Go quick!" The doctor's voice was so sharp and stern that before Shorty knew, he was half way downstairs with the hot-water bottles. With swift, deft movements the doctor went about his work.

"Ah, that's right. Now, Shorty, hold the light again. Now the antitoxin. It's hours, days, too late, perhaps, hardly any use with this mixed infection, but we'll try it. There. Now we'll touch up his heart. Poor chap, he can't swallow. We'll give it to him this way." Again he filled his syringe from another bottle and gave the sick man a second injection. "There. That ought to help him a bit. Now, what fool sent a man in this condition twenty miles through a storm like this? Shorty, don't let that teamster go away without seeing me. Have him in here within an hour." Shorty turned to go. "Wait. Do you know this man's name?"

"I heard Tommy call him Scotty Anderson. He's from the old country, I think."

"All right. Now, go and get the teamster."

The doctor turned to his struggle with death. "There is no chance, no chance. The fools! The villains! It's sheer murder!" he muttered, as he strove moment by moment to bring relief to the sick man fighting to get his breath.

After working with him for half an hour the doctor had the satisfaction of seeing him begin to breathe more easily. But by that time he had given up all hope of saving the man's life. And it seemed to increase his rage to see his patient slipping away from him. For do what he could, the heart was failing rapidly and the doctor saw that it was simply a matter of minutes. Before the hour had elapsed the dying man opened his eyes and looked about. The doctor turned up the light and leaned over him, trying to make out the words which poor Scotty was making such painful efforts to utter. But no words could he hear. Finally the dying man pointed to the chair on which his clothes lay.

"You want something out of your pocket?" inquired the doctor. The eyes gave assent. One by one the doctor held up the articles he found in the pockets of the clothing till he came to a letter, then the eyes that had followed every movement expressed satisfaction.

"Do you want me to read it?"

It was from the mother to her son Andy in far Canada, breathing gratitude for gifts of money from time to time, pride in his well doing, love without measure, and prayers unceasing. It took all the doctor's fortitude to keep his voice clear and steady. The eloquent eyes never moved from his face till the reading was finished. Then the doctor put the letter into his big, hairy hand so muscular and so feeble. The fingers closed upon it and with difficulty carried it to the man's bosom. For a moment the eyes remained closed as if in peace, but only for a moment. Once more they rested entreatingly upon the doctor's face.

"Something else in your pocket?"

The doctor continued drawing forth the articles one by one till he came to a large worn pocketbook.

"This?"

With an effort the head nodded an affirmation. From the innermost pocket he drew a little photograph of a young girl. A light came into the eyes of the dying man. He took the photograph which the doctor placed in his hand and carried it painfully to his lips. Once more the eyes began to question.

"You want something else from your pocketbook? If so, close your eyes." The eyes remained wide open. "No? You want me to do something for you? To write?" At once the eyes closed. "I shall write to your mother and send all your things and tell them about you." A smile spread over the face and the eyes closed as if content. In a few minutes, however, they opened wide again. In vain the doctor tried to catch the meaning. The lips began to move. Putting his ear close, the doctor caught the word "Thank."

"Thank who? The teamster?"

The man moved his hand and touched the doctor's with his fingers.

"Thank me? My dear fellow, I only wish I could help you," said the doctor. "Anything else?"

The eyes looked upward toward the ceiling, then rested beseechingly upon the doctor's face again. Vainly the doctor sought to gather his meaning, till, with a mighty effort, poor Scotty tried to speak. Once more, putting his ear close to the lips, the doctor caught the words, "Mother—home," and again the eyes turned upward toward the ceiling.

"You wish me to tell your mother that you are going home?" And once more a glad smile lit up the distorted face.

For some minutes there was silence in the room. Up from the bar, through the thin partition, came the sounds of oaths and laughter and drunken song. The doctor cursed them all below his breath and turned toward the door. A spasm of coughing brought him back to his patient's side. After the spasm had passed the sick man lay still, his eyes closed, and his breath becoming shorter every moment. Once again the eyes made their appeal, and the doctor hastened to seek their meaning. Listening intently, he heard the word, "Pray." The doctor's pale face flushed quickly and as quickly paled again. He shook his head, saying, "I'm no good at that." Once more the poor lips made an effort to speak, and again the doctor caught the words, "Jesus, tender—." It had been the doctor's child prayer, too. But for years no prayer had passed his lips. He could not bring himself to do it. It would be sheer mockery. But the eyes were fixed upon his face beseeching, waiting for him to begin.

"All right," said the doctor through his set teeth, "I'll do it."

And above the ribald sounds that broke in from below on the solemn silence, the doctor's voice, low but very clear, rose in the verses of that ancient child's prayer, "Jesus, tender Shepherd, hear me." At the third verse,

> *"Let my sins be all forgiven,*
>
> *Bless the friends I love so well,*
>
> *Take me when I die to heaven,*
>
> *Happy there with Thee to dwell."*

there was a deep breath from the sick man, a sigh as of great content, and then all was still. Ere the prayer had been uttered the answer had come, "Happy there with Thee to dwell." Poor Scotty! Out from the sickness and the pain, from the wretchedness and the sin, he had been taken to the place where the blessed dwell and whence they go no more out forever.

Silently the doctor composed the limbs, his eyes dim with unusual tears. As he was thus busied he heard a sniffle behind him and, turning sharply about, he found Tommy and Shorty standing at the door, both wiping their eyes and struggling with their sobs.

"Confound you, Shorty!" burst forth the doctor wrathfully, "what in the mischief are you doing there? Come in, you fool. Did you ever see a dead man before?" The doctor was clearly in a rage. During the weeks Shorty had known him in camp he had never seen him show anything but a perfectly cold and self-composed face. "Is this the teamster?" continued the doctor. "Come in here. You see that man? Someone has murdered him. Who sent him down here through this storm? How long had he been ill? Have you a doctor up there? Are there any more sick? Why don't you speak up? What's your name?" In an angry flood the questions poured forth upon the hapless Tommy, who stood speechless. "Why don't you speak?" said the doctor again.

Recovering himself, Tommy began with the question which seemed to require least thought to answer. "Thomas Tate, sir, av ye plaze. An' sure it's not me ye'd be blamin' at all. Didn't I tell the foreman the man wuz dyin'? An' niver a breath did I draw fer the last twinty miles, an' up an' down the hills like the divil wuz afther me wid a poker."

"Have you no doctor up there?"

"Docthor, is it? If that's what ye call him, fer the drunken baste that he is, wallowin' 'round like Micky Murphy's pig, axin' pardon av the pig."

"Are there any more sick?"

"Sick? Bedad, they're all sick wid fear, an' half a dozen worse than poor Scotty there, God rest his sowl!"

The doctor thought a minute, then turning to Shorty he said, speaking rapidly, "Go and bring to this room the foreman and Swipey. And say not a word to anyone, mind that. And you," he said, turning to Tommy, "can you start back in an hour?"

"I can that same, if I must."

"You know the road. We'll get another team and start within an hour. Get something to eat."

In a short time both the foreman and the saloon-keeper were in the room.

"This man," said the doctor, "is dead. Diphtheria. There is no fear, Swipey. Shut that door. But you must have him buried at once, and you will both see the necessity of having it done quietly. I shall fumigate this room. All this clothing must be burned and there will be no further danger. You will see about this to-morrow. I am going up to No. 2 to-night."

"To-night, doctor!" cried the foreman. "It's blowing a regular blizzard. Can't you wait till morning?"

"There are men sick at No. 2," said the doctor. "The chances are it's diphtheria."

In an hour's time Tommy was at the door with the best team the camp possessed.

"Have you had something to eat, Tommy?" inquired the doctor, stepping out from the saloon.

"That's what I have," replied Tommy.

"All right, then. Give me the lines. You can have a sleep."

"Not if I know it, begob!" said Tommy. "I'll stay wid yez. It's mesilf that knows a man whin I see him."

And off into the blizzard and the night they sped, the doctor rejoicing to find in the call to a fight with death that excitement without which it seemed he could not live.

XVII
THE FIGHT WITH DEATH

At Camp No. 2 Maclennan had struck what was called a hard proposition. The line ran straight through a muskeg out of which the bottom seemed to have dropped, and Maclennan himself, with his foreman, Craigin, was almost in despair. For every day they were held back by the muskeg meant a serious reduction in the profits of Maclennan's contract.

The foreman, Craigin, was a man from "across the line," skilled in railroad building, selected chiefly because of his reputation as a "driver." He was a man of great physical force and indomitable will, and gifted in large measure with the power of command. He knew his business thoroughly and knew just how to get the most out of the machinery and men at his command. He himself was an untiring worker, and no man on the line could get a bigger day out of his force than could Craigin. His men he treated as part of his equipment. He believed in what called his "scrap-heap policy." When any part of the machinery ceased to do first-class work it was at once discarded, and, as with the machinery, so it was with the men. A sick man was a nuisance in the camp and must be got rid of with all possible speed. Craigin had little faith in human nature, and when a man fell ill his first impulse was to suspect him of malingering, and hence the standing order of the camp in regard to a sick man was that he should get to work or be sent out of the camp. Hence the men thoroughly hated their foreman, but as thoroughly they dreaded to fall under his displeasure.

The camp stood in the midst of a swamp, thick with underbrush of spruce and balsam and tamarack. The site had been selected after a month of dry weather in the fall, consequently the real condition of the ground was not discovered until the late rains had swollen the streams from the mountain-sides and filled up the intervening valleys and swamps. After the frost had fallen the situation was vastly improved, but they all waited the warm weather of spring with anxiety.

On the crest of the hill which overlooked the camp the doctor halted the team.

"Where are your stables, Tommy?"

"Over there beyant, forninst the cook-house."

"Good Lord!" murmured the doctor. "How many men have you here?"

"Between two an' three hundred, wid them that are travellin' the road."

"What are your sanitary arrangements?"

"What's that?"

"I mean how do you—what are your arrangements for keeping the camp clean, free from dirt and smells? You can't have three hundred men living together without some sanitary arrangements."

"Begob, it's ivery man fer himsilf. Clane yersilf as ye can through the week, an' on Sundays boil yer clothes in soap suds, if ye kin git near the kittles. But, bedad, it's the lively time we have wid the crathurs."

"And is that the bunk-house close up to the cookery?"

"It is that same."

"And why was it built so close as that?"

"Sure there wuz no ground left by raison av the muskeg at the back av it."

The doctor gave it up. "Drive on," he said. "But what a beautiful spot for a camp right there on that level."

"Beautiful, is it? Faith, it's not beautiful that Craigin calls it, fer ivery thaw the bottom goes clane out av it till ye can't git round fer mud an' the dump fallin' through to the antipods," replied Tom.

"Yes, but up on this flat here, Tommy, under the big pines, that would be a fine spot for the camp."

"It wud that same. Bad luck to the man who set it where it is."

As they drove into the camp the cook came out with some refuse which he dumped down on a heap at the door. The doctor shuddered as he thought of that heap when the sun shone upon it in the mild weather. A huge Swede followed the cook out with a large red muffler wrapped round his throat.

"Hello, Yonie!" cried Tommy. "What's afther gittin' ye up so early?"

"It is no sleep for dis," cried Yonie thickly, pointing to his throat.

The doctor sprang from the sleigh. "Let me look at your throat."

"It's the docthor, Yonie," explained Tommy, whereupon the Swede submitted to the examination.

The doctor turned him toward the east, where the sun was just peeping through the treetops, and looked into his throat. "My man, you go right back to bed quick."

"No, it will not to bed," replied Yonie. "Big work to-day, boss say. He not like men sick."

"You hear me," said the doctor sharply. "You go back to bed. Where's your doctor?"

"He slapes in the office between meals. Yonder," said Tommy, pointing the way.

"Never mind now. Where are your sick men?"

"De seeck mans?" replied the cook. "She's be hall overe. On de bunk-house, on de cook shed. Dat is imposseeb to mak' de cook for den seeck mans hall aroun'."

"What? Do they sit around where you are cooking?"

"Certainment. Dat's warm plas. De bunkhouse she's col'. Poor feller! But she's mak' me beeg troub'. She's cough, cough, speet, speet. Bah! dat's what you call lak' one beas'."

The doctor strode into the cook-house. By the light of the lantern swinging from the roof he found three men huddled over the range, the picture of utter misery. He took down the lantern.

"Here, cook, hold this please, one moment. Allow me to look at your throats, men."

"Dis de docteur, men," said the cook.

A quick glance he gave at each throat, his face growing more stern with each examination.

"Boys, you must all get to bed at once. You must keep away from this cook-house or you'll poison the whole camp."

"Where can we go, doctor? The bunk-house would freeze you and the stink of it would make a well man sick."

"And is there no place else?"

"No. Unless it's the stables," said another man; "they're not quite so bad."

"Well, sit here just now. We'll see about it. But first let me give you something." He opened his bag, took out his syringe. "Here, Yonie, we'll begin with you. Roll up your sleeve." And in three minutes he had given all four an antitoxin injection. "Now, we'll see the doctor. By the way what's his name?"

"Hain," said the cook, "dat's his nem."

"Haines," explained one of the men.

"Dat's what I say," said the cook indignantly, "Hain."

The doctor passed out, went toward the office, knocked at the door, and, getting no response, opened it and walked in.

"Be the powers, Narcisse!" cried Tommy, as the cook stood looking after the doctor, "it's little I iver thought I'd pity that baste, but Hivin save him now! He'll be thinkin' the divil's come fer him. An' begob, he'll be wishin' it wuz before he's through wid him."

But Dr. Bailey was careful to observe all the rules that the punctilious etiquette of the profession demanded. He found Dr. Haines sleeping heavily in his clothes. He had had a bad night. He was uneasy at the outbreak of sickness in his camp, and more especially was he seized with an anxious foreboding in regard to the sick man who had been sent out the day before. Besides this, the foreman had cursed him for a drunken fool in the presence of the whole camp with such vigour and directness that he had found it necessary to sooth his ruffled feelings with large and frequent doses of stimulant brought into the camp for strictly medical purposes. With difficulty he was roused from his slumber. When fully awake he was aware of a young man with a very pale and very stern face standing over him. Without preliminary Dr. Bailey began:

"Dr. Haines, you have some very sick men in this camp."

"Who the deuce are you?" replied Haines, staring up at him.

"They call me Dr. Bailey. I have come in from along the line."

"Dr. Bailey?" said Haines, sitting up. "Oh, I've heard of you." His tone indicated a report none too favourable. In fact, it was his special chum and confrere who had been ejected from his position in the Gap camp through Dr. Bailey's vigorous measures.

"You have some very sick men in the camp," repeated Dr. Bailey, his voice sharp and stern.

"Oh, a little tonsilitis," replied Haines in an indifferent tone.

"Diphtheria," said Bailey shortly.

"Diphtheria be hanged!" replied Haines insolently; "I examined them carefully last night."

"They have diphtheria this morning. I have just taken the liberty of looking into their throats."

"The deuce you have! I like your impudence! Who sent you in here to interfere with my practice, young man? Where did you get your professional manners?" Dr. Haines was the older man and resented the intrusion of this smooth-faced young stranger, who added to the crime of his youth that of being guilty of a serious breach of professional etiquette.

"I ought to apologize for looking at your patients," said Dr. Bailey. "I came in thinking I might be of some assistance in dealing with this outbreak of diphtheria, and I was naturally anxious to see—"

"Diphtheria!" blurted Haines. "Nothing of the sort."

"Dr. Haines, the man you sent out last night had it."

"HAD it?"

"He died an hour after arriving at No. 1."

"Dead? Cursed fool! He WOULD go against my will."

"Against your will? Would you let a man in the last stages of diphtheria leave this camp against your will with the company's team?"

"Well, I knew he shouldn't go. But he wanted to go himself, and the foreman would have him out."

"There are at least four men going about the camp—they are now in the cook-house where the breakfast is being prepared—who are suffering from a severe attack of diphtheria."

"What do you propose? What can I do in this cursed hole?" said Dr. Haines petulantly. "No appliances, no means of isolation, no nurses, nothing. Beside, I have half a dozen camps to look after. What can I do?"

"Do you ask me?" The scorn in the voice was only too apparent. "Isolate the infected at least."

Haines swore deeply to himself while, with trembling hand, he poured out a cupful of whiskey from a bottle standing on a convenient shelf. "Isolate? How can I isolate? There's no building in which—"

"Make one."

"Make one? Young man, do you know what you are talking about? Do you know where you are? Do you know who is running this camp?"

"No. But I do know that these men must be isolated within an hour."

"Impossible! I tell you it is impossible!"

"Dr. Haines, an inquest upon the man sent out from this camp last night would result in the verdict of manslaughter. There was no inquest. There will be on the next man that dies if there is any neglect."

The seriousness of the situation began to dawn upon Haines. "Well," he said, "if you think you can isolate them, go ahead. I'll see the foreman."

"Every minute is precious. I gave those four men antitoxin. Are there others?"

"Don't know," Haines growled, as with an oath he went out, followed by Dr. Bailey. Just outside the door they met the foreman.

"This is Dr. Bailey, Mr. Craigin." Craigin growled out a salutation. "Dr. Bailey here says these sick men have diphtheria."

"How does he know?" inquired Craigin shortly.

"He has examined them this morning."

"Have you?"

"No, not yet."

"Then you don't know they have diphtheria?"

"No," replied Haines weakly.

"These men have diphtheria, Mr. Craigin, without a doubt, and they ought to be isolated at once."

"Isolated? How?"

"A separate camp must be built and someone appointed to attend them."

"A separate camp!" exclaimed Craigin; "I'll see them blanked first! Look here, Haines, let's have no nonsense about this. I'm three weeks, yes, a month, behind with this job here. This blank, blank muskeg is knocking the whole contract endways. We can't spare a single man half a day. And more than that, you go talking diphtheria in this camp and you can't hold the men here an hour. It's all I can do to hold them as it is." And Craigin went off into an elaborate course of profanity descriptive of the various characteristics of the men in his employ.

"But what is to be done?" asked Haines helplessly.

"Send 'em out to the steel. They're better in the hospital, anyway. It's fine to-day. We'll send every man Jack out to-day."

"These men can't be moved," said Dr. Bailey in a quiet voice. "You sent a man out yesterday and he's dead."

"He was bound to go himself. We didn't send him. Anyway, it's none of YOUR business. Look here, Haines, you know me. I'm not going to have any of this blank nonsense of isolation hospitals and all that blankety blank rot. Dose 'em up good and send 'em out."

Dr. Haines stood silent, too evidently afraid of the foreman.

"Mr. Craigin, it would be murder," said Dr. Bailey, "sure murder. Some of them might get through. Some would be sure to die. The consequences to those responsible—to Dr. Haines, for instance—would be serious. I am quite sure he will never give orders that these men should be moved."

"He won't, eh? You just wait till you see him do it. Haines will give the orders right enough." Craigin's laugh was like the growl of a bear. "There's a reason, ain't there, Haines? Now you hear me. Those men are going out to-day, and so are you, you blank, blank interferin' skunk."

Dr. Bailey smiled sweetly at Craigin. "You may call me what you please just now, Mr. Craigin. Before the day is over you won't have enough names left. For I tell you that these men suffering from diphtheria are going to stay here, and are going to be properly cared for."

Craigin was white. That this young pale-faced stranger should presume to come into his domain, where his word was wont to run as absolute law, filled him with rage unspeakable. But there were serious issues at stake, and with a supreme effort he controlled the passionate longing to spring upon this upstart and throttle him. He turned sharply to Haines.

"Dr. Haines, you think these men can go out to-day?"

Haines hesitated.

"You understand me, Haines; these men go out or—"

Haines was evidently in some horrible dread of the foreman. A moment more he paused and then surrendered.

"Oh, hang it, Bailey, I don't think they're so terribly ill. I guess they can go out."

"Dr. Haines," said Craigin, "is that your decision?"

"Yes, I think so."

"All right," said Craigin, with a triumphant sneer. He turned to Tommy, who was standing near with half a dozen men who had just come out from breakfast. "Here you, Tommy, get a couple of teams ready and all the buffalo robes you need and be ready to start in an hour. Do you hear?"

"I do," said Tommy, turning slowly away.

"Tommy," called Dr. Bailey in a sharp, clear tone, "you took a man out from this camp yesterday. Tell the men here what happened."

"Sure, they all know it," said Tommy, who had already told the story of poor Scotty's death and of the doctor's efforts to save him. "An' it's a fine bhoy he wuz, poor Scotty, an' niver a groan out av him all the way down, an' not able to swally a taste whin I gave it to him."

Craigin sprang toward Tommy in a fury. "Here you blank, blank, blank! Do what I tell you! And the rest of you men, what are you gawkin' at here? Get to work!"

The men gave back, and some began to move away. Dr. Bailey walked quickly past Craigin into the midst of the group.

"Men, I want to say something to you." His voice commanded their instant attention. "There are half a dozen of your comrades in this camp sick with diphtheria. I came up here to help. They ought to be isolated to prevent the spread of the disease, and they ought to be cared for at once. The foreman proposes to send them out. One went out yesterday. He died last night. If these men go out to-day some of them will die, and it will be murder. What do you say? Will you let them go?" A wrathful murmur ran through the crowd, which was being rapidly increased every moment by others coming from breakfast.

"Get to your work, you fellows, or get your time!" shouted Craigin, pouring out oaths. "And you," turning toward Dr. Bailey, "get out of this camp."

"I am here in consultation with Dr. Haines," replied Dr. Bailey. "He has asked my advice, and I am giving it."

"Send him out, Haines. And be quick about it!"

By this time the men were fully roused. One of them came forward.

"What do you propose should be done, Doctor?" he inquired.

"Are you going to work, McLean?" shouted Craigin furiously. "If not, go and get your time."

"We're going to talk this matter over a minute, Mr. Craigin," said McLean quietly. "It's a serious matter. We are all concerned in it, and we'll decide in a few minutes what is to be done."

"Every man who is not at work in five minutes will get his time," said Craigin, and he turned away and passed into the office.

"What do you propose should be done, Doctor?" said McLean, ignoring the foreman.

"Build a camp where the sick men can be placed by themselves and where they can be kept from infecting the rest of the camp. Half a day's work of a dozen men will do it. If we send them out some of them will die. Besides, it is almost certain that some more of you have already been infected."

At once eager discussion began. Some, in dread terror of the disease, were for sending out the sick immediately, but the majority would not listen to this inhuman proposal. Finally McLean came again to Dr. Bailey.

"The men want to know if you can guarantee that the disease can be stamped out here if you have a separate camp for an hospital?"

"We can guarantee nothing," replied Dr. Bailey. "But it is altogether the safer way to fight the disease. And I am of the opinion that we can stamp it out." The doctor's air and tone of quiet confidence, far more than his words, decided the men's action. In a minute more it was agreed that the sick men should stay and that they would all stand together in carrying out the plan of isolation.

"If he gives any of us time," said Tommy, "we'll all take it, begob."

"No, men," said the doctor, "let's not make trouble. I know Mr. Maclennan slightly, and he's a just man, and he'll do what's fair. Besides, we don't want to interfere with the job. Give me a dozen men—one must be able to cook—and in half a day the work will be finished. I will be personally responsible for everything."

At this point Craigin came out. "Here's your time, McLean," he said, thrusting a time check at him.

McLean took it without a word and went over and stood by Dr. Bailey's side.

"Who are coming?" called out McLean.

"All of us," cried a voice. "Pick out your men, McLean."

"All right," said McLean, looking over the crowd.

"I'm wan," said Tommy, running over to the doctor's side. "I seen him shtand by Scotty whin the lad wus fightin' fer his life, an' if I'm tuk it's him I want beside me."

One by one McLean called his men, each taking his place beside the doctor, while the rest of the men moved off to work.

"Mr. Craigin, I am going to use these men for half a day." said Dr. Bailey.

For answer Craigin, in mad rage, throwing aside all regard for consequences, rushed at him, but half a dozen men were in his path before he had taken the second step.

"Hold on, Mr. Craigin," said McLean, "we want no violence. We're going to do what we think right in this matter, so you may as well make up your mind to it."

"And Mr. Craigin," continued the doctor, "we shall need some things out of your stores."

Craigin stepped back from the crowd and on to the office steps. "Your time is waiting you, men. And listen to me. If any man goes near that there storehouse door, I'll drop him in his tracks. I've got the law and I'll do it, so help me God." He went into the office and returned in a moment with a Winchester, which he loaded in full view of the men.

"Never mind him, boys," said the doctor cheerily, "I'm going to have breakfast. Come, Tommy, I want you."

In fifteen minutes he came out, with the key of the storehouse in his hand, to find the men still waiting his orders and Craigin on guard with his Winchester.

"Don't go just yet," said McLean to the doctor in a low voice, "we'll get round him."

"Oh, he'll not shoot," said Dr. Bailey.

"He will. He will. I knew him in Michigan. He'll shoot and he'll kill, too."

For a single instant the doctor hesitated. His men were about him waiting his lead. Craigin with his rifle held them all in check. A moment's thought and his decision was taken. He stepped toward Craigin and said in a clear voice, "Mr. Craigin, these stores are necessary to save these men's lives. I want them and I'm going to take them. Murder me, if you like."

"Hear me, men." Craigin's voice was cold and deliberate. "These stores are in my charge. I am an officer of the law. If any man lays his hand on that latch I'll shoot him, so help me God."

"Hear me, Mr. Craigin," replied Dr. Bailey. "I'm here in consultation with Dr. Haines, who has turned over this matter to my charge. In a case of this kind the doctor's orders are supreme. This whole camp is under his authority. These stores are necessary, and I am going to get them." He well knew the weak spot in his position, but he counted on Craigin's nerve breaking down. In that, however, he was mistaken. Without haste, but without hesitation, he walked toward the storehouse door. When three paces from it Craigin's voice arrested him.

"Hold on there! Put your hand on that door and, as God lives, you're a dead man!"

Without a word the doctor turned again toward the door. The men with varying cries rushed toward the foreman. Craigin threw up his rifle. Immediately a shot rang out and Craigin fell to the snow, the smoking rifle dropping from his hand.

"Begob, I niver played baseball," cried Tommy, rushing in and seizing the rifle, "but many's the time I've had the diversion in the streets av Dublin of bringin' down the polismen wid a brick."

A heavy horseshoe, heaved with sure aim, had saved the doctor's life. They carried Craigin into the office and laid him on the bed, the blood streaming from a ghastly wound in his scalp. Quickly Dr. Bailey got to work and before Craigin had regained consciousness the wound was sewed up and dressed. Then giving him over to the charge of Haines, Dr. Bailey went about the work he had in hand.

Before the noon hour had arrived the eight men who were discovered to be in various stages of diphtheria were comfortably housed in a roomy building rudely constructed of logs, tar paper, and tarpaulin, with a small cook-house attached and Tommy Tate in charge. And before night had fallen the process of disinfecting the bedding, clothing, bunk-house, and cookery was well under way, while all who had been in immediate contact with the infected men had been treated by the doctor with antitoxin as a precautionary measure.

Thus the first day's campaign against death closed with the issue still undecided, but the chances for winning were certainly greater than they had been. What the result would be when Craigin was able to take command again, no one could say. But in the meantime, for the next two days, the work on the dump was prosecuted with all vigour, the men feeling in honour bound to support the doctor in that part of the fight which fell to them.

XVIII
THE MEDICAL SUPERINTENDENT
OF THE CROW'S NEST

Mr. Maclennan was evidently worried. His broad, good-humoured face, which usually wore a smile indicating content with the world and especially with himself, was drawn into a frown. The muskeg was beating him, and he hated to be beaten. He was bringing in General Manager Fahey to have a look at things. It was important to awaken the sympathy of the General Manager, if, indeed, this could be accomplished. But the General Manager had a way of insisting upon his contracts being fulfilled, and this stretch in Maclennan's charge was the one spot which the General Manager feared would occasion delay.

"There's the hole," said Maclennan, as they turned down the hill into the swamp. "Into that hole," he continued, pointing to where the dump ended abruptly in the swamp, "I can't tell you how many millions of carloads have been dumped. I used to brag that I was never beaten in my life, but that hole—"

"Maclennan, that hole has got to be filled up, bridged, or trestled, and we can't wait too long, either."

The General Manager's name was a synonym for a relentless sort of energy in railroad construction that refused to consider obstacles. Nothing could stand in his way. The thing behind which he put the weight of his determination simply had to move in one direction or other. The contractor that failed expected no mercy, and received none.

"We're doing our best," said Maclennan, "and we will continue to do our best. Hello! what's this? What's Craigin doing up here? Hold up, Sandy. We'll look in."

At the door of the hospital Dr. Haines met him.

"Hello, Doctor! What have you got here?"

"Isolation hospital," replied the doctor shortly.

"What hospital?"

"Isolation."

"Has Craigin gone mad all at once?"

"Craigin has nothing to do with it. There's a new boss in camp."

A look of wrathful amazement crossed Maclennan's countenance. Haines was beginning to enjoy himself.

"A new boss? What do you mean?"

"What I say. A young fellow calling himself Dr. Bailey came into this camp three days ago, raised the biggest kind of a row, laid up Craigin with a broken head, and took charge of the camp." Maclennan stood in amazement looking from Haines to the General Manager.

"Dr. Bailey? You mean Bailey from No. 1? What has he got to do with it? And how did Craigin come to allow him?"

"Ask Craigin," replied Haines.

"What have you got in there, Doctor?" asked Mr. Fahey.

"Diphtheria patients."

"How many?"

"Well, we began with eight three days ago and we've ten to-day."

"Well, this knocks me out," said Maclennan. "Where's Craigin, anyway?"

"He's down in his own room in bed."

Maclennan turned and got into the sleigh. "Come on, Fahey," he said, "let's go down. Something extraordinary has happened. You can't believe that fellow Haines. What are you laughing at?"

Fahey was too much of an Irishman to miss seeing the humour of any situation. "I can't help it, Maclennan. I'll bet you a box of cigars that man Bailey is an Irishman. He must be a whirlwind. But it's no laughing matter," continued the General Manager, sobering up. "This has a very serious aspect. There are a whole lot of men sick in our camps. You contractors don't pay enough attention to your health."

"Health! When you're driving us like all possessed there's no time to think of health."

"I tell you, Maclennan, it's bad policy. You have got to think of health. The newspapers are beginning to talk. Why, look at that string of men you met going out. Of course, the great majority of them never should have come in. Hundreds of men are here who never used either shovel or axe. They cut themselves, get cold, rheumatism, or something; they're not fit for their work. All the same, we get blamed. But my theory is that every camp should have an hospital, with three main hospitals along this branch. There's one at Macleod. It is filled, overflowing. A young missionary fellow, Boyle, has got one running out at Kuskinook supported by some Toronto ladies. It's doing fine work, too; but it's overflowing. There's a young lady in charge there, a Miss Robertson, and she's a daisy. The trouble there is you can't get the fellows to leave, and I don't blame them. If ever I get sick send me to her. I tell you, Maclennan, if we had two or three first-class men, with three main hospitals, a branch in every camp, we'd keep the health department in first-class condition. The men would stay with us. We'd get altogether better results."

"That's all right," said Maclennan, "but where are you to get your first-class men? They come to us with letters from Directors or some big bug or other. You've got to appoint them. Look at that man Haines. He doesn't know his work and he's drunk half the time. Dr. Bailey seems to be different. He certainly knows his work and he never touches whiskey. I got him up from the Gap to No. 1. In two weeks' time he had things in great shape. Funny thing, too, when he's fighting some sickness or busy he's all right, but when things get quiet he hits the green table hard. He's a wonder at poker, they say."

The General Manager pricked up his ears. "Poker, eh? I'll remember that."

"But this here business is going too far," continued Maclennan. "I didn't hire him to run my camps. Well, we'll see what Craigin has to say."

As they drove into the camp they were met by Narcisse, the cook.

"Bo' jour, M'sieu Maclenn'. You want something for hit?"

"Good-day, cook," said Maclennan. "Yes, we'll take a cup of tea in a few minutes. I want to see Mr. Craigin."

Narcisse drew near Maclennan and in subdued voice announced, "M'sieu Craigin, he's not ver' well. He's hurt hisself. He's lie on bed."

"Why, what's the matter with him?"

Narcisse shrugged his shoulders. "Oh, some leet' troub'. You pass on de office you see de docteur."

"Why, Haines is up at the hospital. We just saw him."

"Hain!" said Narcisse, with scorn indescribable. "Dat's no docteur for one horse. Bah! De mans go seeck, seeck, he can noting. He know noting. He's get on beeg drunk! Non! Nodder docteur. He's come in, fin' tree, four mans seeck on de troat, cough, cough, sore, bad. Fill up de cook-house.

Can't do noting. Sainte Marie! Dat new docteur, he's come on de camp, he's mak' one leet' fight, he's beeld hospital an' get dose seeck mans all nice an' snug. Bon. Good. By gar, dat's good feller!"

The smile broadened on Fahey's face. "I say, Maclennan, he's captured your camp. He's got the cook, dead sure."

The smile didn't help Maclennan's temper. He opened the office door and passed into Craigin's private room at the back. Here he found Dr. Bailey in charge. As he opened the door the doctor put up his hand for silence and backed him out into the office.

"Excuse me, Mr. Maclennan," he said, "he's asleep and must not be disturbed."

Maclennan shook hands with him with a cold "How are you," and introduced him to Mr. Fahey.

"Is Mr. Craigin ill?" inquired Fahey innocently.

"He has met with a slight accident," replied the doctor. "He is doing well and will be about in a day or two."

"Accident?" snorted Maclennan; then clearing his throat as for a speech he began in a loud tone, "Dr. Bailey, I must say—"

"Excuse me," said the doctor, opening the office door and marshalling them outside, "we'd better go somewhere else if we are going to talk. It is important that my patient should be kept perfectly quiet." The doctor's air was so entirely respectful and at the same time so masterful that Maclennan found himself walking meekly toward the grub-house behind the doctor, with Fahey, the smile on his face broader than ever, bringing up the rear. Maclennan caught the smile, but in the face of the doctor's quiet, respectful manner he found it difficult to rouse himself to wrath. He took refuge in bluster.

"Upon my word, Dr. Bailey," he burst forth when once they were inside the grub-house, "it seems to me that you have carried things on with a high hand in this camp. You come in here, a perfect stranger, you head a mutiny, you lay up my foreman with a dangerous wound, with absolutely no authority from anyone. What in the blank, blank do you mean, anyway?" Maclennan was rather pleased to find himself at length taking fire.

"Mr. Maclennan," said the doctor quietly, "it is natural you should be angry. Let me give you the facts before you pass your final judgment. A man was sent to me from this camp in a dying condition. Diphtheria. I learned there were others suffering here with the same disease. I came in at once to offer assistance. Consulted with Dr. Haines. We came to a practical agreement as to what ought to be done. Mr. Craigin objected. There was some trouble. Unfortunately, Mr. Craigin was hurt."

"Dr. Bailey," said the General Manager, "it will save trouble if you will go somewhat fully into the facts. We want an exact statement of what occurred." The authoritative tone drew Dr. Bailey's attention to the rugged face of the speaker, with its square forehead and bull-dog jaw. He recognized at once that he had to deal with a man of more than ordinary force, and he proceeded to give him an exact statement of all that had happened, beginning with the death of Scotty Anderson.

"That is all, gentlemen," said the doctor, as he concluded his tale; "I did what I considered was right. Prompt action was necessary. I may have been mistaken, but I think not."

"Mistaken!" cried Fahey, with a great oath. "I tell you, Maclennan, we've had a close shave. We may, perhaps, explain that one man's death, but if six or eight men had gone out of this camp in the condition in which the doctor says they were, the results would have been not only deplorable as far as the men are concerned, but disastrous to us with the public. Why, good heavens above! what a shave it was! Dr. Bailey, I am proud to meet you," continued Fahey, putting out his hand. "You had a most difficult situation to deal with and you handled it like a general."

"I quite agree with you," said Maclennan, shaking Dr. Bailey warmly by the hand. "The measures were somewhat drastic, but something had to be done. Go right on, Doctor. When Craigin is on his feet again we'll send him out."

"Mr. Craigin will be quite fit to work in a day or so. But I would suggest that he keep his place. You can't afford to lose a man of his force."

"Well, well, we'll see, we'll see."

"Dr. Bailey, I'd like to see your hospital arrangements. Mac will be busy just now and will excuse us."

The next two hours the General Manager spent in extracting from Dr. Bailey his theories in regard to camp sanitation and the care of the sick. Finding a listener at once so sympathetic and so intelligent, Dr. Bailey seized the opportunity of expatiating to the fullest extent upon the theme which, during the last few months, had been absorbing his mind.

"These camps are wrongly constructed in the first instance—every one that I have seen. Almost every law of sanitation is ignored. In location, in relative position of buildings, the disposal of refuse, the treatment of the sick and injured, the whole business reveals atrocious folly and ignorance.

For instance, take this camp. The only thing that prevents an outbreak of typhoid is the cold weather. In the spring you will have a state of things here that will arrest the attention of Canada. Look at the location of the camp. Down in a swamp, with a magnificent site five hundred yards away," pointing to a little plateau further up the hill, clear of underbrush and timbered with great pines. "Then look at the stables where they are. There are no means by which the men can keep themselves or their clothes clean. Their bunks, some of them, are alive with vermin, and the bunk-house is reeking with all sorts of smells. At a very little more cost you could have had a camp here pleasant, safe, clean, and an hospital ready for emergencies. Why, good heavens! they might at least have kept the vermin out."

"Oh, pshaw!" said Fahey, "every camp has to have a few of them fellows. Makes the men feel at home. Besides, you can't absolutely drive them out."

"Drive them out? Give me a free hand and I'll make this camp clean of vermin in two weeks, absolutely, and keep it so. Why, it would pay," continued the doctor. "You would keep your men in good condition, in good heart and spirits. They would do twice the work. They would stay with you. Besides, it would prevent scandal."

"Scandal?" The General Manager looked up sharply.

"Yes, scandal. I have done what I could to prevent talk, but down the line they are talking some, and if I am not mistaken it will be all over the East in a few weeks."

The General Manager was thinking hard. "Look here, young man," he said, with the air of one who has made up his mind, "do you drink?"

"No."

"Do you gamble?"

"When I've nothing to do."

"Oh, well," said Mr. Fahey, "a little poker doesn't hurt a man now and then. I am going to make you an offer which I hope you will consider favourably. I offer you the position of medical superintendent of this line at a salary of three thousand a year and all expenses. It's not much, but if the thing goes we can easily increase it. You needn't answer just now. Think it over. I don't know your credentials, but I don't care."

For answer, Dr. Bailey took out his pocketbook and selected a letter. "I didn't think I would ever use this. I didn't want to use it. But you can look at it."

Mr. Fahey took the letter, glanced through it hurriedly, then read it again with more care.

"You know Sir William?"

"Very slightly. Met him once or twice in London."

"This is a most unusual letter for him to write. You must have stood very high in the profession in London."

"I had a fairly good position," said Dr. Bailey.

"May I ask why you left?"

Dr. Bailey hesitated. "I grew tired of the life—and, besides—well—I wanted to get away from things and people."

"Pardon my asking," said Fahey hastily. "It was none of my business. But, Doctor—" here he glanced at the letter again, "Bailey, you say your name is?"

"They called me Bailey when I came in and I let it go."

"Very well, sir," replied Fahey quickly, "Bailey let it be. My offer holds, only I'll make it four thousand. We can't expect a man of your standing for less."

"Mr. Fahey, I came here to work on the construction. I wanted to forget. When I saw how things were going at the east end I couldn't help jumping it. I never thought I should have enjoyed my professional work so much. It has kept me busy. I will accept your offer at three thousand, but on the distinct understanding that I am to have my way in everything."

"By gad! you'll take it, anyway, I imagine," said Fahey, with a laugh, "so we may as well put it in the contract. In your department you are supreme. If you see anything you want, take it. If you don't see it, we will get it for you."

On their return to the office they found Dr. Haines in Craigin's room with Maclennan. As they entered they heard Haines' voice saying, "I believe it was a put-up job with Tommy."

"It's a blank lie!" roared Craigin. "I have it from Tommy that it was his own notion to fire that shoe, and a blank good thing for me it was. Otherwise I should have killed the best man that ever walked into this camp. Here, keep your hands off! You paw around my head like a blanked bull in a sand heap. Where's the doctor? Why ain't he here attending to his business?"

"Craigin," he said quietly, "let me look at that. Ah, it's got a twist, that's all. There, that's better."

Like a child Craigin submitted to his quick, light touch and sank back in his pillow with a groan of content. Dr. Bailey gave him his medicine and induced him, much against his will, to take some nourishment.

"There now, that's all right. To-morrow you'll be sitting up. Now you must be kept quiet." As he said this he motioned them out of the room. As he was leaving, Craigin called him back.

"I want to see Maclennan," he said gruffly.

"Wait till to-morrow, Mr. Craigin," replied the doctor, in soothing tones.

"I want to see him now."

The doctor called Mr. Maclennan back.

"Maclennan, I want to say there's the whitest man in these mountains. I was a blank, blank fool. But for him I might have been a murderer two or three times over, and, God help me! but for that lucky shoe of Tommy's I'd have murdered him. I want to say this to you, and I want the doctor here not to lay it up against me."

"All right, Craigin," said Maclennan, "I'm glad to hear you say so. And I guess the doctor here won't cherish any grudge."

Without a word the doctor closed the door upon Maclennan, then went to the bedside. "Craigin, you are a man. I'd be glad to call you my friend."

That was all. The two men shook hands and the doctor passed out, leaving Craigin more at peace with himself and with the world than he had been for some days.

XIX
THE LADY OF KUSKINOOK

Soon after Dick's departure for the West, Ben Fallows took up his abode at the Old Stone Mill and very soon found himself firmly established as a member of the family there; and so it came that he was present on the occasion of Margaret's visit, when the offer of the Kuskinook Hospital was under consideration. The offer came through the Superintendent, but it was due chiefly to the influence on the Toronto Board of Mrs. Macdougall. It was to her that Dick had appealed for a matron for the new hospital, which had come into existence largely through his efforts and advocacy. "We want as matron," Dick had written, "a strong, sane woman who knows her work, and is not afraid to tackle anything. She must be cheery in manner and brave in heart, not too old, and the more beautiful she is the better."

"Cheery in manner and brave in heart?" Mrs. Macdougall had said to herself, looking at the letter. "The very one! She is that and she is all the rest, and she is not too old, and beautiful enough even for Mr. Dick." Here Mrs. Macdougall smiled a gentle smile of deprecation at the suggestion that flitted across her mind at that point. "No, she'll never be old to Dick. We'll send her, and who knows, but—" Not even to herself, however, much less to another, did the little lady breathe a word of any 'arriere pensee' in urging the appointment.

With the Superintendent's letter in her hand, Margaret had gone to consult Barney's mother; for to Margaret Mrs. Boyle was ever "Barney's mother."

"It would be a very fine work," said Mrs. Boyle, "but oh, lassie! it is a long, long way. And you would be far from all that knew you!"

"Why, Dick is not very far away."

"Aye, but I doubt you would see little of him, with all the travelling he's doing to those terrible camps. And what if anything should happen to you, and no one to care for you?"

The old lady's hands trembled over the tea cups. She had aged much during the last six years. The sword had pierced her heart with Barney's going from home. And while, in the case of her younger and favourite son, she had without grudging made the ancient sacrifice, lines of her surrender showed deep upon her face.

"What's the matter with me goin' along, Miss Margaret?" said Ben, breaking in upon the pause in the conversation. "There's one of the old gang out there. We cawn't 'ave Barney, but you'd do in his place, an' I guess we could make things hump a bit. W'en the gang gits a goin' things begin to hum. You remember that day down at the 'Old King's' w'en me an' Barney an' Dick—"

"Och! Ben lad," said Mrs. Boyle, "Margaret will be hearing that story many's the time. But what would you be doing in an hospital?"

"Me? I hain't goin' fer to work in no 'ospital! I'm goin' to look after Miss Margaret. She wants someone to look after her, don't she?"

"Aye, that she does," remarked Mrs. Boyle, with such emphasis that Margaret flushed as she cried, "Not I! My business is to look after other people."

But the more the matter was discussed the clearer it became that Margaret's work lay at Kuskinook, and further, that she could not do better than take Ben along to "look after her," as he put it. Hence, before the year had gone, all through the Windermere and Crow's Nest valleys the fame of the Lady of Kuskinook grew great, and second only to hers was that of her bodyguard, the hospital orderly, Ben Fallows. And indeed, Ben's usefulness was freely acknowledged by both staff and patients; for by day or by night he was ever ready to skip off on errands of mercy, his wooden leg clicking a vigorous tattoo to his rapid movements. He was especially proud of that wooden leg, a combination of joints and springs so wonderful that he was often heard to lament the clumsiness of the other leg in comparison.

"W'en it comes to legs," Ben would say, "this 'ere's the machine fer me. It never gits rheumatism in the joints, nor corns on the toes, an' yeh cawn't freeze it with forty below."

As Ben grew in fame so he grew in dignity and in solemn and serious appreciation of himself, and of his position in the hospital. The institution became to him not simply a thing of personal pride, but an object of reverent regard. To Ben's mind, taking it all in all, it stood unique among all similar institutions in the Dominion. While, as for the matron, as he watched her at her work his wonder grew and, with it, a love amounting to worship. In his mind she dwelt apart as something sacred, and to serve her and to guard her became a religion with Ben. In fact, the Glory of the Kuskinook hospital lay chiefly in this, that it afforded a sphere in which his divinity might exercise her various powers and graces.

It was just at this point that Tommy Tate roused his wrath. Dr. Bailey's foreboding regarding Maclennan's Camp No. 2 had been justified by a serious outbreak in early spring of typhoid, of malignant type, to which Tommy fell a victim. The hospitals along the line were already overflowing, and so the doctor had sent Tommy to Kuskinook in charge of an assistant. After a six weeks' doubtful struggle with the disease Tommy began to convalesce, and with returning strength revived his invincible love of mischief, which he gratified in provoking the soul of Orderly Ben Fallows, notwithstanding that the two had become firm friends during the tedious course of Tommy's sickness. It didn't take Tommy long to discover Ben's tender spots, the most tender of which he found to be the honour of the hospital and all things and persons associated therewith. As to the matron, Tommy ventured no criticism. He had long since enrolled her among his saints, and Ben Fallows himself was not a more enthusiastic devotee than he. And not even to gratify his insatiable desire for fun at Ben's expense would Tommy venture any liberty with the name of the matron. In regard to the young preacher, however, who seemed to be a somewhat important part of the institution, Tommy was not so scrupulous, while as to the hospital appointments and methods, he never hesitated to champion the superior methods of those down the line.

It was a beautiful May morning and Tommy was signalizing his unusually vigorous health by a very specially exasperating criticism of the Kuskinook hospital and its belongings.

"It's the beautiful hospitals they are down the line. They don't have the frills and tucks on their shirts, to be sure, but they do the thrick, so they do."

"I guess they're all right fer simple cases," agreed Ben, "but w'en yeh git somethin' real bad yeh got to come 'ere. Look at yerself!"

"Arrah! an' that was the docthor, Hivin be swate to him! He tuk a notion t' me fer a good turn I done him wance. Begob, there's a man fer ye! Talk about yer white min! Talk about yer prachers an' the like! There's a man fer ye, an' there's none to measure wid him in the mountains!"

"Dr. Bailey, I suppose ye're talkin' about?" inquired Ben, with fine scorn.

"Yis, Dr. Bailey, an' that's the first two letters av his name. An' whin ye find a man to stand forninst him, by the howly poker! I'll ate him alive, an' so I will."

"Well, I hain't agoin' to say, Mr. Tate," said Ben, with studied, politeness, "that no doctor can never compare with a preacher, for I've seen a doctor myself, an' there's the kind of work he done," displaying his wooden leg and foot with pride. "But what I say is that w'en it comes to doin' real 'igh-class, fine work, give me the Reverend Richard Boyle, Esquire. Yes, sir, sez I, Dick Boyle's the man fer me!"

"Aw, gwan now wid ye! An' wud ye be afther puttin' a preacher in the same car wid a docthor, an' him the Medical Superintendent av the railway?"

"I hain't talkin' 'bout preachers an' doctors in general," replied Ben, keeping himself firmly in hand, "but I'm talkin' about this 'ere preacher, the Reverend Richard Boyle." Ben's attention to the finer courtesies in conversation always increased with his wrath. "An' that I'll stick to, for there's no man in these 'ere mountain 'as done more fer this 'ere country than that same Reverend Richard Boyle, Esquire."

"Listen til the monkey! An' what has he done, will ye tell me?"

"Well," said Ben, ignoring Tommy's opprobrious epithet, "I hain't got a day to spend, but, to begin with, there's two churches up the Windermere which—"

"Churches, is it? Sure an' what is a church good fer but to bury a man from, forby givin' the women a place to say their prayers an' show their hats?"

"As I was sayin'," continued Ben, "there's two churches up the Windermere. I hain't no saint, an' I hain't no scholar, but I goes by them as is, an' I know that there's Miss Margaret, an' I tell you"—here Ben solemnly removed his pipe from his mouth and, holding it by the bowl, pointed the stem, by way of emphasizing his words, straight at Tommy's face—"I tell you she puts them churches above even this 'ere hinstitution!" And Ben sat back in his chair to allow the full magnitude of this fact to have its full weight with Tommy. For once Tommy was without reply, for anything savouring of criticism of Miss Margaret or her opinions was impossible to him.

"An' what's more," continued Ben, "this 'ere hinstitution in which we're a-sittin' this hour wouldn't be 'ere but fer that same preacher an' them that backs him up. That's yer churches fer yeh!" And still Tommy remained silent.

"An' if yeh want to knew more about him, you ask Magee there, an' Morrison an' Old Cap Jim an' a 'eap of fellows about this 'ere preacher, an' 'ear 'em talk. Don't ask me. 'Ear 'em talk w'en they git time. They wuz a blawsted lot of drunken fools, workin' for the whiskey-sellers an' the tin-horn gamblers. Now they're straight an' sendin' their money 'ome. An' there's some as I know would be a lot better if they done the same."

"Manin' mesilf, ye blaggard! An' tis thrue fer ye. But luk at the docthor, will ye, ain't he down on the whiskey, too?"

"Yes, that's w'at I 'ear," conceded Ben. "But e'll soak 'em good at poker."

"Bedad, it's the truth ye're spakin," said Tommy enthusiastically. "An' it wud do ye more good than a month's masses to see him take the hair aff the tin horns, the divil fly away wid thim! An' luk at the 'rid lights' —"

"'Red lights'?" interrupted Ben. "Now ye're talkin'. Who cleared up the 'rid lights' at Bull Crossin'."

"Who did, thin?"

"Who? The Reverend Richard Boyle is the man."

"Aw, run in an' shut the dure! Ye're walkin' in yer slape."

"Mr. Tate, I 'appen to know the facts in this 'ere particular case, beggin' yer 'umble pardon." Ben's h's became more lubricous with his rising indignation. "An' I 'appen to know that agin the Pioneer's violent opposition, agin the business men, agin his own helder a-keepin' the drug shop, agin the hagent of the town site an' agin the whole blawsted, bloomin' population, that 'ere preacher put up a fight, by the jumpin' Jemima! that made 'em all 'unt their 'oles!"

"Aw, Benny, it's wanderin' agin ye are! Did ye niver hear how the docthor walked intil the big meetin' an' in five minutes made the iditor av the Pioneer an' the town site agent an' that bunch look like last year's potaty patch fer ould shaws, wid the spache he gave thim?"

"No," said Ben, "I didn't 'ear any such thing, I didn't."

"Well, thin, go out into society, me bhoy, an' kape yer ears clane."

"My ears don't require no such cleanin' as some I know!" cried Ben, whose self-control was strained to the point of breaking.

"Manin' mesilf agin. Begorra, it's yer game leg that saves ye from a batin'!"

"I don't fight no sick man in our own 'ospital," replied Ben scornfully, "but w'en yer sufficiently recovered, I'd be proud to haccommodate yeh. But as fer this 'ere preacher—"

"Aw, go on wid yer preacher an' yer hull outfit! The docthor yonder's worth—"

"Now, Mr. Tate, this 'ere's goin' past the limit. I can put up with a good deal of abuse from a sick man, but w'en I 'ears any reflections thrown out at this 'ere 'ospital an' them as runs it, by the livin' jumpin' Jemima Jebbs! I hain't goin' to stand it, not me!" Ben's voice rose in a shrill cry of anger. "I'd 'ave yeh to know that the 'ead of this 'ere hinstitution—"

"Aw, whist now, ye blatherin' bletherskite, who's talkin' about the Head? The Head, is it? An' d'ye think I'd sthand—Howly Moses! here she comes, an' the angels thimsilves wud luk like last year beside her!"

"Good-morning, Tommy. Why, I do think you are looking remarkably well to-day," cried the matron, her brisk step, bright face, and cheery voice eloquent of her splendid vitality and high spirit.

"Och! thin, an' who wudn't luk well in your prisince?" said the gallant little Irishman, with a touch to his hat. "Sure, it's better than the sunlight to see the smile av yer pritty face."

"Now, Tommy, Tommy, we'll have to be sending you away if you go on like that. It's a sure sign of convalescence when an Irishman begins to blarney."

"Blarney, indade! Bedad, it's God's mercy I don't have to blarney, for I haven't the strength to do that same."

"Well, Tommy, don't try. Keep your strength for getting well again. Ben, I think I saw Mr. Boyle riding up. Will you please go and take his horse and show him up to the office. I am just wanting his help in preparing my annual report."

"Report!" cried Ben. "A day like this! No, sez I; git out into the woods an' git a little colour into yer cheeks. It'll do him good, too. This' ere hinstitution is takin' the life out o' yeh."

And Ben went away grumbling his discontent and wrath at the matron's inability to take thought for herself.

The tiny office was bare enough of beauty, but from the window there stretched a scene glorious in its majestic sweep and in its varied loveliness. Down over the tops of second-growth jack pine and Douglas fir one looked straight into the roaring gorge of the Goat River filled with misty light and overhung with an arching rainbow. Up the other side climbed the hills in soft folds of pine tops and, beyond the pines, to the sheer, grey, rocky peaks in whose clefts and crags the snow lay like fretted silver. Far up the valley to the east the line of the new railway gleamed here and there through the pines, while to the west the Goat River gorge issued into the splendid expanse of the Kootenay Valley, forest-clad and lying now in all the sunlit glory of its new spring dress.

For some moments Dick stood gazing. "Of all views I see, this is the best," he said. "Day or night I can get it clear as I see it now, and it always brings me rest and comfort."

"Rest and comfort?" echoed Margaret, coming to his side. "Yes, I understand that, especially with the sunlight upon it. But at night, Dick, with the moon high above that peak there and filling with its light all the valleys, do you know, I hardly dare look at it long."

"I understand," replied Dick, slowly. "Barney used to say the same about the moonlight on the view from the hillcrest above the Mill."

Then a silence fell between them. The deepest, nearest thought with each was Barney. It was always Barney. Resolutely they refused to allow the name to reach their lips except at rare intervals, but each knew how the thought of him lurked in the heart, ready to leap into full view with every deeper throb.

"Come, this won't do," said Margaret, almost sharply.

"No, it won't do," replied Dick, each reading the thought in the other's heart.

"I am struggling with my report," said Margaret in a business-like tone. "What shall I say? How shall I begin?"

"Your report, eh? Better let me write it. I'll tell them things that will make them sit up. What copy there would be in it for the Daily Telegraph! The lonely outpost of civilization, the incoming stream of maimed and wounded, of sick and lonely, the outgoing stream healed and hopeful, and all singing the praises of the Lady of Kuskinook."

"Hush, Dick," said Margaret softly. "You are forgetting the man who travels the lonely trails to the camps and up the gulches for the sick and wounded and brings them out on his broncho's back and his own, too, watches by them and prays with them, who yarns to them and sings to them till they forget their homesickness, which is the sickness the hospital cannot cure."

"Oh, draw it mild, Margaret. Well, we'll give it up. The best part of this report will be that that is never written, except on the hearts and in the lives of the poor chaps who will think of the Lady of Kuskinook any time they happen to be saying their prayers."

"Tell me, Dick, what shall I say?"

"Begin with the statistics. Typhoids, so many—"

"What an awful lot there were, two hundred and twenty-seven of them!"

"Yes," replied Dick. "But think of what there would have been but for that man, Bailey! He's a wonder! He has organized the camps upon a sanitary basis, brought in good water from the hills, established hospitals, and all that sort of thing."

"So you've got it, too," said Margaret, with a smile.

"Got what?"

"Why, what I call the Bailey bacillus. From the general manager, Mr. Fahey, down to Tommy Tate, it seems to have gone everywhere."

"Is that so?" replied Dick, laughing. "Well, there are some who have escaped the tin-horn gang and the whiskey runners. Or rather, they've got it, but it's a different kind. Some day they'll kill him."

"And yet they say he is—"

"Oh, I know. He does gamble, and when he gets going he's a terror. But he's down on the whiskey and on the 'red lights.' You remember the big fight at Bull Crossing? It was Bailey pulled me out of that hole. The Pioneer was slating me, Colonel Hilliers, the town site agent, was fighting me, withdrew his offer of a site for our church unless I'd leave the 'red lights' alone, and went everywhere quoting the British army in India against me. Even my own men, church members, mind you, one of them an elder, thought I should attend to my own business. These people were their best customers. Why, they actually went so far as to write to the Presbytery that I was antagonizing the people and ruining the Church. Well, you remember the big meeting called to protest against this vice? The enemy packed the house. Had half a dozen speakers for the 'Liberal' side. Unfortunately I had been sent for to see a fellow dying up the line. It looked for a complete knockout for me. In came Dr. Bailey, waited till they were all through their talk, and then went for them. He didn't speak more than ten minutes, but in those ten minutes he crumpled them up utterly and absolutely. Colonel Hilliers and the editor of The Pioneer, I understand, went white and red, yellow and green, by turns. The crowd simply yelled. You know he is tremendously popular with the men. They passed my resolution standing on the backs of their seats. Quite true, the doctor went from the meeting to a big poker game and stayed at it all night. But I'm inclined to forgive him that, and all the more because I am told he was after that fellow 'Mexico' and his gang. Oh, it was a fine bit of work. I've often wished to meet him, but he's a hard man to find. He must be a good sort at bottom."

"To hear Tommy talk," replied Margaret, "you would make up your mind he was a saint. He tells the most heart-moving stories of his ways and doings, nursing the sick and helping those who are down on their luck. Why, he and Ben almost came to blows this morning in regard to the comparative merits of the doctor and yourself."

"Ben, eh? I can never be thankful enough," said Dick earnestly, "that you brought Ben West with you. It always makes me feel safer to think that he is here."

"Ben will agree with you," replied Margaret, "I assure you. He assumes full care of me and of the whole institution."

"Good boy, Ben," said Dick, heartily. "And he is a kind of link to that old home and—with the past, the beautiful past, the past I like to think of." The shadows were creeping up on Dick's face, deepening its lines and emphasizing the look of weariness and unrest.

"A beautiful past it was," replied Margaret gently. "We ought to be thankful that we have it."

"Have you heard anything?" inquired Dick.

"No. Iola's letter was the last. He had left London shortly after her arrival, so Jack Charrington had told her. She didn't know where he had gone. Charrington thought to the West somewhere, but there has been no word since."

Dick put his head on the table and groaned aloud.

"Never mind, Dick, boy," said Margaret, laying her hand upon his head as if he had been a child, "it will all come right some day."

"I can't stand it, Margaret!" groaned Dick, "I shut it out from me for weeks and then it all comes over me again. It was my cursed folly that wrecked everything! Wrecked Barney's life, Iola's, too, for all I know, and mine!"

"You must not say wrecked," replied Margaret.

"What other word is there? Wrecked and ruined. I know what you would say; but whatever the next life has for us, there is nothing left in this that can atone!"

"That, too, you must not say, Dick," said Margaret. "God has something yet for us. He always keeps for us better than He has given. The best is always before us. Besides," she continued eagerly, "He has given you all this work to do, this beautiful work."

The word recalled Dick. He sat up straight. "Yes, yes, I must not forget. I am not worthy to touch it. He gave me this chance to work. What else should I want? And after all, this is the best. I can't help the heart-hunger now and then, but God forbid I should ever say a word of anything but gratitude. I was down, down, far down out of sight. He pulled me up. Who am I to complain? But I am not complaining! It is not for myself. If there were only one word to know he was doing well, was safe!" He turned suddenly to Margaret with an almost fierce earnestness. "Margaret, do you think God will give me this?" His voice was hoarse with the intensity of his passion. "Do you know, I sometimes feel that I don't want Heaven without this. I never pray for anything else. Wealth, honour, fame, I once longed for these. But now these are nothing to me if only I knew Barney was right and safe and well. Yes, even my love for you, Margaret, the best thing, the truest thing next to my love of my Lord, I'd give up to know. But three years have gone since that awful night and not a word! It eats and eats and eats into me here," he smote himself hard over his heart, "till the actual physical pain is at times more than I can stand. What do you think, Margaret?" he continued, his face quivering piteously. "Every time I think of God I think of Barney. Every prayer I make I ask for Barney. I wake at night and it is Barney I am thinking of. Can I stand this long? Will I have to stand it long? Has God forgiven me? And when He forgives, does He take away the pain? Sometimes I wonder if there is anything in all this I preach!"

"Hush, Dick!" said Margaret, her voice broken with the grief she understood only too well. "Hush! You must not doubt God. God forgives and loves and grieves with our griefs. He will take away the pain as soon as He can. You must believe this and wait and trust. God will give him back to us. I feel it here." She laid her hand upon her heaving breast.

For some moments Dick was silent. "Perhaps so," he said at length. "For your sake He might. Yes, down in my heart I believe he will."

"Come," said Margaret, "let us go out into the open air, into God's sunlight. We shall feel better there. Come, Dick, let us go and see the Goat cavort." She took him by the arm and lifted him up. At the door she met Ben. "I won't be gone long, Ben," she explained.

"Stay as long as yeh like, Miss Margaret," replied Ben graciously. "An' the longer yeh stay the better fer the hinstitution."

"That's an extremely doubtful compliment," laughed Margaret, as they passed down the winding path that made its way through the tall red pines to the rocky bank of the Goat River. There on a broad ledge of rock that jutted out over the boiling water, Margaret seated herself with her back against the big red polished bole of a pine tree, while at her feet Dick threw himself, reclining against a huge pine root that threw great clinging arms here and there about the rocky ledges. It was a sweet May day. All the scents and sounds of spring filled up the fragrant spaces of the woods. Far up through the great feathering branches gleamed patches of blue sky. On every side stretched long aisles pillared with the clean red trunks of the pine trees wrought in network pattern. At their feet raged the Goat, foaming out his futile fury at the unmoved black rocks. Up the rocky sides from the water's edge, bravely clinging to nook and cranny, running along ledges, hanging trembling to ragged edges, boldly climbing up to the forest, were all spring's myriad tender things wherewith she redeems Nature from winter's ugliness. From the river below came gusts of misty wind, waves of sound of the water's many voices. It was a spot where Nature's kindly ministries got about the spirit, healing, soothing, resting.

With hardly a word, Dick lay for an hour, watching the pine branches wave about him and listening to the voices that came from the woods around and from the waters below, till the fever and the doubt passed from his heart and he grew strong and ready for the road again.

"You don't know how good this is, Margaret," he said, "all this about me. No, it's you. It's you, Margaret. If I could see you oftener I could bear it better. You shame me and you make me a man again. Oh, Margaret! if only you could let me hope that some day—"

"Look, Dick!" she cried, springing to her feet, "there's the train."

It was still a novelty to see the long line of cars wind its way like some great jointed reptile through the woods below.

"Tell me, Margaret," continued Dick, "is it quite impossible?"

"Oh, Dick!" cried the girl, her face full of pain, "don't ask me!"

"Can it never be, Margaret, in the years to come?"

She clasped her hands above her heart. "Dick," she cried piteously, "I can't see how it can be. My heart is not my own. While Barney lives I could not be true and be another's wife."

"While Barney lives!" echoed Dick blankly. "Then God grant you may never be mine!" He stood straight for a moment, then with a shake of his shoulders, as if adjusting a load, he stepped into the path. "Come, let us go," he said. "There will be letters and I must get to work."

"Yes, Dick dear," said Margaret, her voice full of tender pity, "there's always our work, thank God!"

Together they entered the shady path, going back to the work which was to them, as to many others, God's salvation.

There were a number of letters lying on the office desk that day, but one among them made Margaret's heart beat quick. It was from Iola. She caught it up and tore it open. It might hold a word of Barney. She was not mistaken. Hurriedly she read through Iola's glowing accounts of her season's triumph with Wagner. "It has been a great, a glorious experience," wrote Iola. "I cannot be far from the top now. The critics actually classed me with the great Malten. Oh, it was glorious. But I am tired out. The doctors say there is something wrong, but I think it is only that I am tired to death. They say I cannot sing for a year, but I don't want to sing for a long, long time. I want you, Margaret, and I want—oh, fool that I was!—I may as well out with it—I want Barney. I have no shame at all. If I knew where to find him I would ask him to come. But he would not. He loathes me, I know. If I were only with you at the manse or at the Old Mill I should soon be strong. Sometimes I am afraid I shall never be. But if I could see you! I think that is it. I am weary for those I love. Love! Love! Love! That is the best. If you have your chance, Margaret, don't throw away love! There, this letter has tired me out. My face is hot as I read it and my heart is sore. But I must let it go." The tears were streaming down Margaret's face as she read.

"Read it, Dick," she said brokenly, thrusting the letter into his hands.

Dick read it and gave it back to her without a word.

"Oh, where is he?" cried Margaret, wringing her hands. "If we only knew!"

"The date is a month old," said Dick. "I think one of us must go. You must go, Margaret."

"No, Dick, it must be you."

"Oh, not I, Margaret! Not I! You remember—"

"Yes, you, Dick. For Barney's sake you must go."

"For Barney's sake," said Dick, with a sob in his throat. "Yes, I'll go. I'll go to-night. No, I must go to see a man dying in the Big Horn Canyon. Next day I'll be off. I'll bring her back to him. Oh! if I could only bring her back for him, dear old boy! God give me this!"

"Amen," said Margaret with white lips. For hope lives long and dies hard.

XX
UNTIL SEVENTY TIMES SEVEN

The Big Horn flowed by a tortuous and rapid course through rough country into the Goat. The trail was bad and, in places, led over high mountain shoulders in a way heartbreaking to packers. For this reason, all who knew the ways and moods of a canoe chose the water in going up the canyon. True enough, there were a number of lift-outs and two rather long portages that made the going up pretty stiff, but if a man had skill with the paddle and knew the water he might avoid these by running the rapids. Men from the Ottawa or from some other north Canadian river, like all true canoemen, hated to portage and loved to take the risk of the rapids. Though the current was fairly rapid, going upstream was not so difficult as one might imagine; that is, if the canoeman happened to know how to take advantage of the eddies, how to sneak up the quiet water by the banks, how to put the nose of his canoe into the swift water and to hold her so that, as Duprez, the keeper of the stopping place at the Landing, said, "She would walk on de rapide toute suite lak one oiseau."

There was a bad outbreak of typhoid at the upper camp on the Big Horn, and Dr. Bailey had been urgently summoned. The upper camp lay on the other side of the Big Horn Lake, twenty miles or more from the steel. The lake itself was six miles long by canoe, but by trail it was at least twice that. Hence, though there would be some stiff paddling in the trip, the doctor did not hesitate in his choice of route. He knew his canoe and loved every rib and thwart in her. He had learned also the woodsman's trick of going light. A blanket, a tea pail which held his grub, consisting of some Hudson Bay hard tack, a hunk of bacon, and a little tea and sugar, and his drinking cup constituted his baggage, so that he could make the portages in a single carry. Many a mile had he gone, thus equipped, both by trail and by canoe, in his journeyings up and down these valleys, doing his work for the sick and wounded in the railroad, lumber, and tie camps, and more recently in the new-planted mining towns.

It was a great day for his trip. A stiff breeze upstream would help him in his fight with the current and coming down it would be glorious. The sun was just appearing over the row of pines that topped the low mountain range to the east when he packed his kit and blankets under the gunwale in the bow and slipped his canoe into the water. He was about to step in when a voice he had not heard for many days arrested him.

"Hello, Duprez! Did you see the preacher pass this way yesterday? He was—By the livin' jumpin' Jemima! Barney!"

It was Ben Fallows, gazing with open mouth on the doctor. With two swift steps the doctor was at his side. He grasped Ben by the arm and walked him swiftly apart.

"Ben," he said, in a low, stern voice, "not a word. I once did you a good turn?"

Ben nodded, still too astonished for speech.

"Then listen to what I tell you. No one must know what you know now."

"But—but Miss Margaret and Dick—" gasped Ben.

"They don't know," interrupted the doctor, "and must not know. Will you promise me this, Ben?"

"By Jove, Barney! I don't—I don't think—"

"Do you hear me, Ben? Do you promise?"

"Yes, by the livin'—"

"Good-bye, Ben; I think I can depend on you for the sake of old days." The doctor's smile set Ben's head in a whirl.

"You bet, Bar—Doctor!" he cried.

"Good old boy, Ben. Good-bye, lad."

He stepped into the canoe and pushed her off into the eddy just above the falls by which the Big Horn plunged into the Goat.

"Bo' voyage, M'sieu le Docteur!" sang out Duprez. "You cache hup de preechere. He pass on de riviere las' night."

"What? Who?"

"De preechere, Boyle. He's pass on wid canoe las' night. He's camp on de Beeg Fall, s'pose."

Barney held his canoe steady for a moment. "Went up last night, did he?"

"Oui. Tom Martin on de Beeg Horn camp he's go ver' seeck. He send for M'sieu Boyle."

"Did he go up alone?"

"Oui. He's not want nobody. Non. He's good man on de canoe."

It was an awkward situation. There was a very good chance that he should fall in with his brother somewhere on the trip, and that, at all costs, he was determined to avoid. For a minute or more he sat holding his canoe, calculating time and distances. At length he came to a resolve. He must visit the camp on the Big Horn, and he trusted his own ingenuity to avoid the meeting he dreaded.

"All right, Duprez! bon jour."

"Bo' jou' an' bon voyage. Gare a vous on de Longue Rapide. You mak' de portage hon dat rapide, n'est ce pas?"

"No, sir. No portage for me, Duprez. I'll run her."

"Prenez garde, M'sieu le Docteur," answered Duprez, shrugging his shoulders. "Maudit! Dat's ver' fas' water!"

"Don't worry about me," cried the doctor. "Just watch me take this little riffle."

"Bien!" cried Duprez, as the doctor slipped his canoe into the eddy and, with a smooth, noiseless stroke, sent her up toward the point where the stream broke into a riffle at the head of the rapid which led to the falls below. It may be that the doctor was putting a little extra weight on his paddle or that he did not exercise that unsleeping vigilance which the successful handling of the canoe demands, but whatever the cause, when the swift water struck the canoe, in spite of all his strength and skill, he soon found himself almost in midstream and going down the rapids.

"Mon Dieu!" cried Duprez, dancing in his excitement from one foot to the other. "A droit! a droit! Non! Don' try for go hup! Come out on de heddy!"

The doctor did not hear him, but, realizing the hopelessness of the frontal attack upon the rapid, he steered his canoe toward the eddy and gradually edged her into the quiet water.

"You come ver' close on de fall, mon gar'!" cried Duprez, as the doctor paddled slowly up the edge past him. "You bes' pass on de portage. Not many mans go hup on de rapids comme ca."

"All right, Duprez. I hit her too hard, that's all."

Once more the doctor moved toward the riffle. He had done the thing before and he was not to be beaten now. As the eddy bore him toward the swift water again he carefully gauged the angle of attack, so that when the nose of the canoe entered the riffle, with the trick that all canoemen know, he held her up firm against the water, and, with no very great effort, but by skilful manipulations of the force of the current, he shoved her gradually across the riffle into the slow water near the farther bank, and with a triumphant wave of the paddle disappeared around the bend.

"He's good man," said Duprez to Ben Fallows, who had taken all this time to recover from the shock of Barney's sudden appearance. "But de preechere, he's go hup dat rapide lak one oiseau las' night."

"Did, eh?" answered Ben. "Well, he didn't put in three summers on the Mattawa fer nothin'. He's a bird in the canoe, an' so's his bro—that is—the doctor there. Wonder if he'll catch him!" Ben was much excited.

"Mebbe. He's cache heem comin' down, for sure!"

Meanwhile the doctor paddled on with steady, swinging stroke, taking advantage of every eddy and cross current, stealing along the bank under the overhanging trees, sidling across swift water, lifting his canoe over rocky bits, till near mid-day he found himself at the portage below the Long Rapid.

"Guess I'll camp on the other side," he said, talking aloud after the manner of men who live much alone. He adjusted his paddles on the thwarts, hooked his tea pail to his belt, shouldered his canoe, and, taking his blanket pack in his hand, made the half mile portage without a "set down."

"There," he said, setting his canoe carefully on the grass, "my legs are better than my arms. Now we'll grub." He unpacked his tea pail, cut his bacon into strips preparatory to toasting, built a fire, drew a pail of water, threw in a handful of tea, swung it by a poplar sapling over the fire, and sat down to toast his bacon. In fifteen minutes his meal was ready—such a meal as can be had only in the mountains under the open sky and at the end of a ten-mile paddle against the stream of the Big Horn. After dinner he lit his pipe and stretched himself in the warm spring sun for half an hour's quiet think. The old restlessness was coming back upon him. His work as Medical Superintendent of the railway construction was practically completed. The medical department was thoroughly organized and the fight with disease and dirt was pretty much over so far as he was concerned. And with the easing of the strain there came fiercely upon him the soul fever that had for the last three years driven him from land to land. Had it not been that his professional honour demanded that he should hold his post and do his work, he had long ago left a district where he was kept constantly in mind of what he had so resolutely striven to forget. By the exercise of the most assiduous care he had prevented a meeting with his brother during the last three months. But in this he could not hope to be successful much longer.

Before his second pipe was smoked he had reached his resolve. "I'll pull out of this," he said, "once this Big Horn camp is cleaned up."

He packed his kit, carefully extinguished his fire, the mark of a right woodsman, slipped his canoe into the water, and set off again. His meeting with Ben Fallows seemed somehow to have brought his brother near him to-day. Everything was eloquent of those days they had spent together on the upper reaches of the Ottawa. The flowing river, the open sky, the wood, the fresh air, and, most of all, the slipping canoe spoke to him of Dick. The fierce resentment, the bitter sense of loss, that had been as a festering in his heart these years, seemed somehow to-day to have lost their stinging pain. With every lift of the paddle, with every deep breath of the fragrant spring air, with every slip of the canoe, the buoyant gladness of those old canoeing days came swelling into his heart, and ere he knew he caught himself singing, to the rhythmic swing of paddle and shoulders, the old Habitant canoe song:

"En roulant ma boule roulant."

As often as he found his body swinging to the song, so often did he sternly check himself and resolutely set another air going in his head, only to find himself in a short space swinging along again to the old song to which he and his brother had so often made their canoe slip in those great days that now seemed so far away.

"En roulant ma boule,"

sang his paddle in spite of all he could do. He could hear Dick's clear tenor from the bow. "Here, confound it! Quit it, I say!" he said aloud savagely.

"En roulant ma boule roulant,"

in a clear strong voice came the old song from around the bend. The doctor almost dropped his paddle into the stream.

"Heavens above!" he muttered. "What's that? Who's that?"

"Visa la noir, tua le blanc,

Rouli roulant, ma boule roulant,"

sang the voice. There was only one who could sing that verse just that way. With two swift heaves of the paddle he lifted his canoe into the overhanging bushes, noiselessly leaped ashore, and pulled his canoe up the bank after him. Down the river still came the song, and ever nearer.

"O fils du roi tu es mechant,

En roulant ma boule."

The Doctor: A Tale Of The Rockies | 183

The doctor cautiously parted the bushes and looked out. Close to the bank came the canoe, the singer sitting in the stern, his hat off and his face showing brown against the fair hair. How strong he looked and how handsome! Barney remembered his own boyish pride in his brother's good looks. Yes, he was handsome as ever, and yet he was different. "He's older, that's it," said the man in the bushes, breathing hard. No, it was not that altogether. There was a new gravity, a new dignity, upon the face. All at once the song ceased abruptly. The paddle was laid down and the canoe allowed to drift. The current carried her still nearer the shore. Every line in the face could now be seen. The man peering out through the bushes was conscious of a sharp thrust of pain. The lines in that grave, handsome face were lines drawn with some sharp instrument of grief. The change was not that of years, it was more. Not simply the gravity of responsible manhood, it was that, and something else. This was the change, the old careless gaiety was gone out of the face and in its place sadness, almost gloom. Straight down the river the grave, sad face was turned, but the eyes were fixed with unseeing gaze upon the flowing water. The canoe was now almost abreast the hiding place in the bushes and still drifting. Suddenly the man in the canoe, lifting up his face toward the sky, cried out, "I'll bring her back, please God, and I'll find him, too!" The watcher drew back quickly. A stick snapped under his hand. He threw himself face down and gripped his hands hard into the moss as if to hold himself there. "A deer, I guess, but I must get on," he heard a voice say, then a flip of the paddle and, looking out through the bushes, he saw the swaying figure of the man he most longed and most dreaded to see of all men in the world fast disappearing from his view. Twice he raised his hands to his lips to call after him, but even as he did so a vision held his voice, the vision of a room in a city far away, the girl he loved, and this man pressing hot kisses on her face.

"No," he said at length, grinding his foot hard into the moss, "let him go." But still with straining eyes he gazed after the swaying figure till the bend in the river hid it from his sight. Then he sank down on the deep moss bank with the air of a man who has just passed through a heavy fight.

The rest of the journey upstream was to him a weary drag. The brightness had gone out of the light, the sweetness out of the air. A burning pain filled his heart and clutched at his throat. The old sore, which his work for the sick and wounded had helped to heal over, had been torn open afresh, and the first agony of it was upon him again. He arrived at the upper camp late at night and weary. But, weary as he was, he toiled on in his fight with the typhoid outbreak till near the dawning of the day, then, snatching an hour's sleep, he set off down the Big Horn, resolved that ere a week had passed he would seek in some far land the forgetting which here was impossible to him.

Steadily the paddle swung all the long morning, but without awakening any rhythmic song in his heart. It was a heavy grind to be got through with as soon as might be. Even the slip and leap of the canoe failed to quicken his heart a single beat. It was still early in the forenoon when he reached the Long Rapid. It was a dangerous bit of water, but without a moment's considering he stood upright in his canoe and, casting a quick glance down the boiling slope, he made his choice of passage. Then getting on his knees he braced them firmly against the sides of his canoe and before he was well ready found himself in the smooth, steep pitch at the crest of that seething incline of plunging water. Two long swallowlike swoops, then a mad plunging through a succession of buffeting, curling waves that slapped viciously at him as he dashed through, a great heave or two over the humping billows at the foot, then the swirl of the eddy caught him, and lifted him clear over into the quiet water. One minute of wild thrills and the Long Rapid was left behind.

"Didn't take that quite right," he grumbled. "Ought to have lifted her sooner. Next time I'll get through dry. Next time?" he repeated. "God knows if there'll ever be any next time of that water for me." He paddled round the eddy toward the shore, intending to dump the water out of his canoe. "Hello! What in thunder is that?" Up against the driftwood, where it had been carried by the eddy, a canoe was floating bottom upwards. "God help us!" he groaned. "It's his canoe! My God! My God! Dick, boy, you're not lost! He'd run these rapids. That's his style. Oh, why didn't I call him? We could have done it together safe enough!" He stood up in his canoe and searched eagerly among the driftwood. "Dick! Dick!" he called over and over again in the wild cry of a wounded man. He paddled over to the canoe and examined it. "Ah, that's where he hit the rocks, just at the foot. But he shouldn't drown here," he continued, "unless they hit him. Let's see, where would that eddy take him?" For another anxious minute he stood observing the run of the water. "If he could keep up three minutes," he said, "he ought to strike that bar." With a few sweeps of his paddle he was on the sand bar. "Ha!" he cried. A paddle lay on the sand just above the water mark. "That never floated there." He leaped out and drew up his canoe, then, dropping on his knees, he examined the marks upon the bar. There on the sand was stamped the print of an open hand. "Now, God be thanked!" he cried, lifting his hands toward the sky, "he's reached this spot. He's somewhere on shore here." Like a dog on scent he followed up the marks to the edge of the forest where the bank rose steeply over rough rocks. Eagerly he clambered up, his eyes on the alert for any sign. He reached the top. A quick glance he threw around him, then with a low cry he rushed forward. There, stretched prone on the moss, a little pile of brushwood near him, with his match case in his hand, lay his brother. "Oh, Dick, boy!" he cried aloud, "not too late, surely!" He dropped beside the still form, turned him gently over and laid his hand upon his heart. "Too late! Too late!" he groaned. Like a madman he rushed out of the woods, flung himself down the rocky bank and toward his canoe, seized his bag and scrambled back again. Again, and more carefully, he felt for the heartbeat. He thought he could detect a feeble flutter. Hurriedly he seized his flask and, forcing open the closed teeth, poured a few drops of the whiskey down the throat. But there was no attempt to swallow. "We'll try it this way." With swift fingers he filled his syringe with the whiskey and injected it into the arm. Eagerly he waited with his hand upon the feebly fluttering heart. "My God! it's coming, I do believe!" he cried. "Now a little strychnine," he whispered. "There, that ought to help."

Once more he rushed to his canoe and brought his cooking kit and blanket. In five minutes he had a fire going and his tea pail swung over it with a little more than a cupful of water in it. In five minutes more he had half a cup of hot tea ready. By this time the heartbeat could be detected every moment growing stronger. Into the tea he poured a little of the stimulant. "If I can only get this down," he muttered, chafing at the limp hands. Once more he lifted the head, pried open the shut jaws, and tried to pour a few drops of the liquid down. After repeated attempts he succeeded. Then for the first time he observed that his hands were covered with blood. Gently he lifted the head and, examining the back of it, detected a great jagged wound. "Looks bad, bad." He felt the bone carefully and shook his head. "Fracture, I fear." Heating some more water he cleansed and dressed the wound. Half an hour more he spent in his anxious struggle, with intense activity utilizing every precious moment, when to his infinite joy and relief the life began to come slowly back. "Now I must get him to the hospital."

There were still five miles to paddle, but it was down stream and there were no portages. With swift despatch he cut a large armful of balsam boughs. With these and his blankets he made a bed in his canoe, cutting out the bow thwart, then lifting the wounded man and picking his steps with great care, he carried him to the canoe and laid him upon the balsam boughs on his right side. The moment the weight came upon that side a groan burst from the pallid lips. "Something wrong there," muttered the doctor, turning him slightly over. "Ah, shoulder out. I'll just settle this right now." By dexterous manipulation the dislocation was reduced, and at once the patient sank down upon the bed of boughs and lay quite still. A little further stimulation brought back the heart to a steadier beat. "Now, my boy," he said to himself, as he took his place kneeling in the stern of the canoe, "give her every ounce you have." For half an hour without pause, except twice to give his patient stimulant, the sweeping paddle and the swaying body kept their rhythmic swing, till down the last riffle shot the canoe and in a minute more was at the Landing.

"Duprez! Here, quick!" The doctor stood in the door of the stopping place, wet as if he had come from the river, his voice raucous and his face white.

"Mon Dieu!" exclaimed the Frenchman, "what de mattaire?"

The doctor swept a glance about the room. "Sick man," he said briefly. "I want this bed. Get your buckboard, quick." He seized the bed and carried it out before the eyes of the astonished Duprez.

Duprez was a man slow of speech but quick to act, and by the time the bed had been arranged on the buckboard he had his horse between the shafts.

"Now then, Duprez, give me a hand," said the doctor.

"Certainment. Bon Dieu! Dat's de bon preechere! Not dead, heh?"

"No," said the doctor, glancing sharply into the haggard face while he placed his fingers upon the pulse. "No. Now get on. Drive carefully, but make time."

In a few minutes they reached the road that led to the hospital, which was well graded and smooth. Duprez sent along his pony at a lope and in a short space of time they reached the door of the hospital, where they were met by Orderly Ben Fallows on duty.

"Barney! By the livin' jumpin' Jemima Jebbs!" cried Ben. "What on earth—"

But the doctor cut him short. "Ben, get the Matron, quick, and get a bed ready with warm blankets and hot water bottles. Go, man! Don't gape there!"

Still gaping his amazement, Ben skipped in through the hall and up the stair as fast as his wooden leg would allow him. He reached the office door. "Miss Margaret," he gasped, "Barney's at the door with a sick man. Wants a bed ready. We 'aven't got one—and—"

The look upon the matron's face interrupted the flow of his words. "Barney?" she said, rising slowly to her feet. "Barney?" she said again, her hand clutching the desk and holding hard. "What do you mean, Ben?" The words came slowly.

"He wants a bed for a sick man and we 'aven't—"

Margaret took a step toward him. "Ben," she said, in breathless haste, "get my room ready. But first tell Nurse Crane to come to me quick. Go, Ben."

The orderly hurried away, leaving her alone. With trembling hands she shut the door, turned toward her desk, and there stood, both hands pressed hard to her heart, fighting hard to control the tumultuous tides that surged through her heart and thundered in her ears. "Barney! Barney!" she whispered. "Oh, Barney, at last!" The blue eyes were wide open and all aglow with the tender light of her great love. "Barney," she said over and over, "my love, my love, my—ah, not mine—" A sob caught her voice. Over her desk hung a copy of Hoffman's great picture, the Christ kneeling in Gethsemane. She went close to the picture. "O Christ!" she cried brokenly, "I, too! Help me!" A knock came to the door, Nurse Crane entered. Margaret quickly turned toward her desk again.

"Dr. Bailey is at the door with a patient," said the nurse.

"Dr. Bailey?" echoed Margaret, not daring to look up, her trembling hands fluttering among the papers on the desk. "Go to him, Nurse, and get what he wants. Take my room. I shall follow in a moment."

Once more she was alone. Again she stood before the picture of the Christ, the words of the great submission ringing through the chambers of her soul. "Not my will but Thine be done." She pressed nearer the picture, gazing into that strong, patient, suffering face through the rain of welcome tears. "O Christ!" she whispered, "dear blessed Christ! I understand—now. Help me! Help me!" Then, after a pause, "Not my will! Not my will!"

The strife was past. Quietly she went to the lavatory that stood in the corner of her office, bathed her eyes, smoothed away the signs of struggle from her face, and went forth serene to her duty and her cross. In the hall she met Barney. With a quick, light step she was at his side, both hands stretched out. "Barney!" "Margaret!" was all they said. For a moment or two Barney stood holding her hands, gazing without a word into the sweet face, so pale, so beautiful, so serenely strong. Twice he essayed to speak, but the words choked in his throat. Turning abruptly away he pointed to the figure under the grey blanket on the camp bed.

"I've brought—you—Dick," at last he said hoarsely.

"Dick! Hurt? Not—" She halted before the dreaded word.

"No, injured. Badly, I fear, but I hope—"

"The room is ready," said Nurse Crane.

At once all other thoughts and emotions gave way to the immediate demands of their common duty. They had work to do, and they had trained themselves to obey without thought of self that Divine call to serve the suffering. Together they toiled at their work, Margaret noting with delighted wonder the quick fingers and the finished skill that cleansed and probed and dressed the wound in the head and made thorough examination for other injury or ill, Barney keenly conscious of the efficiency of the silent, steady helper at his side whose quick eye and hand anticipated his every want. At length their work was done and they stood looking down upon the haggard face.

"He is resting now," said Barney, in a low voice. "The fracture is not serious, I think."

"Poor Dick," said Margaret, passing her hand over his brow.

At her touch and voice Dick moaned and opened his eyes. Barney quickly stepped back out of sight. For a moment or two the eyes wandered about the room, then rested on Margaret's face in a troubled, inquiring gaze.

"What is it, Dick, dear?" said Margaret, bending over him.

For answer his hand began to move feebly toward his breast as if seeking something.

"I know. The letter, Dick?" A look of intelligence lighted the eye. "That's all right, Dick. I shall get it to Barney. Barney is here, you know."

A hand grasped her arm. "Hush!" said Barney in stern command. "Say nothing about me." But she heeded him not. For a moment longer the sick man's gaze lingered on her face. A faint smile of content overspread the drawn features, then the look of intelligence faded and the eyes closed wearily.

"Come," said Barney, moving toward the door, "he is better quiet."

Leaving the nurse in charge, they went together toward the office.

"Where did you find him?" asked Margaret as she gave Barney a seat. Then Barney told her the story of how he had chanced upon the canoe and had discovered Dick lying insensible in the woods.

"It was God's leading, Barney," said Margaret gently, when the story was done; but to this he made no reply. "Is there serious danger, do you think?" she inquired in an anxious voice.

"He will recover," replied Barney. "All he requires is careful nursing, and that you can give him. I shall wait till to-morrow."

"To-morrow? And then?"

"I am leaving this country next week."

"Leaving the country? And why?"

"My work here is done."

"Surely there is much yet to do, and you have just begun to do such great things. Why should you leave now?"

Barney waited a few moments in silence as if pondering an answer. "Margaret, I must go," he finally burst forth. "You know I must go. I can't live within touch of him and forget!"

"Forgive, you mean, Barney."

"Well, forgive, if you like," he replied sullenly.

"Barney," replied Margaret earnestly, "this is unworthy of you, and in the face of God's mercy to-day how can you hold resentment in your heart?"

"How can I? God knows, or the Devil. For three years I have fought it, but it is there. It is there!" He struck his hand hard upon his breast. "I can't forget that he ruined my life! But for him I believe in my soul I should have won—her to me! At a critical moment he came in and ruined—"

"Barney! Barney, listen to me!" cried Margaret impetuously.

Barney sprang to his feet.

"No, you must listen to me. Sit down." Barney obeyed her word and sat down. "Now, hear me, and hear me fairly. I am not going to say that Dick was free from blame, nor was Iola either. Whose was the greater I can't tell. They were both young and, to a certain extent, inexperienced in the ways of life. Circumstances threw them much together and on terms of almost brotherly and sisterly intimacy. That was a mistake. They ignored conventions that can never be safely ignored. Just at that time Dick's life was made hard for him. His Church had rejected him."

"Rejected him?"

"Yes, rejected him. He was refused license by the Presbytery, was branded as a heretic and outcast from work." Margaret's voice grew bitter. "Do you wonder that he grew hard? Perhaps they could not help it—I can't say—but he grew hard. Yes, and worse than that, grew away from his faith, from his friends, and from those things that keep men straight and strong. He grew weak. The hour of temptation came upon him. You and I have seen enough of that side of life to know what that means. He broke faith with you—no, not with you. He was loyal to you, but he broke faith with himself and with her. For a single moment, that moment at which you appeared, he yielded to passion, and bitterly, terribly, has he suffered since that moment. How terribly no one knows. He has tried to find you, but you would not be found. He wronged you, Barney, but you have made him and all of us suffer much." The voice that had gone on so bravely and so firmly here suddenly trembled and broke.

"Made you suffer!" cried Barney, with bitter scorn. "How can you speak of suffering? You have everything! I have lost all!"

"Everything?" echoed Margaret faintly. "Ah, Barney, how little you know! But, no matter, God has brought you together and you must not do this wicked thing. You must not continue to break our hearts."

"Break your hearts? Margaret, what's the use of words? I had a heart, too, and a brother whom I loved and trusted as myself, yes, more than myself, and—I had—Iola. All I have lost. My work satisfies me for a few months, but try as I can this awful thing hunts me down and drives me mad. There is nothing in life left for me. And there might have been much but for—"

"Stop, Barney!" cried Margaret impulsively. "There is much still left for you. God is good. How much better than we. You can't forgive a fellow-sinner. Oh, shame! But He forgives and forgets, and surely you ought to try—"

"Try! Try! Heavens above, Margaret! Try! Do you think I haven't tried? That thing is there! there!" smiting on his breast again. "Can you tell me how to rid myself of it?"

"Yes, Barney, I think I can tell you. God's great goodness will do this for you. Listen," she said, putting up her hand to stay his words, "God is bringing a great joy to you to shame you and to soften you. Here, read this." She handed him Iola's letter, went to the window, and stood with her back to him, looking out upon the great sweeping valley below.

"Margaret!" The hoarse voice called her back to him. His hard, proud, sullen reserve was shattered, gone. His lips were quivering, his hands trembling. The girl was touched to the heart. "Margaret," he cried brokenly, "what does this mean?" He was terribly shaken.

"It means that she wants you, that she needs you. Dick was going to-morrow to bring her back to you, Barney. That was his one desire."

"To bring her to me? To bring her back to me? Dick? Dear old boy! and I—Oh, Margaret!" He put his trembling hands out to her. "Forgive me! God forgive me! Poor Dick! I'll see him!" He started toward the door. "No, not how," he cried, striving in vain to control himself. "I am mad! mad! For three long years I have carried this cursed thing in my heart! It's gone! It's gone, Margaret! Do you hear? It's gone!" He was shouting aloud. "I feel right toward Dick, my brother!"

"Hush, Barney dear," said the girl, tears running down her face, "you will wake him."

"Yes, yes," he cried, in an eager whisper, "I'll be careful. Poor old boy, he has suffered, too. Dear old Dick! And she wants me! I'll go to-night! Yes, to-night! What's the date?" He tore at the envelope with trembling hands. The letter dropped to the floor. Margaret caught it up and opened it for him. "A month ago and more! Yes, I'll go to-night. Oh, Margaret, what a blasted fool I am! I can't get myself in hand." Suddenly he threw himself into his chair. "Here!" he ground out between his teeth, "get quiet!" He sat for a few moments absolutely still, gathering strength to command himself. At length he got himself in hand. "No," he said in a quiet voice, "I shall not go tonight. I shall wait till Dick is better. Just now he must be kept quiet. In the morning I expect to see him very much himself. We can only wait and see."

Through the night they waited, Barney struggling mightily to hold himself in perfect control, Margaret quietly doing what was to be done, her whole spirit breathing of that self-forgetting love which finds its highest joy in the joy of another. At the break of day the nurse came to the door and found them still waiting.

"Mr. Boyle is awake and is asking for you, Miss Robertson."

"Let me go to him," cried Barney. "Don't fear." His voice was still vibrating, but his manner was calm and steady. He was master of himself again.

"Yes," said Margaret, "go to him." Then as the door closed she stood once more before the Gethsemane scene. "Thank God, thank God," she said softly, "for them the pain is over."

For half an hour she waited and then went up to the sickroom. She opened the door softly, went in and stood gazing till her eyes grew dim.

On the pillow, face down, Barney's head lay close to Dick's, whose arm was thrown about his brother's neck, and on Dick's face shone a look of rapturous peace. As Margaret moved to leave the room Dick called her in a voice faint, but full of joy.

"Margaret," he said, a smile breaking like light through a dark cloud, "my head was broken, but I'd have all the bones in my body broken, just to have Barney set them. We're all right, eh, boy?"

Slowly Barney raised his face, tear-marked, worn, but radiant with a peace it had not known for many a day. "Yes, old chap," he said in a voice still tremulous in spite of all his self-command, "we're right again, and, please God, we'll keep so."

XXI
TO WHOM HE FORGAVE MOST

For three days Dick made steady progress toward health, but his progress was slow. Any mental effort produced severe pain in his head and sufficed to raise his temperature several points. As he gained in strength and became more and more clear in his thinking his anxiety in regard to his work began to increase. His congregations would be waiting him on Sunday, and he could not bear to think of their being disappointed. With no small effort had he gathered them together, and a single failure on his part he knew would have disastrous effect upon the attendance. He was especially concerned about the service at Bull Crossing, which was at once the point where the work was the most difficult, and, at the present juncture, most encouraging. Under his instructions Barney sought to secure a substitute for the service at Bull Crossing, but without result. Preachers were scarce in that country and every preacher had more work in sight than he could overtake. And so Dick fretted and wrought himself into a fever, until the doctor took him sternly to task.

"I don't see that it's your business to worry, Dick," he said. "I suppose you consider yourself as working under orders, and it is your belief, isn't it, that the One who gives the orders is the One who has laid you down here?"

"That's true," said Dick wearily, "but there's the people. A lot of them come a long way. It's been hard to get them together, and I hate to disappoint them."

"Well, we'll get someone," replied Barney. "We're a pretty hard combination to beat, aren't we, Margaret? There will be a man to take the service at Bull Crossing if I have to take it myself—a desperate resort, indeed."

"Why not, Barney?" asked Dick. "You could do it well."

"What? Did you ever hear me talk? I can talk a little with my fingers, but my tongue is unconscionably slow."

"There was a man once slow of speech," replied Dick quietly, "but he was given a message and he led a nation into freedom."

Barney nodded. "I remember him. But he could do things."

"No," answered Dick, "but he believed God could do things."

"Perhaps so. That was rather long ago."

"With God," replied Dick earnestly, "there is no such thing as long ago."

"All the same," said Barney, "I guess these things don't happen now."

"I believe they happen," replied his brother, "where God finds a man who will take his life in his hand and go."

"Well, I don't know about that," replied Barney, "but I do know that you must quit talking and sleep. Now, hear me, drop that meeting out of your mind. I'll look after it."

But Saturday came and, in spite of every effort on Barney's part, he found no one for the service at Bull Crossing next day. There was still a slight hope that one of the officials of the congregation would consent to be a stop-gap for the day.

"I guess I'll have to take that service myself, Margaret," said Barney laughingly. "Wouldn't the crowd stare? They'd hear the sermon of their lives."

"It would be a good sermon, Barney," replied Margaret quietly. "And why should you not say something to the men?"

"Nonsense, Margaret!" cried Barney impatiently. "You know the thing is utterly absurd. What sort of man am I to preach? A gambler, a swearer, and generally bad. They all know me."

"They know only a part of you, Barney," said Margaret gently. "God knows all of you, and whatever you have been you are no gambler today, and you are not a bad man."

"No," replied Barney slowly, "I am no gambler, nor will I ever be again. But I have been a hard, bad man. For three years I carried hate in my heart. I could not forgive and didn't want to be forgiven. And that, I believe, was the cause of all my badness. But—somehow—I don't deserve it—but I've been awfully well treated. I deserved hell, but I've got a promise of heaven. And I'd be glad to do something for—" He paused abruptly.

"There, you've got your sermon, Barney," said Margaret.

"What do you mean?"

"'Forgive and ye shall be forgiven.'"

"It's the sermon someone wants to preach to me, but it's not for me to preach. The thing is preposterous. I'll get one of those fellows at the Crossing to take the meeting."

On Saturday evening Dick again reverted to the subject.

"I'm not anxious, Barney," he said, "but who's going to take the meeting to-morrow night at Bull Crossing?"

"Now, look here," said Barney, "Monday morning you'll hear all about it. Meantime, don't ask questions. Margaret and I are responsible, and that ought to be enough. You never knew her to fail."

"No, nor you, Barney," said Dick, sinking back with a sigh of satisfaction. "I know it will be all right. Are you going down to-morrow evening?" he inquired, turning to Margaret.

"I?" exclaimed Margaret. "What would I do?"

"Of course you are going. It will do you a lot of good," said Barney. "You may have to preach yourself or hold my coat while I go in."

A sudden gleam of joy in the eyes, a flush of red upon the cheek, and the quick following pallor told Dick the thoughts that rushed through Margaret's heart.

"Yes," said Dick gravely, "you will go down, too, Margaret. It will do you good, and I don't need you here."

Many anxious days had Barney passed in his life, but never had he found himself so utterly blocked by unmanageable circumstances and uncompromising facts as he found facing him that Sunday morning. He confided his difficulty to Tommy Tate, whom he had found in "Mexico's" saloon toning up his system after his long illness, and whom he had straightway carried off with him.

"I guess it's either you or me, Tommy."

"Bedad, it's yersilf that c'd do that same, an' divil a wan av the bhoys will 'Mexico' git this night, wance the news gits about."

"Don't talk rot, Tommy," said Barney angrily, for the chance of his being forced to take his brother's place, which all along had seemed to be extremely remote, had come appreciably nearer. With the energy of desperation he spent the hours of the afternoon visiting, explaining, urging, cajoling, threatening anyone of the members or adherents of the congregation at Bull Crossing in whom might be supposed to dwell the faintest echo of the spirit of the preacher. One after another, however, those upon whom he had built his hopes failed him. One was out of town, another he found sick in bed, and a third refused point blank to consider the request, so that within a few minutes of the hour of service he found himself without a preacher and wholly desperate, and for the first time he seriously faced the possibility of having to take the service himself. He returned to the shack of one of his brother's parishioners, where Margaret was staying, and abruptly announced to her his failure.

"Can't get a soul, and of course I can't do it, Margaret. You know, I can't," he repeated, in answer to the look upon her face. "Why, it was only last week I fleeced 'Mexico' out of a couple of hundred. He would give a good deal more to get even. The crowd would hoot me out of the building. Not that I care for that"—the long jaws came hard together—"but it's just too ghastly to think of."

"It isn't so very terrible, Barney," said Margaret, her voice and eyes uniting in earnest persuasion. "You are not the man you were last week. You know you are not. You are quite different, and you will be different all your life. A great change has come to you. What made the change? You know it was God's great mercy that took the bitterness out of your heart and that changed everything. Can't you tell them this?"

"Tell them that, Margaret? Great Heavens! Could I tell them that? What would they say?"

"Barney," asked Margaret, "you are not afraid of them? You are not ashamed to tell what you owe to God?"

Afraid? It was an ugly word for Barney to swallow. No, he was not afraid, but his native diffidence, intensified by these recent years of self-repression and self-absorption, had made all speech difficult to him, but more especially speech that revealed the deeper movements of his soul.

"No, Margaret, I'm not afraid," he said slowly. "But I'd rather have them take the flesh off that arm bit by bit than get up and speak to them. I'd have to tell them the truth, don't you see, Margaret? How can I do that?"

"All that you say must be the truth, Barney, of course," she replied. "But you will tell them just what you will."

With these words she turned away, leaving him silent and fighting a desperate fight. His word passed to his brother must be kept. But soon a deeper issue began to emerge. His honour was involved. His sense of loyalty was touched. He knew himself to be a different man from the man who, last week, in "Mexico's" saloon, had beaten his old antagonist at the old game. His consciousness of himself, of his life purposes, of his outlook, of his deepest emotions, was altogether a different consciousness. And more than all, that haunting, pursuing restlessness was gone and, in its place, a deep peace possessed him. The process by which this had been achieved he could not explain, but the result was undeniable, and it was due, he knew, to an influence the source of which he frankly acknowledged to be external to himself. The words of the beaten and confounded pagan magic-workers came to him, "This is the finger of God." He could not deny it. Why should he wish to hide it? It became clear to him, in these few minutes of intense soul activity, that there was a demand being made upon him as a man of truth and honour, and as the struggle deepened in his soul and the possibility of his refusing the demand presented itself to his mind, there flashed in upon him the picture of a man standing in the midst of enemies, the flickering firelight showing his face vacillating, terror-stricken, hunted. From the trembling lips of the man he heard the words of base denial, "I know not the man," and in his heart there rose a cry, "O Christ! shall I do this?" "No," came the answer, strong and clear, from his lips, "I will not do this thing, so help me God."

Margaret turned quickly around and looked at him in dismay. "You won't?" she said faintly.

"I'll take the service," he replied, setting the long jaws firmly together. And with that they went forth to the hall.

They found the place crowded far beyond its capacity, for through Tommy Tate it had been noised abroad that Dr. Bailey was to preach. There were wild rumors, too, that the doctor had "got religion," although "Mexico" and his friends scouted the idea as utterly impossible.

"He ain't the kind. He's got too much nerve," was "Mexico's" verdict, given with a full accompaniment of finished profanity.

Tommy's evidence, however, was strong enough to create a profound impression and to awaken an expectation that rose to fever pitch when Barney and Margaret made their way through the crowds and took their places, Margaret at the organ, which Dick usually played himself, and Barney at the table upon which were the Bible and the Hymn-book. His face wore the impenetrable, death-like mark which had so often baffled "Mexico" and his gang over the poker table. It fascinated "Mexico" now. All the years of his wicked manhood "Mexico" had, on principle, avoided anything in the shape of a religious meeting, but to-day the attraction of a poker player preaching proved irresistible. It was with no small surprise that the crowd saw "Mexico," with two or three of his gang, make their way toward the front to the only seats left vacant.

When it became evident beyond dispute that his old-time enemy was to take the preacher's place, "Mexico" leaned over to his pal, "Peachy" Bud, who sat between him and Tommy Tate, and muttered in an undertone audible to those in his immediate neighbourhood, "It's his old game. He's runnin' a blank bluff. He ain't got the cards."

But painful experience shook "Peachy's" confidence in his friend's judgment on this particular point, and he only ventured to reply, "He's got the lead." "Peachy" preferred to await developments.

The opening hymn was sung with the hearty fervour that marks the musical part of any religious service in the West. But there was in the voices that curious thrill that is at once the indication and the quickening of intense excitement.

"This here'll show what's in his hand," said "Peachy," when the moment for prayer arrived. "Peachy" was not unfamiliar with religious services, and had, with unusual keenness of observation, noted that when a man undertook to pray he must, if he be true, reveal the soul within him.

"Mexico" grunted a dubious affirmative. But "Peachy" was disappointed, for in a voice reverent, but unimpassioned, the preacher for the day led the people's devotions, using the great words taught those men long ago who knew not how to pray, "Our Father who art in Heaven."

"Blanked if he ain't bluffed again! We've got to wait till he begins to shoot, I guess," said "Peachy," mixing his figures.

The lesson was the parable of the unforgiving debtor and the parallel passage containing the matchless story of the sinful woman and the proud Pharisee. In the reading of these lessons the voice, which had hitherto carried the strident note of nervousness, mellowed into rich and subduing fulness. The men listened with that hushed attention that they give when words are getting to the heart. The utter simplicity of the reader's manner, the dignity of his bearing, the quiet strength that showed itself in every tone, and the undercurrent of emotion that made the voice vibrate like a stringed instrument, all these, with the marvellous authoritative tenderness of the great utterance on a theme so closely touching their daily experience, gripped these men and held them in complete thrall.

When the reading was done the doctor stood for some moments looking his audience quietly in the face. He knew them all, men from the camps and the line, men from the hills and mining claims, men from the saloons and the gambling hells. Many he had treated professionally, some he had himself nursed back to health, others he had rescued from those desperate moods that end in death. Others again—and these not a few—he had "cleaned out" at poker or "Black Jack." But to all of them he was "white." Not so to himself. It was a very humble man and a very penitent, that stood looking them in the face. His first words were a confession.

"I am not worthy to stand here before you," he began, in a low, clear tone, "God knows, you know, and I know. I am here for two reasons: one is that I promised my brother, the Reverend Richard Boyle"—here a gasp of surprise was audible from one and another in the audience—"a man you know to be a good man, better than ever I can hope to be."

"Durned if he is!" grunted "Peachy" to "Mexico." "Ain't in the same bunch!"

"An' that's thrue fer ye," answered Tommy. But "Mexico" paid no heed to these remarks. He was staring at the speaker with the look of a man wholly bewildered.

"And the other reason is," continued, the doctor, "that I have something which I think it fair to tell you men. Like a lot of you, I have carried a name that is not my own." Here significant looks were gravely exchanged. "They gave it to me by mistake when I reached the Pass. I didn't care much at that time about names or anything else, so I let it go. There are times in a fellow's life when he's not unwilling to forget his name. My name is Boyle." And then, in sentences simple, clean-cut, and terse, he told of his boyhood days, the Old Mill, the two boys growing up together, their love for and their loyalty to each other, their struggles and their success. Then came a pause. The speaker had obviously come to a difficult spot in his story. The men waited in earnest, grave, and deeply moved expectation. "At that time a great calamity came to me—no matter what—and it threw me clear off my balance. I lost my head and lost my nerve, and just then—" again the speaker paused, as if to gather strength to continue—"and just then my brother did me a wrong. Not being in a condition to judge fairly, I magnified the wrong a thousand-fold and I tried to tear my brother out of my heart. I could not and I would not forgive him, and I couldn't cease to love him. I lived a life of misery, misery so great that it drove me from everything in earth that I held dear, and for three years I went steadily down from bad to worse. I came to the Crow's Nest a year and a half ago. My life since then most of you know well."

"Bedad we do! An' Hivin bliss ye!" burst forth Tommy Tate, who had found the greatest difficulty in controlling his emotions of indignation and grief during the doctor's self-condemnatory tale. At Tommy's words a quiet thrill ran through the crowd, for few men of those present but held the doctor in affectionate esteem. The sins of which he was conscious and which humiliated him before them were, in their estimation, but trivial.

For a moment the speaker was thrown off his track by Tommy's outburst, but, recovering himself, he went on. "It would be wrong to say that my life here has been all bad. I have been able to serve many of you, but my work has done far more for me than it has for you. But for it I should have long ago gone down out of sight. I confess that it has been a hard fight for me, an awful fight, to stay at my work, but the day that I heard that my brother was your missionary brought me the hardest fight I had had for many a day. I wanted to get away from the past. For nearly four years I had been carrying round a heart with hell in it. I had begun to forget a little, but that day it all came back. This week I met my brother. I found him dying, almost dead, up in the Big Horn Valley. That morning my heart carried hell in it. To-day it is like what I think heaven must be." As he spoke these words a light broke over his face, and again he stood silent, striving to regain control of his voice.

"Blanked if he don't hold the cards!" said "Mexico" in a thick voice to "Peachy" Budd.

"Full flush," answered "Peachy."

"Mexico" was in the grasp of the elemental emotions of his untutored nature. His swarthy face was twisted like the face of a man in torture. His black eyes were gleaming like two fires from under his shaggy eyebrows.

"How it came about," continued the doctor, in a quiet, even tone, "I am not going to tell. But this I am going to say, I know it was God's great mercy, His great kindness it was that took the hate out of my heart. I forgave my brother that day—and—God forgave me. That's all there is to it. It's the biggest thing that has ever come to me. I have got my brother back just as when we were little chaps at the Old Mill." A sudden choke caught the speaker's voice. The firm lips quivered and the strong hands writhed themselves in a mighty effort to master the emotions surging through his soul.

Tommy Tate was openly sniffling and wiping his eyes. "Peachy" Budd was swearing audibly his emotions, but, most of all, "Mexico's" swarthy face betrayed the intensity of his feelings. He had grasped the back of the seat before him and was leaning toward the speaker as if held under an hypnotic spell.

Again the doctor, getting his voice steady, went on. "I have just a word more to say. I would like to give credit for this that happened to me to the One we have been reading about this afternoon, and I do so with all my heart. I came near being coward enough and mean enough to go away without owning this up before you. How He did it, I do not pretend to know. I'm not a preacher. But He did it, and that's what chiefly concerns me. And what He did for me I guess He can do for any of you. And now I've got to square up some things. 'Mexico'—" At the sound of his name "Mexico" started violently and, involuntarily, his hand went, with a quick motion, toward his hip—"I've taken a lot from you. I'd like to pay it back." The voice was humble, earnest, kind.

"Mexico," taken by surprise, shifted his tobacco to the other side of his mouth, stood up and drawled out, "Haow? Me? Pay me back? Blanked if you do! It was a squar' deal, wa'n't it?"

"Yes, I played fair, 'Mexico,' but—"

"Then go to hell!" "Mexico's" tone was not at all unfriendly, but his vocabulary was limited, and he was evidently deeply stirred. "We're squar' an'—an' blanked if I don't believe ye're white! Put it thar!" With a single stride "Mexico" was over the seat that separated him from the platform and reached out his hand. The doctor took it in a hard grip.

"Look here, men," he said, when "Mexico" had resumed his seat, "I've got to do something with this money. I've got at least five thousand that don't belong to me."

"'Tain't ours," called a voice.

"Men," continued the doctor, "I'm starting out on a new track. I want to straighten out the past all I can. I can't keep this money. I'd feel like a thief."

But such an ethical code was beyond the men, and one and all protested to each other, in tones that were quite audible over the hall and with anathemas of more or less terrible import, that the money was not theirs and that they would not touch it. The doctor listened for a minute or more and then, with the manner of one closing a discussion, he said, "All right. If you won't help me I'll have to find some way, myself, of straightening this up. This is all I have to say. I'm no preacher and I'm not any better than the rest of you, but I'd like to be a great deal better man than I am, and, with God's help, I'm going to try. That's my religion."

And with these words he sat down, leaving the people still staring at him and waiting for something in the way of closing exercises to what must have been the most extraordinary religious service in all their experience. Softly, Margaret began to play the old hymn, "Nearer, My God, to Thee!" The men, accepting it as a signal, rose to their feet and began to sing, and with these great words of aspiration ringing through their hearts they passed out into the night.

Among the many who lingered to speak to the doctor were "Mexico," "Peachy," and, of course, his faithful follower, Tommy Tate. "Mexico" drew him off to one corner.

"Say, pard," he began, "you've done me up many a time before, but blanked if yeh haven't hit me this time the worst yet! When you was talkin' about them two little chaps—" here "Mexico's" hard face began to work and his voice to quiver—"you put the knife right in here. I had a brother once," he continued in a husky voice. "I wish to God someone had choked the blank nonsense out of me, for I done him a wrong an' I wasn't man enough to own up. An' that's what started me in all this hell business I've been chasin' ever since."

The doctor took him by the arm and walked him out of the room. "Take Miss Robertson home," he said to Tommy as he passed.

An hour later he appeared, pale and as nearly exhausted as his iron nerve and muscle would allow him to be. "I say, Margaret, this thing is wonderful! There's no explaining it by any physical or mental law that I know." Then, after a pause, he added, with an odd thrill of tenderness in his voice, "I believe we shall hear good things of 'Mexico' yet."

And so they did, but that is another tale.

XXII
THE HEART'S REST

There is no sweeter spot in all the west Highlands of Scotland than the valley that runs back from that far penetrating arm of the sea, Loch Fyne, to Craigraven. There, after a succession of wild and gloomy glens, one comes upon a sweet little valley, sheltered from the east and north winds and open to the warm western sea and to the long sunny days of summer. It is a valley full of balmy airs, fragrant with the scents of sea and heather, and shut in from the roar and rush of the great world, just over the ragged rim of the craggy hills that guard it. A veritable heaven on earth for the nerve-racked and brain-wearied, for the heart-sick and soul-burdened; for it was the pleasure of the lady of Ruthven Hall, a kindly, homely mansion house that stood at the valley's head, to bring hither such of her friends or her friends' friends as needed the healing that soft airs and sunny days, with long quiet hours filled with love that understands, can give.

To this spot Lady Ruthven herself had been brought, a girl fresh from the shelter of her English home, the bride of Sir Hector Ruthven; and here for five happy summers they had come from the strenuous life of Diplomatic Service to find rest. Here, too, came Sir Hector, when his work was done, still a young man, to rest under the yews in the little churchyard near the Hall, leaving his lady with her little daughter and her infant son to administer his vast estates. After the first sharp grief had passed, Lady Ruthven took up her burden and, with patient courage, bore it for the sake of the dead first, and then for the sake of the living. Round her son, growing into sturdy young manhood, her heart's roots wound themselves, striking deep into his life, till one day he, too, was laid beneath the yew trees in the churchyard. From that deep shadow she came forth, bearing her cross of service to her kind, to live a life fragrant with the airs of Heaven, in fellowship with Him who, for love of man, daily gave Himself to die.

It was through her nephew, Alan Ruthven, artist and poet, pure of heart and clean of life, that Jack Charrington came to know Ruthven Hall and its dwellers. The young men first met in London, and later in Edinburgh, where both were pursuing their professions with a devotion that did not forbid attention to sundry social duties, or prevent them from taking long walks over the Lammermuirs on Saturday afternoons. To Ruthven Hall, Alan was permitted to bring his young Canadian friend, who, he was secretly convinced, stood sorely in need of just such benediction as his saintly aunt could bestow. The day of Jack Charrington's coming to Ruthven Hall was the birthday of his better life, when he had a vision of his profession in the light of that great ministry to the world's sick and wounded and weary by Him who came to the world "to heal." In another sense, too, it was for him the beginning of days, for it was the day on which his eyes first fell upon sunny, saucy Maisie Ruthven. Thenceforth the orbit of Jack's life swung round Ruthven Hall, and thus it fell that when, on one of his visits to the great metropolis, he found Iola exhausted after her season's triumphs and forbidden to sing again for a year, and so well-nigh heart-broken, he bethought him of the little valley of rest in the far western Highlands. Straightway he confided to Lady Ruthven his concern for his co-patriot and friend, giving as much of her story as he thought it well that both Lady Ruthven and her daughter should know. Hence, when they went north to their Highland valley again, they carried with them Iola, to be rested and nursed, and to be healed in heart, too, if that could be. For Lady Ruthven, with her eyes made keen by grief and love, had not been long in discovering that, with Iola, the deeper sickness was that which no physician's medicine can reach.

Through the early summer they waited for signs of returning health to their guest, but neither the most watchful care nor the most tender nursing could keep the strength from gradually waning.

"She is fretting her heart out. That's the chief cause of this terrible restlessness," said Alan Ruthven to his friend, who was visiting at the Hall.

"Partly," replied Charrington gloomily, "but not altogether, I fear. This restlessness is symptomatic. We must have Bruce Fraser out again. But if we only could get track of Boyle it would greatly help. She wrote yesterday to her great friend, Miss Robertson, who, more than anyone, has kept in touch with him."

"Charrington," inquired Alan hesitatingly, "would you advise that he should be looked up? Of course, you credit me with being perfectly disinterested. I gave up my dream some time ago, you know."

"Oh, certainly, Ruthven, I know, but—"

"You fear I'm prejudiced. Well, I confess I am. I hate to think of a girl like that having anything to do with a man unworthy of her, as from what you have told me of him he must be."

The Doctor: A Tale Of The Rockies | 205

"Unworthy!" cried Jack. "Did I ever call him unworthy? It depends upon what you mean. He gambles. He has terrific passions; but he's a man through and through, and he's clean and honourable."

"Ah," said Ruthven, drawing a deep breath, "then would to Heaven she could find him! For this fretting is like a fever in her bones."

"At present, we can only wait for an answer to her letter."

And so they waited, each one of the little group vying with the other in providing interest and amusement for the weary, restless, fevered girl. Often, at the first, the old impatience would break out, mostly in her talk with Charrington, at rare times to her hostess, too, but at such times followed by quick penitence.

"Dear Lady Ruthven," she said one day after one of her little outbreaks, "I wish I were like you. You are so sweetly good and so perfectly self-controlled. Even I cannot wear out your patience. You must have been born good and sweet."

For a few moments Lady Ruthven was silent, her mind going back swiftly to long gone years. "No, dear," she said gently; "I have much to be thankful for. It was a hard lesson and slowly learned, but He was patient and bore long with me. And He is still bearing."

"Tell me how you learned," asked Iola timidly, and then Lady Ruthven told her life story, without tears, without repinings, while Iola wondered. That story Iola never forgot, and the influence of it never departed from her. Never were the days quite so bad again, but every day while she struggled to subdue her impatience even in thought, she kept looking for word from across the sea with a longing so intense that all in the house came to share it with her.

"Oh! if we only knew where to get him!" groaned Jack Charrington to her one day, for to Jack, who was the only link with her happy past, she had opened her heart. "Why does he keep away?" he added bitterly.

"It is my fault, Jack," she replied. "He is not to blame. No one is to blame but me. But he will come some day. I feel sure he will come, I only hope he may be in time. He would greatly grieve if—"

"Hush, Iola. Don't say it. I can't bear to have you say it. You are getting better. Why, you walked out yesterday quite smartly."

"Some days I am so well," she replied, unwilling to grieve him. "I would like him to see me first on one of my good days. I am sure to hear soon now."

They had hardly turned to enter the house when they saw a messenger wearing the uniform of the Telegraph Department approaching.

"Oh, Jack!" she cried, "there it is!"

"Come, Iola," said Jack, almost sternly, "come in and sit down." So saying, he brought her into the library and made her recline upon the couch, in that sunny room near the window where many of her waking hours were spent.

It was Alan who took the message. They all followed him into the library. "Shall I open it?" he asked, with an anxious look at Iola.

"Yes," she said faintly, laying both hands upon her heart.

Lady Ruthven came to her side. "Iola, darling," she said, taking both her hands in hers, "it is good to feel that God's arms are about us always."

"Yes, dear Lady Ruthven," replied the girl, regaining her composure; "I'm learning. I'm not afraid."

Opening, Alan read the message, smiled, and handed it to her. She read the slip, handed it to Jack, closed her eyes, and, smiling, lay back upon her couch. "God is good," she whispered, as Lady Ruthven bent over her. "You were right. Teach me how to trust Him better."

"Are you all right, Iola?" said Jack, anxiously feeling her pulse.

"Quite right, Jack, dear," she said.

"Then hooray!" cried Jack, starting up. "Let's see, 'Coming Silurian seventh. Barney.'" he read aloud. "The seventh was yesterday. Six days. She'll be in on the thirteenth. Ought to be here by Monday at latest."

"Saturday, Jack," said Iola, opening her eyes.

"Well, we'll plan for Monday. We're not going to be disappointed. Meantime, you're not to fret." And he frowned sternly down upon her.

"Fret?" she cried, looking up brightly. "Never more, Jack. I shall never fret again in all my life. I'm going to build up for these five days, every hour, every minute. I want Barney to see me well."

It was a marvel to all the house how she kept her word. Every hour, every minute, she appeared to gain strength. She ate with relish and slept like a child. The old feverish restlessness left her, and she laid aside many of her invalid ways.

"You are going down to Glasgow to-morrow, I suppose, Charrington?" said Alan on Thursday, after the Silurian had been reported.

"I've just been thinking," replied Jack, with careful deliberation, "that it would be almost better you should go, Ruthven. You see you're the man of the house, and it would be easier for a stranger to tell him."

"Come, Charrington," replied his friend, "you don't often play the coward. You've simply got to go. But why should you tell?"

"Tell? He'll see it in my face. That last report of Bruce Fraser's he would read in my eyes. I see the ghastly words yet, 'Quite hopeless. Heart seriously involved. Cannot be long delayed.' I say, old man, I suppose I ought to go, but you've got to come along and make talk. I'll simply blubber right out when I see him. You know I'm awfully fond of the old boy."

"I say, Charrington, I've got it! Take my aunt with you."

Jack gasped. "By Jove! The very thing! It's rough on her, but she's the saintly kind that delights to bear other people's burdens."

And so it was arranged that Jack and Lady Ruthven should meet the boat and bring Barney, with all speed, to Ruthven Hall.

At the Silurian's gangway Jack received his friend with outstretched hands, crying, "Barney, old boy, we're glad to see you! Here, let me present you to Lady Ruthven, at whose house Iola is staying." With feverish haste he hurried Barney through the crowds, bustling hither and thither about his luggage and giving himself not a moment for conversation till they were seated in the first-class apartment carriage that was to carry them to Craigraven. But they had hardly got settled in their places when the conversation, in spite of all Jack's efforts, dropped to silence.

"You have bad news for me," said Barney, looking Lady Ruthven steadily in the face. "Has anything happened?"

"No, Dr. Boyle," replied Lady Ruthven, a little more quickly than was her wont, "but—" and here she paused, shrinking from delivering the mortal stab, "but we are anxious about our dear Iola."

"Tell me the worst, Lady Ruthven," said Barney.

"That is all. We are very anxious. It is her lungs chiefly and her heart. But she is very bright and very hopeful. It is better she should be kept so."

Barney listened with face growing grey, his eyes looking out of their deep sockets with the piteous, mute appeal of an animal stricken to death. He moistened his lips and tried to speak, but, failing, kept his eyes fixed on Lady Ruthven's face as if seeking relief. Charrington turned his head away.

"We feel thankful for her great courage," said Lady Ruthven, in her sweet, calm voice, "and for her peace of mind."

At last Barney found his voice. "Does she suspect anything?" he asked hoarsely.

"I think she must, but she has said nothing. She has been eager all summer to get back to her home—to you—to those she loved. She will rejoice to see you."

Suddenly Barney dropped his face into his hands with a low, long moan. Jack looked out upon the fleeting landscape dimmed by the tears he dared not wipe away. A long silence followed while, drop by drop, Barney drank his cup to the bitter dregs.

"We try to think of the bright side," at length said Lady Ruthven gently.

Barney lifted his face from his hands, looked at her in dumb misery.

"There is the bright side," she continued, "the side of the immortal hope. We like to think of the better country. That is our real home. There, only, are our treasures safe." She was giving him time to get hold of himself after the first deadly stab. But Barney made no reply except to gravely bow. "It is, indeed, a better country," she added softly as if to herself, "the only place we immortals can call home." Then she rose. "Come, Jack," she said, "I think Dr. Boyle would like to be alone." Before she turned away to another section of the carriage, she offered him her hand with a grave, pitying smile.

Barney bowed reverently over her hand. "I am grateful to you," he said brokenly, "believe me." His face was contorted with the agony that filled his soul. A quick rush of tears rendered her speechless and in silence they turned away from him, and for the long hour that followed they left him with his grief.

When they came back they found him with face grave and steady, carrying the air of one who has fought his fight and has not been altogether beaten. And with that same steady face he reached the great door of Ruthven Hall.

"Jack, you will take Dr. Boyle to his room," said Lady Ruthven; "I shall see Iola and send for him." But just then her daughter came down the stairs. "Mamma," she said in a low, quick tone, "she wants him at once."

"Yes, dear, I know," replied her mother, "but it will be better that I—"

But there was a light cry, "Barney!" and, looking up, they all saw, standing at the head of the great staircase, a figure slight and frail, but radiant. It was Iola.

"Pardon me, Lady Ruthven," said Barney, and was off three steps at a time.

"Come, children." Swiftly Lady Ruthven motioned them into the library that opened off the hall, where they stood gazing at each other, awed and silent.

"Heaven help them!" at length gasped Jack.

"Let go my arm, Dr. Charrington," said Miss Ruthven. "You are hurting me."

"Your pardon, a thousand times. I didn't know. This is more than I can well stand."

"It will be well to leave them for a time, Dr. Charrington," said Lady Ruthven, with a quiet dignity that subdued all emotion and recalled them to self-control. "You will see that Dr. Boyle gets to his room?"

"I shall go up with you, Lady Ruthven, a little later," replied Jack. "Yes, I confess," he continued, answering Miss Ruthven's look, "I am a coward. I am afraid to see him. He takes things tremendously. He was quite mad about her years ago, fiercely mad about her, and when the break came it almost ruined him. How he will stand this, I don't know, but I am afraid to see him."

"This will be a terrible strain for her, Lady Ruthven," said Alan. "It should not be prolonged, do you think?"

"It is well that they should be alone for a time," she replied, her own experience making her wise in the ways of the breaking heart.

When with that quick rush Barney reached the head of the stairs Iola moved toward him with arms upraised. "Barney! Barney! Have you come to me at last?" she cried.

A single, searching glance into her face told him the dread truth. He took her gently into his arms and, restraining his passionate longing to crush her to him, lifted her and held her carefully, tenderly, gazing into her glowing, glorious eyes the while. "Where?" he murmured.

"This door, Barney."

He entered the little boudoir off her bedroom and laid her upon a couch he found there. Then, without a word, he put his cheek close to hers upon the pillow, murmuring over and over, "Iola—Iola—my love—my love!"

"Why, Barney," she cried, with a little happy laugh, "don't tremble so. Let me look at you. See, you silly boy, I am quite strong and calm. Look at me, Barney," she pleaded, "I am hungry to look at your face. I've only seen it in my dreams for so long." She raised herself on her arm and lifted his face from the pillow. "Now let me sit up. I shall never see enough of you. Never! Never! Oh, how wicked and how foolish I was!"

"It was I who was wicked," said Barney bitterly, "wicked and selfish and cruel to you and to others."

"Hush!" She laid her hand on his lips. "Sit here beside me. Now, Barney, don't spoil this one hour. Not one word of the past. You were a little hard, you know, dear, but you were right, and I knew you were right. I was wrong. But I thought there would be more in that other life. Even at its best it was spoiled. I wanted you. The great 'Lohengrin' night when they brought me out so many times—"

"I was there," interrupted Barney, his voice still full of bitter pain.

"I know. I saw you. Oh! wasn't that a night? Didn't I sing? It was for you, Barney. My soul, my heart, my body, went all into Ortrud that night."

"It was a great, a truly great thing, Iola."

"Yes," said Iola, with a proud little laugh, "I think the dear old Spectator was right when it said it was a truly great performance, but I waited for you, and waited and waited, and when you didn't come I found that all the rest was nothing to me without you. Oh, how I wanted you, Barney, then—and ever since!"

"If I had only known!" groaned Barney.

"Now, Barney, we are not to go back. We are to take all the joy out of this hour. Promise me, Barney, you will not blame yourself—now or ever—promise me, promise me!" she cried, eagerly insistent.

"But I do, Iola."

"Oh, Barney! promise me this, we will look forward, not back, will you, Barney?" The pleading in her voice swept away all feeling but the desire to gratify her.

"I promise you, Iola, and I keep my word."

"Yes, you do, Barney. Oh, thank you, darling." She wreathed her arms about his neck and laid her head upon his breast. "Oh!" she said with a deep sigh, "I shall rest now—rest—rest. That's what I've been longing for. I could not rest, Barney."

Barney shuddered. Only too well he knew the meaning of that fateful restlessness, but he only held her closer to him, his heart filled with a fierce refusal of his lot.

"There is no one like you, Barney, after all," she murmured, nestling down with a delicious sigh of content. "You are so strong. You will make me strong, I know. I feel stronger already, stronger than for months."

Again Barney shuddered at that cruel deception, so characteristic of the treacherous disease.

"Why don't you speak to me, Barney? You haven't said a word except just 'Iola, Iola, Iola.' Haven't you anything else to say, sir? After your long silence you might—" She raised her head and looked into his eyes with her old saucy smile.

"There is nothing to say, Iola. What need to speak when I can hold you like this? But you must not talk too much."

"Tell me something about yourself," she cried. "What? Where? How? Why? No, not why. I don't want that, but all the rest."

"It is hardly worth while, Iola," he replied, "and it would take a long time."

"Oh, yes, think what a delicious long time. All the time there is. All the day and every day. Oh, Barney! does one want more Heaven than this? Tell me about Margaret and—yes—and Dick," she shyly added. "Are they well and happy?"

"Now, darling," said Barney, stroking her hair; "just rest there and I'll tell you everything. But you must not exhaust yourself."

"Go on then, Barney," she replied with a sigh of ineffable bliss, nestling down again. "Oh, lovely rest!"

Then Barney told her of Margaret and Dick and of their last few days together, making light of Dick's injury and making much of the new joy that had come to them all. "And it was your letter that did it all, Iola," he said.

"No," she replied gently, "it was our Father's goodness. I see things so differently, Barney. Lady Ruthven has taught me. She is an angel from Heaven, and, oh, what she has done for me!"

"I, too, Iola, have great things to be thankful for."

A tap came to the door and, in response to their invitation, Lady Ruthven, with Jack in the background, appeared.

"Dinner will be served in a few minutes, Iola, and I am sure Dr. Boyle would like to go to his room. You can spare him, I suppose?"

"No, I can't spare him, but I will if you let me go down to-night to dinner."

"Is it wise, do you think?" said Lady Ruthven gravely. "You must save your strength now, you know."

"Oh, but I am strong. Just for to-night," she pleaded. "I'm not going to be an invalid to-night. I'm going to forget all about it. I am going to eat a good dinner and I'm going to sing, too. Jack, tell them I can go down. Barney, you will take me down. You may carry me, if you like. I am going, Jack," she continued with something of her old imperious air.

Barney searched her face with a critical glance, holding his fingers upon her wrist. She was growing excited. "Well, I think she might go down for a little. What do you think, Charrington? You know best."

"If she is good she might," said Jack doubtfully. "But she must promise to be quiet."

"Jack, you're a dear. You're an angel. I'll be good—as good as I can." With which extremely doubtful promise they had to content themselves.

At dinner none was more radiant that Iola. Without effort or strain her wit and gaiety bubbled over, till Barney, watching her in wonder, asked himself whether in his first impression of her he had not been mistaken. As he still watched and listened his wonder grew. How brilliantly clever she was! How quick her wit! How exquisitely subtle her fancy! Her mind, glowing like a live coal, seemed to kindle by mere contact the minds about her, till the whole table, catching her fire, scintillated with imagination's divine flame. Through it all Barney became conscious of a change in her. She was brighter than of old, cleverer by far. Her conversation was that of a highly cultured woman of the world. But it was not these that made the change. There was a new quality of soul in her. Patience had wrought her perfect work. She exhaled that exquisite aroma of the spirit disciplined by pain. She was less of the earth, earthy. The airs of Heaven were breathing about her.

To Barney, with his new sensitiveness to the spiritual, this change in Iola made her inexpressibly dear. It seemed as if he had met her in a new and better country where neither had seen the other before. And yet it filled him with an odd sense of loss. It was as if earth were losing its claim in her, as if her earthward affinities were refining into the heavenly. She was keenly interested in the story of Dick's work and, in spite of his reluctance to talk, she so managed the conversation, that, before he was aware, Barney was in the full tide of the thrilling tale of his brother's heroic service to the men in the mountains of Western Canada. As Barney waxed eloquent, picturing the perils and privations, the discouragements and defeats, the toils and triumphs of missionary life, the lustrous eyes grew luminous with deep inner light, the beautiful face, its ivory pallor relieved by a touch of carmine upon lip and cheek, appeared to shed a very radiance of glory that drew and held the gaze of the whole company.

"Oh, what splendid work!" she cried. "How good to be a man! But it's better," she added, with a quick glance at Barney and a little shy laugh, "to be a woman."

It was the anxiety in Charrington's eyes that arrested Lady Ruthven's attention and made her bring the dinner somewhat abruptly to a close.

"Oh, Lady Ruthven, must we go?" cried Iola, as her hostess made a move to rise. "What a delightful dinner we have had! Now you are not going to send me away just yet. 'After dinner sit a while,' you know, and I believe I feel like singing to-night."

"My dear, my dear," said Lady Ruthven, "do you think you should exert yourself any more? You have had an exciting day. What does your doctor say?"

"Barney?"

"Barney, indeed!" echoed Jack indignantly. "Oh, the ingratitude of the female heart! Here for all these weeks I have—"

"Forgive me, Jack. I am quite sure you won't be hard-hearted enough to banish me."

"An hour on the library couch, whence one can look upon the sea, in an atmosphere of restful quiet, listening to cheerful but not too exciting conversation," said Jack gravely.

"And music, Doctor?" inquired Iola, with mock humility.

"Well, I'll sing a little myself," replied Jack.

"Oh, my dear Iola," cried Miss Ruthven, "hasten to bed, I beg of you, and save us all. And yet, do you know, I rather like to hear Dr. Charrington sing. It makes me think of our automobile tour in the Highlands last year," she continued with mischievous gravity.

"Ah," said Jack, much flattered, "I don't quite—"

"Oh, the horn, you know."

"Wretch! Now I refuse outright to sing."

"Really? And after we had prepared ourselves for the—ah—experience."

"How do you feel now, Iola?" said Jack, quietly placing his fingers upon her pulse.

"Perfectly strong, I assure you. Listen." And she ran up her chromatics in a voice rich and strong and clear.

"Well, this is most wonderful!" exclaimed Jack. "Her pulse is strong, even, steady. Her respiration is normal."

"I told you!" cried Iola triumphantly. "Now you will let me sing—not a big song, but just that wee Scotch thing I learned from old Jennie. Barney's mother used to sing it."

"My dear Iola," entreated Lady Ruthven, "do you think you should venture? Do you think she should, Dr. Boyle?"

"Don't ask me," said Barney. "I should forbid it were it anyone else."

"But it isn't anyone else," persisted Iola, "and my doctor says yes. I'll only hum, Jack."

"Well, one only. And mind, no fugues, arpeggios, double-stoppings, and such frills."

She took her guitar. "I'll sing this for Barney's dear mother," she said. And in a voice soft, rich and full of melody, and with perfect reproduction of the quaint old-fashioned cadences and quavers, she sang the Highland lament, "O'er the Moor."

"O'er the moor I wander lonely,
Ochon-a-rie, my heart is sore;
Where are all the joys I cherished?
With my darling they have perished,
And they will return no more.

"I loved thee first, I loved thee only,
Ochon-a-rie, my heart is sore;
I loved thee from the day I met thee.
What care I though all forget thee?
I will love thee evermore."

And then, before anyone could utter a word of protest, she said, "You never heard this, I think, Barney. I'll sing it for you." And in a low, soft voice, thrilling with pathetic feeling, she sang the quaint little song that described so fittingly her own experience, "My Heart's Rest."

"I had wandered far, and the wind was cold,
And the sharp thorns clutched, and the day was old,
When the Master came to close His fold
And saw that one had strayed.

"Wild paths I fled, and the wind grew chill,
And the sharp rocks cut, and the day waned, till
The Master's voice searched vale and hill:
I heard and fled afraid.

"Dread steeps I climbed, and the wind wailed on.
And the stars went out, and the day was gone,
Then the Master found, laid me upon
His bosom, unafraid."

A hush followed upon her song. Far down the valley the moon rose red out of the sea, the sweet night air, breathing its fragrance of mignonette and roses, moved the lace of the curtains at the open window as it passed. A late thrush was singing its night song of love to its mate.

"I feel as if I could sleep now," said Iola. "Barney, carry me." Like a tired child she nestled down in Barney's strong arms. "Good-night, dear friends, all," she said. "What a happy evening it has been." Then, with a little cry, "Oh, Barney! hold me. I'm slipping," she locked her arms tight about his neck, lifting her face to his. "Goodnight, Barney, my love, my own love," she whispered, her breath coming in gasps. "How good you are to me—how good to have you. Now kiss me—quick—don't wait—again, dear—good-night." Her arms slipped down from his neck. Her head sank upon his breast.

"Iola!" he cried, in a voice strident with fear and alarm, glancing down into her face. He carried her to the open window. "Oh, my God! My God! She is gone! Oh, my love, not yet! not yet!"

But the ear was dull even to that penetrating cry of the broken heart, and the singing voice was forever still from words or songs that mortal ears could hear. In vain they tried to revive her. The tired lids rested upon the lustrous eyes from which all light had fled. The weary heart was quiet at last. Gently, Barney placed her on the couch, where she lay as if asleep, then, standing upright, he gazed round upon them with eyes full of dumb anguish till they understood, and one by one they turned and left him alone with his dead.

For two days Barney wandered about the valley, his spirit moving in the midst of a solemn and mysterious peace. The light of life for him had not gone out, but had brightened into the greater glory. Heaven had not snatched her away. She had brought Heaven near.

At first he was minded to carry her back with him to the old home and lay her in the churchyard there. But Lady Ruthven took him to the spot where her dead lay.

"We should be glad that she should sleep beside our dear ones here," she said. "You know we love her dearly."

"It is a great kindness you are doing, Lady Ruthven," Barney replied, his heart responding with glad acceptance to the suggestion. "She loved this valley, and it was here she first found rest."

"Yes, she loves this valley," replied Lady Ruthven, refusing to accept Barney's tense. To her, death made no change. "And here she found peace and perfect love again."

A single line in the daily press brought a few close friends from London to bury her. Old Sir Walter himself was present. He had taken such pride in her voice, and had learned to love his pupil as a daughter, and with him stood Herr Lindau, the German impresario, under whose management she had made her London debut in "Lohengrin." There in the sunny valley they laid her down, their faces touched with smiles that struggled with their tears. But on his face who loved her best of all there were no tears, only a look of wonder, and of gladness, and of peace.

XXIII
THE LAST CALL

Dick was discouraged and, a rare thing with him, his face showed his discouragement. In the war against the saloon and vice in its various forms he felt that he stood almost alone.

At the door of The Clarion office the editor, Lemuel Daggett, hailed him. He hesitated a moment, then entered. A newspaper office was familiar territory to him, as was also that back country that stretches to the horizon from the back door of every printing office. The Clarion was the organ of the political Outs as The Pioneer was that of the Ins. Politics in British Columbia had not yet arrived at that stage of development wherein parties differentiate themselves from each other upon great principles. The Ins were in and the Outs opposed them chiefly on that ground.

"Well," said Daggett, with an air of gentle patronage, "how did the meeting go last night?"

"I don't suppose you need to ask. I saw you there. It didn't go at all."

"Yes," replied Daggett, "your men are all right in their opinions, but they never allow their opinions to interfere with business. I could have told you every last man of them was scared. There's Matheson, couldn't stand up against his wholesale grocer. Religion mustn't interfere with sales. The saloons and 'red lights' pay cash; therefore, quit your nonsense and stick to business. Hutton sells more drugs and perfumes to the 'red lights' than to all the rest of the town and country put together. Goring's chief won't stand any monkeying with politics. Leave things as they are. Why, even the ladies decline to imperil their husbands' business."

Dick swallowed the bitter pill without a wink. He was down, but he was not yet completely out. Only too well he knew the truth of Daggett's review of the situation.

"There is something in what you say," he conceded, "but—"

"Oh, come now," interrupted Daggett, "you know better than that. This town and this country is run by the whiskey ring. Why, there's Hickey, he daren't arrest saloonkeeper or gambler, though he hates whiskey and the whole outfit worse than poison. Why doesn't he? The Honourable McKenty, M. P., drops him a hint. Hickey is told to mind his own business and leave the saloon and the 'red lights' alone, and so poor Hickey is sitting down trying to discover what his business is ever since. The safe thing is to do nothing."

"You seem to know all about it," said Dick. "What's the good of your paper? Why don't you get after these men?"

"My dear sir, are you an old newspaper man, and ask that? It is quite true that The Clarion is the champion of liberty, the great moulder of public opinion, the leader in all moral reform, but unhappily, not being an endowed institution, it is forced to consider advertising space. Advertising, circulation, subscriptions, these are the considerations that determine newspaper policy."

Dick gazed ruefully out of the window. "It's true. It's terribly true," he said. "The people don't want anything better than they have. The saloon must continue to be the dominant influence here for a time. But you hear me, Daggett, a better day is coming, and if you want an opportunity to do, not the heroic thing only, but the wise thing, jump into a campaign for reform. Do you think Canadians are going to stand this long? This is a Christian country, I tell you. The Church will take a hand."

Daggett smiled a superior smile. "Coming? Yes, sure, but meantime The Pioneer spells Church with a small c, and even the Almighty's name with a small g."

"I tell you, Daggett," said Dick hotly, "The Pioneer's day is past. I see signs and I hear rumblings of a storm that will sweep it, and you, too, unless you change, out of existence."

"Not at all, my dear sir. We will be riding on that storm when it arrives. But the rumblings are somewhat distant. I, too, see signs, but the time is not yet. By the way, where is your brother?"

"I don't see much of him. He is up and down the line, busy with his sick and running this library and clubroom business."

"Yes," replied Daggett thoughtfully, "I hear of him often. The railroad men and the lumbermen grovel to him. Look here, would he run in this constituency?"

Dick laughed at him. "Not he. Why, man, he's straight. You couldn't buy him. Oh, I know the game."

Daggett was silenced for some moments.

"Hello!" said Daggett, looking out of the window, "here is our coming Member." He opened the door. "Mr. Hull, let me introduce you to the Reverend Richard Boyle, preacher and moral reformer. Mr. Boyle—Mr. Hull, the coming Member for this constituency."

"I hope he will make a better fist of it than the present incumbent," said Dick a little gruffly, for he had little respect for either of the political parties or their representatives. "I must get along. But, Daggett, for goodness' sake do something with this beastly gambling-hell business." With this he closed the door.

"Good fellow, Boyle, I reckon," said Hull, "but a little unpractical, eh?"

"Yes," agreed Daggett, "he is somewhat visionary. But I begin to think he is on the right track."

"How? What do you mean?"

"I mean the West is beginning to lose its wool, and it's time this country was getting civilized. That fool editor of The Pioneer thinks that because he keeps wearing buckskin pants and a cowboy hat, he can keep back the wheels of time. He hasn't brains enough to last him over night. Boyle says he sees the signs of a coming storm. I believe I see them, too."

"Signs?" inquired Hull.

"Yes, the East is taking notice. The big corporations are being held responsible for their men, their health, and their morals. 'Mexico,' too, has something up his sleeve. He's acting queer, and this Boyle's brother is taking a hand, I believe."

"The doctor, eh? Pshaw! let him."

"Do you know him?"

"Not well."

"You get next him quick. He's the coming man in this country, don't forget it."

Hull grunted rather contemptuously. He himself was a man of considerable wealth. He was an old timer and cherished the old timer's contempt for the tenderfoot.

"All right," said Daggett, "you may sniff. I've watched him and I've discovered this, that what he wants to do he does. He's an old poker player. He has cleaned out 'Mexico' half a dozen times. He has quit poker now, they say, and he's got 'Mexico' going queer."

"What's his game?"

"Can't make it out quite. He has turned religious, they say. Spoke here at a big meeting last spring, quite dramatic, I believe. I wasn't there. Offered to pay back his ungodly winnings. Of course, no man would listen to that, so he's putting libraries into the camps and establishing clubrooms."

"By Jove! it's a good game. But what do the boys, what does 'Mexico' think of it?"

"Why, that's the strangest part of it. He's got them going his way. He's a doctor, you know, has nursed a lot of them, and they swear by him. He's a sign, I tell you. So is 'Mexico.'"

"What about 'Mexico'?"

"Well, you know 'Mexico' has been the head centre of the saloon outfit, divides the spoil and collects the 'rents.' But I say he's acting queer."

Hull was at once on the alert. "That's interesting. You are sure of your facts? It might be all right to corral those chaps. The virtue campaign is bound to come. A little premature yet, but that doctor fellow is to be considered."

But the virtue campaign did not immediately begin. The whole political machinery of both parties was too completely under the control of the saloon and "red light" influence to be easily emancipated. The business interests of the little towns along the line were so largely dependent upon the support of the saloon and the patronage of vice that few had the courage to openly espouse and seriously champion a campaign for reform. And while many, perhaps the majority, of the men employed in the railroad and in the lumber camps, though they were subject to periodic lapses from the path of sobriety and virtue, were really opposed to the saloon and its allies, yet they lacked leadership and were, therefore, unreliable. It was at this point that the machine in each party began to cherish a nervous apprehension in regard to the influence of Dr. Boyle. Bitter enemies though they were, they united their forces in an endeavour to have the doctor removed. The wires ordinarily effective were pulled with considerable success, when the manipulators met with an unexpected obstacle in General Manager Fahey. Upon him the full force of the combined influences available was turned, but to no purpose. He was too good a railway manager to be willing to lose the services of a man "who knew his work and did it right, a man who couldn't be bullied or blocked, and a man, bedad, who could play a good game of poker."

"He stays while I stay," was Fahey's last word in reply to an influential director, labouring in the interests of the party machine.

Failing with Fahey, the allied forces tried another line of attack. "Mexico" and the organization of which he was the head were instructed to "run him out." Receiving his orders, "Mexico" called his agents together and invited their opinions. A sharp cleavage immediately developed, one party led by "Peachy" being strongly in favour of obeying the orders, the other party, leaderless and scattering, strongly opposed. Discussion waxed bitter. "Mexico" sat silent, watchful, impassive. At length, "Peachy," in full swing of an impassioned and sulphurous denunciation of the doctor, his person and his ways, was called abruptly to order by a peremptory word from his chief.

"Shut up your fool head, 'Peachy.' To hear you talk you'd think you'd do something."

A grim laugh at "Peachy's" expense went round the company.

"Do somethin'?" snarled "Peachy," stung to fury, "I'll do somethin' one of these days. I've stood you all I want."

"Peachy's" oaths were crude in comparison with "Mexico's," but his fury lent them force. "Mexico" turned his baleful, gleaming eyes upon him.

"Do something? Meaning?"

"Never mind," growled "Peachy."

"Git!" "Mexico" pointed a long finger to the door. It was a word of doom, and they all knew it, for it meant not simply dismissal from that meeting, but banishment from the company of which "Mexico" was head, and that meant banishment from the line of the Crow's Nest Pass. "Peachy" was startled.

"You needn't be so blanked swift," he growled apologetically. "I didn't mean for to—"

"You git!" repeated "Mexico," turning the pointing finger from the door to the face of the startled wretch.

With a fierce oath "Peachy" reached for his gun, but hesitated to draw. "Mexico" moved not a line of his face, not a muscle of his body, except that his head went a little back and the heavy eyelids fell somewhat over the piercing black eyes.

"You dog!" he ground out through his clenched teeth, "you know you can't bring out your gun. I know you. You poor cur! You thought you'd sell me up to the other side! I know your scheme! Now git, and quick!"

The command came sharp like a snap of an animal's teeth, while "Mexico's" hand dropped swiftly to his side. Instantly "Peachy" rose and backed slowly toward the door, his face wearing the grin of a savage beast. At the door he paused.

"'Mexico,'" he said, "is this the last between you and me?"

"Mexico" kept his gleaming eyes fastened upon the face of the man backing out of the door.

"Git out, you cur!" he said, with contemptuous deliberation.

"Take that, then."

Like a flash, "Mexico" threw himself to one side. Two shots rang out as one. A slight smile curled "Mexico's" lip.

"Got him that time, I reckon."

"Hurt, 'Mexico'?" anxiously inquired his friends.

"Naw. He ain't got the nerve to shoot straight." The bartender and some others came running in with anxious faces. "Never mind, boys," said "Mexico." "'Peachy' was foolin' with his gun; it went off and hurt him some."

"Say, there's blood here!" said the bartender. "He's been bleedin' bad."

"Guess he's more scared than hurt. Now let's git to business."

The bartender and his friends took the hint and retired.

"Now, boys, listen to me," said "Mexico" impressively, leaning over the table. "Right here I want to say that the doctor is a friend of mine, and the man that touches him touches me." There was an ominous silence.

"Just as you say, 'Mexico,'" said one of the men, "but I see the finish of our game in these parts. The doctor's got the boys a-goin' and you know he ain't the kind that quits."

"You're right an' you're wrong. The Doc ain't the whole Government of this country yet. His game's the winnin' game. Any fool can see that. But we hold most of the trumps just now. So for the present we stay."

As the meeting broke up, "Mexico's" friends warned him against "Peachy."

"Pshaw! 'Peachy'!" said "Mexico" contemptuously. "He couldn't hold his gun steady at me."

"He's all right behind a tree, though, an' there's lots of 'em round."

But "Mexico" only spat out his contempt for anything that "Peachy" could do, and went calmly on his way, "keeping the boys in line." But he began to be painfully conscious of an undercurrent of feeling over which he could exercise no control. Not that there was any lack of readiness on the part of the boys to "line up" at the word, but there was no corresponding readiness in pledging their support to the "same old party." There was, on the contrary, a very marked reserve on the part of the men who formerly, especially after the lining up process had been several times repeated, had been distinguished for unlimited enthusiasm for all "Mexico" represented. They "lined up" still, but beyond this they did not go.

The editor of The Pioneer, too, became conscious of this change in the attitude of the men he had always counted upon to do his bidding at the polls. "It's that cursed doctor!" he exclaimed to McKenty, the Member for the district. "He's been working a deep game. Of course, his brother's putting up all kinds of a fight, but we expect that and we know how to handle him. But this fellow is different. I tell you I'm afraid of him."

"Pshaw! He hasn't got any backing," said McKenty.

"How?"

"Well, he hasn't got any grease, and you can't make anything go without grease." McKenty spoke out of considerable experience.

"That's all right as an ordinary thing, but the doctor has grease of another kind. This library and clubroom business is catching the boys all round."

"I've heard about it," said McKenty. "I guess the Government could take a hand in libraries and institutes and that sort of thing, too."

"That's all right," replied the editor. "Might do some good. But you can't beat him at that game. It isn't his libraries and his clubs altogether or chiefly, it's himself and his work. He's a number one doctor, and night and day he's on the road. By Jove! he's everywhere. He's got no end of stay, confound him! I tell you he's a winner. He can get a thousand men in a week to back him for anything he says."

McKenty thought deeply for some moments. "Well," he said, finally, "something has got to be done. We can't afford, you and I, at this stage to get out of the game. What about 'Mexico'?"

"'Mexico'!" exclaimed the editor, breaking out into profanity. "There's the weakest spot in the whole combination, just where it used to be strongest. The doctor's got him, body and soul. Why, 'Mexico' 'd be after him with a gun if he stayed anywhere else when he visits town. The best in 'Mexico's' saloon isn't quite good enough for the doctor. No, sir! He's got a line on 'Mexico,' all right."

"Can't you shake him loose? There are the usual ways, you know, of loosening up people."

"But, my dear sir, I'm just telling you that the usual ways won't work here. This combination is something quite unusual. I believe there's some religion in it."

McKenty laughed loud. It was a good joke.

"I tell you I mean it," said the editor, testily. "The doctor's got it hard. Talk about conversion! You weren't at that meeting last spring—I was—when he got up and preached us a sermon that would make your hair curl." And the editor proceeded to give a graphic account of the meeting in question.

"Well," said McKenty, "I guess we can't touch the doctor. But 'Mexico,' pshaw! we can keep 'Mexico' solid. We've got to. He knows too much. You've simply got to get after him."

This the editor of The Pioneer proceeded to do without delay, for, looking out through the dusty windows of The Pioneer office, he perceived "Mexico" sauntering down the other side of the street.

"There he is now," he cried, going toward the door. "Hi! 'Mexico'!" he called, and "Mexico" came slouching across. "Ugly looking beggar, ain't he?" said the editor. "Jaw like a bulldog. Morning, 'Mexico'!"

"Mornin'," grunted "Mexico," nodding first to the editor and then to McKenty.

"How is things, 'Mexico'?" said the editor, in his most ingratiating manner.

"How?"

"How are the boys? Vote solid? Election's coming on, you know."

"Comin' on soon?"

"Well, it looks that way, but really one can't say. We ought to be ready, though."

"Can't be too soon," said "Mexico."

"How is that?"

"Time's agin ye. Leather pants goin' out of fashion," with a glance at the schapps which the editor delighted to wear. "People beginnin' to go to meetin' in this country."

"I hear you're going yourself a little, 'Mexico,'" said McKenty, facetiously.

"Mexico" turned his eyes slowly upon the Member.

"Anything to say agin it?"

"Not at all, 'Mexico,' not at all. Good thing; but they say the doctor's got the boys rather away from you, that you're losing your grip."

"Who says?"

"Oh, I hear it everywhere."

"Guess it must be right, then," replied "Mexico," grimly.

"And they say he's got a line on you, 'Mexico,' getting you right up to the mourners' bench."

"Do, eh?"

"Look here, 'Mexico,'" said McKenty, dropping his bantering tone, "you're not going to let the blank preacher-doctor combination work you, are you?"

"Don't know about that."

"You don't?"

"No. But I do know that there ain't any other combination kin. I'm working for myself in this game. If any combination wants to shove my way, they can jump in. They'll quit when it don't pay to shove, I guess. Me the same. You fellers ain't any interest in me, I reckon."

"Well, do you imagine the doctor has?"

"Mexico" paused, then said thoughtfully, "Blanked if I can git on to his game!"

"Oh, come, 'Mexico,' you can't get on to him? He's working you. You don't really think he has your interest at heart?"

"Can't quite tell." "Mexico" wore a vexed and thoughtful air. "Wish I could. If I thought so I'd —"

"What?"

"Tie up to him tight, you bet your eternal life!" There was a sudden gleam from under "Mexico's" heavy brows and a ring in his usually drawling voice, that sufficiently attested his earnestness. "There ain't too many of that kind raound."

"What do you think of that?" inquired the editor, as "Mexico" sauntered out of the door.

"Think? I think there's a law against gamblers in this province and it ought to be enforced."

"That means war," said the editor.

"Well, let it come. That doctor is the whole trouble, I can see. I'd give a thousand dollars down to see him out of the country."

But there was no sign that the doctor had any desire to leave the country, and all who knew him were quite certain that until he should so desire, leave he would not. All through the winter he went about his work with a devotion that taxed even his superb physical strength to the uttermost. In addition to his work as Medical Superintendent of the railroad he had been asked to take oversight of the new coal mines opening up here and there in the Pass, which brought him no end of both labour and trouble. The managers of the mines held the most primitive ideas in regard to both safety in operating a mine and sanitation of miners' quarters. Consequently, the doctor had to enter upon a long campaign of education. It was an almost hopeless task. The directors were remote from the ground and were unimpressed by the needs so urgently reported by their doctor. The managers on the ground were concerned chiefly with keeping down the expenses of operation. The miners themselves were, as a class, too well accustomed to the wretched conditions under which they lived and worked to make any strenuous objection.

How to bring about a better condition of things became, with the doctor, a constant subject of thought. It was also the theme of conversation on the occasion of his monthly visits to the Kuskinook Hospital, where it had become an established custom for Dick and him to meet since his return from Scotland.

"We'll get them to listen when we kill a few score men, not before," grumbled Barney to Dick and Margaret.

"It's the universal law," replied Dick. "Some men must die for their nation. It's been the way from the first."

"But, Barney, is it wise that you should worry yourself and work yourself to death as you are doing?" said Margaret, anxiously. "You know you can't stand this long. You are not the man you were when you came back."

Barney only smiled. "That would be no great matter," he said, lightly. "But there is no fear of me," he added. "I don't pine for an early death, you know. I've got a lot to live for."

There was silence for a minute or two. They were thinking of the grave in the little churchyard across the sea. Ever since Barney's return, and as often as they met together, they allowed themselves to think and speak freely of the little valley at Craigraven, so full of light and peace, with its grave beside the little church. At first Dick and Margaret shrank from all reference to Iola, and sought to turn Barney's mind from thoughts so full of pain. But Barney would not have it so. Frankly and simply he began to speak of her, dwelling lovingly and tenderly upon all the details of the last days of her life, as he had gathered them from Lady Ruthven, her friend.

"It would be easier for me not to speak of her," he had said on his return, "but I've lost too much to risk the loss of more. I want you to talk of her, and by and by I shall find it easy."

And this they did most loyally, and with tender solicitude for him, till at length the habit grew, so that whenever they came together it only deepened and chastened their joy in each other to keep fresh the memory of her who had filled so large a place, and so vividly, in the life of each of them. And this was good for them all, but especially for Barney. It took the bitterness out of his grief, and much of the pain out of his loss. The memory of that last evening with Iola, and Lady Ruthven's story of the purifying of her spirit, during those last few months, combined to throw about her a radiance such as she had never shed even in the most radiant moments of her life.

"There is only place for gratitude," he said, one evening, to them. "Why should I allow any mean or selfish thought to spoil my memory of her or to hinder the gratitude I ought to feel, that her going was so free from pain, and her last evening so full of joy?"

It was with these feelings in his heart that he went back to the camps to his work among the sick and wounded in body and in heart. And as he went in and out among the men they became conscious of a new spirit in him. His touch on the knife was as sure as ever, his nerve as steady, but while the old reserve still held his lips from overflowing, the words that dropped were kinder, the tone gentler, the touch more tender. The terrible restlessness, too, was gone out of his blood. A great calm possessed him. He was always ready for the ultimate demand, prepared to give of his life to the uttermost. To his former care for the physical well-being of the men, he added now a concern for their mental and spiritual good, and hence the system of libraries and clubrooms he had initiated throughout the camps and towns along the line. It mattered not to him that he had to meet the open opposition of the saloon element and the secret hostility of those who depended upon that element for the success of their political schemes. His love of a fight was as strong as ever. At first the men could not fathom his motives, but as men do, they silently and observantly waited for the real motive to emerge. As "Mexico" said, they "couldn't get onto his game." And none of them was more completely puzzled than was "Mexico" himself, but none more fully acknowledged, and more frankly yielded to the fascination of the new spirit and new manner which the doctor brought to his work. At the same time, however, "Mexico" could not rid himself of a suspicion, now and then, that the real game was being kept dark. The day was to come when "Mexico" would cast away every vestige of suspicion and give himself up to the full luxury of devotion to a man, worthy to be followed, who lived not for his own things. But that day was not yet, and "Mexico" was kept in a state of uncertainty most disturbing to his mind and injurious to his temper. Day by day reports came of the doctor's ceaseless toil and unvarying self-sacrifice, the very magnitude of which made it difficult for "Mexico" to accept it as being sincere.

"What's his game?" he kept asking himself more savagely, as the mystery deepened. "What's in it for him? Is he after McKenty's job?"

One night the doctor came in from a horseback trip to a tie camp twelve miles up the valley, wearied and soaked with the wet snow that had been falling heavily all day. "Mexico" received him with a wrathful affection.

"What the—ah—what makes you go out a night like this?" "Mexico" asked him with indignation, struggling to check his profanity, which he had come to notice the doctor disliked. "I can't get onto you. It's all just d—, that is, cursed foolishness!"

"Look here, 'Mexico,' wait till I get these wet things off and I'll tell you. Now listen," said the doctor, when he sat warm and dry before "Mexico's" fire. "I've been wanting to tell you this for some time." He opened his black bag and took out a New Testament which now always formed a part of his equipment, and finding the place, read the story of the two debtors. "Do you remember, 'Mexico,' the talk I gave you last spring?" "Mexico" nodded. That talk he would not soon forget. "I had a big debt on then. It was forgiven me. He did a lot for me that time, and since then He has piled it up till I feel as if I couldn't live long enough to pay back what I owe." Then he told "Mexico" in a low, reverent tone, with shining eyes and thrilling voice, the story of Iola's going. "That's why," he said, when he concluded his tale. "That was a great thing He did for her and for me. And then, 'Mexico,' these poor chaps! they have so little. Who cares for them? That's why I go out on a night like this. And don't you think that's good enough?"

Then "Mexico" turned himself loose for five minutes and let off the sulphurous emotion that had been collecting during the doctor's tale. After he had become coherent again he said with slow emphasis:

"You've got me, Doc. Wipe your feet on me when you want."

"'Mexico,'" replied the doctor, "you know I don't preach at you. I haven't, have I?"

"Blanked if—that is, no, you haven't."

The Doctor: A Tale Of The Rockies | 229

"Well, you say I can have you. I'll take you right here. You are my friend." He put out his hand, which "Mexico" gripped and held fast. "But," continued the doctor, "I want to say that He wants you more than I do, wants to wipe off that debt of yours, wants you for His friend."

"Say, Doc," said "Mexico," drawing back a little from him, "I guess not. That there debt goes back for twenty years, and it's piled out of sight. It never bothers me much except when I see you and hear you talk. It would be a blank—that is, a pretty fine thing to have it cleaned off. But say, Doc, your heap agin mine would be like a sandhill agin that mountain there."

"The size makes no difference to Him, 'Mexico,'" said the doctor, quietly. "He is great enough to wipe out anything. I tell you, 'Mexico,' it's good to get it wiped off. It's simply great!"

"You're right there," said "Mexico," emphatically. Then, as if a sudden suspicion flashed in upon him, "Say, you're not talkin' religion to me, are you? I ain't goin' to die just yet."

"Religion? Call it anything you like, 'Mexico.' All I know is I've got a good thing and I want my friend to have it."

When the doctor was departing next morning "Mexico" stopped him at the door. "I say, Doc, would you mind letting me have that there book of yours for a spell?"

The doctor took it out of his bag. "It's yours, 'Mexico,' and you can bank on it."

The book proved of absorbing interest to "Mexico." He read it openly in the saloon without any sense of incongruity, at first, between the book and the business he was carrying on, but not without very considerable comment on the part of his customers and friends. And what he read became the subject of frequent discussions with his friend, the doctor. The book did its work with "Mexico," as it does with all who give it place, and the first sign of its influence was an uncomfortable feeling in "Mexico's" mind in regard to his business and his habits of life. His discomfort became acute one pay night, after a very successful game of poker in which he had relieved some half a dozen lumbermen of their pay. For the first time in his life his winnings brought him no satisfaction. The great law of love to his brother troubled him. In vain he argued that it was a fair deal and that he himself would have taken his loss without whining. The disturbing thoughts would not down. He determined that he would play no more till he had talked the matter over with his friend, and he watched impatiently for the doctor's return. But that week the doctor failed to appear, and "Mexico" grew increasingly uncertain in his mind and in his temper. It added to his wretchedness not a little when the report reached him that the doctor was confined to his bed in the hospital at Kuskinook. In fact, this news plunged "Mexico" into deepest gloom.

"If he's took to bed," he said, "there ain't much hope, I guess, for they'd never get him there unless he was too far gone to fight 'em off."

But at the Kuskinook Hospital there was no anxiety felt in regard to the doctor's illness. He was run down with the fall and winter's work. He had caught cold, a slight inflammation had set up in the bowels, and that was all. The inflammation had been checked and in a few days he would be on his feet again.

"If we could only work a scheme to keep him in bed a month," groaned Dick to his nurse as they stood beside his bed.

"There is, unhappily, no one in authority over him," replied Margaret, "but we'll keep him ill as long as we can. Dr. Cotton," and here she smilingly appealed to the newly appointed assistant, "you will help, I am sure."

"Most certainly. Now we have him down we shall combine to keep him there."

"Yes, a month at the very least," cried Dick.

But Barney laughed their plans to scorn. In two days he promised them he would be fit again.

"It is the Superintendent of the Hospital against the Medical Superintendent of the Crow's Nest Railway," said Dr. Cotton, "and I think in this case I'll back the former, from what I've seen."

"Ah," replied Margaret, "that is because you haven't known your patient long, Doctor. When he speaks the word of command we simply obey."

And that is just what happened. On the afternoon of the second day, when both the doctor and Dick had gone off to their work and Barney had apparently fallen into a quiet sleep, the silence that reigned over the flat was broken by Ben Fallows coming up the stair with a telegram in his hand.

"It's fer the doctor," said Ben, "an' the messenger said as 'ow 'Mexico' had got shot and—"

Swiftly Margaret closed the door of the room in which Barney lay. Ben's voice, though not loud, was of a peculiarly penetrating quality. Two words had caught Barney's ear, "Mexico" and "shot."

"Let me have the wire," he said quietly, when Margaret came in.

"I intended to give it to you, Barney," she replied as quietly. "You will do nothing rash, I am sure, and you always know best."

Barney opened the telegram and read, "'Mexico' shot. Bullet not found. Wants doctor to come if possible."

"Dr. Cotton is not in?" inquired Barney.

"He is gone up the Big Horn."

"We can't possibly get him to-night," replied Barney.

Silently they looked at each other, thinking rapidly. They each knew that the other was ready to do the best, no matter at what cost.

"Take my temperature, Margaret." It was nine-nine and one-fifth. "That's not bad," said Barney. "Margaret, I must go. It's for 'Mexico's' life. Yes, and more."

Margaret turned slightly pale. "You know best, Barney," she said, "but it may be your life, you know."

"Yes," he replied gravely. "I take that chance. But I think I ought to take it, don't you?" But Margaret refused to speak. "What do you think, Margaret?" he asked.

"Oh, Barney!" she cried, with passionate protest, "why should you give your life for him?"

"Why?" he repeated slowly. "There was One who gave His life for me. Besides," he added, after a pause, "there's a fair chance that I can get through."

She threw herself on her knees beside his bed. "No, Barney, there's almost no chance, you know and I know, and I can't let you go now!" The passionate love in her voice and in her eyes startled him. Gravely, earnestly, his eyes searched her face and read her heart. Slowly the crimson rose in her cheeks and flooded the fair face and neck. She buried her face in the bed. Gently he laid his hand upon her head, stroking the golden hair. For some moments they remained thus, silent. Then, refusing to accept the confession of her word and look and act, he said, in a voice grave and kind and tender, "You expect me to do right, Margaret."

A shudder ran through the kneeling girl. Once more the cup of renunciation was being pressed to her lips. To the last drop she drained it, then raised her head. She was pale but calm. The bright blue eyes looked into his bravely while she answered simply, "You will do what is right, Barney."

Just as he was about to start on his journey another wire came in. "Didn't know you were so ill. Don't you come. I'm all right. 'Mexico.'" A rumour of the serious nature of the doctor's illness had evidently reached "Mexico," and he would not have his friend risk his life for him. A fierce storm was raging. The out train was hours late, but a light engine ran up from the Crossing and brought the doctor down.

When he entered the sick man's room "Mexico" glanced into his face. "Good Lord, Doctor!" he cried, "you shouldn't have come! You're worse than me!"

"All right, 'Mexico,'" replied the doctor cheerfully. "I had to come, you know. We can't go back on our friends."

"Mexico" kept his eyes fastened on the doctor's face. His lips began to tremble. He put out his hand and clutched the doctor's hard. "I know now," he said hoarsely, "why He let 'em kill Him."

"Why?"

"Couldn't go back on His friends, eh?"

"You've got it, 'Mexico,' old man. Pretty good, eh?"

"You bet! Now, Doc, get through quick and get to bed."

The bullet was found in the lung and safely extracted. It was a nasty wound and dangerous, but in half an hour "Mexico" was resting quietly. Then the doctor lay down on a couch near by and tossed till morning, conscious of a return of the pain and fever. The symptoms he well knew indicated a very serious condition. When "Mexico" woke the doctor examined him carefully.

"You're fine, 'Mexico.' You'll be all right in a week or two. Keep quiet and obey orders."

"Mexico's" hand grasped him. "Doc," he said anxiously, "you look awful bad. Can't you get to bed quick? You're going to be terrible sick."

"I'm afraid I'm going to be pretty bad, 'Mexico,' but I'm glad I came. I couldn't have stayed away, could I? Remember that, 'Mexico.' I'm glad I came."

"Mexico's" fierce black eyes softened. "Doc, I'm sorry and I'm glad. I had a lot of things to ask, but I don't need to. I know now. And I want to tell you, I've quit all that business, cut it right out." He waved his hand toward the bar.

"'Mexico,'" said Barney earnestly, "that's great! That's the best news I've had all summer. Now I. must get back quick." He took the gambler's hand in his. "Good-bye, 'Mexico.'" His voice was earnest, almost solemn. "You've done me a lot of good. Good-bye, old boy. Play the game. He'll never go back on a friend."

"Mexico" reached out and held him with both hands. "Git out," he said to the attendant. "Doc," his voice dropped to a hoarse whisper as he drew the doctor down to him, "there ain't nobody here, is there?" he asked, with a glance round the room.

"No, 'Mexico,' no one."

"Doc," he began again, his strong frame shaking, "I can't say it. It's all in here till it hurts. You're—you're like Him, I think. You make me think o' Him."

Barney dropped quickly on his knees beside the bed, threw his arms about his friend, and held him for a few moments in a tight embrace. "God bless you, 'Mexico,' for that word," he said. "Goodbye, my friend."

They held each other fast for a moment or two, looking into each other's eyes as if taking a last farewell. Then Barney took his journey through the storm, which was still raging, his fever mounting higher with every moment, back to the hospital, where Margaret received him with a brave welcoming smile.

"Dr. Cotton has returned," she announced. "And Dr. Neeley of Nelson is here, Barney."

He gave her a look of understanding. He knew well what she meant. "That was right, Margaret. And Dick?"

"Dick will be here this afternoon."

"You think of everything, Margaret dear, and everybody except yourself," said Barney, as he made his way painfully up the stairs.

"Let me help you, Barney," she said, putting her arms about him. "You're the one who will not think of yourself."

"We've all been learning from you, Margaret. And it is the best lesson, after all."

The consultation left no manner of doubt as to the nature of the trouble and the treatment necessary. It was appendicitis, and it demanded immediate operation.

"We can wait till my brother comes, can't we, Doctor?" Barney asked, a little anxiously. "An hour can't make much difference now, you know."

"Why, certainly we shall wait," cried the doctor.

Twenty miles through the storm came Dick, in answer to Margaret's urgent message, to find his brother dangerously ill and preparing for a serious operation. The meeting of the brothers was without demonstration of emotion. Each for the sake of the other held himself firmly in hand. The issues were so grave that there was no room for any expenditure of strength and indulging in the luxury of grief. Quietly, Barney gave his brother the few directions necessary to the disposal of his personal effects.

"Of course, Dick, I expect to get through all right," he said, with cheerful courage.

"Of course," answered Dick, quickly.

"But it's just as well to say things now when one can think quietly."

"Quite right, Barney," said Dick again, his voice steady and even.

The remaining minutes they spent in almost complete silence, except for a message of remembrance for the mother and the father far away; then the doctor came to the door.

"Are you ready, Doctor?" said Dick, in a firm, almost cheerful voice.

"Yes, we're all ready."

"A minute, Doctor, please," said Barney.

The doctor backed out of the room, leaving the brothers alone.

"Just a little, word, Dick."

"Oh, Barney," cried his brother, his breast heaving in a great sob, "I don't think I can."

"Never mind then, old chap," replied Barney, putting out his hand to him.

"Wait a minute, Barney. I will," said Dick, instantly regaining hold of himself. As he spoke he knelt by the bed, took his brother's hand in both of his and, holding it to his face, spoke quietly and simply his prayer, closing with the words, "And O, my Father, keep my brother safe." "And mine," added Barney. "Amen."

"Now, Dick, old boy, we're all ready." And with a smile he met the doctor at the door.

In an hour all was over, and the grave faces of the doctor and the nurse told Dick all he dared not ask.

"How long before he will be quite conscious again?" he inquired.

"It will be an hour at least," replied the surgeon, kindly, "before he can talk much."

Without a word to anyone, Dick went away to his room, locked the door upon his lonely fight and came forth when the hour was gone, ready to help his brother if he should chance to need help for "the last weariness, the final strife."

"We must help him," he said to Margaret as they stood together waiting till he should waken. "We must forget our side just now."

But he need not have feared for her, nor for Barney. Through the night they watched him grow weaker, watched not in growing gloom, but, as it were, in an atmosphere bright with the light of hope and warm with strong and tender love. At times Barney would wander in his delirium, but a word would call him back to them. As the end drew near, by Nature's kindly ministry the pain departed.

"This is not too bad, Dick," he said. "How much worse it might have been. He brought us two together again—us three," he corrected, glancing at Margaret.

"Yes, Barney," replied Dick, "nothing matters much beside that."

"And then," continued his brother, "He let me do a little work for the boys, for 'Mexico.' Poor 'Mexico'! But he'll stick, I think. Help him, Dick. He is my friend."

"Mine, too, Barney," said Dick; "mine forever."

"Poor chaps, they need me. What a chance for some man!—for a doctor, I mean!"

"We'll get someone, Barney. Never fear."

"What a chance!" he murmured again, wearily, as he fell asleep.

Day dawned clear and still. The storm was gone, the whole world was at peace. The mountains and the wide valleys lay beautiful in their unsullied robes of purest white, and, over all, the rising sun cast a rosy sheen. As Margaret rolled up the blinds and drew back the curtains, letting in the glory of the morning, Barney opened his eyes and turned his face toward the window, moving his lips in a whisper.

Bending over him his brother caught the words, "Night no more." The great day was dawning for him. With a long, lingering look upon the mountains, he turned his eyes away from the window and let them rest upon his brother's face. "It is near now, Dick—I think—and it's not hard at all. I'd like to sleep out there—under the pines—but I think mother—would like—to have me near."

"Yes, Barney, my boy. We'll take you home to mother." Dick's voice was steady and clear.

"Margaret," said Barney. She came and knelt where he could see her. An odd little smile played over his face. "I wasn't worth it, Margaret—but I thank you—I like to think of it now—I would like you—to kiss me." She kissed him on the lips once, twice, for a single moment her superb courage. faltering as she whispered in his ear, "Barney, my love! my love!"

Again he smiled up at her. "Margaret," he said, "take care—of Dick—for me."

"Yes, Barney, I will." The brave blue eyes and the clear, sweet voice carried full conviction to his mind.

"I know you will," he said with a sigh of content. For a long time he lay still, his eyes closed, his breathing growing more rapid. Suddenly he opened his eyes, turned himself toward his brother. "Dick, my boy," he cried, in a clear, strong voice, "my brother—my brother." He lifted up both his arms and wound them round Dick's neck, drew a deep breath, then another. They waited anxiously. Then one more. Again they waited, tense and breathless, but the eternal silence had fallen.

"He's gone, Margaret!" cried Dick, in a voice of piteous surprise, lifting up a white appealing face to her. "He's gone! Oh! he has left us!"

She came quickly round to him and knelt at his side. "We have only each other now, Dick," she said, and took him in her arms. And so, in the strength of the great love that bound them to the dead, they found courage to turn again and live.

Three days later, when the road was clear again, they bore him through the Pass, the General Manager placing his private car at their disposal. It was no poor funeral. It was rather the triumphal procession of a king. At every station stood a group of men, silent and sorrow-stricken. It was their friend who was being carried past. At Bull Crossing a longer stay was made. The station house and platform and the street behind were blocked with men who had gathered in from the lumber camps and from down the line. One of their number came up, bearing a large wreath of the costliest flowers brought from the far south, and laid it on the bier. The messenger stood there a moment and then said, hesitatingly, "The men would like to see him again, if you think best."

"Tell them to come," replied Dick, quickly, proceeding to uncover the face. For almost an hour they filed past, solemn, silent for the most part, but many weeping as only strong men can weep. But as they looked upon the strong dead face, its serene dignity, its proud look of triumph subdued their sobbing, and they passed out awed and somewhat comforted. The look on that dead face forbade pity. They might grieve for the loss of their friend, but to him the best had come.

By Margaret's side stood Tommy Tate, till the last. "Ochone!" he sobbed, "when I think of mesilf me heart is bruck entirely, but when I luk at him I feel no pain at all." It was the feeling in the hearts of all. For themselves they must weep, but not for him.

At length, all had gone. "Could you say a word to them, Dick?" said Margaret. "I think he would like it." And Dick, drawing a deep breath, went forth to them. His words were few and simple. "We must not speak words of grief to-day. He was glad to help you and he grew to love you as his friends. In his last hours he thought of you. I know you will not forget him. But were he giving me my words to-day, he would not ask me to speak of him, but of the One who made him what he was, Whom he loved and served with his life. For His sake it was, and for yours, that he gave himself to you."

As his voice ceased a commotion rose at the back of the crowd. A sleigh dashed up, two men got out, helping a third, before whom the crowd quickly made way. It was "Mexico," pale, feeble, leaning heavily upon his friends. He came up to Dick. "May I see him?" he asked humbly.

"Come in," said Dick, giving him both his hands and lifting him on to the platform, while a great sob swept over the crowd. They all knew by this time that it was to save "Mexico" the doctor had given his life. With heads bared they waited till "Mexico" came out again. As he appeared on the platform of the car with Dick's arm supporting him, the men gazed at him in deathly stillness. The ghastly face with its fierce, gleaming eyes held them as with a spell. For a moment "Mexico" stood leaning heavily upon Dick, but suddenly he drew himself erect.

"Boys," he said, his voice hoarse and broken, but distinctly audible over the crowd, "he died because he wouldn't go back on his friend. He gave me this." He took from his breast the New Testament, held it up and carried it reverently to his lips. "I'm a-goin' to follow that trail."

Two thousand miles and more they carried him home to his mother, and then to the old churchyard, where he sleeps still, forgotten, perhaps, even by many who had known and played with him in his boyhood, but remembered by the men of the mountains who had once felt the touch of that strong love that gave the best and freely for their sakes, and for His Whom it was his pride and joy to call Master and Friend.

XXIV
FOR LOVE'S SAKE

Again it was June, and over all the fields Nature's ancient miracle had been wrought. The trees by the snake fences stood in the full pride of their rich leafage, casting deep shadows on the growing grains. As of old, the Mill lane, with its velvet grassy banks, ran between snake fences, sweet-scented, cool, and shaded. Between the rails peeped the clover, red and white. Over the top rail nodded the rich berries of the dogwood, while the sturdy thorns held bravely aloft their hard green clusters waiting the sun's warm passion. The singing voices of summer were all a-throb, filling the air with great antiphonies of praise, till this good June day was fairly wild with the sheer joy of life.

At the crest of the hill Margaret paused. This was Barney's spot. "I'll wait here," she said to herself, a faint flush lighting up the chaste beauty of her face. But the hot sun beat down upon her with his fierce rays. "I must get into the shade," she said, climbed the fence, and, on the fragrant masses of red clover, threw herself down in the shade of the thorn tree. On this spot, how vividly the past came to her. How well she remembered the heartache of that day so long ago. The ache would never quite be gone, but with it mingled now a sweetness that only love knows how to distil from pity where trust is and high esteem.

A year had passed since she had sent Dick back alone to his work, remaining herself to bring the lonely hearts of the Old Mill such help and comfort as she could. At the parting with him, Barney's words, "Take care of Dick for me," had moved her to offer with shy courage to go back with him. But Dick was far too generous to avail himself of any such persuasion.

"You must not come to me for pity," he said, bidding her good-bye.

But throughout the year she had waited, listening to her heart and wondering at its throbs, as from time to time the story of Dick's heroic service came to her ears; and now the year was done. Last night he had returned. To-day he would come to her. She would meet him here. Ah, there he was now. On the crest of the hill he would turn and look toward her. There, he had turned.

As Dick caught sight of her he raised his voice in a shout, "Margaret!" and came running toward her.

She rose, and with her hands pressed hard upon her heart to quiet the throbbing that threatened to choke her, she stood waiting him.

Touching a top rail, he vaulted lightly over the fence and stood there waiting. "Margaret!" he cried again, with a note of anxiety in his voice that trembled under the intensity of his feeling.

But still she could not move for the tumult of joy that possessed her. "Oh, I am so glad," she whispered to herself. Dick came toward her slowly, almost timidly, it seemed to her. He took her hands down from her breast, held her at arm's length, seeking to read the meaning in the blue eyes lifted so bravely to his.

"For pity's sake, Margaret?" he asked, the note of anxiety deepening in his voice.

For a moment she stood pouring her heart's love into his eyes. "Yes," she said, shyly dropping her eyes before his ardent gaze, "and for love's sake, too."

And for Dick the day's gladness grew riotous, filling his world full from earth to heaven above.